Nonfiction

A NOVEL

COURTING CARRIE IN WONDERLAND

FROM BEST-SELLING AUTHOR

CARLA KELLY

WINNER OF TWO SPUR AWARDS
FROM WESTERN WRITERS OF AMERICA

A NOVEL

COURTING CARRIE IN WONDERLAND

FROM BEST-SELLING AUTHOR

CARLA KELLY

WINNER OF TWO SPUR AWARDS
FROM WESTERN WRITERS OF AMERICA

SWEETWATER
BOOKS

An Imprint of Cedar Fort, Inc.
Springville, Utah

This is a work of historical fiction which, by definition, contains certain historical figures prominent in history. In addition to the real persons which inhabit this work, other characters, names, incidents, places, and dialogue are products of the author's imagination and are not to be construed as real. The opinions and views expressed herein belong solely to the author and do not necessarily represent the opinions or views of Cedar Fort, Inc. Permission for the use of sources, graphics, and photos is also solely the responsibility of the author.

ISBN 13: 978-1-4621-1872-4

Published by Sweetwater Books, an imprint of Cedar Fort, Inc.,
2373 W. 700 S., Springville, UT 84663
Distributed by Cedar Fort, Inc. www.cedarfort.com

LIBRARY OF CONGRESS CATALOGING-IN-PUBLICATION DATA

Names: Kelly, Carla, author.
Title: Courting Carrie in Wonderland / Carla Kelly.
Description: Springville, Utah : Sweetwater Books, an imprint of Cedar Fort,
    Inc., [2017]
Identifiers: LCCN 2016055719 (print) | LCCN 2016059935 (ebook) | ISBN
    9781462118724 (mass market) | ISBN 9781462126637
Subjects: LCSH: Yellowstone National Park, setting. | LCGFT: Romance fiction.
    | Historical fiction.
Classification: LCC PS3561.E3928 C68 2017 (print) | LCC PS3561.E3928 (ebook)
    | DDC 813/.54--dc23
LC record available at https://lccn.loc.gov/2016055719

Cover design by Priscilla Chaves
Cover design © 2017 by Cedar Fort, Inc.
Edited and typeset by Deborah Spencer and Jessica Romrell

Printed in the United States of America

10 9 8 7 6 5 4 3 2

Printed on acid-free paper

*In memory of Dan Christie Kingman
(1852–1916), and Hiram Martin
Chittenden (1858–1917),
US Army Corps of Engineers.
Gentlemen, thank you from
the depths of my heart.
And to my dad, Kenneth Carl Baier (1923–
2010), who shared his Yellowstone stories
with me and my dear sisters.*

Why, No One to Love?

Chorus:

No one to love!
Why, no one to love?
What have you done in this beautiful world,
That you're sighing for no one to love?

Stephen Foster, 1862

Chapter One

*F*ull dress uniform? Check. Xerxes brushed to a fare-thee-well, including a new saddle blanket? Check. That medal on his chest centered properly by the wife of B Company's first sergeant? Check.

Sergeant Major Ramsay Stiles edged Xerxes into line next to Captain Hiram Chittenden, Army Corps of Engineers, with the comment, "No one really knows where to put me, Captain, so here I am."

"And you're welcome here, Sergeant Major," Captain Chittenden said most formally. He lapsed quickly enough. "Ramsay, this is a how-de-do for Yellowstone Park. I hear Teddy had a great two weeks, swapping lies with our fair major and making rough camps where there wasn't too much snow."

The men grinned at each other; so much for rough camping in Yellowstone. Ramsay was well aware of the commodious tents, the horse docile enough not to throw the president of the United States, and better food than usually found among the troops in the back country.

3

Logistics seemed to be Ramsay's lot in life, now that he had accepted the exalted promotion of sergeant major, which had the unfortunate consequence of throwing him out of B Company and into a private office in Admin. This was not his idea, of course.

They waited for Major Pitcher and President Roosevelt to take their places at the head of the column of troopers, some still in blue, and others—especially Philippine war veterans like Ramsay—in the new khaki mandated last year. *Can a man be too ambitious?* he asked himself.

He decided the answer was yes. If he had turned down the honor, he would still be First Sergeant Stiles of B Company, First Cavalry Regiment, better known as Sarge. Now he was Sergeant Major Stiles, addressed by the full title in excessive syllabic splendor. Granted, the title gave him more of a free rein, but Ramsay knew some of his work this coming summer would be to assure the men of the First (and best) Cavalry Regiment that he hadn't changed much, not really.

The day was mild for April 24. The winter of '02–03 had been a bit of a tease, with snow beginning in September as usual, but melting by early April, when Roosevelt arrived for two weeks of private camping. Even a president can't control the weather, but fortune seemed to smile on Teddy.

Ramsay Stiles and Captain Chittenden saluted smartly when the two men in question passed them and moved to the head of the column, right behind the American flag, regimental colors, and a presidential flag. As much as his new promotion still hadn't quite settled onto his shoulders, Ramsay Stiles could not deny the pleasure of riding so close to the front as sergeant major, First Cavalry. No more eating dust for him.

As the column began to move, he couldn't resist looking back down the line at B and F companies, everyone smartly attired, every horse stepping in unison. He noticed with amusement and some nostalgia that the first sergeants in those companies were doing exactly the same thing he was. Once, one of Ramsay's lieutenants, when he was more drunk than usual—long dead now because he never could pay attention in Indian country—had remarked that sergeants really ran the army. Ramsay, stone cold sober, already knew that but he had smiled and nodded anyway.

As they approached Gardiner at a dignified trot, Ramsay stared at the size of the crowd. "Captain, is there any chance that Gardiner will eventually be home to more saints than sinners?"

"Not anytime soon!" the engineer said with a laugh. "That fence I built to keep our antelope and elk inside and away from poachers has made me a target for any number of nasty letters."

"I didn't know, sir," Ramsay said.

"They can't spell, so I save them for Nettie to laugh over when she gets here in June."

"She won't laugh, sir."

"Probably not." Chittenden pointed toward the partially built rock wall in the distance, their destination. "That, my friend, might someday be a silk purse from the proverbial sow's ear."

Ramsay nodded. Last year, he and the captain had indulged in occasional late-night visits after the day's work was done. Chittenden had mulled over some way to make this north entrance into something more remarkable, rather than a bleak expanse of blown-out sagebrush country. Ramsay had probably been the first person to see Chittenden's rough drawings of a stone wall with an arch for park traffic to pass beneath. Ramsay had been more impressed with Chittenden's message in stone, *For the Benefit and Enjoyment of the People.* "It's in the National Park Enabling Act, so why not?" Chittenden had asked his audience of one.

The drawings had made their way up the chain of command, with an architect given the actual duty to lay it out. The result stretched before them—the stone wall, at least. The arch would follow, but here was President Roosevelt, a handy tourist. Why not turn his camping trip into a dedication, complete with cornerstone and the inevitable speech?

The cornerstone mortaring came first, with everyone crowding around. Ramsay knew the Northern Pacific Railroad had run four extra trains to Cinnabar, three miles north of Gardiner and the current terminus of the rail, which by June would be through to Gardiner. Stagecoaches had brought more than three thousand spectators from Cinnabar to this place. Fort Yellowstone's two companies of cavalry had worked themselves into place to help with crowd control, Ramsay among them.

Speechifying followed, always the tedious but necessary part when leaders and people of some influence from Montana and Wyoming preened and patted themselves on the back. Captain Chittenden, a modest man, had already declined to say anything, confident—as he mentioned to Ramsay—that his initial idea would be remembered long after the windbags blew away.

In his clipped, staccato style, the president had assured Major Pitcher, acting superintendent of the park, that he wanted his constituents to crowd as close as they could, the better to hear.

It was a big gathering and a noisy one. Ramsay frowned to see brown bottles passed around and a certain amount of belligerence in evidence. No teetotaler he, the sergeant major knew there was a time and place for most things, and a cornerstone dedication wasn't one for booze. Hopefully the crowd was a friendly one, but who knew?

Captain Chittenden seated himself on the stand, which had been erected by his carpenters right next to the new stone wall. Ramsay counted the other dignitaries and angled Xerxes as close as he could until he reined in next to the platform, decked in patriotic bunting. He turned his attention to the crowd, scanning east to west, and then back, constantly surveying the rowdy, enthusiastic citizens.

After an effusive introduction by Major Pitcher, who knew Roosevelt well, the great man himself stepped forward, notes in hand. True to form, he leaned over the wooden railing, shook a few hands, and made some laughing remarks. Ramsay smiled when the president even kissed a baby some father held up.

Ramsay searched the crowd again, and rose in the saddle when he heard a commotion and glimpsed sudden movement. Two men hung onto a bearded old boy with a bottle in one hand and a gun in the other.

The man broke free and started for the stand. Sergeant Major Stiles stepped from his horse onto the platform. Quicker than speech, he pushed Roosevelt behind him. He stood in front of the president, shielding him from the drunk. He'd thrown away his bottle and stopped not ten feet away, blinking his eyes and swaying, gun in hand.

There was no time to take out his Navy Colt, so Ramsay Stiles stood still, ready for whatever came, calm because he knew the president of the United States was behind him and protected. It was all a soldier could do.

To his relief, others in the crowd tackled the drunk and disarmed him. Privates from B Company hustled the man away, his arms held tight behind his back, as he protested loudly, and then threw up over a second lieutenant's boots.

Ramsay sighed with relief, then he turned around to face President Roosevelt. "I'm sorry that happened, Mr. President. Gardiner is a no-account town."

"Western rough and tumble," Roosevelt said calmly enough. "I remember it well from my Dakota days." He held out his hand. "Shake, Sergeant Major. Thank you for your vigilance." He gave his toothy grin, the one that signaled to the other dignitaries that all was well. He lowered his voice for Ramsay's ears only. "This little incident will never make it into any newspapers or history books, but you were ready to protect me with your life."

Ramsay shook hands with President Theodore Roosevelt. "I'd do it again, sir."

"I know you would. I see it in your eyes."

Dignitaries on the platform crowded close and Roosevelt waved them back. "I'm fine and this speech needs to be given, eh, Sergeant Major?"

Ramsay laughed. "If you say so, sir."

Roosevelt took him by the elbow this time and looked into Ramsay's face. "I believe I know you." He touched the medal on Ramsay's uniform. "In fact, didn't I pin on that little gem in January?"

"You did, sir."

"Is it heavy?"

He could tell Roosevelt was deeply, deadly serious now. "It weighs even more than you can fathom, sir. Or maybe you can. You know combat."

"I do, indeed. Medal of Honor for the Philippine Insurrection, wasn't it?"

"Yes, sir."

"Nasty place."

"Yes, sir."

Roosevelt looked down at the notes he still clutched in his hand, then over at Major Pitcher, who ushered him back to the lectern, the crisis over. Roosevelt walked toward it, and then turned around.

"I won't forget this, Sergeant Major."

Chapter Two

Sergeant Major Ramsay Stiles had never expected much ease in life. All the same, was it too much to ask for a peaceful night's sleep without having to stare down barely visible enemies in a stinking, sweltering cave? Didn't dead men know the difference between the Philippines in 1900 and Fort Yellowstone in 1903? Apparently not.

With a sigh, he knifed one Moro insurrectionist again and then another, pushed them aside, and took the cave with his men right behind him, at least the ones still alive. He was used to heavy enemy fire, but did it have to seem louder within the confines of a cave?

Here it came: claustrophobic blankets needing to be tossed aside with all swiftness so he could leap out of bed and stand there a moment, wondering why he was continually retaking that stupid cave in his union suit. Once his heart stopped pounding, he had to smile. No man looks great in a union suit.

He did what he always did. Sergeant Major Stiles laughed off the whole matter, scratched, and started to crawl back into bed. He knew it would only take him a few minutes to return to slumber, and he knew he wouldn't be bothered again. Lately, the dreams were wider and wider spaced apart, so a soldier couldn't complain too much. He knew it would pass.

One knee up, ready to climb back in, he changed his mind. The moon outside was full to the point of bursting, and he liked the way it rose over the mountains. After his return from the hospital in November, Ramsay had watched the moon, as well as the gradual retreat of the constellation Orion, and winter stars he had seen in many a state and territory, and also in the Philippine Islands, where Orion seemed out of place because nights were hot and muggy, and not cold.

He padded downstairs and out the front door to stand on the porch, lifting one foot and then the other because even June in Wyoming is not a warm month. They had finally put away the skis for the season—dried, sanded, waxed, and stacked until next winter. At least there weren't any repeats this winter of Private W. H. Davis's death by freezing while skiing alone from Lake to West Thumb. That cautionary tale from six years ago still served to keep troopers alert, traveling by twos, and, for the most part, sober. Dragging a stiff body from Thumb to Fort Yellowstone's dead house on the man's own skis created an image destined to linger. Companies came and went, but the story remained as a warning.

The winter had gone well enough, all things considered. Poachers had caused their usual nuisance amongst the overly plentiful elk and few remaining bison, but there had also been the satisfaction of arresting some of the miscreants. Trouble was, the wretched men usually pleaded starvation and untold misery for the wife and kiddies before Judge Meldrum gave his patently heavy judicial sigh, stamped his official stamp on official papers, fined the bad men, and sent them to Rawlins to think about their sins for a few months. It was better than nothing.

Ramsay took a deep lungful of brisk air, and blew it out, already looking forward to summer, when breath didn't hang in mid-air, and a man could put away a few of those blankets; not all, but some.

Summer brought the Wylie Camping Company to the park. Sergeant Major Stiles smiled at the thought of cherry pie, with real whipped cream from Wylie Camping Company cows, and peach pie ditto. One thin dime of heaven, or maybe only a nickel, if Mr. Wylie himself was there and feeling benevolent.

He leaned his elbows on the porch railing and watched the elk hunkered down not far from noncommissioned officers' quarters, here in the easterly end of the fort. Another deep breath brought the always-present fragrance of sulfur from Mammoth Hot Spring's magnificent terraces. Soon summer would bring tourists with their Kodaks to take enough pictures to bore any number of relatives back home, or maybe convince them to see Wonderland.

Merciful heavens, what a stupid advertising gimmick Wonderland was, except that at times, Wonderland seemed exactly right. Ramsay thought about a summer of patrolling, keeping the visitors from doing stupid things, eating cherry pie, and experiencing the sheer pleasure of life in Yellowstone National Park. It was a long way from the Philippines, which could not possibly have made him more grateful. He stood there a moment more before the cold defeated his bare feet, then he turned to go inside.

The howl of a wolf stopped him. Alert now, he listened to that lonely sound, hoping to hear an answering call, wishing no one would expect him to order his men to kill those lovely creatures, along with coyotes and mountain lions. He knew he hoped in vain. All he could wish was that the wolves, at least, would retreat of their own volition and save themselves.

Truth to tell, the bigger nightmare that made him toss and turn was the annual directive he received to make sure each soldier station, supplied for the winter, had traps on hand, plus two pounds per station of strychnine to poison wolves by dumping the strychnine inside slit-open, winter-killed elk and deer.

According to the directive, the predator hides were to be taken as evidence and later brought to Fort Yellowstone headquarters for the winter count. In Ramsay's nightmare, he was always the trooper putting poison inside the carcasses, his arms red up to the elbows.

Ram, you're a sap, he thought. *You love this job, but you know your duty.*

He smiled to hear an answering howl, then smaller, chirpier yips. Puppies were baying to the moon like their parents. "Hide somewhere, little buddies," he said softly.

He went upstairs, tired now and ready to sleep, except there was another ritual, one that the Philippine Islands dream required. Needing no more than the glow of the full moon, Ramsay opened the top drawer of his bureau and took out a red case. He pushed on it. The lid snapped to attention to reveal a gilt-colored five-pointed star with a red, white, and blue ribbon. An eagle perched on a cannon with some goddess or other striking an enemy.

He knew the citation by heart, mainly because he wanted to say it out loud at times like this in memory of those men of his who were equally brave and who did not get out of that cave alive, including his lieutenant.

"'First Sergeant Ramsay Andrew Stiles with other men entered a cave occupied by a desperate enemy. After the death of his lieutenant and in the face of a heavy fire, with utter disregard for his personal safety, aided in forcing the outlaws to abandon their stronghold, which resulted in their destruction by our force,'" he whispered. "Thank you, men. I wish you were still alive. Sincerely, your sergeant."

Then Ramsay Stiles could go back to bed and sleep until reveille, except that his usually orderly thoughts took another turn. Perhaps he could blame June's full moon, which everyone who ever heard a Tin Pan Alley tune knew rhymed with croon and spoon and other delectable ideas. He lay there thinking he wouldn't be so cold in this bed if he shared it with someone.

He yawned and scratched the stubble on his face. It was time to stand closer to his straight edge razor—army polish was lax during a Yellowstone winter—and pat on a little hopeful aftershave. Marriageable women didn't materialize out of nowhere in Wyoming, but summer was coming. For the first time in nearly forever, Sergeant Major Ramsay Stiles—Medal of Honor recipient, a man kind to horses, and general all-around capable fellow—wanted a little more.

Chapter Three

The paperwork is going to kill me, Ramsay thought, and not for the first time since his return to Fort Yellowstone from the Philippines. He looked around Major Pitcher's office at the others, and wondered why the Almighty, in His infinite wisdom, had ever allowed staff meetings in the first place. Perhaps it was Adam's special punishment after ejection from the Garden of Eden.

None of the officers seemed to mind sitting in unforgiving chairs, taking such notes as warranted their attention, their backs straight, their eyes forward. He glanced at Captain Hiram Chittenden sitting next to him and revised his opinion. The Corps of Engineers officer, back from winter's duty on the Upper Missouri, was doodling little rows of lodgepole pines, maybe planning his own assault on the trees as he built more roads for Yellowstone Park this summer.

What in the world was he, Ramsay Stiles, Iowa farm boy, doing here? He gave a hopefully unnoticed glance at the insignia on his sleeve: three gold chevrons, three gold rockers with a simple star in the middle, and hash marks slanting down both sleeves. A lesser man could crumble under the weight of all that gilt.

He took another glance at the light blue Medal of Honor service ribbon, with its five silver stars which Major Pitcher had informed him would always be worn on his uniform blouse. "No argument, Sergeant Major," his commanding officer had told him firmly. "You won it; you wear it."

Here he sat in a staff meeting with the officers, still amazed he even had his own office just down the hall in the admin building. He wasn't the only enlisted man in the room, because there sat Corporal Myers, command clerk, at his tall desk, taking minutes. Myers didn't sit in the exalted half circle around Major Pitcher's desk though.

Major Pitcher cleared his throat. While no one came to attention, everyone did sit a little taller.

"Gentlemen, here we are at the start of another tourist season at Yellowstone Park," Major Pitcher said and tapped on his paperwork. "Why the army has been here since 1882, goodness only knows. Heaven help us all."

General laughter of the polite, officer type followed. Ramsay thought it best to just smile, his natural modesty unwilling to call attention to himself.

He hoped in vain. Major Pitcher looked directly at him and then at his officers. "Gentlemen, I have the unheard of luxury to introduce Sergeant Major Ramsay Stiles, former first sergeant of B Company and new Medal of Honor recipient. Yes, we all know him well, but glory be, this is his first summer with an impressive rank and a medal. And a seat in my staff meeting." He glanced at the command clerk. "Corporal Myers, I want this in the record too, if just for my benefit. Can't think of another time I escorted someone to Washington, D.C., for a Medal of Honor ceremony."

Ramsay felt heat rush past his tight stand-up collar to bloom on his face.

"And he blushes," Pitcher continued, while the others chuckled. He looked at the officer seated on the other side of Captain Chittenden. "Captain Bouvier, I know you will hate me until I die for usurping B Company's first sergeant—"

"Not quite that long, sir," Captain Bouvier interrupted. "Only every time I think about it." More laughter.

Major Pitcher joined in the laughter and answered, "You are kindness, itself, Jack." Ramsay watched the major's face grow serious. "For the record now in this meeting, I did some amazing groveling—no, not that in the record, Corporal—let us say persuasive argument to get Sergeant Major Stiles kept here instead of booted upstairs to regimental headquarters at Fort Clark, where he rightfully belongs now. You don't mind, do you, Stiles?"

"Not even slightly, sir," Ramsay said. He looked down at the paucity of notes on his tablet. "Headquarters would mean more meetings, and you know how I love those."

Chuckles this time. No one liked meetings, apparently.

Major Pitcher said something pithy, which was also left out of those minutes after a hard-eyed squint at the clerk. Pitcher looked down at his own agenda. "Because Sergeant Major Stiles just mumbles and blushes when asked, let me tell the rest of you and the record: After our fair-haired boy was awarded that hard-earned piece of metal, it was my privilege to request a promotion for First Sergeant Stiles from General Nelson Miles himself.

Told him I wanted a sergeant major to help with the dirty work here in the park, if that was allowed."

Pitcher looked at Ramsay, his expression kindly. "In case you want to thank them or cross them off your Christmas card list after this summer, depending, Sergeant Major, you can also thank your former captain and also the whiz bang engineer seated next to you for their additional letters of recommendation."

Ramsay knew about Captain Bouvier's recommendation, but he felt a warm spot in his chest to know that the fort's engineer had sent a letter too. He gave Captain Chittenden a sideways glance of appreciation.

"Of course it didn't hurt that General Miles and I know each other from early years in Appleton, Wisconsin." Major Pitcher's expression turned serious again. "It's a big step up, lad. I have no doubt you're equal to the task. Gentlemen, let me turn your attention to the agenda."

Had he blushed this much during the medal award ceremony in January? Probably. Men with reddish blond hair had almost no choice in the matter. Ramsay sat now with his typical stillness, watching the others, grateful the major had directed his attention to the business at hand, and away from the army's newest, and probably youngest, sergeant major, who just wanted to do his duty and be left alone.

Once the blush died down, Ramsay took his own notes on summer events familiar to him from a previous tour here at Yellowstone with Bouvier's B Company. The perspective was different now. Usually Captain Bouvier held his own staff meeting, once the word had been distributed from on high in this august gathering. Ramsay would be given his orders there, and he gave his orders in turn, placing corporals and privates at various strategic points in this district of the park from Mammoth Hot

Springs to the Lower Geyser Basin, the better to assist tourists and/or stop them from stupidity.

Now he took notes on everyone's duties and listened, wishing himself smaller, but that was impossible too. He was tall for a cavalryman, and took his share of good-natured abuse from his fellows in rank, who commiserated with his horse until the jokes got old and everyone forgot. For the hour of the meeting, Ramsay did what he did best—listened and absorbed.

Captain Chittenden's report on continuing road construction toward what would eventually become the park's east entrance was a masterpiece of information without superfluity, much like the man himself. This summer Chittenden's crew, already in residence, might finish the road to Cody, Wyoming. "We need an east entrance," Captain Chittenden announced with a smile. "Too many of you have been complaining how long it takes to get home to Pennsylvania and New York for Christmas."

That's right, Ramsay thought. *Officers can leave. Oh, winter, where is thy sting for the men who sport shoulder straps?*

Captain Chittenden's enthusiasm was nearly palpable when he described the bigger event of his summer—a steel-girded concrete bridge at a suitable crossing above the upper falls of the Grand Canyon of the Yellowstone. "I'll be using one thousand laborers this summer on this and the roads," he said. He held up a drawing of a graceful arch bridge. "With any luck . . ."

"It's no mistake that the smartest men at West Point go into the Corps of Engineers," Major Pitcher remarked. "Then it's artillery, followed by infantry, and then us, the cavalry. How were your engineering grades, Captain Bouvier?"

The captain's wry face and two thumbs down met with answering nods from the other cavalry officers. Captain Chittenden just shook his head and smiled.

The meeting ran from the dry details of commissary stores and horseshoes on hand, to the tasks that made patrolling Fort Yellowstone among the most interesting of assignments in the entire army. "Gentlemen, I know some of you deplore the spectacle of feeding bears at the hotels . . ." Major Pitcher began.

Without moving his head, Ramsay glanced at his former captain and saw his expected frown. Captain Bouvier had railed long and hard against the practice, and the major knew it.

"I would remind you all that we are here to protect the wildlife and remarkable formations and geysers, but we also owe something to our visitors, who do see this place as Wonderland," Major Pitcher said. "They want bears, and we have bears for them."

Ramsay watched Captain Bouvier open his mouth and prudently close it.

"And now back to you, Sergeant Major Stiles," the major said, just when Ramsay thought his ordeal was over. "Don't think for a minute you will have nothing to do this summer. Far from it." Yellowstone's acting superintendent leaned forward across his desk, and all eyes swiveled toward Ramsay again, perhaps also wondering what use a sergeant major would be in this remote place.

"I trust you have no problem with piles," Pitcher said, and everyone laughed.

All of a sudden it became abundantly clear what the park's chief enforcer was up to, and Ramsay smiled. This was his indoctrination, his entry into the club of higher command he had never sought, but which he had earned in a terrible place, doing extraordinary things to keep his men alive. So be it. He would play along, because he understood this army and he understood hard duty as well as every man seated here.

"Not a hemorrhoid in sight or otherwise, Major," he said. "No dyspepsia, either. Sir, I am a nearly perfect specimen," he said to laughter, getting his own digs in.

"That's a relief, Sergeant Major, because I intend to keep you in the saddle this summer. You're going to have free rein over this park and spare me any number of headaches. Are you in so far?"

"Yes, sir," Ramsay said promptly, knowing his place.

"I want you to become familiar with every geyser, every paint pot, every bear, every elk herd, and the occasional moose," Major Pitcher continued, a smile on his face. "Watch what goes on at the soldier stations and the hotels and the camping companies. If you see problems or complaints, keep me informed and be my eyes. Are you still in agreement?"

"Yes, sir," he replied.

"I will request all sergeants and corporals in each of our companies to report to you with issues regarding tourists who come into conflict with geysers, paint pots, and wildlife. You will hear the problems and solve them promptly, if you can."

Ramsay sat back, struck by the weight of responsibility as it settled on his shoulders like concrete. He nodded, wondering how on earth anyone could manage all this.

"You're good with people, Sergeant Major Stiles," Pitcher said. "You always have been."

Ramsay looked around the half circle, heartened to see nods of agreement from the captains in the room, men he had known here, at other garrisons, and in battle in the Philippines. "Thank you, sir," he said, flattered and puzzled at the same time.

"I'll give you letters to carry to park concessionaires and hoteliers, letting them know to contact you if difficulties arise."

Dazed at the duty ahead, Ramsay nodded, but then remembered himself. "Yes, sir."

"You are probably wondering what these captains and their lieutenants will be doing this summer to wile away their leisure moments as you slave with this assignment. Go ahead, admit it."

"It did cross my mind, sir," he said, to general laughter.

"Every few days, you will report to me," Pitcher said. "What you cannot solve—and I know there will be plenty of ladies and gents caught redhanded trying to chip away at a geyser for a souvenir or carve initials on a tree—you will inform me and I will send out these captains and lieutenants to apply some higher-level pressure, if needed."

"Very well, sir," Ramsay said. "When they start to demand, 'Don't you know who I am, Sergeant Major?' I, uh, send in the cavalry."

"Precisely," Pitcher said when the laughter died down. "It's a loose assignment, but one requiring that you get to know a lot of people from stable boys to hotel managers. People need to trust you." He chuckled. "I imagine you'll pose with a lot of pretty ladies who want their pictures taken with a stalwart representative of Uncle Sam's Army. You'll have all these lovely memories to fall back on when winter sets in and the work changes."

Ramsay looked around again and saw altered expressions, serious ones. Winter was always another matter at Yellowstone Park. It came too soon and it stayed too long, with mounds of snow, faltering animals, and endless poachers. He knew his brother soldiers were remembering last winter's disaster at the remote Sylvan Pass Station, where a sergeant shot and killed one private and wounded another private he thought were conspiring against him. Winters in Yellowstone could do that to ordinarily sane men.

Major Pitcher clapped his hands together to break the mood. "But this is summer and we are going to enjoy it, eh, men? That is all. Sergeant Major, I will speak to you this afternoon about another assignment. You will enjoy this one." He looked at his agenda. "I forgot one thing. It's not listed here."

The major stood and everyone else did too, except Corporal Myers taking notes at his high desk. "There is one remaining matter, brought to my attention by my dear wife, Matilda, over breakfast this morning. Pay attention, you captains, as I expect some assistance in this."

And why was everyone looking at him again? Ramsay smelled a rat and knew his indoctrination into this new world of power and hierarchy was only beginning. He stifled a sigh. At least he wasn't crawling through caves on Palong Batan, dragging out insurgents. Surely nothing could be worse than that. He stood at attention, because he was a man possessed of much ability to take what came his way.

"Sergeant Major, are you a man of temperate habits? No cursing or swearing?"

"Temperate habits, sir," he said, wondering where this was going, especially if the major's wife had called Pitcher's attention to the matter over breakfast.

"You already told us you are a nearly perfect specimen. Do you smoke or drink to excess?"

"No, sir. Just a little hot toddy at Christmas and a beer now and then."

"No diseases you would blush to tell us about?"

Ramsay stifled a smile. "No, sir."

"You save your money?"

"Yes, sir, safely tucked in a bank in Bozeman."

Pitcher shook his head. "This is much as I suspected, and which Matilda confirmed to me over porridge." He pointed his finger at Ramsay. "Sergeant Major, she cannot think of a single reason why you haven't found a wife yet."

The officers burst into laughter, and Ramsay knew he had been set up. Maybe this would satisfy them and his indoctrination would be over. He had to smile because it was funny, and because he liked Mrs. Pitcher.

"Not so easy in Wyoming, sir," he said, regretting his statement the moment such a lame excuse came out of his mouth.

"Beg to differ," his own former captain said. "Stiles, there are women all over this park in the summer. Major Pitcher told me only this morning that we're anticipating a record crowd of more than ten thousand visitors, some of whom will be female and unencumbered."

Ramsay put up his hands. "I surrender, sirs. A wife?"

Major Pitcher gave him another kindly look; drat it if the man wasn't full of them. "At least get started, Sergeant Major. That is all, gentlemen. You are excused."

Chapter Four

*R*amsay hoped that Captain Chittenden, always a busy man, was waiting for him when he finally escaped from the laughter and jibes of the officers, and he was.

"I thought you wanted to say something to me, Sergeant Major," the captain said, pocketing his watch.

"Thank you for your letter of commendation, sir," Ramsay said, after his salute.

Chittenden may have looked like the most spit and polish officer in the army, but appearance were deceiving. He touched one finger to his forehead in a lazy returning salute. "I may have languished in Alabama doing piddly stuff during the war while you were with the glory boys, but I heard plenty about your exploits in that cave."

"My men and I, sir," Ramsay amended. "Wish I could have got them all out."

"Only thoughtless, careless men would wish otherwise. When the major asked several of us to add to his letter of recommendation for promotion, I had no qualms. You're splendidly qualified, Sergeant Major."

Chittenden started walking. With his clipboard, he beckoned Ramsay to join him, which pleased the sergeant major as nothing else could have.

"I feel amazingly inadequate, sir," Ramsay admitted.

"So you should, but it doesn't follow that you can't do all the major requires." The engineer smiled then, more to himself than to Ramsay, or so it seemed. "Sorry about the ribbing at your expense, but that's what we do."

"I thought as much, sir. I do want to tell you that if you find yourself stretched thin, I can usually rout out men for extra duty. They might grumble, but they don't mind an extra fifty cents a day."

"I will call on you if I need them. I'm still amazed that Congress coughed up the money I asked for. Once they all arrive, I should have enough men for once."

Chittenden paused on the front steps of his nearly completed residence, a steep-roofed house with a surrounding porch. "Watch your step there when you leave. I've staked out the dimensions for an engineering office that might also get done this summer. The house came first. Mrs. Chittenden loves Sioux City, but she wants to see my sorry carcass."

"You have so many projects, sir. How far ahead do you plan?" Ramsay asked impulsively.

"As far as I can, Sergeant Major," came the reply Ramsay expected from an officer who didn't seemed surprised at a question another officer might consider impertinent. "I'd advise you to do the same thing." Chittenden sighed. "And now to work."

Where was this impulse coming from? Ramsay touched Chittenden's sleeve to detain him, realized his error, and stepped back, ready to apologize. The captain shook his head. "Say on, Stiles."

"It's this, sir," Ramsay said, taking the man at his word. "I am out of line and I know it. I intend to take Major Pitcher's assignment to heart, only I will include the enlisted men and officers, if I see a necessity. Sir, lights burn here so late at night, and by the end of the summer, I see how tired you are."

Chittenden's slight nod seemed to give Ramsay permission to continue. "I've observed that projects big and small always seem to be there next season, sir. Don't wear yourself out completely, Captain Chittenden. I worry."

"You and my wife." Chittenden looked at the house, which appeared to only lack trim and glass in the upstairs windows. "Nettie will be here in a few weeks, and she'll tell me the same thing. Thank you for your concern."

"Captain, there's not a man on post who knows less than I do on the matter," Ramsay said, plunging forward because it was his nature, "but I encourage you to listen to her."

Chittenden laughed at that. "You keep up such comments, and you'll be the best husband in history!"

"I believe I need a wife first, sir," Ramsay joked.

Captain Chittenden turned serious quickly. He patted his heart. "Sergeant Major Stiles, I am forty-three years old. My father died when he was forty-eight. Who knows how much time we have? You might think about that. Mrs. Pitcher's admonition is worth considering."

To Ramsay's continuing surprise, the engineer held out his hand. Ramsay shook it. He saluted smartly, and turned on his heel, wondering at his effrontery and, thinking about time, himself. He was thirty-four, an army man since the age of fourteen, six feet tall and mature for his years. He knew a lie about his age would go unnoticed and free him from the tyranny of an Iowa farm where he had watched his parents, who struggled

27

with drought and grasshoppers, wither and die. His uncle, who bought the farm for unpaid taxes, made it clear Ramsay could leave anytime.

One enlistment had turned into two, first in Arizona, then in Montana, then back to chasing Apaches in Arizona, followed by a wrenching summer giving battle to Nez Perce and taking some lumps, other assignments, then on to the blessing that was Fort Yellowstone.

The US Army threw the Philippines and fierce jungle warfare at him, and then a welcome return to Fort Yellowstone, which suited Ramsay Stiles right down to the ground. He smiled inside to recall that bit of army doggerel, patched together from a sentimental poem: "Backward, turn backward, O Time in your flight, make me a child again just for this fight!" He had fought his fight, and now it was Yellowstone again, to his great relief.

He sniffed sulfur in the air and looked toward the massive calcium carbonate formations of Mammoth Hot Springs, often the first sight of what the tourists called Wonderland and what Ramsay knew as the majesty of land set aside for the benefit of America's citizens. The view never got old. Looking at it now, he reminded himself how he had slept in jungle mud in the Philippines, dreaming of travertine terraces, wolves howling, and the splendor of the few remaining bison, anything but where he was then.

He had a moment of leisure. From the sounds of Major Pitcher's plans for the summer, he wouldn't have many. Mess call was coming, and then a private afternoon interview with the major. He followed another impulse and turned to Officers Row again instead of the barracks where he usually ate, because he wasn't much of a cook.

He climbed up a short flight of steps and he knocked on a door. He knew Tillie Jackson would open the door, and he had a smile ready for her. Her broad face brightened to see him, and she tugged him inside the house.

"What's your title again now, chile?" she asked, with no waste of words.

"Sergeant major," he replied. "But it's still Ramsay to you."

The housekeeper-cook threw back her head and laughed, a deep, rich sound that never failed to warm him. "And you remember that it's Tuesday and I always make cinnamon buns on Tuesday, rain or shine."

Truth to tell, he had forgotten, but he wasn't about to admit it to the Negro servant as tall as he was who outweighed him. He wanted to remember, even though his year in the Philippines had scrubbed the fun out of him. Or had it?

He knew better than to fib. "Tillie, I didn't remember," he said frankly. "It's been a tough year."

To his dismay, tears came to her eyes. "Poor, poor chile. I know you got a fancy medal, but they don't make up for much, do they?"

Ramsay shook his head, and then his native optimism resurfaced. It always did, if a bit slower now. "Not much, but I can still smell cinnamon buns."

On surer ground apparently, she steered him toward the kitchen. He stopped her.

"If you'll give me a minute with Mrs. Pitcher, I'll be more than happy to separate a cinnamon bun from the pack and take it with me," he said.

Tillie nodded and gestured him toward the parlor instead. He stood there and heard her ponderous footsteps on the central stairway. In a matter of minutes, Mrs. Pitcher appeared in the doorway of the parlor. It amused Ramsay that her expression was entirely unrepentant.

"Yes, I did tell the major over breakfast this morning that you needed to find a wife," she began, also without any small talk. It hardly surprised him that the entire Pitcher household didn't waste time on inane pleasantries; he sensed the major's influence. "I hope I am not in your black book now, Sergeant Major."

"No, ma'am," he replied. "Only thing is, I haven't the slightest idea how to go about finding such a commodity. If you're going to give me an order, then give me advice."

Her expression softened, reminding him of his mother, gone so many years now he could barely remember what she looked like, beyond that same kindness in her eyes.

He knew he could trust this woman not to blab anything throughout the fort. He had been garrisoned at other isolated posts where anyone's news quickly became everyone's news. Fort Yellowstone was not such a place, or he would never have said anything.

She motioned to a chair and he sat. She went to the bookcase, stood there a moment with her head cocked, then pulled a volume from a low shelf. She handed it to him and he looked at the title—*Rules of Etiquette and Home Culture*, he read. The subtitle made him smile: *Or What To Do and How To Do It.*

"I gave that to our son James before he went to West Point," she said. Her expression turned wistful. "It was returned with his other personal effects after the battle for Manila. I want you to have it."

Her concern touched his heart. He ruffled through the pages, and stopped at her inscription. "To my son, James William Pitcher—May you always know what to say, when, and to whom. Your loving mother."

"I'm sorry for your loss, ma'am," he told her. "It was a nasty war. Still is."

She nodded and stared out the window for a moment. When she looked back, she was in control of her emotions again. "Thank you, Sergeant Major. You'll find everything in there you need to know about how to meet ladies and what a gentleman should say to them."

"I'm not a gentleman," he reminded her. "I grew up on a farm with more weeds than corn and went barefoot to school."

"Of course you are a gentleman," she said firmly. "You always have been, no matter what your rank or where you came from." She leaned forward and touched the book, her finger tracing the raised lettering. "It's small enough to fit in your saddlebag. If my husband is determined you will travel about the Grand Loop this summer, you have time for a little reading. Life is not all duty and dispatches, in spite of what he says."

She stood there, silent, and he knew that was his signal to thank her for the dubious gift, and leave. He knew that much etiquette already. "I'll take good care of it, Mrs. Pitcher," he assured her.

"Read it," she said, and it didn't sound like a suggestion. Obviously life as wife of a field officer who was now acting superintendent at America's first national park knew something of command herself. "Keep it, please, and someday pass it on to your sons."

He couldn't help himself. "Is that an order, Mrs. Major Pitcher?"

"Most certainly," she replied. "As much a one as I can issue."

She turned when Tillie came from the kitchen with a cinnamon bun wrapped in waxed paper. "Tillie, I've told this nice young man to find a wife."

Ramsay waited for the housekeeper to laugh, but Tillie merely nodded and handed him the sweet-smelling package. "You'd better do what Mrs. Pitcher says," she told him, and again, it was no suggestion, not with that militant gleam in her eyes. This was an army household through and through.

"It's a conspiracy," he said as he took his hat from Tillie. He nodded to them both and found himself on the porch. There was no dignified way for a sergeant major to carry both a book and a cinnamon bun too far, so he returned to his office, closed the door, and ate the cinnamon bun.

It was the first one baked by Tillie that he had eaten in more than two years and it went down easily. He ate slowly, appreciating the rare treat and mulling over the Philippines and the cave of Palong Batan.

His little office afforded him a view of Mount Everts behind Fort Yellowstone. Officers got the view of the parade ground, but all things considered, he liked watching the storehouses, the horses grazing in their corrals, the foothills, and the mountains.

As he ate and watched, he saw two big horn sheep picking their careful way from rock to rock. He smiled to see two little ones booming along behind, fearless and leaping about with the vigor of the young. For a small moment, he wondered where his own energy had gone. As he watched, he felt his shoulders relax. Yellowstone could do that to a person, even a person tired from war. He leaned back in his swivel chair, enjoying the comfort, savoring the last of the cinnamon bun.

He licked his fingers—surely an activity frowned upon in what he reached for—and picked up Mrs. Pitcher's etiquette book, given first to a son who died too young in a distant land, and now to him, a sergeant too old for his thirty-four years.

He landed first on "Chapter Seven—Introductions." It seemed a good place to start, so he turned the page and scanned it. *Circumstances often determine the beginning of an acquaintanceship without an introduction*, he read. He shook his head, wondering how a soldier on horseback was going to meet anyone, casually or otherwise.

He looked to the next heading, "How to Give an Introduction." "Me oh my," he said out loud and tried not to laugh. *In giving the introduction, one should bow to the lady, or make a slight wave of the hand toward her, and say, 'Miss A, permit me to introduce my friend Mr. B.'*

Since it was his office and the door was closed, he said something salty out loud. "This will happen precisely never," he said and set the book aside.

Chapter Five

*N*ever a man to put off any duty, onerous or otherwise, Ramsay was in the saddle directly after guard mount the next morning. He had stayed up too late reading the etiquette book, finding the whole thing amusing and totally useless. He stowed shaving gear, a change of smallclothes, and socks in one saddlebag. Then he thought a moment and added the how-to-do-it book to the other bag, next to the journal he used for wolf observations. The red book went in his back pocket as usual.

He stopped by the admin building to pick up the letters from Major Pitcher that Corporal Myers had prepared for the managers of the park's hotels and concessions, each one neatly labeled.

"Major Pitcher says you are to visit each manager and hand over the letter," Corporal Myers detailed. "Wait for them to read it and note any replies that will be helpful to you in the coming season, Sergeant Major." Myers was a bit of a priss.

Ramsay accepted the letters and the sleeve of thicker paper to stick them into. Knowing the corporal's eyes were on him, he carefully folded them for his saddlebag, all the time wondering why and how clerks became so superior. Arizona Territory or Wyoming, clerks were all the same.

His next stop was south of his own quarters at the buffalo corral he had heard about even in the distant Philippines. In yesterday's afternoon meeting with Major Pitcher, his boss had invited him to visit the corral and make inquiries from the current man in charge, a remarkably taciturn Crow by the name of Sam Deer Nose.

"Give Sam a medal," Major Pitcher had said. "I hired him last year as an assistant to Buffalo Jones and he managed to survive. You remember Buffalo Jones?"

Everyone did, and no one was sorry when the major fired him for all-around irritating behavior, even if he did understand bison.

"One seldom meets a more self-righteous fellow," Ramsay had said. "Still, he knew buffalo."

"So does Deer Nose. Stop by and take a look. When you have time, I also want you to visit Jack Strong and see if he has any horses for us. I know Jack and Sam are relatives of some sort. Jack might recommend another cousin or uncle to assist Sam."

"That is a pleasant assignment," Ramsay said.

"I figure it was the least I can do, after ribbing you about a wife," Major Pitcher had said, sounding as unrepentant as Mrs. Pitcher.

"Sam? Sam Deer Nose?" Ramsay called, stopping Xerxes outside the enclosure, which he had to admit was chosen with a practiced eye to buffalo terrain. Buffalo Jones knew his business, but why was it some talented people worked so hard to muddy their own nests? Look in the dictionary under "self-righteous prig," and Ramsay was certain Mr. Webster had posted a drawing of Buffalo Jones.

"Over here."

Ramsay looked around and saw a tall Indian coming from the log house that probably used to belong to Buffalo Jones. He didn't wear his hair braided, but free-flowing as Crows preferred. Ramsay smiled to see two little ones peeking around the door, until their mother moved them inside.

He dismounted and crossed the distance between them. He held out his hand, and Sam Deer Nose gave him that familiar but always surprisingly gentle Indian handshake.

"I'm Sergeant Major Stiles," Ramsay said. "I hear you're in charge now."

Sam nodded. "I hear you're the tall horse soldier with the big medal."

"For what it's worth. Major Pitcher wanted me to ask if you need an assistant. I'm going to visit Jack Strong sometime soon. I can pass your recommendation on to him, and we'll see."

Sam nodded. "I'll think on it. I can leave you a note in your office."

He gestured for Ramsay to follow him. They ended up with arms resting on the top fence post, watching the bison that had started traveling slowly toward them, no one in a hurry, no sense of alarm or danger: just the way Ramsay liked to see bison.

The two of them watched the little herd approach. After silent observation, Sam spoke. "I hear your shoulder strap officer who builds roads made a survey of the whole park to count these boys."

"Captain Chittenden sure did. Came up with twenty-nine, he told me," Ramsay said. "Buffalo Jones added some bulls brought up from Texas."

"I was here last spring when we rounded up more big boys, little red dogs, and their mamas from Lamar Valley," Sam said. He pointed toward the approaching herd. "Look now. Thirty-nine."

"I've spent some time watching the herd," Ramsay said. "Probably too much time to suit Uncle Sam. I watch wolves too."

Deer Nose looked around elaborately. "Don't see Uncle Sam out here, do you?"

"Nope."

"Keep watching."

Ramsay remembered his first spring at Yellowstone, when the bison calved their red offspring. He knew he had wasted a lot of Uncle Sam's pay, comfortable in a tree with his binoculars, watching the little ones trucking about on stiff legs. He could have stayed there for hours, and probably did, truth be told.

Time to push off, as much as he wanted to remain in the little draw with a frozen stream starting to run free again, and suitable gullies and swales to keep a buffalo happy. The fenced enclosure was the surest protection against poachers, some of whom valued bison heads for trophies in some back east board room.

"Yeah, just leave me a note if you need me, but it looks like you have things in hand, Sam," he said.

"More like the buffalo do," Sam commented.

Ramsay mounted his horse and tapped his forefinger against his campaign hat. He stifled a laugh when he saw Sam start to scuff the ground with his moccasin in—hopefully—unconscious imitation of a bearded and burly gentleman behind the stout fence. Yep, Sam was a buffalo man. No worries here.

He pointed Xerxes toward the travertine beauty that constituted Mammoth Hot Springs. He rode slowly by, ticking off the names in his head: Opal Terrace, Palette Spring, Jupiter Terrace, and Canary Spring. He liked Jupiter the best and reined in to watch the deep blue water play over the edge to another pool below.

No tourists walked the terraces yet, but he knew they would come soon: the women with their wide-brimmed, impractical hats and wearing linen dusters, and the men in suits and bowlers—so improbable, so overdressed, but visitors deserving of his best attention.

As he turned toward distant Norris Geyser Basin, Ramsay found himself envying the sergeant who had replaced him in B Company. It would be his duty to place privates at vantage points to keep visitors from stepping where they shouldn't, and answering questions—some silly, some thoughtful—that came the guardian-trooper's way on an average day.

He had visited last night with Sergeant Chambers of B, advising him to learn what he could about the terraces, because there would be questions. "You'll never learn enough about the place," he had told the sergeant and meant it. Yellowstone was a lifetime's duty.

He stayed at the hot springs long enough to soak in the sight of elk lying down on the terraces, savoring, in their elk way, the warmth after a long winter. For the few months since his return he had watched this particular band struggle through deep snow, peeling bark from trees to stay alive. It was a reward to their tenacity to see them at leisure now. Another layer of wartime funk slid away, and he hadn't even left the terraces yet.

Glory be, no wind blew down on him as he ambled along in no hurry, doing his own savoring of earth reawakening and sky so blue it looked postcard fake. He took a deep breath and another, relishing the fragrance of nothing more glamorous than fresh-turned dirt. Given enough time, he knew he could forget the stink of the jungle, where everything seemed to rot, from damp socks to leather hatbands.

I am here and I am happy, he thought, as he followed a water wagon up a moderate incline made much less difficult to travel by the work of Captain Chittenden's road crews two summers ago.

He reined in Xerxes again where the road turned and he saw a black bear and two cubs minding their own business in a cluster of lodgepole pines. In a mere week, tourists would be crowding too close, taking too many snapshots, blocking the roads and offering bread and apples and licorice and other stuff bears didn't need. He could argue with visitors, telling them all the reasons that such largess only turned bears into beggars, because that was their nature. Some tourists might listen, but most would look apologetic, turn away, and keep doing what they were doing, once they thought he was out of sight.

Maybe he was wrong. Maybe Yellowstone was a place for visitors to be entertained at the expense of bears growing daily more accustomed to licorice and Jujubes. After he returned, worn out from war, there had been discussions veering into heated debate about this very issue. He knew Major Pitcher didn't mind visitors feeding the park's year-round citizens. "We're here for the enjoyment of the public," the major had reminded Ramsay on more than one occasion. "Visitors want to see bears."

"But what about the animals?" Ramsay asked a mountain jay that swooped in for a closer view, and then soared off, either frightened or satisfied. "What's best for you, little buddy? Hey, don't fly away. You're not taking this seriously."

Amused at himself, Ramsay looked around, hopeful no one on two feet stood anywhere near to hear a sergeant major talking to critters so early in the season. *Worry about it later, Stiles*, he thought. It was enough to feel the sun on the left side of his face and down his leg, warmth without humidity, silence without fear of insurgents in the jungle, hunkered down and alert.

He rode along in solitude, bullied by mother swallows that wanted him far away from the cliffs where their babies waited, open-mouthed, for worms or grubs. Always there was the roar of water moving fast, rivers free from snow and ice.

Once through the Golden Gate Canyon, he touched his finger to his hat in salute to Captain Chittenden's new concrete viaduct that had widened the road, much to the relief of terrified tourists. Now two wagons could easily pass each other without major fear or more than usual cussing. He and Xerxes had the road to themselves.

He didn't have far to go to reach his first stop. Ramsay ignored a chipmunk scolding him for some infraction or other and walked Xerxes across the road. He looked south to Willow Park and smiled to see the red-and-white-striped tents of the Wylie Camping Company, as sure a sign of summer as red dogs, bear cubs, and what one of his privates in B Company had called little moosettes.

He wondered if it was too early in the day, or even the summer to wish for cherry pie. The memory of cherry pie, canned cherries but still tart and sweet, had sustained him through terrible times in the Philippines, where he had promised himself he would eat pie at Willow Park again before he died.

He rode closer, taking in the company's permanent structures, which included a small storeroom, combination dining hall and dance floor, kitchen, and Wylie store with postcards, candy, and other tourist attractions. Only some of the striped tents had been installed so far. From their location, these were probably tents for the cooks, chore girls, custodians or camp men, and wranglers. Before another week went by, he knew there would be at least twenty tents in two rows, tents with wooden floors and partitioned areas for sleeping and for sitting around a pot-bellied stove in the evenings. Wylie advertised comfort for tourists used to the easy life, and he meant it.

Ramsay recalled finding some excuse during summer evenings to visit this Willow Park camp with one of the other sergeants, and maybe a corporal, to sit around a campfire, eat popcorn, and listen to one of the girls sing. Mr. Wylie hired college students from Montana Agricultural College in Bozeman to staff his summer-time camps. Lately, some came from even farther afield at the University of Washington, or Oregon, and others were teachers wanting summer work. It was soon obvious to anyone who didn't have a tin ear that the chore girls, camp men, and kitchen flunkies weren't hired for their singing ability, but who cared when there was a roaring fire and popcorn?

Now the place was empty of guests, with the dishevelment that accompanied windows, shuttered all winter, needing to be washed, mouse nests swept out, and chairs dusted. Give the crew a week, and summer visitors would never even suspect the housecleaning chaos going on now. He watched two girls scrubbing away, one on each side of the same window in the dining room, the better to catch all the streaks. A camp man wearing a UW letter

41

sweater walked by and stopped to chat with the girl on the outside. She looked coy and he laughed and Ramsay felt eighty years old.

It was enough to make a man all surly and mean, except the sun still shone and the air had a whiff of sulfur to it now, certainly not every man's eau de cologne, but a well-remembered fragrance for someone who had been missing Yellowstone Park.

Ramsay guided Xerxes behind the dining hall and its attached kitchen, wondering where Mr. Wylie might be located when he heard someone pounding on a door. He looked around, wondering what sort of prank one of the college boys might be playing on a sweet young thing.

"Yes?" he asked, willing to appear foolish, if someone really was in dire straits.

Nothing, and then another bang on a door to one of the privies. This time he heard someone. "Um, is anyone there? Is the bear still sitting in front of the door? Anyone?"

Laughing to himself, he looked around just to make sure. Xerxes had a sixth sense about bruins, and he was looking as bored as a horse can look. Ramsay dismounted.

He walked to the privy where the banging had originated, thinking of the chapter on introductions in *Rules of Etiquette and Home Culture* and wondering what its authors, all seven of them, would make of this situation. The matter had most emphatically not been covered in the entire chapter, and he had read it carefully.

"Miss?" he asked, for she sounded young. "There's no bear in sight. You're quite free to come out."

"You're positively certain?"

He heard the tiniest lilt in her voice, but he couldn't place it. *Sartain*, with a little twist to the r.

"I am more certain of this than nearly anything in my entire life," he replied. "No bears."

He stepped back, not sure how to pretend he didn't know what a privy was and what she had been doing in there. He considered his options, which were slim to none. He decided to assume she was a grownup and wouldn't make any fuss at being rescued from nonexistent bears camped around a backhouse. He might see whoever she was again sometime this summer, and Ramsay hoped she wouldn't carry to the grave any embarrassment over this delicate situation.

Trying not to grin, he watched as the door opened slowly. He had been right about her probable age. She didn't look any older than the Wylie chore girls cleaning the windows, but gloriosky, she was a pretty thing.

Oddly, her hair, what he could see of it peeking from under a bandanna, was the same color as his. He made a snap judgment and decided strawberry blond looked much more appropriate on a female head than on his. Her eyes were deep blue, unlike his own brown ones. Nature had certainly not stinted on the combination of blue eyes and reddish-blond hair. One of the B Company corporals given to slang would probably have called her a real pip.

To his relief, she looked him in the eye and he saw no embarrassment. In fact, she smiled and then took an exaggerated look around, as though peering over imaginary spectacles. "Sergeant, when I opened the door, there he sat, as if waiting his turn. I am surprised he did not knock."

Ramsay knew it was useless to fight the mirth that bubbled up from some place inside where it must have been stored for a while. He tipped back his head and laughed. To his pleasure, she joined in, as she came out of the privy and shut the door behind her.

She looked around and pointed. "Watch your step, sir. It appears he couldn't wait."

Sure enough. *I need to stop laughing*, Ramsay thought, as he stepped sideways to avoid a still-steaming pile.

He took a chance. "Bears being what they are, I now understand why it's referred to as a call of nature," he said, and was rewarded with a great peal of laughter.

He didn't know her at all, but her good humor seemed not even slightly dampened by what could only be deemed an awkward rescue. "Mr. Wylie says we should carry a frying pan and a stick and bang on it, but that seemed unnecessary for such a short visit. I will consider this a lesson."

Again he heard that little bit of a burr in her words, one that a man with the name of Ramsay might recognize. Blowing away everything he had read last night, he held out his hand. "Sergeant Major Stiles, miss. And you are?"

She pointed to her name tag with its red and white border. "Mostly just Carrie to everyone, sir," she said.

"Carrie McKay," he said. She had a nicely proportioned bosom, as much as he could tell of someone swathed in a black dress and all-encompassing apron. He didn't stare, because that wasn't polite, but she had pointed to her name tag, and it did reside so nicely on a pleasant slope, a bit south of her collarbone.

Her charming face brightened. "You know how to pronounce it!" she declared. "Nearly everyone rhymes McKay with hay. You know better."

He could have wriggled like a puppy at such praise, but he was thirty-four after all, and a grown man. "If I had a name tag, I'd point to my first name, which is Ramsay," he said. "Surely a Ramsay should know how to pronounce McKay."

She nodded as if he had said something sage and packed with wisdom. She raised her eyebrows, which only made her prettier, because her eyes were round like a child's. "You saved me from a privy, Sergeant Major Stiles. I suppose you've had harder duties."

"One or two," he replied, dismissing Apaches in the Southwest and Moros in the Philippines. He was also deeply aware that absolutely nothing either of them had said bore any relation to proper introductions. *Now what?* he thought, feeling the heat rise up his neck.

"Are you looking for Mr. Wylie, or do you just rescue random people?"

"I am looking for the boss," he said, relieved she had just rescued him. After all, the army didn't pay him to ogle pretty girls. "Might you know where he is?"

"In his office. He also calls it the storeroom, but I told him he needs to dignify it with a title. Come with me."

To the ends of the earth, he thought, happy to walk alongside Carrie McKay, a Wylie girl who didn't seem to mind a ham-handed introduction by a privy. As he matched his stride to hers with surprising ease, considering she was short, he made a singular discovery.

He didn't feel eighty anymore.

Chapter Six

Even though she was short, Carrie McKay had a purposeful stride. She led him past the dining hall toward a nondescript shed with a sign reading, "Mr. Wylie's Office" tacked above the door. He noticed a daily chore board outside the door, where employees wrote in their names and hours.

He waited for her to open the door, or at least knock, then he felt flattered when she seemed content to stand there with him.

"When I was a little girl, I saw a tall lady in Bozeman who walked her really small dog on a leash. My, but that little fellow could move. His feet were a blur." She laughed. "Thanks for slowing down a bit."

He smiled, because the picture she painted of the little dog trucking along was so vivid. "You have a way with a phrase. Are you one of Mr. Wylie's storytellers around the campfire?"

"I'm a kitchen flunkie, and I sing at the campfires. I worked mostly at Lake Yellowstone camp last summer, and in Gardiner the summer before, where Mr. Wylie keeps a temporary office. Lots of times the soldiers came over from their station at Lake to listen. Were you one of those? I don't remember you, sir."

"I was in the Philippines last year," he said.

He thought he had tossed off the sentence with a certain unconcerned air, but maybe not, since she gave him a gentle look. He didn't know how else to explain that look. "And now you're here," she said, so matter-of-fact. "I'll wager this is better."

She knocked on the door and then opened it and stuck her head in. "Mr. Wylie, you have a visitor of an official nature, I think." She looked back at Ramsay, eyeing his chevrons and hash marks. "He's some sort of sergeant, but maybe a bit more."

"Send the man in, Carrie, no matter what sort of sergeant he is."

Carrie opened the door and ushered him inside. Ramsay removed his campaign hat because the ceiling was low but then wondered what to do with the thing that seemed to grow to enormous proportions, because he felt suddenly awkward.

He shouldn't have worried. Carrie deftly plucked his hat from his hand and hung it by the chin strap from a hook. She stood there, hands clasped in front of her, so proper but still with that amazing twinkle in her eyes, as if life itself was the adventure.

Mr. Wylie stood up and held out his hand. "Will Wylie," he said.

"Sergeant Major Stiles," Ramsay said, glad to have something to do with his hands. Gadfreys, where was this sudden shyness coming from?

"Mr. Wylie, would you like me to get you two some pie?" Carrie asked.

Pie. He couldn't help himself and sighed. "Mr. Wylie, I dreamed about cherry pie from this very dining room for the last year and a half."

"He was in the Philippines," Carrie added, frowning. "I'm afraid it's only a reconstituted dried apple pie. We haven't unpacked the canned cherries yet, but there is whipped cream. Mounds of it, if you'd like."

Shoot me dead right now and I will die a happy man, Ramsay thought.

"Will apple pie be an adequate substitute?" Mr. Wylie asked him. "I hate to disappoint the army." He looked closer and Ramsay saw the respect in his eyes. "Sergeant major, are you?"

"As of February, Mr. Wylie. You might remember me from B Company. We patrol this district."

"Indeed I do," Mr. Wylie replied. "I remember more than that." He gestured toward a Nabisco box. "Have a seat in my well-appointed office. Carrie, bring us some pie, and while you're at it, get a piece for yourself and join us."

Thank you, Mr. Wylie, Ramsay thought.

"Bring a note pad and pencil too. I suspect Sergeant Major Stiles is here on business, even though he'd like pie."

"On my way," she said, closing the door quietly behind her.

"The Philippines?" Mr. Wylie asked. He leaned back in his swivel chair and regarded Ramsay with inter-est. "Stiles, Stiles. There was an article about you in the Bozeman paper last winter, wasn't there?"

Here it came. "Yes, sir, there was."

"Something about a Medal of Honor."

"That's the one." He took a chance. "It's good to be back here in Yellowstone, sir."

"I feel that way at the start of every season," Mr. Wylie said, letting him change the subject, to Ramsay's relief. "You have some business with us?"

No, I'm just here to eat pie and admire the help, he thought but had the sense not to say it. "Out in my saddle bag. I'll be right back," Ramsay said.

Xerxes gave him a patient look, the look that told Ramsay he wasn't measuring up, but a horse is just a horse, even a smart one. Ramsay took the letter from the saddlebag, gave Xerxes a pat, and turned around in time to open the door for Carrie, who held a tray of pie.

She was about to hoist the tray to her shoulder to get a free hand when he made his move. He opened the door with what he wished was a flourish, except that it's hard to give a grand gesture to a door on a shed.

"Yours is the one with all the whipped cream," she said as he stepped back for her to pass.

She set the tray on another Nabisco box and handed a plate to Mr. Wylie and the other to him, after he resumed his perch on his box. He set the letter on Mr. Wylie's desk, but the man just waved it away.

"Pie first. That's my rule. Dig in, Sergeant Major Stiles."

After tucking a napkin into the neck of his uniform blouse, he dug in with no hesitation. It took every ounce of discipline not to utter small cries of delight as the first bite went down so smoothly, well-lubricated with whipped cream. He glanced at Carrie, who was watching him, her face full of good humor.

"It's edible?" she asked.

"You cannot imagine how good this is," he assured her.

"I made it," she said and took a bite of her own, one not burdened with too much whipped cream.

"In addition to shorthand and some secretarial classes, Carrie is taking the domestic science course at Montana Agricultural College in Bozeman," Mr. Wylie explained, after he took his own bite. "Did you make an A in pie?"

"Fruit and cream pie, plus eclairs, creampuffs, and cookies," she told Mr. Wylie. "Cake is fall semester this year."

"You know shorthand too?" Ramsay asked, knowing he was here on business, but tossing all discipline to the wind, if only for the moment.

Carrie gave a kind look in her employer's direction. "Mr. Wylie says I should maximize my efficiency in all areas, because we live in a modern century."

Who could argue with that? Ramsay nodded and applied himself to the more important issue of eating pie, grateful down to his boots that the First Cavalry was still garrisoned at Fort Yellowstone and not back in Arizona Territory, staring down surly Apaches.

The three of them ate in silence. Carrie finished first because she had only cut herself a sliver of pie. She wiped her mouth with some delicacy and picked up the notepad and pencil from the tray.

Ramsay took his time, savoring the nearly unimaginable delight of crust flaky enough to make a grown man weep and apples lightly dusted with cinnamon and some other spice he couldn't identify. He rolled one bite around in his mouth, trying to figure it out, then he looked at Carrie.

"Mace," she said. "And now you know all my secrets."

He probably did. There was something open about Carrie McKay. He hadn't known her more than thirty minutes, but he understood her. She was a western woman, the frank and fair kind not found in urban areas. She bore herself with an air of capability he had long noticed in the ladies who inhabited the Rocky Mountains and Southwest. And maybe his mind was wandering too. Still, he wanted to know more about her, even as he knew he had to hurry up a bit, because he was wasting time, something Uncle Sam frowned upon.

He held up a fork in salute. "Until only recently, every private in each company, skilled or not, took a weekly turn cooking for the company. Miss McKay, you are a prodigy."

"No, I'm not," she said softly, but he saw the pleasure in her eyes. "I like to eat, and that is all."

Ramsay happened to glance at Mr. Wylie as she spoke, and saw a shadow of something close to melancholy cross his face. He might have imagined it; the lighting wasn't too good in a shed for food storage that happened to have a desk crammed in it.

He finished his pie and handed the letter to Mr. Wylie. "I'm taking similar letters to all the concessionaries and hoteliers in the park, sir," he explained. "Major Pitcher wants me to be his troubleshooter this summer." He couldn't help a self-deprecating laugh. "I suppose there are better ways to put it, but that's what I am."

Mr. Wylie nodded while Carrie took notes.

"I've been thinking about my job on the ride this morning," he said and then made an executive decision, the kind that perhaps sergeant majors in more traditional posts might make. How would he know, stuck out here in the wilderness? "I believe I will be making a twice-monthly circuit of the Grand Loop, just to find out what's going on."

Before he had rescued Carrie McKay from the backhouse, Ramsay had decided to ask each recipient of each letter to shoot a memo to the nearest soldier station, where, depending on the seriousness of the offense, it could be telephoned to Fort Yellowstone if the lines were operating, or carried on a fast horse. Miss McKay was right; this was a modern century. Since the rescue, he decided it might be better to make the circuit himself, especially if there was dessert at Willow Park.

"You're always welcome here," Mr. Wylie said. He leaned back in his chair again. "Take note of this, Carrie. When we're done, you can type up a memo for me on my fancy new typewriter."

She bent diligently over her tablet. Ramsay watched a tendril of hair escape from her red bandanna and rest against the back of her neck. She must have felt the hair bolt for freedom because she tried to stuff it in among its brethren, with little success.

"Major Pitcher wants everyone to be aware of visitor misconduct and to make a note of it, particularly if certain offenses seem to be repeated," he explained. "It's all in the letter, but with some ten thousand tourists anticipated this summer, we need to stay on top of events. We can establish patterns and see what changes to make."

Mr. Wylie nodded. "That's forward thinking. We'll be mindful, Sergeant Stiles. "I wonder—would your major be receptive to a comment from me about his soldiers?"

"It works both ways," Ramsay said. "You'll let me know, and I'll see what I can do."

"Carrie can tell you right now, eh? Remember our chief complaint each summer?"

Ramsay braced himself for some misdemeanor and thought of the times he had dropped in on Wylie campgrounds in the evening to enjoy the singing and stories and popcorn. "Maybe you'd rather the soldiers didn't come around in the evenings for the campfires?" he suggested, hoping he was wrong.

Somehow, Carrie's response didn't surprise him. "Don't worry, Sergeant Major. It's not that." She cleared her throat. "How to explain this: We know your men are stationed at the geysers and paint pots and rivers to keep visitors from trouble, but I . . . we . . . wish some of them knew more about what they are guarding."

"That's it in a nutshell, Sergeant Major," Mr. Wylie said. "Some soldiers say nothing when spoken to." He chuckled. "And others tell the tallest tales. Last summer, one lady at our Lake campground asked one of our chore girls if she knew there were certain birds with nests near the geysers that laid boiled eggs."

"Remember the visitor who said a soldier told him all geysers were set on a timer?" Carrie asked.

Ramsay understood. "We discussed this only yesterday in a staff meeting, Miss McKay," he told her. "Some of the company commanders want their men to be as silent as sentries guarding Buckingham Palace, and others think fooling the tourists with tall tales is funny."

"What do you think?" Carrie asked.

"I think we ought to do better than hard boiled eggs and timers," Ramsay admitted.

Mr. Wylie shrugged. "It's not a big thing, in the scheme of events, I suppose. I came to Bozeman from Iowa to be superintendent of schools, so I am in favor of education. At my Wylie camps, we pride ourselves on answering visitors' questions about Wonderland. Could you help us with this?"

"I can, sir," Ramsay said. The vagueness of his summer's assignment, unsettling to a fellow used to crisp orders, began to gel in his mind. "I'll ask the other businessmen I see on the Loop if they have a similar concern. Can I help you with anything else?"

"We're bothered by bears more and more," Mr. Wylie said. "At each of my campgrounds, I have to assign men to stay awake at night and pound on pans to move them away."

Ramsay nodded, thinking of the bleachers at each hotel, set not too far from the hotel garbage dumps, where the nightly feeding of scraps was a well-established routine. So far most of the freeloaders were black bears, but how long would that last?

"It would help if the hotels, and your camps too, didn't toss out garbage for the bears," he said. "I know the tourists want to see bears, but is that wise? Could you find better ways to dispose of garbage?"

Ramsay watched Mr. Wylie's face for some sign of anger, but he saw only interest.

"I'll give it some thought. Visitors want to see geysers and bears," Mr. Wylie said, after a pause. "Isn't the mandate of this national park to provide for the enjoyment of all Americans?"

"It is, sir."

"I've heard your own Major Pitcher talk about the bears as entertainment, so he's on my side," Mr. Wylie said.

"He is," Ramsay said, already pretty certain he was going to lose this round. "But that's why bears come around more often, isn't it?"

"No argument from me. We walk a delicate line, don't we, Sergeant Major?"

Ramsay nodded, wondering just how delicate that line was going to become. He thought about the wolf pups he had heard yesterday morning, and the buffalo behind wire fences because they were scarce. "I worry about visitors being mauled, Mr. Wylie, but I have another concern. Bears eating garbage and marshmallows are not healthy bears. They're on their way to becoming beggars, fun to watch, to be sure, but beggars."

"Whose side are you on, Sergeant Major?" Mr. Wylie asked.

Mr. Wylie had tipped himself back in his swivel chair and was staring at the ceiling. Ramsay glanced over at Carrie and saw concern writ large on her face. Was it for the tourists, or the bears?

"I am on the side of the bears," he replied. He wondered if his answer would get him in trouble. He touched his medal of honor ribbon. Who is brave now? "What if this park, and others to come, turn out to be the last stronghold of our national wildlife?"

Mr. Wylie tipped his chair down. "We may have to agree to disagree on this issue, Sergeant Major Stiles," he said, and again Ramsay heard no animosity. He held out his hands, as if encompassing the entire region. "There's so much space here. I believe your worries are unfounded. This wilderness will never disappear."

Ramsay wanted to ask how he could be so certain, but he said nothing.

Mr. Wylie looked at Carrie, who sat with her pencil poised and her eyes troubled. "What about you, Carrie? Your summer employment keeps you in tuition money for college. What if visitors couldn't see any bears? What if I had to lay off workers if too many visitors go elsewhere?"

You're putting her on the spot, Ramsay thought, irritated. Somehow it surprised him that a person as charming as Miss Carrie McKay worked for tuition money. From her carefree demeanor, he had thought she did this as a lark. He thought indulgent parents let their darling daughter earn some money and have a good time during the summer. Why he thought that he couldn't have said, except that her easy ways and kindness pointed to someone well cared for. Well, he had been wrong before.

She put down her pencil. "I am on the side of the bears, Mr. Wylie," she said, her voice firm.

Her employer smiled. "I believe you are, Carrie." He gestured to the tray. "You can take this now. I'll get back to you later about a memo."

She nodded and picked up the tray. She smiled at Ramsay and left the shed quietly.

"People like Carrie McKay need the jobs I provide, Sergeant Major," Mr. Wylie said. "She has tuition and room and board to pay."

Ramsay wished she hadn't left. The room seemed smaller somehow. "I guess I assumed she was working here for fun," he said, and it sounded lame.

"Some of my workers do precisely that. They come from good homes in Washington, Oregon, and Montana," he said. "Not Carrie. You'll have to ask her about her life sometime."

"I can't imagine a situation where I would ever have that opportunity," Ramsay said honestly. He looked around for his hat. This interview was obviously over.

"Don't be such a pessimist, Sergeant Major," Mr. Wylie said. He stood up and extended his hand again. "I don't think Carrie has ever piled that much whipped cream on anyone else's pie before. Stop by on your return around the Grand Loop."

He felt that traitor blush spread up his neck again. "I just might."

"I would," Mr. Wylie said. "Something tells me Carrie will move mountains to find some canned cherries between now and the end of the week. Good day, Sergeant Major Stiles."

Chapter Seven

$\mathcal{R}$amsay Stiles could hope all he wanted, but he had no excuse to keep from mounting Xerxes and continuing south to the Norris soldier station. Carrie was not in sight. He thought about dumping the etiquette book in the nearest burn barrel. He hadn't done a single thing that the book recommended, but did it matter?

Someone had left a bucket of water for Xerxes, someone kind. He looked around again and there she was, her hair tucked up better under her bandanna and a broom in her hand.

"Stop by on the way back," she said. "There might be some canned cherries around here, desperate to escape confinement. And thank you, Sergeant Major Stiles."

"I will stop by, Miss McKay," he replied formally, uncertain if he could resurrect some good manners that would satisfy a reader of an etiquette book. "Are you thanking me for your rescue?"

"No, sir," she said firmly. "I would probably have taken my chances sooner or later. Thank you on behalf of the bears."

He looked in her eyes and she returned his gaze. "I'll do what I can for them."

"They were here first, after all," she said. She started sweeping the back steps. Unable to help himself, he looked back at her several times as he left.

As the apple pie and whipped cream settled in his still-amazed stomach, Ramsay prodded Xerxes into something more ambitious than a stroll, but not much. They sauntered through Swan Lake Flats, their traverse of that lovely meadow heralded by nesting birds who squawked and wished them elsewhere. He watched a mother plover drag herself over the ground, one wing awkwardly extended, trying to lure him to follow an injured bird and not a path close to her babies. A bird is a bird, but her instinctive action touched him.

He crossed the meadow and reined in Xerxes in silent wonder closer to the tree line when a black bear mama idled along under the warm sun, two cubs behind her. They followed her dutifully enough, but with the stop, start, roll, and play of youngsters. Mama gave him a hard stare from a distance, decided he was harmless, and left him alone.

He paused longer at Roaring Mountain, listening to the sound—something between a hiss and a growl—emitted by fumeroles hard at work tossing up water so hot that it turned to steam on the surface of the mountain. *Sulfate gives the mountain its ashy gray color*, he thought, remembering one of Captain Chittenden's informal lectures to visitors lounging on the Mammoth's National Hotel porch. The engineer was a one-man Chautauqua, ready to dispense information if anyone asked.

He thought about Mr. Wylie's wish that soldiers could furnish factual information. "Why not?" he asked Xerxes, who only shook his big head. "Seriously, Xerxes. Who is in a better place to teach than soldiers guarding park treasures?"

He was approaching the soldier station near Norris Geyser Basin, idling along the Gibbon River, when he reined in to watch a moose and her baby work their way down the bank toward the water. The mother went in easily in a spot where the water was shallow and protected by a fallen tree. The baby paced back and forth, tossing its head, uncertain.

"You can do it, little guy," Ramsay whispered, even as he fingered the coiled rope looped on his saddle. Jack Strong ranched in Paradise Valley north of Gardiner and had taught him to rope one summer. Ramsay wondered if he remembered anything.

Ramsay watched the moose calf come closer to the water a step at a time. Mama cow stayed right there. Over the hiss and hum of the water, Ramsay heard her low encouragement.

"You can do this, Mama," he said and took his hand off the rope. In another moment, the calf went in, flailed a bit, then was nudged upright by Mama's long nose. They stood nose to nose a moment, and soon Moose Junior munched on vegetation at the water's edge.

He sat there in appreciation of motherhood and thought that Carrie McKay might like to spend a day along this bank too, doing nothing more than watching critters. Too bad she had to work for her living, same as he did. A chipmunk sassed him from a rock and he took it as a sign to move along.

He spent the night at the Norris Soldier Station, happy to sit on the porch with the corporal and two privates from B Company. It was no imaginary supposition they had looked at him warily at first, he who knew them well, but who now held a significantly more exalted rank and wore those silver stars on their little blue ribbon. Better to clear the air right now, or it would be a long summer and longer winter.

"Let's get one thing straight, troopers," he said, returning to the porch after he had removed Xerxes's saddle and bridle, hobbled him, and left him happy in belly-high grass. "I still look out for you and I suppose in formal settings I should be Sergeant Major. My job has changed, but let's understand one thing: at times like this, I'm Sarge."

He watched them relax. "Don't think I've forgotten how this works," Ramsay continued. "I'm the odd man out and I showed up without any warning. Unless something has changed in the year and a half some of us were overseas, that means I do the dishes tonight, doesn't it?"

The men laughed. Ramsay knew he was home again when the corporal handed him a fishing pole and pointed toward the fast-moving river. "Sarge, try that spot behind the log where it's running quieter. We've already caught dinner, but we'll wait."

"If you don't take too long, Sarge," someone said and the men laughed again.

He took the pole with a smile of his own and a private handed him a glop of something stinky from the bait can by the front door. He walked downstream to the well-remembered spot. Four casts landed him a cutthroat trout and then another. The tree stump close to the bank still served as the clean and filet station. He tossed the head closer to the bank, knowing the bears would appreciate it. The scales left his fingers iridescent.

They dined in high style at the table in the great room on trout and crisp slices of potato well-salted and drenched in ketchup. Someone opened a can of peaches and they took turns spearing the soft goodness until nothing was left but peach juice. In time-honored fashion, the corporal silently chose a number. Everyone wrote down a number and put it facedown on the table. The corporal called out the number, and Private Costello was closest. He drank the juice from the can and everyone sat back, satisfied.

They talked of the coming tourist invasion, road and bridge-building, and when the paymaster could be expected. Content to listen, Ramsay sat back and felt his shoulders relax and his eyes grow heavy. Someone speculated about how pretty the Wylie Camping Company girls might be this season, and Ramsay smiled inside, thinking of Carrie McKay, who cared about bears and made pie.

"Sarge?"

"H'mm? What?" he asked, surprised out of his reverie.

"What do you think?"

About what? Somewhere in contemplating Carrie's childlike round eyes he must have missed the ebb and flow of conversation around him. He yawned. "I'm old. Tell me again."

Polite laughter. "Think we'll be called back to the Philippines anytime soon?" the corporal asked.

Great gobs of monkey meat I hope not, Ramsay thought. The jungle seemed as far away as another planet, sitting there as they were in front of a massive fireplace nearly as noisy as Roaring Mountain.

"I doubt it," he said, but how did he know? Somehow the high command in Washington, D.C., made its decisions without his suggestions. It was enough to be back in Yellowstone, warm and well-fed and trying to figure out a strategic move that would land him in Carrie McKay's orbit again.

As he looked around, he could tell the men wanted more of an answer. "Two more years here," he said, basing that on nothing except his own wishes.

He must have said it with some conviction because most of the men nodded. He looked at the corporal, who had returned with him in November from that former Spanish possession in the Pacific Ocean, and saw the same wariness in his eyes that Ramsay saw when he looked in a mirror. The two privates hadn't been to war yet.

"Two years at least, Corporal," he said. "I'd like to think we did our job."

"We did, Sarge, but who listens to us?" the corporal asked.

Who indeed? One of the privates stretched and stood up. Ramsay remembered Xerxes hobbled out front and rose too. He stopped at the door, remembering what he wanted to ask all the soldiers he saw on this ride-about of his through Yellowstone.

"Men, think about this and let me know before I ride out tomorrow: would you like to learn enough about the geyser basin here to give our visitors good information, if they asked?"

"You mean not feed them some tall tale, Sarge?" one of the privates asked.

"Exactly. We're in a unique position to provide some education, in addition to following orders of a more military nature."

Ramsay looked around at his little audience, seeing skepticism on one face, but interest on two others. That was about the ratio he expected. "Share your ideas with me tomorrow," he concluded. "I have better things to do right now."

"Sarge, are you heading to Norris's chief reason for existence?" the corporal asked with a smile.

"Besides protecting wildlife and natural phenomena? Are roses red?" Ramsay replied. "After I see to Xerxes, of course."

"Of course. Remember the rule, Sarge."

He waved a hand and walked onto the porch, looking for Xerxes. He removed the hobbles and led his horse to the stables, staying there a moment to make sure the men were taking adequate care of their mounts. All was well. He knew the corporal understood the equine business better than most.

And now for something he had been waiting to do for eighteen months at least. Ramsay pulled a towel, washrag, and soap from his saddlebag and headed for the wooden shack down by the Gibbon. Now and then a June rise would carry off the structure, but someone at the Norris Station always replaced it.

He opened the door and breathed in the rotten egg odor he took for granted. His towel went on its handy nail. Sure enough, there was a box of matches by the kerosene lamp, primed and ready.

He shucked his clothes and looked in appreciation at the handiwork of some enlisted man in distant days who must have been a mason in a previous career, or more likely an enterprising thief. Whoever that person was, he had lined a portion of the dugout bank with bricks probably brought down from Bozeman, maybe a few at a time, perhaps carefully swiped from some brick yard and stuffed in saddle bags. It was hard to say about some soldiers, but no one who ever used the Norris bathhouse ever questioned the matter, not even the officers.

As he settled himself onto the brick shelf, he sank back with a sigh into a judicious natural mixture of water from some little hot spring as it meandered into the Gibbon. Mammoth had a so-so bathhouse open to visitors, but the degree of hot to cold at the Norris's brick-lined soak apparently could not be duplicated anywhere else in the park. It was perfect.

Amply informed about their bathhouse, the troopers had dictated that no one could soak longer than twenty minutes at a time. Staying in much longer could make even the toughest soldier lightheaded.

After a lengthy soak, in which whatever cares he hauled around took a distinct back seat in his brain, Ramsay soaped himself and washed. The soapy water flowed away down the river, taking with it another layer of guerilla warfare in the Luzon Peninsula. "Take it all, river," he said out loud. "I sure don't want it."

Somehow, another much more pleasant layer seemed to attach itself to his bare skin, one that involved blue eyes and a cheerful face. There was apple pie and whipped cream jumbled into the mix, and a bucket of water for Xerxes. It all began to swirl together like the hot spring water meeting the cold river, which suggested he was getting lightheaded.

It was too soon to feel dizzy from the heat. He smiled to think of how thoroughly he had trashed every bit of good advice in the etiquette book. Maybe some things were just meant to happen, polite manners or not. Maybe the wheel was finally turning in his favor. Or maybe he was a bit dizzy from the heat. That was the more logical explanation for his dreamy kaleidoscope.

Getting out was nearly as much fun as getting in. He stood up and moved more into the stream of the river, letting the cold smack his body until he felt invigorated and ready to slay dragons, should any appear in this district.

He toweled off, pulled on his smallclothes and carried his uniform back to the station. The great room was dark now. Even if it hadn't been, there wasn't anyone who would be shocked by his less-than-soldierly appearance. He couldn't be so casual in a week, when tourist traffic ran past the station until nightfall. Right now, it didn't matter.

Back inside the cabin, he prepared to spread his bedroll on the floor in front of the fireplace when the corporal stepped out of his own room and pointed to the empty officer's room. "You're entitled, Sarge," he said.

"Not really," Ramsay said.

The corporal nodded. He leaned against the doorframe of his room. "Sergeant Major, if you don't mind the observation, you're neither fish nor fowl now, are you?"

"I've been thinking that same thing, Corporal," Ramsay said, appreciating the man's frank observation.

"How do you like it?"

"Ask me in a year."

The corporal said goodnight and went into his room. Ramsay started to shake out his bedroll onto the floor, but then changed his mind. "Since I'm neither fish nor fowl," he said and opened the door to the officer's room. He took the mattress from the empty bed into the great room and plopped it on the floor. His blankets and pillow went down next. He stretched out and sighed with pleasure. Perfect.

He thought through the day, starting with Sam Deer Nose, moving to Carrie McKay and her apple pie, and finishing with trout for dinner, hot-potting, and now a comfortable bed. As his eyes closed, he made a mental note to visit Jack Strong soon at his ranch in Paradise Valley, per Major Pitcher's orders, but also for his own pleasure.

He thought about Carrie again, touched by her unabashed interest in what he was doing in the park, and interested in her easy camaraderie with Mr. Wylie, who had suggested he, Sergeant Major Stiles, find out more about her by stopping now and then. Why would Mr. Wylie do that?

He turned on his side and tugged up his blanket. He drifted toward sleep, thinking how much he would like to twine one of Carrie's curls around his finger. Such a bold act would earn him a slap in the chops, which made him decide to do no such thing. She was just a kid, anyway. Probably had her eye on one of the college men, some pup more her age, whatever that was. Someone as pretty as Carrie would never want for stalwart company.

All the same, Carrie McKay wasn't that easy to dismiss. He thought about small talk that might engage her interest but discarded that avenue. He already knew she wasn't a trivial sort of woman, not someone who cared about bears and didn't mind admitting it.

He tried to think of a way to spend some time in Carrie's vicinity this summer. Nothing came to mind, but that didn't mean a man couldn't dream. An hour later, he was still staring at the beams overhead, almost wishing one would drop down, conk him on the head, and send him into unconsciousness, if not slumber.

Supremely dissatisfied with himself, Ramsay got up and opened the front door. He leaned his elbows on the railing and stared at the Gibbon River whispering along. He heard coyotes tuning up in the meadow, their series of yips and barks so different from the howl of a lone wolf.

The corporal's observation of his neither fish nor fowl status made him pause and consider. Lone wolves didn't belong in anyone's pack. They hunted in solitary, traveled by themselves, and eventually moved on to another valley, looking for something. When he was supposed to have been trapping and hunting them down, per government orders, Ramsay had observed lone wolves trying to work their way into an established pack. The result was usually a fight and a chase.

I don't want to be a lone wolf, he thought.

Chapter Eight

*C*arrie McKay turned over her pillow for the umpteenth time, searching for that elusive cool spot. She had reached that state of weariness after a long day cooking, cleaning, and scrubbing that usually ushered in a good night's sleep.

Usually. She flopped onto her back and stared up at the red and white striped ceiling. She decided to count the stripes and laughed at herself. She had learned in the hard school of life that it was better to make the most of small moments. Carrie felt herself relax as she reminded herself how nice it was to sleep in a room—well, a tent—all by herself, with no one snoring or chattering with a roommate.

Any day now, there would be at least two other Wylie girls sharing Tent Twenty-Six for the summer. She hoped they would be congenial and pleasant, at least until Millie Thorne started gossiping and passing on unfounded rumors.

She turned her head at the sound of laughter from the nearest tent, where two girls from the University of Washington had staked their claim.

Two days ago and newly arrived herself, Carrie had gone to their tent to see if she could join them for the summer. She went no farther than the pathway because Millie Thorne, a fellow Montana Agricultural College student, had showed up first, making the third tent-mate. After that, Carrie knew better than to suggest she make up the fourth. Sure as the world, Millie had already acquainted the U-Dub girls with Carrie McKay's moral deficiencies as a human being. She could ask, but Millie would tell her nicely that a fourth girl from the University of Oregon was due any day now. So sorry.

Better to back away without saying anything and pretend it didn't matter. She could say she didn't care what people thought of her, but Carrie McKay couldn't fool herself; what's more, she never tried to fool herself. She did care.

It was also true she found it nice to lie in bed with no one else around, warm in her blankets, and stomach full. She finally allowed herself to sink into the mattress, mull over the day, and contemplate tomorrow. The cook had asked her after dinner tonight if she would clean out the dry goods storeroom, then whispered that Carrie could keep whatever crackers she wanted that were left over from the 1902 summer season and not too stale.

"Only if you see a need," Bonnie Boone had added. She understood, because Mr. Wylie must have told his Willow Park cook something about the little strawberry-blond who worked so hard.

Carrie had thought she would not see the necessity of extra food this summer, but a girl had to be cautious. Maybe next summer she could go to bed without squirreling away a little something to eat. It never amounted to much: a heel of bread, a handful of oyster crackers— something easy to slip into her apron pocket and then put in the cubbyhole by her bed. Sometimes she ate it during the night, sometimes it was still there in the morning, which Carrie considered a modest victory. Right now, it gave her some peace to see food when she went to sleep, and when she woke.

She couldn't tell what the girls in the next tent were talking about, but since Millie had wormed her way into their twosome, it was only a matter of time before it became obvious in the way they treated her. *Millie, I know you're eager to tell them that my father was a drunk and deserted me and Mam*, she thought, *and then tell them Mam was an upstairs woman at the saloon. It's not true, but that's what you'll pass on, because you're spiteful.*

Papa was a drunk; that much was true. He left one night, saying vaguely that he was stepping out with the boys; she and Mam never saw him again. She was only twelve when he left, but the memory of the relief they both felt had never faded. Mam always saw the positive side of the worst events. "At least we don't have to walk on eggshells when he's drinking, or worry about a beating any more," Mam had said.

As for her mother, Mam worked hard in the kitchen of Bozeman's Railroad Hotel, which did boast a stable of sporting women on the second floor. Mam cooked, cleaned, and scrubbed in the main floor café, and Carrie worked right beside her. As Mam grew more and more deaf, the result of one of Papa's beatings, Carrie found herself speaking for both of them. They managed, but barely. School for Carrie was out of the question, so she didn't complain.

Two years of this, and then Mam took ill and died. The city of Bozeman buried her, but didn't see the necessity of anything beyond a wooden marker with Mary McKay and date of death, written in grease pencil. Carrie touched it up every year and wished she could afford a proper headstone.

Carrie lay there, wondering why she was reminding herself of those bad years. Usually she daydreamed herself to sleep, remembering how Mam always sang to her before she drifted off to slumber. Now she mostly wished she could remember Mam's voice.

Carrie sang to herself then, keeping her voice low and singing partly under the blankets. Mam's repertory hadn't been huge, but there was a song for most moods. Since today had been a good day, she sang the chorus of "Love's Old Sweet Song," first in her mind, just to savor the words privately with Mam somehow, and then aloud.

Just a song at twilight, when the lights are low,
And the flick'ring shadows softly come and go,
Tho the heart be weary, sad the day and long,
Still to us at twilight comes Love's old song,
Comes Love's old sweet song.

"That's for you, Mam," she said and closed her eyes, expecting sleep to come, as it usually did after her favorite ritual.

Not tonight. She knew why and admitted it to herself because she had never learned how to gild a lily. "Mam, I really think Sergeant Major Stiles is a handsome man," she said out loud, but soft. She liked that his hair color was the same as hers, even though his eyes were brown. She knew he must have trouble in the summer with sunburn, same as she did, and wondered if he used zinc oxide on his nose. Probably not; it wasn't dignified, and he did look dignified.

No horsewoman herself, she had long admired the posture of the cavalrymen who regularly patrolled the roads, geysers, and hot springs. Carrie wondered if Sergeant Major Stiles ever leaned back in a chair, and doubted it. From the deferential sound in Mr. Wylie's voice, a sergeant major must be someone special. Maybe a man didn't get to that rank if he slouched in his chair.

He had been kind to rescue her from the backhouse, but she knew he had performed more notable tasks. After Sergeant Major Stiles left, Mr. Wylie told her about the article in the Bozeman paper last winter concerning the trooper earning a Medal of Honor in a terrible place. Carrie laughed to herself about her rescue from the privy by a medal winner. A person could be embarrassed by such a rescue, considering that real ladies probably pretended that they never ever even used a backhouse, or burped, or passed a little gas.

She relished again in Sergeant Major Stiles's evident appreciation of her dried apple pie with that nearly obscene mound of whipped cream on it. When she had whispered to Bonnie Boone that there was a really spiffy-looking trooper in Mr. Wylie's office who had been thinking about pie for ages, the cook had done the honors herself. "Give this to him, dearie," Bonnie had insisted. "He won't turn it down."

She had watched his face grow serious when he talked about bears and park duties, and she wished he could take her around the park some day, just to show her more animals than she saw at Willow Park Camp. She knew it would never happen, but just thinking about it put a smile on her face.

She slept then, only waking up once when one of the camp men banged a metal spoon on a frying pan to scare away bears. Once the camp filled up with horses and wagons, tourists and more summer help, Carrie hoped the bears would retreat more to the edge of the camp.

She knew how much the visitors from the Midwest and back East yearned to see bears, photograph and feed them, but Sergeant Major Stiles was right. Feeding bears Vienna sausages and bread fried in lard probably wasn't a way to keep them healthy.

Once the spoon on the frying pan clatter stopped, Carrie closed her eyes, thinking that it wouldn't be hard to convince Bonnie Boone to let her make a cherry pie every other day, on the chance that Sergeant Major Stiles might actually stop on his return to Mammoth Hot Springs and Fort Yellowstone.

After all, a girl can dream, and Carrie McKay did precisely that.

Just as an experiment—nothing more, mind you—Ramsay Stiles tested the pie at Fountain Hotel when he delivered Major Pitcher's letter there, and again at Lake Hotel the following day. He was scrupulous about paying for the food he ate, and then remembered he hadn't even offered to pay for that apple pie at Willow Park.

Fountain Hotel did have cherry pie, but the crust lacked the feathery lightness of Carrie McKay's dried apple offering. Lake Hotel's rendition of black bottom pie, something he hadn't eaten since B Company was garrisoned in Texas, did give him pause. He told Mr. Marsh, the manager at that grandest park hotel, that he would happily give the cook a peck on the cheek. He had a good laugh at his expense when Mr. Marsh told him the author of all that magnificence was a Hungarian chef who probably wouldn't take kindly to a kiss.

The pastry chef at Canyon Hotel specialized in sponge cake, but he ate a slice anyway and came away suitably impressed with the bits of lemon and orange peel in the glaze. Ramsay also realized that if he kept sampling the wares at each hotel, he would have to trot alongside Xerxes so he could continue to button his trousers without straining.

Never one to shy away from stories that put him in a less-than-glorified light, he told his fellow cavalrymen at every soldier station where he spent each night about his quest for cherry pie. He did it for the reason that had become obvious to him at the first stop in Norris. The men of the First Cavalry Regiment, garrisoned here and there in the West, had known him for years as a first sergeant, someone they called Sarge. This sergeant major was a horse of a different color, and so was the hero—oh, that word—wearing the Medal of Honor ribbon Major Pitcher insisted upon. The men knew Sarge; they didn't know the sergeant major yet.

Ramsay had explained the whole matter to Xerxes on the boring ride from Norris to the Lower Geyser Basin and the Fountain Hotel, where the only view was one lodgepole pine after another for many miles. Maybe he could even twit Captain Chittenden about a stretch of Yellowstone Park that verged on dullness. He could tease him that he expected better from a Corps of Engineers road builder and get that slow smile and then a good laugh from an officer who knew his worth and didn't mind a joke.

Ramsay's horse was always a useful sounding board, if no one was around except ravens and chipmunks. "Xerxes, the men have to know me as the same sergeant if they're ever going to let me mold them into serious guides who will want to educate tourists instead of prey on their gullibility with tall tales."

Xerxes had no comment beyond a shake of the reins. "My men knew they could trust Sarge," Ramsay said. "They have to trust Sergeant Major Stiles too, don't you think? They already know I expect them to be the best troopers. Now I want something more."

His notebook was full of commentary from hoteliers about his men, and how they could improve. The concessionaires at the lunch counters had some thoughts on soldiers who liked handouts, which made Ramsay even more conscientious about paying for every bite he ate on this little jog around the park. His men at each station had their own opinions about tourists trying to knock off bits of geyser cones to take home, or to bottle the water from hot springs. This vandalism invariably led to burns, which meant the soldiers were to blame for letting them get that close to danger in the first place. Everyone had a side to take, and each side was valid.

By the time he returned to Norris Soldier Station, his head ached from the accumulation of praise and complaints and good ideas and bad ones. He soaked in the hot water again, fished for his dinner, wrote down more ideas from the Norris soldiers, and slept fitfully, wondering why he had agreed to this promotion in the first place. Could a soldier request a reduction in rank that had nothing to do with felonies or misdemeanors? He thought not, and kept his worries to himself.

Before he swung into the saddle in the morning, he sat on the porch, watching the Gibbon River sparkle in the sunlight and listening to magpies picking a fight with each other. He heard something crashing through in the willows near the river bank and assumed a moose was blundering by. Surrounded by so much beauty, his late-night doubts returned to their crypt, much like the actor portraying Dracula in the play he saw last winter while in

Washington, D.C. He was pretty sure other men doubted, even though most never spoke of their moments of real uncertainty. Maybe that was another good use for wives. The poor things had to listen; maybe they even enjoyed it.

He smiled to himself, thinking that a wife would at least answer him, unlike Xerxes. In his next breath he thought of Carrie McKay and wondered how in the world he could ever see her again without appearing like a bumbler or an opportunist.

Then it hit him, and he nearly laughed out loud. He hadn't even offered to pay for that magnificent piece of apple pie he had gulped down like a drowning man taking on water. Some leader he was. He had just finished advising companies of soldiers to be more scrupulous about paying for food at the hotels and lunch counters. Sergeant Major Hypocrite owed a debt to the Willow Park Wylie Camping Company.

"Xerxes, we have a stop to make," he told his horse as he mounted and started at a sedate pace to Willow Park. "A gentleman always pays his own way."

Chapter Nine

$\mathcal{I}$'m going to be out of a job before the tourists even arrive, if Mr. Wylie finds out what a pastry maker you are," Bonnie Boone teased as Carrie lifted her fourth cherry pie in as many days out of the oven.

"Bonnie, your job is safe," Carrie teased back. "I have so much to learn."

"Seriously, let's change your title from kitchen flunkie to assistant cook," Bonnie told her.

"That has a certain ring to it, but probably the same salary," Carrie teased back. She put the second cherry pie of the morning into the oven, then held her hand there. "If my fingernails don't start to tingle, then I need to add another stick of wood?"

"Or two. Between you and me, Mr. Wylie likes cherry pie as well as your sergeant," the cook said.

"He's not my sergeant," Carrie said quickly, hoping Bonnie would blame her red face on a cook stove. "You should have seen the wistful look on his face when he said he'd been thinking about cherry pie for a whole year in the Philippines. I . . . I . . . took pity on him. That's all."

"How do you know he's not your sergeant?" Bonnie countered, not one to give up an interesting line of inquiry. "You might not have noticed, because you were sweeping the steps as he rode off, but he looked back several times."

"Oh, Bonnie, he didn't! Did he?"

Bonnie patted her cheek. Carrie put up her hand to keep it there. "Mam used to do that," she said softly. "I like it."

"I had a daughter once," Bonnie said. She patted Carrie's cheek again, then turned to the prep table. Carrie noticed that the cook didn't do anything except stare at the table and then sigh, before she reached for a cookery book.

We all have our stories, Carrie thought. *Who is ever brave enough to tell them? Who cares enough to listen?* She set the finished pie on a window ledge, the pie for Sergeant Major Stiles, should he ever return in a million years.

Still, pie is pie and everyone likes it, Carrie knew. When the tourists started arriving soon in huge numbers, she was going to ask Bonnie if she could start making the twenty or so pies a day that were one of the many reasons people liked camping—call it what you will for Eastern visitors—in what was increasingly known as the Wylie Way.

She breathed deep of the pie and looked out the window to watch the camp men put up the last of the striped tents. The place that had been a jumble of canvas and ropes at the beginning of the week was now a colorful tent city, ready for the first tourists to arrive on a Wylie coach, tired of bumpy travel but eager for adventure because they were in Wonderland.

Mr. Wylie had given his annual employee pep talk last night around a campfire, with everyone seated on logs and bowls of popcorn already circulating. He reminded them that tourists were their guests and deserved of every attention.

"They have paid $35 each for our best six-day tour, and I depend upon you savages . . ." Everyone chuckled. They knew the park nickname for Mr. Wylie's summertime help. ". . . to be on your best behavior, and show these Easterners our Yellowstone Park enthusiasm."

Carrie had waited for that moment when the former educator, who knew how to command a classroom, held up one finger. "Remember this, my savage friends: our little national park system is based on eight simple words. Who knows them?"

Several hands went up, Carrie's among them. "Say them with me," Mr. Wylie commanded.

"For the benefit and enjoyment of the people," Carrie said in company with others, with all the pride in her heart, because she believed it. Never mind that stupid old Millie Thorne and her already indoctrinated tentmates snickered at her. *For the benefit and enjoyment of even the little people*, Carrie thought. *I know who I am.*

She had done something then that was still on her mind this morning. Instead of turning away in embarrassment from Millie Thorne—a definite thorn in her side—she smiled and nodded with what must have been serenity, and enjoyed the quiet satisfaction of seeing dismay on Millie's face.

Maybe if she ever saw Sergeant Major Stiles again and felt courageous, Carrie could tell him she could be brave too. She knew her kind of bravery would seem silly to a real hero. It was enough to realize she could learn from someone else, whether he ever knew it or not.

Mr. Wylie had left early this morning on horseback to give the same message to the other campsites, most of the others located close to the posh, traditional hotels of the

Yellowstone Park Association. Their little camp at Willow Park stood by itself, as though announcing its independence from stuffiness and elegance.

Carrie took another deep breath, hoped, and then turned back to preparing the dining tables for lunch in an hour. She had finished setting out knives, forks, and spoons rolled in their napkins and was starting on the plates when Bonnie stepped into the dining room, her eyes lively.

"I'm to ask if Miss Carrie McKay has any cherry pie," the cook announced. She stepped aside to usher in Sergeant Major Stiles, who took off his campaign hat and set it on a hook by the door, indicating to Carrie a willingness to stay a while.

Carrie had to move her feet, but she felt rooted to the spot, weighed down by sudden shyness. When had she ever hoped for something and seen a result as positive as this one? She couldn't remember a time, but there he was.

"I wondered if you had . . ."

"I've been hoping you might . . ."

They laughed, which somehow seemed to make Carrie capable of movement again. She set down the plates and came closer, still shy, but determined not to waste a moment of this soldier's time. His hat already hanging on the nail suggested that he wasn't in a hurry.

"I certainly do have cherry pie, Sergeant Major Stiles," she said, wishing she didn't sound so breathless. She couldn't blame it on the altitude, because she already lived at altitude in Bozeman the rest of the year. She worked up the nerve to look into his honest eyes and decided she should be honest too. Somehow, it was starting to matter. "I've made a cherry pie every day this week."

"For the other employees?" he asked, and there was no overlooking his blush.

Don't stop now, Carrie, she advised herself. "They enjoy it, but I did it for you, because I know you wanted it, and you've been in tough places. Would you like some now?"

"More than just about anything," he replied, "but first I need to make a confession and suggest a restitution."

"Um . . .well . . ." That sounds intelligent, Carrie, she scolded herself. "Should I sit down, in case this is life-shattering?" she joked, relieved to think of something, no matter how stupid.

He gestured toward the nearest bench, and sat beside her. "I've been traveling the Grand Loop, as I told you and Mr. Wylie. I've advised the troopers to make sure they offer to pay for everything they eat that isn't an army ration." He hung his head in mock contrition. "And here I am, a major offender, who didn't pay a red cent for that apple pie and enough whipped cream for three slices. I came to make amends, Miss McKay."

Carrie laughed out loud, and stopped herself just in time from putting her hand on his arm. "As I remember it, Mr. Wylie invited you to have that piece of pie. You don't owe a thing."

"You're certain?" he asked.

"Positive," she said firmly. She stood up and went to the window, where the still-warm pie was sending out its come-hither fragrance. "That'll be ten cents for this and another nickel for whipped cream."

He was already reaching into his pocket. "How about thirty cents, so you can have some too? I mean, if you can spare fifteen minutes with me?"

Carrie glanced at the door into the kitchen, which was slightly ajar. "I'll go ask the cook. I think I have time."

81

She opened the door on Bonnie, her eyes bright. She had obviously been eavesdropping, which made Carrie smile. "Can you spare me for fifteen minutes?"

"Twenty, but not a minute more," Bonnie said. "Hand over that pie and I'll slice it."

"Fifteen minutes, and maybe even twenty," Carrie told the sergeant major as she retrieved the pie and took it to Bonnie, who cut two pieces and put only a dignified amount of whipped cream on both.

Carrie turned around to carry the pie back to the table, but Sergeant Major Stiles stood right behind her, his hand out. She laughed and gave him a plate and a fork, and stepped aside so he could hand Bonnie thirty cents.

"Twenty minutes?" he asked Bonnie.

Bonnie nodded. "I'm strict and tough," she told him.

Sergeant Major Stiles reached for his hat, put it on and gave the cook a smart salute, right down to a click of his heels. He crooked out his arm and Carrie did not hesitate to put her arm through his. Bonnie kindly opened the screen door and shooed them out.

"Where's a good spot to eat this pie?" he asked. "Somewhere not too crowded so no one will hear if I whimper in sheer delight. I'm certain there is nothing in the red book about eating pie."

"Red book?"

"I'll show you later."

Carrie led him toward last night's campfire, with the logs arranged so carefully and ready for the first visitors of summer. "We had our summer pep talk here last night," she said.

"How to be good savages and treat the tourists as though you were related to them?"

"That one, Sergeant Major. Even better than relatives," she added, and he laughed.

When they walked past the dining room and Wylie store, she held her breath to see Millie Thorne stare at her and glower from the red and white tent where she was making beds. She waited for that familiar fear to turn around a few times in her stomach like a demon dog, but nothing happened. Maybe this was what Mam meant when she told Carrie years ago how nice it must be to have a dependable man around. Whatever she felt, she liked it and smiled at Millie, who looked away.

To her amusement, Sergeant Major Stiles let go of her arm, took out a red bandanna and elaborately wiped the log before indicating that she seat herself. He sat beside her and removed his hat again.

"I suppose I should make some small talk but it's not happening, not with this bit of heaven in my hand," he said, then took a bite, and another one. Carrie watched with lively interest.

"Sergeant Major, your eyes might get stuck if you keep rolling them back in your head," she teased, which made him smile and dig in again.

Shy, delighted, and unsure of herself all at the same time, Carrie did what anyone so afflicted would do and took a bite of her own.

Sergeant Major Stiles finished first. "Do you think I could talk the cook out of what remains of that pie?"

"There is every hope," Carrie told him. "She might charge you fifty cents."

"Worth every penny." He pulled out his timepiece. "I have roughly another ten minutes. Let me run something by you, Miss McKay." He hesitated, and she watched his face redden again, the curse of the strawberry blond. "Oh, hang it. I could read a library of etiquette books and never do the right thing. Let's do this: I'll call you Carrie if you call me Ramsay."

This doesn't happen to people like me, Carrie reminded herself. Not ever. She hung onto her fork, but handed him the rest of her pie, not because he was eyeing it, but because she wanted to. "I'm full, and you're not, Ramsay," she said simply.

"Thanks, Carrie," he said with no embarrassment, and ate her pie too. "Here's what's on my mind," he began when he had finished and had set the two plates on the ground. "I want to write something about each hot spring and geyser, or . . . or Roaring Mountain—just a little something—and put it in a booklet. So every soldier standing patrol at one of Wonderland's features will be able to answer simple questions visitors might ask. What do you think?"

"You mean, as opposed to telling them that breathing too much sulfur will make a man go bald?" she teased.

"Hadn't heard that one," he said and ran his hand across his thick head of hair, probably an unconscious gesture.

Good thing she hadn't added she overheard the teamsters telling one wide-eyed tourist that sulfur made a man bald *and* sterile. She bit back a smile. "I think your idea is a great one. Would all the soldiers go along with it?"

"Carrie, you forget what organization I work for. If Major Pitcher likes the idea, he'll make it an order."

She could see from the enthusiasm in his eyes that enough solitary miles on horseback equaled a well-considered plan.

"It can be a small book, something the size of the red book we already carry."

He pulled a worn, red leather notebook from his back pocket. The curve told her he had carried it on his hip for years. Somehow that touched her heart, even though she couldn't have told a jury of her peers precisely why. Maybe it spoke of duty, and lots of it.

He handed it to her. "Take a look. If you ever want to know what to do in Yellowstone, here's your bible, right down to arresting poachers."

"Oh, I don't think I'd . . . You're teasing."

She leafed through the book, feeling her face grow rosy again because the book was still warm. She stopped at random on page twenty-one and read out loud. "'Scouts and noncommissioned officers in charge of stations throughout the park are authorized and directed to kills mountain lions, coyotes, and timber wolves.'" She looked up and watched the light go out of Ramsay's eyes. "My goodness. I don't think you like this much. Not sure I do, either."

"You found my least favorite page," he said. He took the book from her, closed it, and slipped it back in his hip pocket. He gazed into the distance then and she knew he was quoting from memory: "'They will do this themselves, and will not delegate the authority to anyone else.'"

She stared at him, not knowing what to say, all the while certain he had so much he wanted to tell her. "Why?" she asked finally, wondering if he had anyone to unburden himself to. Come to think of it, did she? "Why?"

"Someone in the Department of the Interior, someone who has probably been no farther west than Pittsburgh, is convinced he knows what we need out here," he said, and there was no mistaking his disdain.

"No one can change this man's mind, whoever he is?"

"We're talking about the government, Carrie," he said and seemed to almost age before her eyes. "They don't seem to grasp that when the predators are finally gone—and gone they will be, mark my word—what's to prevent the elk and deer herds from growing to uncontrollable size? What will that do to the grass and foliage in this park? Tree bark even?"

"I . . . I could write a letter," she offered, which made the sergeant major smile and look not quite so old. "Don't make fun of me!"

"I'm not," he said. "I appreciate your concern. You're not afraid of man-eating wolves and slavering mountain lions, ready to pounce?"

When had this conversation gone from cherry pie to hard duty? Carrie could nearly feel the sergeant major's concern. She was silent, thinking what it was that made her care about creatures she should probably fear.

"I guess I believe every living creature deserves a chance," she said finally, hoping she didn't sound silly, which was the last thing she wanted to seem before this thoughtful man. "I hope that doesn't make me sound silly."

"It makes you sound kind," he said.

"All I ever want is a chance," she told him, remembering dark days in the too-recent past, and worry about making enough money this summer for tuition.

Maybe her face clouded over then. She didn't mean to air out her problems in front of someone she barely knew.

"Life's kinda tough?" he asked gently.

She nodded before she could stop herself. "Could be worse," she amended hastily.

He looked at his timepiece again. "We only have three minutes."

Carrie took a deep breath, uncertain she could laugh this off. She could try. "My worries are not your worries," she told the sergeant major, striving for a light tone. "I'm not in charge of wolves or mountain lions." She chuckled and felt better. "Only pie. Come on. Let's see if Mrs. Boone will sell you that pie."

He put on his hat, picked up the dishes which she took from him, and walked beside her, in no particular hurry. They passed the tent where Millie Thorne stood, hands on her hips, watching them. When they were closer to the dining room, Ramsay gave Carrie a sidelong glance and whispered, "That one back there was giving one of us the hairy eyeball, and I don't know her."

Carrie smiled at his slang. "Wasn't you," she assured him. "The things I could tell you." *There I go again*, she thought, exasperated with herself. *He'll think I am the most helpless female in Gallatin County.* "I can't tell you in three minutes," she concluded, hoping that would put him off.

It didn't, and she wasn't certain if she was relieved or dismayed. "Is the Willow Park Camp having its usual evening entertainment with popcorn and singing?" he asked, opening the dining room door for her.

"Same as always," she said.

"Maybe if I stopped by some night, you could squeeze out more than twenty minutes?"

She could have said no, and ended all this. Heaven knows why she decided to look at his face again and into the kindest eyes. He was tall; he was dignified; he wore a Medal of Honor service ribbon on his uniform blouse, for heaven's sake. He was a grown man, and not one of the Wylie camp men or the college students in Bozeman. For all she knew he was forty years old. A man doesn't get that many wrinkles around his eyes and not have a lot of years to accompany them.

"How old are you?" she blurted out, amazed at herself the moment the words left her mouth. Had she never heard of proper manners?

"Thirty-four," he said promptly. "Time's up, but I have all my own teeth, plus a scar or two. No tattoos. I've never been that drunk. Good day, Miss Carrie McKay. Close your mouth or you'll catch flies. Now where is that cook?"

Silent, eyes big, she pointed toward the kitchen. "Where's my broom?" she asked, desperate to be doing something because she felt young, awkward, and silly.

She couldn't help but laugh when the sergeant major pointed to the broom in plain sight beside the back door. "Planning a quick flight?"

"You are perfectly wretched," she said and felt better again.

"See you some night when the moon is full, so my trusty horse won't stumble into a geyser or fall off the Golden Gate Canyon," he said and then went into the kitchen. "Mrs. Boone," she heard him say. "I have a proposition. Fifty cents and you're in."

"My goodness," Carrie said softly as she returned to setting the table. "My goodness."

Chapter Ten

*B*onnie Boone gave Ramsay the pie for forty cents and wrapped the tin in great swaths of waxed paper. "Make sure I get that tin back," she ordered.

"Without fail," he assured her.

"Don't send it along with someone else," the cook said, and Ramsay couldn't ignore the twinkle in her eyes. "Make sure you bring it back."

He did something so out of character that it amazed him the moment he did it. He kissed Mrs. Boone's forehead.

He could tell he had flustered her, but Mrs. Boone was not a woman to be trifled with. "Bring back the tin, Sergeant Major," she said. "It's a good idea."

"Preferably during a campfire when some of your staff might be otherwise off duty?"

"You are wise beyond your years."

Ramsay secured the pie in his saddlebag and swung aboard Xerxes. He knew he had a friend and ally already. "Mrs. Boone, tell me, please: Does Carrie McKay have a fellow?"

His shoulders slumped when she frowned. Too late. "Guess I missed out."

"No, you didn't!" Mrs. Boone said emphatically. "It's like this." She moved closer to Xerxes, who stood still like the gentleman he was. "Lots of new summertime help seem interested, same as last year, and then Millie Thorne gets her hooks in them, tells lies, and everyone backs off."

"Why would anyone lie about Miss McKay?" he asked, dismayed for Carrie and curious to know more.

"Ask Carrie." She shook her finger at him. "And if you do, you'd better find a way to help her!"

I've been threatened, Ramsay thought, amused in spite of his misgivings, even though he didn't see a smile on the cook's face. So Carrie needed help? Didn't Major Pitcher tell him in that staff meeting that one of his summer duties was seeing to the welfare of everyone in the park, and not just soldiers? If ever a soldier was given a mandate . . .

He gathered his reins. "Let's leave it at this until I return, Mrs. Boone: You might be surprised what authority I have over everyone in this park. Good day now, and thank you."

"For what?" Mrs. Boone asked.

"For rationing me twenty minutes with Carrie McKay. I'm an amateur at all this, but I think I used my time well. See you later."

Ramsay kept a smile on his face until he was back on the Grand Loop road heading north to Fort Yellowstone. His pleasure at seeing Carrie McKay turned contemplative. He thought of Major Pitcher teasing him about finding a wife, if teasing it was. His next emotion was chagrin, wondering at startling complications in his life, especially when he was feeling his way through new responsibilities and a promotion he doubted he deserved. He stewed next over Millie Whoever for dealing in rumor and innuendo about someone who already struck him as a straight shooter.

But a person can only stew so long on the beautiful road to Mammoth Hot Springs, courtesy of Lieutenant Dan Kingman, the first engineer to envision the Grand Loop, incorporating the major features of the park into one roadway. He was also the first engineer brave enough to tackle what was now called the Golden Gate, where Kingman's wooden-trestle road cantilevered out over a canyon of some depth and terror.

Kingman had built the impossible road and timbered the bridges through the Golden Gate nineteen years ago, when Yellowstone boasted nothing grander than dusty roads steep enough to terrify even the most intrepid tourist. Captain Chittenden had replaced the Gate last year with the concrete viaduct sporting graceful arches, the engineer's stock in trade.

He paused a moment at the entrance to Kingman Pass, named after that intrepid engineer, and looked around, willing the beauty to sink into his tired heart and soul. It took a bit longer than usual, but Yellowstone did not fail him. He snapped off a sharp salute at the familiar sight of the monster stone Lieutenant Kingman had used on the Golden Gate to buttress the death-defying road naturally. Captain Chittenden had carefully raised the twenty-three-ton stone column into its new home last year as his own way of honoring Kingman's work. There it stood. Ramsay hoped no future engineer would ever remove it.

"Thank you, Lieutenant Kingman!" he shouted. For reasons unknown, some trooper from an earlier company when Kingman worked his engineering magic had started the salute and the shout and the tradition continued.

Feeling immeasurably better, he let Xerxes set the pace, knowing better than to crowd his horse, any horse, onto a road that still demanded careful attention. All was silent, once the irritated ravens turned their tail feathers to him and tried to get back to sleep after his vocal disturbance. A mountain jay told him what it thought, and then flew away on slow wing beats, intent on whatever it was jays liked to do.

Once through the canyon, Ramsay indulged in bit of daydreaming. He had never been a particular fan of strawberry blond hair, considering it vaguely unmanly on him. He was even less pleased with the beard he always grew in winter—they all bearded up then—because it came in distressingly red. But by golly, reddish-blond hair on Carrie McKay's head was totally acceptable. While he sat by her on the campfire log a mere hour ago, he had tried to angle his head a little to catch the sparkling highlights in her hair.

She wore her hair in one long braid down her back, maybe because it was early times yet, and Mr. Wylie probably didn't care what his help looked like before the tourists started arriving. A deep breath had brought that fragrance of almond. Even if he never saw Carrie again, he knew he was doomed to think of her every time he ate cherry pie and breathed what he thought was almond extract.

Thinking of Carrie occupied his thoughts pleasantly all the way to Mammoth Hot Springs. On the Upper Terrace, he paused a moment to admire the fierce blue of Jupiter Terrace. In mere days, there would be soldiers standing there to protect both the natural wonders and the tourists. The summer season had arrived.

One huge perk of his new rank was the ability to turn over Xerxes to a private in company stables for grain and a good rubdown. He knew he'd be back to check on his horse later that day, because he was a cavalryman before any rank entered the picture. Still, it was nice.

He went into his office, closed the door, and wrote a concise summary of his tour around the park, noting the comments and suggestions of concessionaires and soldiers on duty. He added his ideas, then left it on the admin clerk's desk for Major Pitcher, who was currently in the quartermaster storehouse, according to the clerk. After going back once to pick up a book on his desk, Ramsay said he would return.

He enjoyed the walk down Officers Row toward Captain Chittenden's house, which now appeared to have all its windows. New recruits to B Company were drilling on the parade ground. He watched them for a few minutes, wishing he were drilling the men in equitation, instead of their perfectly qualified sergeant.

He knew he was starting to wallow in self-pity, stuck in an office, filling out reports. *I should have considered that before I accepted this promotion*, he told himself. He was known as a man who thought things through—quickly on the field of battle, and more deliberately when time and tide didn't matter. He hadn't really considered the responsibility of such a rank, which made him feel more remorse than pleasure as he watched the troops at work.

"I'm a hands-on man," he quietly announced to his boots as he stared down at them. "Maybe a fool too. I hate sitting at a desk."

He crossed the road and noticed the stakes Captain Chittenden had put in place to mark off this year's Corps of Engineers building. *Maybe I'll not re-enlist this fall when it comes up and I'll go to working on the captain's road crew*, he thought, but then shook his head at his own folly. *Maybe you'd better start learning to like what you're doing now, Sergeant Major Idiot.*

The front door to the captain's quarters was wide open, but Ramsay knocked anyway. Captain Chittenden stuck his head into the hall and gestured him forward. Ramsay saluted and went into what was the dining room. At least there was a dining table in place, even though the chairs were shoved back and the table was covered with blueprints.

"I gather your wife hasn't arrived yet, Captain," Ramsay said.

"You're perceptive, Sergeant Major," the engineer replied cheerfully. "Wise beyond your years, even. Two more weeks, and this mess will be relegated to a back room. An unfinished back room, I might add. It's a small price to pay for excellent feminine company."

Ramsay looked at the blueprints. "A corkscrew road, sir?" he asked, winding his finger around an impossible route.

"Only way I can think of to get through Sylvan Pass to open an east entrance. Would you use it? We started the approaches last year, so the answer had better be yes."

"Only if you continue building it, sir."

Chittenden smiled and perched on the edge of the table. He pointed to the book in Ramsay's hand, the one he had been reading off and on all winter. "Looks familiar, Sergeant Major. Nettie thinks I should have named it something more tantalizing than *The Yellowstone National Park*."

"Maybe something with Wonderland in the title, Captain?"

Both men laughed. "Wonderland Revealed," Captain Chittenden said, holding up his hand as if outlining the words.

"Or maybe Dallying in Wonderland."

"I like that," Chittenden said. "You know, suggestive without being scurrilous."

Ramsay knew better than to waste too much of the man's time. "I'd like your permission to take some of the information from your book, shorten it considerably, and issue it in pamphlet form to the men who stand patrol at the geyser basins and other prominent sites," he said. "Tourists have questions and they deserve proper answers, sir."

"You mean, when a tourist asks in all earnestness, 'Does Old Faithful go off at night?' the answer won't be, 'No. Everyone is asleep so no one can turn it on,'" Chittenden said, his eyes lively.

"Not even if they ask, 'How long does it take for a deer to turn into an elk?'" Ramsay responded, getting into the humor of the situation. "Captain, these are silly questions to us, but many visitors truly don't know the West, or wilderness, or roads with no street cars on them. They come here ignorant, and sometimes we make fun of them. Is that what we should be doing?"

"You want the troopers to become educationists?" Captain Chittenden asked.

"I think we owe it to the American public, sir."

"I do too, Sergeant Major Stiles," Chittenden said promptly and straightened up. "Yes, you have my permission. Let me see how it turns out, and come to me if you have any questions." He laughed. "If you can find me. I'll be wearing my oldest clothes and mucking about on that east muddy bog we laughingly call a road right now." His eyes took on a thoughtful gaze. "I will also be at that bridge site over the Yellowstone."

"Thank you, sir. I will stop by." Ramsay hesitated. How well did he know this man? Might as well blunder ahead and blurt it out. "Sir, I'm not sure how to say this, but I . . . well, I met a girl at the Wylie Willow Park Camp."

He sighed and looked at the engineer, who was staring at him in frank astonishment. As he gazed back, Captain Chittenden's expression mellowed into what appeared to be genuine, kindly interest.

"Say on. Don't leave me dangling."

"First stop on my Grand Loop tour, sir," Ramsay said. "There she was."

Chittenden pointed to one of the chairs against the wall. He sat in one and Ramsay sat in the other. "I'm impressed," the captain said. "You didn't squander a minute dealing with Major Pitcher's suggestion, did you?"

Ramsay could tell Captain Chittenden was teasing him, but he took it in stride, as a noncommissioned officer should, with humor of his own. "Guess I'm just in the habit of following orders, sir."

"Perhaps. Maybe the major was right; maybe you needed a little prodding to be reminded that man does not live by bugle calls and paperwork alone," Chittenden told him. He shrugged and his eyes grew thoughtful, as if thinking of his own life. "Or maybe it was just the right time. How old are you?"

"Thirty-four, sir."

"I succumbed at twenty-six. I met Nettie when we were sixteen and studying at the same academy near my father's farm." He smiled at the memory. "We wrote to each other for years and married when I graduated from West Point. How did you meet your Wylie girl?"

My Wylie girl, Ramsay thought, struck by the notion. "There she was, and so pretty. I rescued her from a privy where a bear had apparently been sitting earlier, blocking her exit."

Chittenden laughed until he had to wipe his eyes. Ramsay smiled in embarrassment first, but then he couldn't help joining in.

"That's one for the books, Sergeant Major," Chittenden said when he could speak again. "Tell your children some day! Where does it go from here?"

"That's my concern. I have to return a pie tin when it's empty, but what then? She's eight miles away with her duties, and I have mine, sir. She might as well be on the moon."

The engineer seemed inclined to give the matter serious consideration. He gave Ramsay a long look.

"Think creatively, Sergeant Major Stiles. That's an order."

Chapter Eleven

*B*uried under his own mound of early-season paper-work, Major Pitcher was only too happy to agree to an educational pamphlet and send Ramsay on his way.

"With your permission, Major, I'll pay that visit to Jack Strong now. His cousin Sam Deer Nose left some suggestions about an assistant with the clerk."

"Do it." The major rubbed his hands together. "Nothing this spring gave me more satisfaction than to fire Buffalo Jones, the old prissy meddler. Sam's better. And do ask Jack about remounts. We could use some."

Ramsay went back to the stable and requested a remount. The sun was high and spring days were long. He could take along that pie, eat it in the saddle, and get to Jack's ranch by late afternoon. Maybe he'd even save a piece for Jack, a man who never saw too many of life's frills.

A private led out a sorrel that Ramsay rode occasion-ally. Ramsay had to walk right by Xerxes in his loose box and knew if his personally bought-and-paid-for compan-ion could speak, it wouldn't be pretty.

"Xerxes, take a break for the day. You took me every-where this past week," he said, making an overhand catch of a carrot another stable boy, grin on his face, tossed his way. "Thank you, Private Angelo. Xerxes takes offense too easily."

Ramsay gave the carrot to his horse, who lipped it delicately and then turned away to eat, not ready to be placated. "I swear, Xerxes, you're touchier than a cat."

"Horses know, Sergeant Major Stiles," Private Angelo said.

"Indeed they do. Do me a favor and distract him until I'm out of here."

He balanced the cherry pie on his lap and finished half of it long before he reached Gardiner, not his favor-ite little town in the world, mainly because it was filled with poachers of even thinner skin than Xerxes. He kept a weather eye out for any familiar-looking ones. There wasn't a thing he could do but give the one he recognized a hard glare, but Ramsay felt some satisfaction, anyway.

During an earlier duty in the park, Captain Chittenden and his road crew had built the macadam road from Gardiner north through Yankee Jim Canyon. Ramsay passed the railroad crew at work farther south of Cinnabar.

He saw the crew chief, so he stopped to inquire about completion.

"Everyone wants to know, Sarge," the chief said, wiping his hands on an oily rag that did no discernible good. "I'm thinking end of June." He looked back down the tracks. "Then poor old Cinnabar, whish! Gone."

"Life in the West," Ramsay said with a shrug. Once the NPRR reached Gardiner, who would need a seedy hotel, general store, and blacksmith shop three miles from the town boasting a new terminus?

Ramsay looked for Yankee Jim in the canyon already bearing his name, but the old rip wasn't in sight. James George, more properly, had squatted there for years and operated, from all accounts, a pretty good toll road into Yellowstone Park. Captain Chittenden and then the railroad ended that, but Yankee Jim was a philosophical sort and continued serving food to travelers and railroad men. No telling what kind of lies vaguely described as the truth he had been spinning for unwary tourists.

Ramsay felt his heart lift when he passed through the canyon and turned west toward Jack Strong's ranch. The old mixed blood Mountain Crow had been there long enough to claim the best land in what was increasingly coming to be known as Paradise Valley. Ramsay stopped his well-mannered gelding with a word and raised up in the saddle, happy to admire a fine piece of ground with cattle grazing on tender grass. There weren't any flies on Jack Strong. He had been the first to ranch there, and the first to bring in good Hereford stock tough enough for Montana winters—they were in Montana now—tough, but, me oh my, what tender beef.

Ramsay admired the young calves strutting around on stiff legs, as if still getting the hang of ambulation. Some came right up to the barbed wire as if to question his right to be there. Others hung back behind their mothers, who looked mean enough to tangle with even a sergeant major, if he thought to threaten their little ones. "No thank you, ma'am," Ramsay said to one mama pawing the ground. "I didn't get a medal by being stupid."

He was greeted at the ranch house by the same yellow dog Jack claimed had been hanging around the place when Jack first rode into the valley. Like many of Jack's declarations, it may have been tinged with truth at one time. The old gent waved his feathery tail and pointed his nose up, waiting for the scratch under the chin that well-informed visitors knew to administer. Ramsay was no exception.

"Brute, you're a good old lad," Ramsay said, and scratched in the right place. "Where's the rascal that you own?"

"Sarge, is that you?" he heard from inside the cabin.

"No one else, Jack."

He dropped the reins and waited to see what Brute would do. Sure enough, the yellow dog took the reins in his mouth and led the horse into the pasture. Smart dog.

He ducked his head and went inside the log cabin, pleased to see how well-kept everything was. A person might imagine the fine hand of a woman in Jack Strong's life, but it wasn't so. Jack just ran a tidy house and ranch.

Jack sat by the fire. He started to rise, but Ramsay waved him down. He knew what effort that took and couldn't help but think of the first time he saw the rancher nearly dead from a broken leg left untended. He and his little patrol had wasted not a minute in draping him over a placid horse, leaving behind one of their number to tend to the ranch, and trotting back to Fort Yellowstone. After hours of additional agony for the played-out man, the post surgeon was able to set the leg. It never worked as well as before, but at least the leg was still attached to its owner.

Without a word, Ramsay plunked down the rest of the cherry pie into Jack's lap. He went in search of a fork, and found one just as Jack was about to skirt around the niceties and pick up the pie with his hands. He ate the slice and smacked his lips.

"That's the best thing I've had in years. You get married, Sarge?"

"No such luck," Ramsay said as he took the tin and set it on the table. "I've been advised by Major Pitcher to do that. He also wanted me to tell you he'd be by in a month or so to look at horses you might want to sell."

"The major can order you to get married?" Jack asked.

"I think it was a joke," Ramsay replied, wishing he hadn't said anything, because it was time he got his mind off pretty ladies with strawberry blond hair, and back on duty. "Besides, who'd marry an army man?"

"More women than you'd think. You do have an annual income," Jack pointed out.

"That I do."

A man of few words, Jack pointed to a brown jug on the table and requested two glasses, his only two glasses, from the apple crate cupboard. Ramsay fetched the glasses and popped the cork stopper. Jack Strong's apple jack—famous in some circles, notorious in others—went down raw and harsh, only to puddle peacefully in the stomach and create a peculiar, if brief, sense of well-being.

Lubricated sufficiently, Ramsay answered Jack's questions about the Philippines, and how he won that little scrap of light blue material with five stars embroidered into it. He brought Jack up to date on his new promotion and what a trial it was proving to be and then sat back to take another sip.

"Your turn, Jack," Ramsay said. Pleasantly tired, he closed his eyes to listen to his old friend describe his winter, with too much snow, too much isolation, too many beans and beef. He also heard the affection in Jack's voice and noticed how steady his hand was on the yellow dog's big head.

"All in all, okay then?" Ramsay asked, opening his eyes.

"Pretty much," came the reply, followed by a laugh. "I don't have to deal with tourists, so better'n you!"

Ramsay couldn't argue with that. He came right to the point, reminding Jack of Captain Chittenden's bison count a year or two ago that had returned a dismal twenty-nine.

"You'll like this," he said. "Major Pitcher finally fired that old priss Buffalo Jones, and your cousin Sam Deer Nose has proved to be a good replacement."

Jack spat in the fireplace. "Buffalo Jones can't help but muddy his nest. Good for Sam."

"I got Sam to suggest his brother David as a possible assistant, now that Sam's in charge. He also suggested Wesley Plenty Coups. Major Pitcher wants your opinion."

"Either one's good," Jack said. He leaned back and shook his head. "Nice to know someone wants an old man's opinion, even a man part Crow. Ramsay, I probably stole some of Pitcher's horses when he was a skinny lieutenant and I was a bit of a warrior."

"You probably did. Some of mine too, maybe. Plans change and so did the West."

They both stared into the fireplace then, Ramsay thinking about Carrie McKay and Jack thinking about whatever it was Indians liked to reflect on, considering the kind of West they knew now, and what went before.

Ramsay looked out the still-open door to watch dusk move into Paradise Valley. "Mind if I hole up here tonight, and maybe do a little practice roping in the morning?"

"Suit yourself. You're one soldier who's always going to have a welcome here, but you know that already."

He did. Jack never talked much about that bad time when Ramsay and his troopers found him nearly dead.

He had grabbed Ramsay's hand once and kissed it, which told him all he ever needed to know about gratitude.

They spent the evening in restful talk, none of it involving medals or the Philippines. Jack Strong seemed to have an innate sense of what suited the moment, for which Ramsay was profoundly grateful. He talked mainly of the ranch, and how he had grown it into an outfit large enough to run three hundred cattle, if he wanted to. Ramsay enjoyed listening, stretched out in his favorite canvas-backed reclining chair, a glass of apple jack close by but only sipped from now and then. The foul stuff made him burp.

He didn't know at what point his eyes finally closed, only that Jack shook him and said it was time to wake up so he could go to bed. He followed his host down the hall to the bedroom reserved for what few visitors came to the J Bar 81. He took his boots off, wondered how he would get to sleep after slumbering through most of the evening, fell back, and promptly returned to the comforting arms of Morpheus.

His roping practice in the morning didn't begin well. He had been too long away from a rope, and needed to be reminded how to ride Jack's nimble—but patient—cutting horse. A few reminders from his host set his hips swaying with his mount in cow-cutting fashion. By the time the sun was high overhead and his stomach was starting to rumble, Ramsay had scored a few good tosses.

"Come back more often, if you can," Jack told him after they took care of the horses and Ramsay saddled his army remount. "You might amount to a rancher yet."

Ramsay knew the old-timer well enough to be aware that Jack Strong administered praise with an eye dropper. "Thanks," he replied and meant it. "If only I had arrived in Paradise Valley in 1881 like you did, and found a piece of unclaimed land . . ."

Jack shrugged. "I got lucky. One of the few times, but my word, I did." He slapped Ramsay between his shoulder blades. "Not many men with some part Crow blood can say that even now. Maybe you'll get lucky too."

He considered that all the way back to Fort Yellowstone, wondering about luck and about Captain Chittenden's admonition to think creatively. He grained and groomed his horse, even though several privates were willing to do it for him. He turned the gelding loose in the pasture, after Private Angelo promised to return him to the stable later on. A few carrots for Xerxes placated his usual horse.

Duty loomed. Ramsay went to his office and pulled out a notepad. He opened Captain Chittenden's book and started to read. He made some notes, knew he could do this, and settled in for an evening of reading, writing, and wondering how one officer could be so talented.

He finished for the night after Extinguish Lights, which surprised Ramsay, because he hadn't been aware so much time had passed. Last man out of Admin, he locked the door. He ambled back to his dark, empty quarters. He stopped a moment on the front steps, looking toward the next noncom officer's house, small like his, but well lit. He heard Sergeant Mathieu playing his harmonica, and his wife and son singing along.

He stood in his dark sitting room, cold because there was no one to lay a good fire in the pot-bellied stove before he came home. The only fragrance was metal polish, the only food a few carrots for Xerxes. He lit the lamp, and knew he was heading to the Willow Park Wylie Camp before the week was out. A man has to return a pie tin, after all.

Chapter Twelve

*P*atience, patience. Carrie had never been inclined to wish a week to hurry by. She knew she was a deliberate kind of person, the kind who likes to see every side to an issue. If she could look around corners, she knew she would have. There had been too many ugly surprises in her life.

After a long look in the scrap of a mirror allotted to Tent Twenty-Six, Carrie decided to become more tidy in her appearance. There wasn't a thing she could do about the occasional freckle—she didn't care anyway—but she could pile her hair on top of her head into something resembling a pompadour. A single braid down the back was never going to impress anyone.

She decided against a corset, wishing she could afford one of those lacy brassieres found in the women's magazines that Mr. Wylie liked to spread about at one end of the Wylie Store, where there were comfortable chairs for ladies. Miss Janeway of Montana Ag's domestic science faculty had shaken her head over brassieres, calling them "the devil's tool to ruination," but Carrie still wanted one.

She had to admit there wasn't any real need for a corset, considering that her brown dress was made of some fabric perilously close to sackcloth, without additional ashes, and decidedly shapeless. Her heavy-duty apron complete with bib meant that she wasn't likely to jiggle. Carrie wondered if Miss Carter, a more liberal member of the domestic science department, might let her make a brassiere for her fine sewing class in the fall. It wouldn't hurt to ask, provided she earned enough money this summer for tuition and books, and had something for extras.

Carrie tried to remember a time she had wasted even a quarter on anything. Luckily she wasn't one to envy others' good fortune, or working at a tourist camp could have been purgatory. As it was, she never minded assisting some of the more helpless ladies who had never ironed a thing in their lives, because it usually meant a nickel tip. She made mental notes of stylish shirtwaists and skirts she ironed that she could create herself, now that she had passed last spring's pattern-making class with a B plus.

She dressed quietly, hoping not to wake her three new tentmates—two girls from other colleges, and a new teacher—who had arrived just yesterday. All she knew so far was that Sophie was destined for the Wylie Store, and that Amy and Pru would be house maids. So far they were friendly, but Carrie knew it was only a matter of time before Millie Thorne decided to inform them of her lower than low background. Then they would be polite, and probably nothing more, until the season wore on and they learned otherwise for themselves.

I should not be afraid of Millie Thorne, Carrie told herself as she put her last hairpin in place. She stood still a moment, thinking of all the jabs and slights Millie had inflicted since that awful morning when Millie's father and uncle had grabbed Carrie by the arms, sat her down, shouted at her, and told her on pain of jail not to breathe a word of what had happened, or nearly happened.

That should have been the end of the matter. Carrie had been too terrified to even move, let alone blab, and those men knew it. She sighed, knowing how easy it is for word to get around the family to someone like Millie, who seemed to enjoy tormenting people. Some folks were just natural bullies, and others, less self-assured, were probably destined to grit their teeth and bear it.

She stood there and thought about Sergeant Major Stiles, who probably wasn't afraid of anything or anyone. He wore a ribbon on his uniform that declared him a hero. *Could I ever be that brave?* she asked herself. She thought of her mother, the bravest person on earth, who had never knuckled under abuse or hunger. Mam had worked hard every day of her life with that single-minded Scottish grit of hers until work became impossible. She died from overwork or exhaustion, or even from discouragement that she never, ever disclosed to her only child until the very end when a person could be excused a little complaining. Carrie never knew what killed her because a doctor never came.

"Mam," she whispered.

Usually just saying Mam was enough to put the heart back into Carrie, but not today, not when her examination of her hair had surprisingly turned into a handsome pompadour, and when cinching her apron tighter turned into a trimmer figure. Standing there in the cherry red and white striped tent, she resolved to be braver. She suddenly knew she needed to do more, to be more. Might as well start today.

Kitchen work began before any other duties in Mr. Wylie's Willow Park Camp. She paid a cautious visit to the privy, which still made her laugh inside, thinking of the bear and the sergeant major, and returned to the tent to wash her face and hands in ice cold water. Next stop was the work board outside Mr. Wylie's summer office, where she signed her name and time: Carrie McKay, 4:00 a.m.

Mrs. Boone and her silent Shoshone assistant, Alice, were already elbow deep in roll dough for cinnamon buns when Carrie came into the kitchen. She looked at the breakfast board and smiled to see cherry pie and apple pie by her name.

Bonnie Boone looked up from her prep table and said so casually, "It's tourist season. You make a good pie, so the job is yours."

"Thanks, Bonnie. I might need some instruction with cream pies."

"Just ask."

It was still early in the season, so ten pies each at eight slices per pie would do for the day. The tourists who arrived today near noon from Cinnabar would lunch in Gardiner, tour Mammoth Hot Springs and arrive at Willow Park for dinner, famished and ready to gnaw off their left leg, as Jake Trost, camp man from the University of Washington, put it.

Right now, the tourists still sleeping would straggle into the dining tent no later than six thirty, where coffee waited to revive them, oatmeal to fortify them, and fried eggs, bacon, and cinnamon rolls to see them out of the tent and onto the waiting coaches by seven a.m., ready to tackle the geyser basins.

Carrie had finished rolling out pie dough into waiting tins when the tourists came in, some hesitating at the door, others (perhaps they had been here before) moving with all deliberate speed, but not exactly racing each other to a bench. She stopped what she was doing and circulated among the long tables, pouring coffee and standing back when Alice brought in the oatmeal, followed shortly by platters of eggs and bacon.

The room was silent now. Maybe no one had breakfast at six thirty, wherever they came from. Carrie poured milk next, then more coffee. If she had a watch, she could have glanced down to see six forty-five, when newly revived diners began to talk and laugh.

Sticky buns came last. Carrie looked around. Long experience after two summers had taught her that people who didn't smile at the mere sight of Mrs. Boone's sticky buns probably weren't going to have a good time in Wonderland, no matter how remarkably heavenward the geysers shot, or how magnificent the lower falls of the Yellowstone sparkled against multi-hued canyon walls. Everyone appeared to be smiling, so Carrie smiled too.

She looked up from pouring a final mug of coffee when the coach driver stood in the doorway and whistled between what remained of his teeth. Chatter stopped and the tourists rose like marionettes.

"All aboard for the geysers!" the driver called. In minutes the room was deserted. For the next hour, while Alice's glum-faced children washed dishes, the employees took their turn at the table. The coffee went around again and Carrie finally sat down. Oatmeal and half a sticky bun were enough for her, and she had unfinished duties. In another hour, the pies were ready for both ovens.

She sat on a stool in the kitchen, her eyes on the ovens and the clock. Mr. Wylie wandered through, his ink-stained fingers testifying to a morning's-worth of accounting in various ledgers, each with the name of a Wylie camp or lunch station. He always knew when the first pies were ready to come out of the ovens.

He gestured for Carrie to sit with him. Pleased, she did as he asked, hopeful of what was coming. A few bites and he put down his fork.

"Carrie, how's your Stephen Foster?"

She laughed and cleared her throat. It was their summer ritual. "'Mid pleasures and palaces, though we may roam, be it ever so humble, there's no place like home,'" she sang, giving the last word a two-note warble because she felt like it.

"Lovely as ever," he said. "Looks like you're stuck singing Stephen Foster for the campfire again this summer."

"Thanks, Mr. Wylie," she said. "Would you be interested in some harmony too?"

"I'm quite satisfied with your voice alone," he said, "but what do you have in mind?"

"Sophie Baxter, that first year teacher you hired to run the Wylie store, has a very nice contralto," Carrie said. "She's a tentmate and I've heard her humming."

"She's the teacher from Idaho?" he asked.

"Yes. We could branch out a bit from Stephen Foster and maybe sing 'Annie Laurie' together. I'll have to ask her, of course."

"Do that. For now, you're my singer. Jake Trost from U-Dub told me last night that he knows a few magic tricks." He looked down at his empty plate. "Amazing how quickly food disappears around here."

"More, sir?" she asked.

He patted his stomach. "Mrs. Wylie will be disappointed if she has to take out the waist band in my trousers. Carry on, Carrie," he said. He leaned in closer for a moment. "Any problems?"

Only that my heart will probably break if a certain sergeant major doesn't show up again this season, she thought, but knew what wasn't what he meant. "No problems yet."

He must have heard the worry in her voice. "I can always move you to Lake, like I did last summer."

Then I'm even less likely to see Sergeant Major Stiles, she thought. "No, sir, not this summer."

She knew Mr. Wylie felt uncomfortable about the whole conversation, and she also knew of his own problems with the Thornes. Too bad that Millie's father was a banker and had deep ties to both the Yellowstone Park Association that ran the park's hotels, and the Northern Pacific Railroad that brought them there. Too bad other people were bullies.

"Going to tough it out?" he asked.

She saw the sincere concern in his eyes. "Mr. Wylie, there was a bona fide hero sitting in your office last week. He has a medal for it. Maybe I can be a little braver about my own situation, which isn't really a life or death matter."

"He certainly liked that apple pie." He leaned a little closer again. "I heard a rumor that he came back for cherry pie too."

"He did," Carrie said in a low voice. Her face felt as warm as she knew it would tonight by that campfire.

"Will he return again?"

She shrugged. "It's probably hard for him to get away."

"But you keep making cherry pie," he observed as he stood up and pushed back his sleeves, as if preparing to battle again with the ledgers.

"Mr. Wylie, it's my job," she said, and picked up his dishes. "Will it be 'Old Kentucky Home' and 'There's No Place Like Home' tonight?"

"Throw in that sad song about the dog too, and you'll get a lot of tips," he advised.

" 'Old Dog Tray'?" she asked. "When I sing that one, you always seem to get some dust in your eye or something, Mr. Wylie."

"I should speak to the army about getting those water wagons going, to cut some of that dust," he said with a smile.

"You should."

And so the day went and the days that followed until the week was nearly done: a casual lunch for employees, then a few hours of calm to prepare the evening meal. The coaches from Mammoth Hot Springs usually arrived about four o'clock, when the call went out for tea and biscuits to the ladies' tents. Everyone seemed to be drooping by four, including the staff. Bonnie Boone usually found a few stray meat pies for savages and hungry coachmen who needed fortification.

Once the dinner dishes were washed, dried, and on the shelves again, Bonnie and Carrie made bowls of buttered popcorn to circulate among the visitors who had perked up and were walking toward the roaring fire in the middle of the campground, husband and wives arm in arm, and children running around because children never seemed to wear out. With a pang, she watched soldiers arrive from the not-too-distant Norris station, ready to strike up conversations with young ladies, many of them teachers on holiday. She looked but Sergeant Major Stiles wasn't among them.

A week had never seemed longer, even though she knew that was silly. All weeks had the same minutes and hours. Thankfully, she never had time to mope or pine, but she couldn't stop her mind from going over their conversation by the dead campfire last week.

At the beginning of the week, Carrie had told herself that a man with as many responsibilities as a sergeant major must surely have was too busy to waste his time at a campfire. By the end of the week, she wrote it off as a pleasant twenty minutes with an interesting man and quietly closed that little door in her heart.

Now it was Friday and her turn to sing. Sophie Baxter had said she would be ready tomorrow night for the duet they had practiced all week, but Carrie appeared to be on her own, as she had been since the age of thirteen. She looked toward the fire to see the U-Dub engineering major who performed magic tricks pull a handful of scarves out of a hat, and then a quarter from behind a little girl's ear. He wasn't very good, but no one seemed to mind.

The magic tricks gave her time to hurry to her tent and change into a tan skirt that had earned her an A minus in last spring's tailoring class, and a green-and-white-checked gingham shirtwaist that she had found at the Lake Wylie Camp last summer, left behind by a visitor because it had a tiny tear on one buttonhole that was easily mended. Her hair had started to curl from the heat in the kitchen, but it was dark and no one would notice.

After the popcorn bowls circulated, Carrie stepped forward. The magician pulled out a pitch pipe and gave her a note. She sang "We Wandered Today Through the Hills, Maggie," gratified to see an older couple on the second row of logs look at each other and smile. She sang to them and had the delight of watching the husband take out his handkerchief and dab at the tears in his wife's eyes.

She finished to applause, gave a little curtsy, then did something Mr. Wylie had wanted her to do, but which her hard-earned caution had vetoed. She held up her hand, pleased when her little audience quieted. Maybe this wasn't so hard, after all. A frown on her face, Millie Thorne stood there holding a bowl of popcorn. Carrie decided to give her sweetest smile to someone who wished her nothing but hard times and bad news. That wasn't so hard, either. Too bad Ramsay Stiles wasn't around so Carrie could tell him that she had decided to be brave.

"We have a sweet couple sitting on the second row," Carrie said, marveling at her own courage. "I think maybe that was a favorite song of theirs. Would you kindly tell us where you are from and why the song seems to mean so much to you?"

The gentleman stood up and helped his wife to her feet. They looked like Easterners, well-dressed and so out of place and tidy in a national park in the middle of basically dusty nowhere.

"Since you asked, miss, we are from Darien, Connecticut. Our children sang that song to us only last week on the occasion of our fortieth wedding anniversary," the man said. "This little trip was their idea of a second honeymoon." He smiled at his wife. "We were married in 1863, when I had two weeks' furlough from the Army of the Potomac."

Everyone burst into applause, including Carrie. The lady leaned her forehead into her husband's coat sleeve, shy and looking much younger than a woman married forty years. Maybe that was what Yellowstone did to some people; maybe love did it too. Whatever it was, Carrie felt her own heart lift. It had been a discouraging week, but she vowed to put it behind her. Next week would be better. She wasn't sure how, except that it would be.

She sang "Old Dog Tray," because Mr. Wylie liked it. As usual, some of the softer-hearted dog owners sniffed into their handkerchiefs. She put what she hoped was sufficient feeling into the song, which was never easy. There was a time once when she had competed with stray dogs for scraps, but these people didn't know that. She hadn't even told Mr. Wylie, and he knew the worst.

She finished to more applause and waited for her audience to leave. No one moved. They didn't know she was tired, and four in the morning came early. There had to be a way to shuffle visitors off to their tents, or it was going to be a really long summer. Carrie raised her hand again for silence.

"There is only time for one more song," she said. "Morning comes early around here and you will want to be in the dining hall by six thirty for Mrs. Boone's sticky buns."

She heard good-natured laughter. "Does anyone have a favorite Stephen Foster song? If I know it, I'll sing it for my finale."

"I'd like to hear 'Why, No One to Love,'" came a voice from the shadow.

She knew the voice, but held her breath anyway; she had been wrong before. Besides, she had already decided Sergeant Major Stiles wasn't going to return to the Wylie Camp. What would he be doing here?

"I know that song," she said softly, and didn't even need a pitch to begin it.

"'No one to love in this beautiful world, full of warm hearts and bright beaming eyes! Where is the lone heart that nothing can find that is lovely beneath the blue skies.'"

A young couple standing close to the sergeant major, their arms around each other, had started to sway to the melody. Carrie sang to them, partly because Mr. Wylie had told her to target people in her little audience and make everything personal, and partly because she didn't have the courage to sing to a sergeant major stepping out of the shadow now and holding an empty pie tin.

Chapter Thirteen

Ramsay was grateful Carrie chose to sing to the couple standing next to him, a couple practically reeking of orange blossoms and newness. Personally, he had never given much thought to the idea of honeymooning in Yellowstone Park, but then, he hadn't thought to honeymoon anywhere. He laughed inside and remembered Captain Chittenden's comment about thinking creatively.

When Carrie started the chorus, she waved to her audience to join in. He decided to take a page from her book and sing to Carrie McKay. " 'No one to love! Why, no one to love! What have you done in this beautiful world, that you're sighing of no one to love?' "

As she began the next verse, he had to ask himself that question. What had he done? He listened to Carrie's lovely voice—not loud, but so pure—and wondered how any man ever worked up the nerve to talk seriously to a lady. He'd better consult the etiquette book Mrs. Pitcher had given him.

He sang the chorus with the others, then listened to the final verse, the one that seemed almost out of place. "'Many a fair one that dwells on the earth who would greet you with kind words of cheer, many who would gladly join in your pleasures or share in your grief with a tear.'" Glory be, but Stephen Foster was a melancholy, maudlin songwriter. Share people's griefs?

He couldn't be melancholy, not as he sang and watched the singer. He had never seen Carrie McKay in anything but a drab dress and that all-encompassing apron. Here she stood in a trim skirt and checked shirt-waist that showed to perfection her small waist. He still preferred the single braid down her back, but the pompa-dour was dignified in a way that touched his heart. She was a woman to be admired, maybe even cherished. That errant thought made him take a deep breath and remind himself he was too busy this summer for anything more than admiration.

He stayed where he was as some in the audience left tips in a jar and headed to their tents. Carrie shook the coins from the jar and divided them with the magi-cian wearing a University of Washington letter sweater who stood close to her. He tried to hand back some of the coins, but Carrie waved him off. He said, "Maybe it would be fair if I sang *and* pulled scarves out of hats," and she still shook her head, refusing to take anything back. He gave her a thumbs up and strode toward the employee tents, whistling.

"Fifty cents, Ramsay," she said as he came closer. "I save my tips all summer for extra things during the school year, like food."

She laughed but he didn't think she was joking. Closer now, he could tell her shirtwaist was faded from many washings. Mr. Wylie had hinted that some of his summertime help needed every dime they earned for college. Ramsay already knew Carrie was one of those. Her gesture in making sure that the tips were divided evenly, even though she did the lion's share to earn them tonight, struck him as gallant as anything he had ever seen.

"Why that song?" she asked, with no preamble, as if they were continuing a conversation broken off only minutes ago, instead of a week. "You'll make me worry about you, and I don't really want to."

"No worries," he said, amused. "My mother used to sing that to me. She had a lovely voice too."

"Thank you," she said simply, which touched him again. Not for Carrie McKay the flowery denials, the simper. He liked that.

Major Pitcher had noticed once and remarked to Ramsay that he was a great observer of people, a valued skill in a sergeant. It was true. Saying less and watching more had helped Ramsay through many a fraught situation. Maybe it was his imagination, but from their first meeting outside the backhouse, he had noticed how high Carrie held her shoulders, as though she were carefully picking her way through life and its troubles

He had also noticed last week when they sat together for Mrs. Boone's twenty minutes that Carrie's shoulders dropped as she relaxed. Maybe this charming person felt she could lower her guard around him. Maybe he was imagining the whole thing. Major Pitcher had also told him that he had a tendency to overthink a situation. Better just let that observation rest among a pile of sleeping dogs.

For a brief moment, Ramsay thought of his wolves in the Lamar Valley. He had made many entries in his journal about their watchfulness. Was this a wolf trait he had unconsciously adopted? Nothing would surprise him.

He held out the pie tin. "The kitchen seems to be buttoned up for the night. I didn't want you to think I wasn't going to return it."

She took it from him and started to walk toward the kitchen. *No, you don't*, he thought and sat down on a log in the now-deserted campfire circle. She looked back and sat down next to him, the pie tin in her lap, her hands folded across it, feet together. He had never seen a more proper woman, until he found the courage to look into her eyes, which were lively with interest.

"I hope you shared some of it," she said.

"A very small slice," he said. "I took it with me to Jack Strong's ranch, just the other side of Yankee Jim Canyon." He couldn't help smiling back at those lively eyes. "He told me he'd marry you in a minute."

Thank goodness she didn't blush and turn away. She laughed and set the tin aside. "My first proposal! Will I like him?"

"If you don't mind that he's somewhere north of sixty and has a bum leg. Owns a nice piece of property, though." He wanted to nudge her shoulder, but didn't. "If I were a lady, I'd propose to him. It's a good ranch."

She shook her finger at him. "That's no reason to marry someone. I thought you liked the army."

"I thought I did too," he said, then wondered where that came from. "I mean, of course I do."

"Mr. Wylie told me that your new rank is a pretty exalted one," Carrie said. "Do you . . . do you sometimes wish you were still just a sergeant?"

"First sergeant," he corrected, "the perfect rank. I suppose I do wish that."

She nodded and stared into the coals. "When I'm studying for an English test, or trying to understand

120

algebra, I sometimes wish myself back in the kitchen washing dishes."

"At the Railroad Hotel?"

He didn't imagine her intake of breath, or the way she moved away from him. "Did . . . did Mr. Wylie mention that to you?" she asked, long after he thought she was not going to say another word to him.

"No. It was Mrs. Boone. She told me you had some hard times in Bozeman in a bad place."

"Still do, I suppose," she said quickly. "Do you ever have trouble forgetting stuff you don't want to remember? Ramsay, it's awfully late."

Stuff I don't want to remember, he thought. *Now and then.* He pulled out his timepiece. "Only eight o'clock. Look, I didn't mean to make you nervous. I won't mention the Railroad Hotel again."

"Thank you," she said, with an innate dignity that was hers alone.

"I am curious about one thing, though." He took a breath and blew it out, knowing he was going far beyond the letter of Major Pitcher's charge to him. "Like it or not, my new job means I am responsible for everyone in this entire park."

"Come now! That's a hummer."

In for a penny, in for a dollar, he thought. "I mean it. The US Army, in the form of the First Regiment of Cavalry, is literally in charge of everything in this park's three thousand and some four hundred square miles. Major Pitcher told me I am to keep an eye on the people, the geysers, and the animals. Oh, we all do that, but I'm supposed to be some sort of exalted buffer between irate campers, geysers that don't play on cue, and . . . and angry bears, maybe."

He wanted her to laugh and she did. She moved an infinitesimal bit closer to him again.

"You don't sound too happy about that," she observed, her chin on her palm now as she stared into the fire.

"I need to get used to more responsibility," he said, "but you're right. Life used to be simpler."

"It's simpler now for me." She glanced up. "I wondered if anyone would come back."

He looked to see couples returning to the logs with long forks and plates.

"Mrs. Boone makes marshmallows. Sugar syrup, gelatin, and egg whites," Carrie said. "Six per customer. They're a little too sweet for me, but tourists like them."

To Ramsay's gratification, the couples sat on the other side of the fire circle. He didn't know Carrie well, but he was pretty sure she wouldn't leap up and run, now that others were close by.

"It's just something I noticed when I was here last, and again tonight," he said, keeping his voice low. "Why does Millie . . . Millie . . ."

". . . Thorne . . . stare daggers at me?" she finished, and gave a gusty sigh. "We're back to the Railroad Hotel."

"Then you'd better tell me what happened there," he said, suddenly aware he was taking the biggest chance of his life, even bigger than crawling into a muddy, dark cave after his lieutenant was killed, when any sane man would have backed out and declared the task impossible.

"Why do you need to know?" Carrie asked, as he knew she would. "You can say what you want, but it's not your business, Sergeant Major Stiles."

Ouch, that hurt. Might as well plunge ahead and fulfill the objective, whatever it was. "You looked wary around Millie. You also told me that she makes a point to turn everyone against you."

"I did, didn't I?"

"Why does she do that?"

She resumed her position, chin in hand. As he watched her, she put her face in the palm of her hand, covering eyes suddenly seeing too much. He thought for a long moment, then lightly touched her shoulder. She turned to look at him. "Are you telling me I am not alone?"

"I think I am, Carrie." He couldn't help his smile, because he knew she saw right through him. "It's for the good of the US Army."

"Liar, liar pants on fire," she said softly. "What time did you say it was?"

"A little after eight now."

"I go to bed at nine," she told him. "I'd better start at the beginning. You need to know something right away."

"All right," he said. "How bad can it be?"

"I nearly killed Millie's cousin."

Chapter Fourteen

*H*e didn't mean to swear, but she surprised him. "I'm sorry," he apologized.

"Do you want to hear this or not?" she asked. Ramsay heard her irritation, but he also heard the dignity.

"Tell me."

"My parents came from Scotland—Mam from Dumfries and Papa near Gate of Fleet," she said, sitting up straight now, but not looking at him. "Papa got work on the Northern Pacific and we ended up here when I was nine or so."

"What did he do?"

"He switched cars in the roundhouse," she said. "He also spent most of his spare time drinking with his buddies. Mam called it Cù Dubh."

"Koo doo?"

"Close enough," she said and edged closer to him. "It means black dog, but it also means foul moods. We never knew where we stood, Mam and I. Sometimes Papa would come home cheerful. Sometimes he would yell at us. Usually he beat us both, but Mam the hardest, until he made her deaf."

Shocked, Ramsay thought of his own parents, Mama always singing, and Pa with a joke even when times were hard, as they often were on a farm. He realized Carrie had moved even closer.

"Papa said he was going out with his friends. We never saw him again." Carrie sighed. "I admit it was a bit of a relief, but there we were, evicted from railroad housing. Millie's uncle owns the Railroad Hotel and her father is a banker with some connections to the Northern Pacific. They got Mam a job washing dishes—me too—and doing some cooking at the restaurant. We slept upstairs at the back of the hotel." Her head went up and he heard the defiance in Carrie's voice. "Kept that door locked too, I assure you! The second floor was not a good place."

"Neither is the first floor," Ramsay said. "There was a shooting in the bar a few years ago. The previous super-intendent at Fort Yellowstone declared it off limits to all soldiers."

"The restaurant was good," Carrie assured him. "We worked together. Mam taught me to read, but I didn't have much to read except food labels."

"No school for you?"

"I had to work." She laughed, the tone soft and low and so beguiling. "I read a few of the Police Gazettes the men left around, until Mam found out."

"You're a woman with a checkered past," he teased, then regretted it. "I mean . . ."

"Don't be so sensitive," she chided. "I know what you mean." She started to lean into him then, and he knew the hard part of a hard story was coming. "When I was thirteen, Mam took sick. Her stomach hurt all the time. I don't know what it was, and she never went to a doctor."

"No money?"

"Partly. Mam didn't want Mr. Thorne to know she was sick. She was afraid he'd just throw us out. He's not really kind. She didn't want me on the streets." She turned to face him. "Life is hard on women, in case you don't know."

What could he say to that?

She jumped when some coals dropped and set up sparks. He looked around. The marshmallow roasters had gone and they were alone again.

"I took over Mam's work whenever I could." He heard a sound low in her throat. He remembered that sound from a funeral he went to for one of his mother's Scottish aunts. It wasn't a sound a person could forget, and it chilled him now.

"It was February. I worked a long day and part of a night. When I dragged myself upstairs, Mam was dead. I wasn't there for her last breath."

Ramsay put his arm around her shoulder without thinking about it, and she turned her face into his shirt. They sat there in silence while the coals grew dim.

"The city of Bozeman buried her and I kept working at the Railroad Hotel. What else could I do? Two more years and then it happened."

Carrie leaped to her feet and walked away from the dead campfire. He started to follow her and she put her hand up. "I can't say any more now. Maybe later. Goodnight."

He watched her walk away, and his heart felt completely hollow. He listened to the crunch of her shoes on the gravel by the dining hall and closed his eyes.

He opened them when he heard her walking back toward him, with her now-familiar quick step. She stood in front of him and he could just make out the concern on her face.

"You're not going to go to Norris tonight, are you?" she asked. "It's late and dark and I would worry."

She sounded so much like his mother that he smiled. He also realized that for the first time in many years since his parents died, someone felt concern for him. Ramsay touched the little Medal of Honor ribbon pinned to his uniform. "Carrie, I'm a hero, remember?"

She laughed and he felt relief cover him. "I paid Mr. Wylie fifty cents to sleep in Tent Twenty with the camp men," he told her.

"Good! I won't worry about you then."

She stood there, as if uncertain what came next. He had no idea, either, so there they were, just looking at each other. But he was the sergeant major and he thought he had better say something, even something stupid or possibly unwanted.

"I want to hear the rest of this. What time do you go to work, Carrie?"

"Four in the morning," she told him in a small voice, practically a child's voice. "If you must, come to the kitchen. Mrs. Boone knows the rest of the story."

"I will."

She turned to go, but he touched her hand and she stopped. "I have something you can borrow tonight."

His eyes on hers, he worked the little clasp and took off his Medal of Honor ribbon. Carrie watched, her mouth open, as he pinned it carefully to the collar of her shirtwaist.

"I need it back before I leave tomorrow morning, but I think it's your turn to wear it," he said. "Where is Number Twenty?"

Her eyes huge in her face, she pointed toward the end of the row. "I'm no hero, Ramsay," she whispered.

"Yeah, you are," he said. "See you at four."

Ramsay thought he might not sleep, but he did. He had enough blankets, and none of the young guys he shared the tent with snored. He drifted to sleep thinking of his mother singing, " 'No one to love in this beautiful world, Full of warm hearts and bright beaming eyes!' "

He must have been about eight and had dragged himself home from school, sad about something he couldn't remember now, and truth to tell, had probably forgotten not soon after the incident. Ma must have noticed his bleak face, because he remembered her asking him if he was too old at eight years old to sit on her lap. He decided he wasn't, and she sang to him. As he lay in the Wylie tent, he thought through the song, and by the chorus, his mother's voice had changed into Carrie's.

Ramsay had scribbled a note and left it next to one of the tentmates, asking him to wake him up. It was still dark when he felt a hand to his shoulder and a little shake. "Sir? Sir?"

"I'm awake. Thanks," he said as he sat up, thought a second, and remembered where he was.

A glance out the door showed a lightening sky. A squint at his watch told him it was slightly after four. He dressed quickly, sharing the space with three college students who stared at him when he turned into a sergeant major, once his clothes were on.

"Too dark to ride on to Norris soldier station. Glad you had a spare bed in here," he said.

He started to leave the tent but then looked back at the others. "Tell me something. Have you heard rumors about Miss Carrie McKay?"

His heart sank when they looked at each other, but he plunged ahead. "From Millie Thorne?"

One reluctant nod, and then two. "You'd be wise not to believe a single thing you hear from that source," he said, putting enough command into his voice to make one of the students stand up straight. "Good day, gentlemen. I hope a word to the wise is sufficient."

All three said "Yessir," promptly, but thank goodness no one tried to salute.

After a stop behind the row of tents, which made him think of bears hanging out, waiting for a Wylie girl, he walked to the dining room. It was already set for early arrivals eager to snag a good seat on the Wylie coaches heading to the lower and upper geyser basins.

The kitchen was well-lit and warm from the ovens. Mrs. Boone waved a flour-covered hand in his direction and pointed toward the long prep table, where Carrie McKay was rolling out pie dough for waiting tins. He watched a moment, enjoying the economy of her movements. He knew he was looking at a well-trained, hard-working cook. He doubted she ever wasted a single motion.

He pulled a stool up beside the table, sitting far enough away not to impede her activity, but close enough so neither of them had to speak loud. "I came back for the rest of the story, Carrie, if you're inclined to share it."

"I told myself I wasn't going to," she said, her eyes on the circle of dough she was rolling out now. "I changed my mind."

He settled in and waited for her to speak. She folded the dough over and carefully arranged it in the pan, pushing it down to line the walls. She moved quickly to the next empty tin and began the same motions all over again.

"I was fifteen and Mam was two years gone," she began. "I was cleaning up in the kitchen after a long night. The Odd Fellows had finished their monthly meeting, and there were so many dishes. I think it was near midnight."

She deftly folded dough around the rolling pin and spread it across the next pie tin. "Millie's cousin George came into the kitchen and called for me. I turned around, and he was on me before I could do anything. He stuffed a napkin in my mouth when I opened it to scream."

Ramsay felt a cosmic presence suck the air right out of his body. He took a deep breath to start himself going again. "Sounds premeditated. He must have been planning this."

"Probably," she said and attacked the pie dough as though it was something predatory, and not just flour, water, and lard. "He had been making some suggestive comments, but I heard those from others too."

She turned around, her eyes angry. "Why do some men think women are fair game?" She shook the rolling pin at him. "I hope you don't, because if you do, I'm never going to speak to you again." Her face hardened. "And no, I'm not joshing."

Ramsay thought of past relationships, some successful, others soul-sucking. "My parents taught me manners," he told her.

She thumped the rolling pin on the dough. "Good!" She turned to the prep table. "He knocked me down."

Shocked, he watched her shoulders begin to shake. He thought she might be crying, but he heard no tears in her voice. She shook with anger.

"What did you do?" He felt like a churl asking, but he wanted to know.

Carrie turned around again to face him. She leaned back against the prep table and picked at the pilled dough on her palms. "I reached behind me to a low shelf where we kept frying pans. I grabbed the closest one by the handle and slammed it against the side of his head."

"Bravo, Carrie," he said.

"There was blood everywhere," she said, with a look in her eyes that told him she was seeing every detail in her mind.

He did something then that no one in Mrs. Pitcher's etiquette book would have approved of. He crossed the space between them and put his hand over her eyes. She started in surprise, then leaned toward him until her forehead touched his chest. He did nothing to draw her closer, but kept his hand firmly over her eyes until she straightened up and took his hand away. She gazed at him out of clear eyes full of something besides fear now.

"I needed that," she said, her voice soft.

She turned back to the table, leaned on it, and started to sag. He helped her onto the stool he had vacated and she sat there, head bowed. Ramsay looked over his shoulder at Mrs. Boone. The cook motioned to him and he came to the prep table where she was rolling up sticky buns.

"Stay with her. The pies can wait," the cook said.

"Am I doing the right thing?" he asked.

"Yes, if you do something about Millie Thorne."

"What . . . what has Miss Thorne been saying?"

"That Carrie works on that second floor and spend her summers in the park trolling for a rich husband." She slammed the unsuspecting buns, then stared in surprise at what she had done. "May have to do that section over," she muttered. "What she could say keeps Carrie frightened."

"What is it?"

"She'll tell you." Mrs. Boone turned back to her flattened sticky buns and shook her head. "Could be I have to give these to you, since I daren't feed them to visitors."

"I'll never turn down a sticky bun, flattened or not," he said, and returned to the pie table, where Carrie was doggedly rolling out pie dough again. He lifted the rolling pin from her fingers, took her hand and led her into the empty dining room, where he sat her down.

"I need to . . ." She started to rise.

"Mrs. Boone said the pies can wait. Finish your story and I'll see what I can do to help you."

She gave him a doubtful look, which he countered with a benign version of what his men called Sarge's Stare. Apparently it worked on ladies too.

"There was blood everywhere, on the floor, on him, on me." She shuddered. "I toed him just to make sure he was alive, and he grabbed my ankle. I've never been so frightened!"

Fifteen and no one to help you, he thought. He felt a great rage building inside him, but he knew better than to show it.

"I hit his hand with . . . something . . . and he let go," she said, her breath coming faster. "I ran upstairs, yanked the pillowcase off my bed, stuffed everything I owned in it and ran outside. I ran like a crazy person."

"You don't have to run too far to run out of Bozeman," he said.

Carrie smiled at that. "No! When I calmed down, I remembered something Mam told me the morning of the day she died."

He waited, certain Carrie would speak when she was ready.

"She must have known something like this might happen. She told me that when things couldn't get any worse, I was to go to the First Presbyterian Church on Babcock Street. I was to sit there and cry until someone helped me."

She gave him a little-girl look that touched the deepest place in his heart. For a tiny second, she was a child again, and not the capable woman he was coming to know and already admired.

"You went there?"

"I couldn't right then. It was only Saturday. I found a safe place in an alley between two ash cans and stayed there." He watched her resolution return. "Had to convince a dog that I needed the spot worse than he did, and the scraps." Her look softened. "Another dog, a big yellow one, came along and scared that one off. He curled up beside me and I stayed warm."

He turned away then, trying hard not to cry. My word, he hadn't cried in years. Carrie reached out and touched his arm lightly. "I'm sorry it's such a grim story," she said, apologizing to him.

"Please tell me it gets better soon," he said.

"Not right away," she admitted. "On Sunday morning I started for Babcock Street and the Thorne brothers found me." Her breath came fast again. "They took me by my arms and dragged me into a warehouse. They sat me down hard into a chair, shouted so loud right in my face . . ." She sobbed out loud. ". . . and said if I ever breathed a word of what happened they would summon the magistrate and charge me with assault. They promised I would go to prison where worse would be done to me. Ramsay, I was fifteen!"

"That's the limit!" Ramsay shouted and regretted his too-loud words immediately, because Carrie sank back against the table and put her hands over her ears.

"Never shout at me," she said when she could talk. "Never shout or I will never speak to you again."

"I won't," he said, dismayed to see how white in the face she was. "Never again."

She looked toward the kitchen as if yearning to escape into pie dough and filling, a world she could control. Ramsay understood her longing, thinking of the mornings after that dark, endless age in the cave, killing and fighting to stay alive and keep his men alive too, wounded himself, blood everywhere.

"I had an awful time once when all I could do was count tiles in the hospital ceiling," he told her. "I'm not proud of it, but I finally quit counting and went back to work." He stood up. "Carrie, I won't keep you here if you want to finish those pies. Accept my profoundest apology for frightening you."

She gave him a patient glance, one he knew belonged exclusively in the domain of women. He had seen it at Wounded Knee and in the Philippines. "The pies can wait." She patted the spot on the bench he had vacated. "Sit down, Sergeant Major."

"Yes, ma'am."

"Oh, you!" she said and he heard her humor. It didn't last long. "They terrified me and threatened me, but let me go. I ran to the Presbyterian Church, sat in the back row as the parishioners filed in, and cried every tear I had not cried since the first time my father beat me." She spoke calmly. "Mr. Wylie and his wife took me home with them. It's no wonder I admire that man."

"I often think the acting superintendents see the Wylie Camping Company as a nuisance," he said. "The Northern Pacific Railroad and the Yellowstone Park Association are powerful and would like to see him squashed. Funny, isn't it? People with power always want more. Mr. Wylie is a good man, though."

"I know. Then tell me why it is that so many people who can afford to stay in those fancy hotels like to camp with us?" she asked, her hands folded in her lap, her eyes cheerful again.

"Because that's where the adventure in Wonderland lies," he said promptly. "Mr. Wylie understands and more power to him."

They gazed at each other with real charity. Somewhere in the back of his brain was Duty with a capital D, tugging on his sleeve and leaping about to get his attention. Ramsay looked at his timepiece.

"There's more to your story, but you have pies to make and I have to see the manager of the Fountain Hotel about a bear that keeps staring in the first floor windows and sending old ladies into spasms."

Carrie laughed and stood up. "I'd rather make pies! Yes, there's more to my story, but it's easier." Her expressive eyes turned wistful. "I just wish Millie Thorne didn't need to tell the world that I work on the second floor of the Railroad Hotel, because it's a lie."

"Is that one way the Thornes still try to keep you afraid?" he asked.

"It works." She looked down at her shoe tops, but he could see that her face had gone rosy. "Rumor is that her awful cousin left Bozeman quietly because he was accused of . . . of interfering with young girls like me."

She looked up and Ramsay saw the quiet resolution on her face. "I was lucky."

"It's time you got luckier, Carrie," he said. "You can't always depend on a handy frying pan. I'll see what I can do about Millie."

He stood quiet and straight while she removed his Medal of Honor ribbon from her collar, hesitated a moment, then pinned it on his uniform.

"Thanks for the loan," she said quietly. "I needed it."

Chapter Fifteen

*C*arrie went back to rolling pie dough and Ramsay hung around until Bonnie Boone's assistant took the oatmeal pan from the oven and cut him a square. He took out a nickel, but Bonnie glowered at him. She also gave him her version of The Stare when he tried to pay for the flattened sticky buns she handed him, securely bound into a pasteboard box.

"Give these to that motley crew of worthless men at Norris soldier station," she said gruffly, daring him to do anything about her philanthropy.

"Yes, ma'am," he said and snapped off a salute worthy of a sergeant to a colonel, which made her giggle. Carrie laughed out loud back at the prep table, where she was pouring in apple pie filling now.

He stood there to watch her work and smiled when Mrs. Boone gave him a little shove against the small of his back, and sent him in the direction of the prep table.

"Nothing's cooked yet," she said, "but you know that."

Carrie gave him her clear-eyed honest look, the one that made him wish he were the competent, capable, and thoughtful man she seemed to think he was. Who was he to tell her how he was floundering about his promotion, that stupid medal, a problem with wolves he knew was coming, and his own feelings at this very moment? Should he be the sergeant major, or maybe the friend he knew he was becoming? The push in Carrie's direction that Bonnie gave him seemed to indicate he was wasting time.

He chose something between the two and held out his hand. Carrie wiped the flour off her fingers and shook his hand, a firm pressure that told him this was not a frivolous woman, if he ever had any doubts.

"Thanks for listening to me," she said and looked away because her face was blushing. "I don't usually spill the beans like that. Maybe it was the campfire."

"That was it," he said but then realized what a cowardly comment he had just made. "Nope. It was more than that. I pried into your life because I want to know you better, Miss Carrie McKay."

"Did you find anything salvageable?"

What does a man say to that? Ramsay knew there wasn't anything in that confounded etiquette book to answer her. Mentally he dumped the book into the Gardner River, watched it bob away and said, "Without question. See you around." Before he lost his nerve, he kissed her cheek.

Her eyes opened wide in surprise, then grew small as her smile increased. "Was that scarier than taking the cave in the Philippines?"

He opened his mouth to assure her it wasn't but changed his mind. "Yes. I only took that cave once. Have a good day, Carrie. I'll see what I can do about Millie Thorne."

He left the kitchen walking about a foot off the ground. Luckily, no one noticed. Xerxes might have had an opinion, but the big gelding declined any comment. Ramsay balanced the pasteboard box of slightly flattened sticky buns in one hand and managed to mount his horse with something close to skill. Too bad no one was watching. He started through the Willow Park meadow toward the Grand Loop road when he heard, "Wait up, Sergeant Major," behind him.

He turned in the saddle to see Mr. Wylie himself riding toward him. He had watched the camping company impresario on the trail before, and admired the way he sat a horse. He knew Mr. Wylie had acquired a ranch in the Gallatin Valley and was no stranger to the saddle. Ramsay hoped he could still ride that elegantly when he was on the shady side of fifty.

"I trust you slept well enough last night, Sergeant Major," Mr. Wylie said as his horse fell in step with Xerxes, who never minded company.

"I did, indeed, sir. You heading my way?" Ramsay asked.

"I'm going to the camp at Lake. I make my own circuit during the season."

"I'll keep you company to Norris station. I have to go on to Fountain after I visit with the men. Apparently there is a bear playing Peeping Tom in the windows of the hotel. Major Pitcher thinks convincing the bear to stop is a good use of my time."

Mr. Wylie nodded. "You must admit that soldiering in Yellowstone probably bears—excuse that—bears no resemblance to life in another garrison."

"No doubt," Ramsay agreed. "Some of the men like it, some can't stand it, but the park suits me. Well enough, anyway," he added, thinking of winter and wolves that someone in the Department of the Interior thought needed to be killed. "No assignment is perfect."

"I noticed you chatting with Carrie McKay last night," Mr. Wylie said after two magpies stopped their harsh chatter and flew into the nearest lodgepole pine. "She's a hard-working employee and I value her." He sighed. "I'm at a bit of a loss to know what to do about Millie Thorne."

Then it wasn't Ramsay's imagination or Carrie's disquiet. "She seems to enjoy ruining reputations. Can't you fire her?"

"Wish I could," Mr. Wylie admitted. "Let me tell you what I think is going on."

I was hoping someone would, Ramsay thought. "Be my guest," he said, and slowed Xerxes.

"She told you how we found her?" Mr. Wylie asked.

"Said her mother told her to go to the Presbyterian Church and cry until someone helped her."

"What a jolt that was," Mr. Wylie said, slowing his horse even more. "There she was, covered in blood, hair wild, eyes terrified, shivering in the cold because she had snatched up a few possessions and run from the Railroad Hotel. Maybe she didn't even own a coat."

Ramsay thought of the tidy and self-possessed lady who had sat beside him at the campfire. As well as he claimed to have slept, he saw that fear as the last thing that crossed his mind before he slept, and the first thing in the morning.

"Mary Ann and I took her home immediately," Mr. Wylie said. "My wife helped her clean up, gave her something to eat—she was a polite child, but she fell on that food. She slept around the clock, when she wasn't covering her ears and crying out."

"Oof. That's an image," Ramsay said, startled even though Carrie had shared her story. "She said the Thorne brothers found her, bullied her, and threatened her if she breathed a word of anything about what happened."

"A more worthless young man never lived than George Thorne," Mr. Wylie said. He reined in his horse. "Here we are at Apollinaris Springs. How about a drink?"

"It won't be stiff enough," Ramsay said as he dismounted and walked Xerxes to the spring. The men sat together on a log, sharing the tin cup chained to a spigot.

"Carrie said he was Millie's cousin. Had he done this sort of thing before?" Ramsay asked.

"That's the rumor," Mr. Wylie said, drinking the last of the fizzy water. "John Thorne, who owns the Railroad Hotel, probably paid off the local constabulary to say nothing when women complained." He shrugged. "George Thorne—what a useless waste of space! He mostly preyed on those second floor women, and who ever listens to them?"

"Even when they have an honest complaint," Ramsay said, making it a statement and not a question. "Please tell me he's in prison now."

"Wish I could. As near as Mary Ann and I could find out, and believe me, we kept our inquiries discreet, he's back East, doing what I don't know, but I could probably speculate."

"No justice for Carrie. Why is Millie Thorne even involved in this?" Ramsay asked. "For that matter, why didn't anyone speak out?"

"John Thorne runs a business that, however shady, brings good revenue into Bozeman," Mr. Wylie explained. "Millie's father Alfred Thorne is a banker with considerable holdings in the Northern Pacific Railroad, which has its tentacles in the Yellowstone Park Association."

Ramsay understood. "Everyone with a complaint would have to do battle with the man who holds the valley's purse strings."

"I am numbered among that cowardly roster," Mr. Wylie said. "We all keep quiet because we need the goodwill of our banker. Who would believe anything Carrie has to say? I can only assume that Millie's father sent her to keep an eye on Carrie, tell some lies, and make certain no one believes Carrie, if she decides to talk."

"That's a mean supper," Ramsay said.

"It is," Mr. Wylie agreed. "Carrie goes about her business with rumors hanging over her head." He smiled, but there was no overlooking his wistful expression. "I can tell you that by the end of the summer, my employees who are paying any attention at all have no grounds to accuse Carrie of anything. Still, in Bozeman she's a second floor woman, and that's the Thornes's doing."

"Why hasn't Carrie bailed out of Bozeman?" Ramsay commented as they continued their leisurely trip down the Grand Loop.

"Probably my doing. I also believe she likes living here and is too stubborn to be run off by rumors," Mr. Wylie said.

"I call that courage more than stubbornness," Ramsay said, and touched his medal of honor ribbon. "What do you mean, 'my doing'?"

"Mary Ann and I could quickly see how much Carrie wanted to go to school, to read something . . ."

". . . besides the Police Gazette?" Ramsay asked with a laugh.

"She told you that story?" Mr. Wylie said. "Carrie McKay has spunk and brains enough for three people. Without even asking, she started cooking for us and cleaning. My younger daughter Mary Grace was a freshman at Montana Ag the year Carrie came to live with us. You should have seen Carrie's eyes follow Gracie out the door and down the street as she walked to college. I doubt she'd have said anything. I know Carrie was grateful to have a safe place to live . . ." His voice trailed off. "I came here from Iowa to become the county's superintendent of schools."

"You're an educationist. You couldn't ignore that look, could you, sir?"

"Not with a Christian conscience. Mary Ann and Gracie brought Carrie up to snuff with her reading, taught her how to write better, and coached her on numbers."

"I'll wager she was a quick study."

"Indeed. When she was eighteen, I took her to Montana Agricultural College to enroll her in the high school prep course. It's a three-year course for students Carrie's age and younger who don't have opportunities for schooling, living on remote ranches. Or in Carrie's case, working too hard since she was nine years old."

"That must have pleased her," Ramsay said, imagining Carrie's delight.

"You'd be wrong," Mr. Wylie said, surprising him. "She cried and said she wouldn't be an expense to me." He looked away and Ramsay focused his own attention on Roaring Mountain, which was hissing more than usual this morning as they rode by.

"That's Carrie," Mr. Wylie said simply. "Desperate to learn, but far too well brought up by a deaf mother who worked herself to death in a seedy hotel kitchen. Carrie had been taught to be beholden to no one. She refused to go inside that building until I promised her I would let her keep working for me until she paid me back."

"Stubborn little button," Ramsay commented. He could see Carrie behaving that way, proud and determined, without a penny to her name.

"She is that, as well as persuasive," Mr. Wylie said. "Carrie talked the prep school principal into letting her take a typewriting course. For three years she typed all my correspondence, kept up her prep grades, and cooked for us. She has a hunger for education."

Yikes, I was so happy to finish the eighth grade and leave school behind, Ramsay thought. *I don't think my record of scholarship will impress Carrie too much.* "Uh, schooling is a fine thing," he said, and winced to hear his lame words.

Mr. Wylie either didn't notice, or kindly overlooked Ramsay's tepid response.

"I was walking by her room one night and heard her crying inside as if her heart were breaking."

"Don't stop there," Ramsay spoke up, suddenly anxious.

"I wasn't sure what to do, and Mary Ann was out playing bridge at the neighbor's. I finally knocked on the door. I heard her blow her nose really loud, and then she opened the door." He laughed, and Ramsay thought he almost heard the fondness of a parent. "Seems she had just finished reading *A Tale of Two Cities*, one of those prep-required books, and was sobbing her heart out over poor Sydney Carton. You've read the book?"

"A few years back," Ramsay admitted. "School was never my number one idea of how to spend my youth." He read it only two winters ago when he was in charge of the super-isolated West Thumb soldier station and even Charles Dickens started to look good, along about

February. He even owed his horse's name to a dusty book about the Persian Wars, just dying to be read in the West Thumb station.

It took no imagination for him to see Carrie weeping over the death of a reformed rascal—a lawyer, of course—who chose to go to the guillotine to spare the husband of the woman he secretly loved. It also took no imagination for him to know that someone with his lack of scholarly interest would have no appeal for a Carrie McKay.

He had no more to say. Ramsay rode in silence, wondering how long it would take him to quit thinking about the strawberry blond who had sung his mother's favorite song so sweetly, and who didn't mind sharing her life's story with him, for some reason. He reasoned it was going to be a busy summer, once the bulk of the tourist trade started. He had desk work to do, and probably an entire summer of tasks like the strange one waiting for him in Fountain Hotel. Uncle Sam wasn't paying him the princely sum of ninety-four dollars a month plus quarters, food, and forage to moon over a pretty lady, even if Major Pitcher and his wife thought it was a good idea.

He had nothing to say beyond casual comments when Mr. Wylie mentioned his summer expectations, or groused mildly about the way the drivers seemed to punctuate every sentence with a curse, or the irritation of dust on the roads that hadn't been graveled yet. Finally even Mr. Wylie stopped talking.

He was yanked out of his self pity when Mr. Wylie grabbed Xerxes' reins and forced his horse to a standstill. Ramsay lurched forward and grabbed the pommel of his saddle like a pea-green private. "What in the world?" he exclaimed as he righted himself.

"Are you moping because Carrie likes school and you didn't?" Mr. Wylie asked, and he didn't sound like he wanted a stupid answer.

All Ramsay had was a stupid answer. "I guess I . . . I didn't think this whole thing through, or even very far, Mr. Wylie. She has big plans, hasn't she? She's probably studying to be a teacher."

Mr. Wylie took his hand off Xerxes's reins but he stayed where he was, glowering at Ramsay as if he were a misbehaving high schooler sent to the office for some living, breathing misdemeanor of monumental proportions.

"She's taking the domestic science course because she wants to sew and cook and take care of children and probably make some knuckleheaded imbecile like you really happy some day," Mr. Wylie said, with considerable asperity. "I thought you were a smart man."

"The older I get, the less I seem to know, sir," Ramsay said frankly. "I think I came home from the Philippines about as dumb as a man can be."

The Norris soldier station was coming into view. Ramsay felt some relief at the sight. Mr. Wylie probably wouldn't have time to say everything he thought.

He said enough, exhibiting the triumph of great powers of condensation over irritation, and maybe even the kindness Will Wylie was known for, whether a man deserved it or not. "Sergeant Major Stiles, could this be the beginning of wisdom? Most nincompoops have no earthly idea how little they know. You at least are willing to admit it. Don't throw in the towel so soon," Mr. Wylie said.

Ramsay nodded, too unsure of himself to speak. Was Mr. Wylie in cahoots with Major Pitcher in want to see a perfectly capable sergeant major turn into a blithering idiot in five easy steps?

"One thing to consider, Sergeant Major," Mr. Wylie said, when Ramsay thought he wouldn't say anything more on what was obviously a delicate subject. "Plans change. "

He didn't feel up to debating the matter with Mr. Wylie. "They can, sir," he admitted. "I thought I would spend the rest of my career as a first sergeant."

"And I thought nothing was better than being superintendent of schools in Bozeman," Mr. Wylie said. "Then I fell in love with Wonderland."

"So did I, sir," Ramsay said, feeling himself on sure ground again. Well, nearly. Was he destined to overthink everything? Could a man fall in love *in* Wonderland too? And so quickly? He sighed and shook his head.

Mr. Wylie leaned over in his saddle and gave Ramsay a quick punch on his arm. "Be a bit more creative, Sergeant Major."

That's the second time someone has told me that, Ramsay thought as he gave his riding companion a casual salute and peeled off toward the soldier station.

"Let me know what you decide to do about that thorn in everyone's side," Mr. Wylie called after him. "Maybe the other matter too."

When pigs fly, Ramsay thought.

Chapter Sixteen

$\mathcal{T}$he soldiers were overjoyed to see the sticky buns, no matter their shape. Ramsay ate one, shook his head over it, and left the rest for the men. He argued with himself all the way from Norris to Fountain Hotel, a four-story wooden monster that seemed to exude comfort, stability, and old money. The ladies in the lobby wore the requisite linen dusters, the best protection in the park from dusty roads, even this early in the season. Their flowery hats were fetching and useless.

While he waited for the hotelier, Ramsay watched the leisurely class promenade through the lobby, looking so out of place in their rustic surroundings. He tried to imagine them sitting around a campfire and couldn't.

As he stood there wondering where to find Mr. Bell, the hotelier he remembered from his last visit, an older lady bore down upon him. She walked with a cane, but he suspected it was merely ornamental when she raised it inches from his campaign hat and slapped it on his shoulder. Suddenly thinking of the jungle, he nearly grabbed the stick and thrashed her with it. He stopped just in time.

"You there! I have been waiting for a bellboy five minutes and more!"

Startled, Ramsay wondered if she really meant to address him. Humiliated, he saw several ladies titter in a well-bred way behind their gloved hands.

"There is some mistake," he started, then stopped when she poked his chest with that cane. "Oww!"

Employing what he thought was great restraint, he took the cane out of her hand. "Ma'am, I am not your bellhop. I am a sergeant major in the United States Army," he said, giving her The Stare in a medium-sized glance.

Unimpressed, she snatched back her cane. "What on earth is the army doing in this national park?" she asked in the kind of voice that demanded an explanation from someone obviously her inferior.

"We work here," he tried to explain, "protecting the park from poachers and tourists."

The tittering behind him turned into laughter but the woman was undeterred. The artificial bird among the flowers on her hat started to shake as though preparing to fly.

"You should be chasing Indians or apprehending road agents, not mingling with your betters," the lady said, her voice still full of command, but her cane under more control, as she leaned on it now. She reminded him of an eagle glaring at road kill. "Find me a bellboy."

Happy to get a little farther from the cane, he looked around for the bellhop stand and saw two young men in a uniform vaguely resembling his own, if one were remarkably nearsighted, as the woman probably was. He gestured to them, but both men shook their heads.

"Cowards," he muttered under his breath. What was the republic coming to?

"They appear not to want to get your luggage," he said to the lady, who was beginning to resemble his lower grades teacher, who had no tolerance for boys who came to school barefoot.

"Why do you think that is?" she demanded, a bully in full flower.

"Perhaps because you are a dragon with no manners," he told her.

The woman gasped and turned the color of raw liver. "Do you know who I am, and what I can do to your rapidly vanishing career?"

"I have no idea who you are, ma'am. Do your worst to my career," he said, tired of bullying, and ready to tell Carrie McKay to punch Millie Thorne in the face.

"I know General Nelson Miles!" the woman said, firing what he hoped was her last shot.

"So do I, ma'am," he said. "He stood beside me while President Roosevelt pinned a Medal of Honor on me in January. Where do you want your luggage?"

Gaping like a fish now, she pointed her walking stick toward the door.

Ramsay fixed The Stare on the bellboys. "Now," he said, pointing down at the floor in front of him. "Front and center."

To his relief, both bellboys did as he ordered. "You heard the lady."

He turned on his heel and stalked across the lobby, where absolute silence reigned now. *I hate my job*, he thought in misery.

He saw Mr. Bell, worried expression on his face, standing by an open door. Even if it had been a broom closet, Ramsay felt like diving in headfirst, anything to get out of that lobby.

The men shook hands. Mr. Bell closed the door behind him and gestured to a chair. Ramsay sat and watched as the hotelier poured them each a drink from a flask he pulled from his desk drawer. Ramsay knocked his back and shook his head at another.

"I apologize for that," Ramsay said. He leaned forward. "Do you deal with people like her every day?"

"'All the livelong day. Doo dah, doo dah,'" Mr. Bell sang, which made the low level in the flask not too surprising to Ramsay. *And it's not even high season yet*, he thought, his mind back on Carrie for a moment, and her lovely voice. He doubted she had sung "Camptown Races," anytime recently.

"I could never do your job," Ramsay said, taking in Mr. Bell's wan expression.

"I feel that way at the end of every season, when snow flies and we are closing this hotel," Mr. Bell said. "It's early in the year, but I feel it now." He stood up and went to the window. "Every day, when the touring coaches arrive, I look out over a sea of eager, disgruntled, irritated, enthusiastic faces and ask myself, 'Which one of you is it?'"

"Is what?" Ramsay asked.

Mr. Bell turned back to his desk and plopped himself into his chair. "The guest from the Infernal Regions, who causes nothing but trouble and whom we would gladly pay to leave."

"Are you pretty good at telling?"

"You'd be amazed. That woman who ordered you about is the wife of a steel magnate from New York City. She likely treats her own help like dirt, and they are probably happy to see her off to Yellowstone, in hopes that a bear will eat her. By the time she leaves, I predict we will hope she gets squashed by a hansom cab in Central Park."

"It's more fun at a Wylie Camp," Ramsay said, embarrassed at his scene in the lobby. "I should have kept my temper." *Maybe I needed a little humility*, he thought, wondering if Carrie would have scolded him. "What can I do for you? Something about a peeping bear?"

"Yes," Mr. Bell said, rubbing his hands together. He looked pleased to discuss something besides the Gorgon in the lobby. "For the last few nights, a bear has been observed peering into one of the main floor windows. We moved the lady in question to another room—she doesn't care to climb stairs—and the same thing repeats itself, no matter the room. The woman hasn't slept a wink and she's developed a nervous tic."

And you brought me here for this? Ramsay thought, but wisely kept his counsel, something he regretted not doing in the lobby. "Could you station a bellhop or a custodian outside to watch for the bear? You know, just to yell 'Hey bear!' and swat it with a broom?"

Mr. Bell poured himself another drink with shaking hands. "None of us are that brave, Sergeant Major Stiles."

"You'd like me to set up shop outside the hotel and watch for a bear?"

"That sums it up." Mr. Bell's color had improved with each sip; so had his good cheer. He raised his glass to Ramsay. "Here's to the army."

"Uh, yes, sir." He sat there, waiting for Mr. Bell to offer him a room at the Fountain Hotel where he could wait until dark. The longer he sat the more he realized that neither Mr. Bell nor the outraged lady in the lobby saw him as a responsible, well-trained, noncommissioned officer. He was someone convenient to do their work, but not stay in a hotel. Maybe I needed this comeuppance, he told himself grimly. I'm one of the little people, just like Carrie.

Still, a man has some pride. "Where should I stay tonight so I can do this?" he asked.

"I assumed you'd be more comfortable among your own kind at the Fountain Soldier Station," Mr. Bell said, and gave him an owlish look that hinted at over-involvement in the bottle.

There it was; his own kind. "It's three miles to the soldier station, Mr. Bell."

"So it is. You can eat there and be back here by dark."

Someone knocked on the door. Mr. Bell reached for a small box on his desk and shook what looked like Sen-Sen into his hand. He tossed them into his mouth and chomped down. Ramsay shook his head in amazement at his own naivete, and vowed to be smarter as soon as tomorrow, if not before.

Ramsay didn't bother with saying good-bye, because Mr. Bell was busy composing himself for his next problem. He opened the door on a fetching little thing in summer white and smelling of rose talcum powder who looked ready to chew nails. *I don't want to know*, Ramsay thought, as he quietly closed the door.

He retrieved Xerxes and rode behind the hotel, looking at the window ledges. An older lady with white hair and a winning smile waved to him from one of the rooms, and he waved back. She looked like his grandmother.

The three miles to the middle geyser's soldier station restored his equanimity, particularly since his trip through the geyser basin coincided with Old Faithful at play. Xerxes was used to geysers, so Ramsay rested his leg across his saddle and thought of what he had written, based on Captain Chittenden's excellent study: Old Faithful is a cone geyser that erupts every sixty-five minutes, give or take, to a height of some one hundred and fifty feet. The play lasts from three to ten minutes, day and night.

"Xerxes, I could cuddle Carrie McKay here on a log, provided she and I could ever find a time to get together on said log," he told his horse. Impossible.

At the Fountain soldier station, he ate with the regiment's newest sergeant and two privates and then spent a thoughtful hour walking with the sergeant, listening to his concerns about duty at Fountain, with tourists getting too close to geysers.

"We caught one yahoo tossing a bar of Ivory soap into a hot spring," the sergeant said. "When we asked him why, he said he heard it would make it erupt sooner."

"Did you explain the difference between hot springs and geysers?" Ramsay asked.

"Sergeant Major Stiles, I assured him that hot springs don't erupt, and soap's for people," the sergeant said. "I don't think he believed me."

"They seldom do."

The sergeant nodded, a wiser man. "What I really don't like is watching the hotel toss out garbage for the bears," he said. "They have bleachers and a fenced-off area for visitors. It doesn't seem right."

"It isn't."

He spent another hour with the men, taking notes on their grievances and listening, always listening. When the sun started to head toward the pines, he saddled up Xerxes and headed back to Fountain Hotel, where snobs and drunks held court.

He rode behind the hotel and tied Xerxes to a strut on the bleacher by the distant garbage dump, where visitors were starting to assemble. He watched their faces, noting the bored self-interest of the youths—it came with the age—contrasted with the jump up and down enthusiasm of the children, soon to return to their lives back East and writing essays about what they did during their summer vacation.

He breathed in the odd fragrance of sulfur and pine oil, which reminded him that no matter how vexing this particular assignment, patrolling Yellowstone Park was always going to be the highlight of his army career.

He admitted to some curiosity about the bear feeding. He had never seen one, although he was well-acquainted with the park's brown bears, lumbering masses of flesh and teeth that generally minded their own business in the meadows and forests. He knew the sows with cubs would keep their babies at a distance from crowds. He took out his binoculars to look for the little ones sitting on the periphery of the clearing, following Mama's first lesson—obedience.

He shared his binocs with a girl no older than eight or so, who wore a starched dress, her hair in ringlets. He answered her questions about geysers and bears, and thought of another girl working long hours in the Railroad Hotel in Bozeman, hoping for enough to eat, and to not be yelled at.

Dusk was settling fast when kitchen flunkies from the Fountain Hotel dragged up a cart containing two 42-gallon drums of kitchen leavings and scraps from the dining room. The bleachers were full of spectators, everyone leaning forward in anticipation.

Ramsay saw orange peels mixed with coffee grounds, and seasoned with hunks of lard and bones, a perfect bear stew far easier to obtain than hunting all day in the woods, snuffling bugs from rotten logs and trying to snag trout from fast-moving rivers. Stale bread and old cake amounted to a recipe no bear should eat and remain healthy and independent of people.

His heart turned over as he thought of bears nosing around the closed-down hotels in the fierce grip of sudden winter, wondering when the free meal was coming. They waited too long sometimes, putting off hibernation until they froze outside hotels empty now. Sitting there with the visitors on the bleachers, waiting for the bears to arrive, he knew it was wrong.

"Here they come!" someone shouted, and Ramsay looked beyond the man's pointing finger. Sure enough, three bears walked toward the garbage pit, their heads swaying from side to side.

Unable to help themselves, some of the more impetuous tourists left the bleacher and raced to the wooden rail separating them from the garbage and the approaching bears. Some of them waved pieces of bread in their hands, calling to the bears as though they were pets.

Ramsay left the bleacher too. He hesitated only a moment but then waded into the middle of the group, shouting at them to move back. He stared down the angry faces and ignored calls of "Killjoy!"

"These are bears," he shouted, "not pets. Move back or I'll ask you to leave."

Grumbling, the visitors did as he commanded. He turned his back on the bleacher and tried not to hear demands for his name and unit, and the who-do-you-think-you-are question he had heard earlier from a woman out of her element who could still sling around her prestige in a hotel lobby.

The bears came at a run now, veterans of this garbage treat. Ramsay kept waving the spectators back to the bleachers, wishing he could take each tourist one by one, to sit with him by a fast-moving river and watch bears pull trout from the stream, instead of crunching down egg shells and slobbering over gravy. Watching these beautiful animals slurp down leavings from breakfast, luncheon, and dinner both appalled and saddened him. He might ask Captain Chittenden about that fine line between entertainment and education, between observing cheap tricks like this, and watching wildlife in nature.

The crowd dispersed when it was too dark to see anything else, and the bears lumbered away, full of garbage. Dutiful now, the tourists followed an escort from the hotel who led the way with a lantern. Discouraged, Ramsay stayed where he was until everyone had gone.

His melancholy didn't last long. A young family still remained in the bleachers. He recognized the girl who had looked through his binoculars and seemed interested when he told her about bears hibernating, and mother bears coming out of their dens in the spring with little ones to teach and train.

"Sergeant, tell us more about this," the father said.

"Happy to," Ramsay replied, and asked them where they were from. As it turned out, Papa was a stockbroker who worked on Wall Street and took a train home to New Rochelle every night. Mama, a bright-eyed, intelligent-looking woman, probably maintained a lovely home in the suburbs.

Their two daughters sat next to him on the bleacher seat. "What can I tell you about Wonderland?" he asked the one—Alice, she informed him—who had shared his binoculars.

"Everything," Alice said solemnly. Her parents chuckled, obviously used to this child of theirs.

As the sky darkened, he told them about cone geysers and hot springs, and bears and even wolves, which meant little Alice scooted closer to him. She assured him magpies, ravens, and blue jays were more to her taste, and her little sister wanted to know about chipmunks. The wolves could wait.

When the younger daughter started yawning, Papa pulled the plug on more questions, but with regret. He shook Ramsay's hand, wished him well, and let Ramsay set the girls on Xerxes as he walked with them back to the hotel.

In the lobby, Ramsay shook hands all around again. Alice held his hand the longest. He squatted down to look her in the eye, which made her mother say, "You have excellent instincts, Sergeant Major Stiles."

"Some day I want to do what you do," Alice told him.

"Be in the army?"

"No, no. I want to tell people about Yellowstone."

"Honey, I don't know if it's something the ladies can do," Papa said.

"Why not?" Ramsay replied, and smiled inside to see the huge grin on Mama's face. "I know a sweet lady who sticks up for the bears. You can too."

"Your wife?" Mama asked.

Ramsay was all set to blush and deny. Instead, he looked at the kind woman, took heart from her interested expression, and replied, "Not yet. We'll see."

"You can probably do what you want because you are a man," Alice pointed out, ever practical.

Ramsay glanced at Papa, who shook his head. "Honey, even I don't get everything I want," Alice's father said.

"We should all get what we want," Alice said firmly.

Ramsay admired this child, who had opportunity and ease ahead of her, and maybe enough gumption to tell visitors about bears, if the army ever left Yellowstone to another as-yet-unknown agency. He thought of Carrie, and wished she could meet Alice. He took the thought a crazy step farther and imagined a daughter of his own like this. In the lobby of the Fountain Hotel, with a string quartet playing something Mozart-y, anything seemed possible.

"I have no doubt that you might teach tourists someday," he said, and straightened up. "Start by studying animals and fish and birds in school, and go where your fancy takes you."

Alice nodded, her eyes serious. "Thank you, sir," she said, and gave him a small curtsy that went straight to his heart.

He watched them head toward the elevator, his mind clear of the discouragement that had descended as he watched the bears guzzle down food nature never intended them to eat. Even the lobby, where he had spent some awful moments earlier in the day, had turned into a friendly place.

At the elevator, Alice turned to wave at him. In return, Ramsay snapped off a salute better than any salute he had ever given, including the one to President Roosevelt in January. She saluted back.

"Now I have to see a bear about an indiscretion," he murmured, as pretty ladies flirted with equally elegant gentlemen in the lobby, and the quartet played on.

Chapter Seventeen

With Xerxes stabled for the night, Ramsay went back to the hotel and knocked on Mr. Bell's door. He opened it on Mr. Bell's invitation and told him he was headed outside to watch for the bear. "Will you be here if I need your assistance?" he asked.

Mr. Bell promptly turned pale, the second time in their brief acquaintance, leaving Ramsay to wonder how the Yellowstone Park Association chose its fearless managers. "I . . . I . . . ," he began, and got no farther.

"Stay in your office until I turn up something," Ramsay ordered, speaking in the voice that always worked wonders with mint-green privates. "And lay off the sauce. That is an order."

Mr. Bells raised his arm as if to salute but then stopped and stared at his hand as though it belonged to someone else. "Just get rid of the bear. That's all I ask."

Ramsay found a broom and a place to sit on the back steps of the Fountain Hotel. Sitting in the shadows, he observed a maid and a chef wander hand in hand toward the gravel path that led to a campfire in the distance. They stopped to smooch and then disappeared behind one of the outbuildings.

"Going rotten-logging, are we?" he asked and envied them.

In the distance, he saw the bonfire of the Wylie Camp at Fountain, too far away to provide any warmth as he shivered in the shadows. His conversation with Alice from New Rochelle still warmed his heart and left him with questions of his own. He knew the army couldn't stay in Yellowstone Park forever. Cavalry troops had been patrolling here for twenty-one years. He wondered how long the army could shoulder such additional duties. It remained for more exalted ranks than his up the chain of command to make decisions. When it happened, Ramsay hoped there was a place for Alice's Adventures in Wonderland.

He chuckled over that bit of Lewis Carroll humor, then sat up, alert, as something materialized out of the shadows so close to him that he felt the hair rise on his arms. Improbably, he sniffed the fragrance of rose talcum powder. He watched in open-mouthed amazement as the shadowy form turned into the young lady in the lacy dress who had pushed her way into Mr. Bell's office as he had left it earlier today.

Silent and stunned, he watched as she took a handful of what looked like cookies from her handbag and set them on a window ledge. She stepped back, and Ramsay heard another sound that made the hairs rise even higher.

Moving slowly, but coming closer with every step was a bear of epic proportions. Ramsay held his breath then let it out slowly, relieved not to see the telltale hump of a grizzly. How brave to you feel right now? he asked himself, and decided he was brave enough.

He spoke quietly to the oblivious young lady who stood by the ledge. "Freeze. There is a bear behind you. Don't move or speak."

The woman froze. He heard her whimper and he told her to stop. She did.

"I'm going to try to scare the bear away," he said. "When I move and yell, kneel down where you are and put your hands over your neck and head."

Ramsay unsnapped the cover on his sidearm, wincing at how loud that little noise sounded. He gripped the broom and leaped off the porch, shouting, "Hey bear! Hey bear!" at the top of his lungs. The woman shrieked, but she did as he commanded and dropped to the ground by the window, hands over her neck.

Startled, the bear reared back, sank onto his haunches and flopped over as if someone had shot him. Ramsay charged toward him, yelling and swinging the broom in front of him, which seemed suddenly to have shrunk from a broom into a coat whisk. With the same singleminded fury that had driven him deep into the cave at Palong Batan, he ran close enough to the bear to shoot him at pointbank range, not that his little popgun of a Navy Colt would have made a dent.

He smelled a powerful odor and realized with a jolt just how terrified the bear was. Thank goodness he hadn't eaten much in the last six hours; better let the bear be indiscreet. Ramsay stood still, breathing hard, and watched as the bear righted himself and took off in the opposite direction, knocking over some barrels but making good time.

Ramsay let out his breath in a rush until he felt dizzy. He leaned forward, hands on his knees, until the blood returned to his head. He looked at the young woman still crouched by the window ledge and knew what his next step was.

He kicked aside the broom he had dropped while regaining his balance and walked to the window. As she still crouched there, looking up, her eyes still fearful, he swept the cookies into his hand, pocketed them, and then picked up the girl around her waist and slung her over his shoulder. He knew he could keep her there no matter what she tried.

Tourist over his shoulder and pounding on his back now, Ramsay banged on Mr. Bell's office door and opened it without waiting for an invitation to enter. Mr. Bell stared at him, mouth open, as he set Miss Talcum Powder down in one of the chairs and closed the door. Heads had started to pop out of doorways and this didn't need an audience.

"Why are you manhandling one of our honored guests?" Mr. Bell managed to stammer.

Ramsay yanked the cookies from his pocket and slammed them on Mr. Bell's tidy desk, where they disintegrated into chaff. "Because your honored guest put these on the window ledge of . . . of that nearest numbered room!" He turned to glare at the young woman, who tried to look defiant and failed. He watched as her lips quivered and her big eyes filled with tears. "If you think I can be swayed by tears, miss," he said, "you are wasting your time!"

She burst into tears, which sent Mr. Bell scuttling around the desk, handkerchief in hand. He darted angry glances at Ramsay, which lasted until Sergeant Major

Stiles gave him The Stare. Quietly, Mr. Bell returned to his seat and cowered there.

Ramsay took a deep breath and then another. He sat in the chair next to the weeping woman. He picked up the handkerchief Mr. Bell had dropped in his terror and put it in her hand. "Blow," he commanded, and she blew.

"Did you realize there was a bear about twenty feet behind you?" he asked, his voice calm now.

From the depths of the handkerchief, she shook her head.

"How many times have you put something on one ledge or another?" he asked. "Give me a straight answer." And then he couldn't resist, because it wouldn't hurt to impress Mr. Bell too. "The guardhouse at Fort Yellowstone is not a good place for young ladies, but believe me, I'll put you there."

He let her cry, feeling a bit like the Thorne brothers who had terrified Carrie, but only a little. "Your answer?"

"Four days."

Ramsay turned to Mr. Bell. "The lady who occupied that room . . . had you been moving her too, with each disturbance?"

"Yes, Sergeant."

"That's Sergeant Major," Ramsay snapped, weary of both of these sillies.

"Sergeant Major," the hotelier said. "I've moved her four times and every time the bear found her." He had his own question for the young woman, who blew her nose again. "Miss Marchant, isn't she your grandmother?"

Miss Marchant nodded.

Ramsay couldn't help his own stupefaction. "Why, in heaven's name, were you doing this?"

Miss Marchant sat up in the chair. She looked around and must have seen no sympathy in the room.

She retreated to the handkerchief again and took a deep breath. "I just wanted to scare her so bad that she would go back to Mammoth Hot Springs and let the rest of us enjoy Wonderland."

"What was she doing?" Mr. Bell asked.

Silence from Miss Marchant.

"I suspect she was acting like a grandmother," Ramsay said. "Making you behave, and not wanting you to go off with one of the drivers, or maybe a camp man or bellhop? Was that it?"

Miss Marchant nodded and retreated to the soggy safety of the handkerchief. Ramsay turned his attention to Mr. Bell. "Sir, go get the grandmother."

"It's after midnight," he started to protest.

"I don't care. Do it."

Mr. Bell scurried from the room. Ramsay leaned back in his chair, at a loss. He thought about the kind and practical Carrie McKay and asked himself what she would do. It didn't take long. Maybe he knew her better than he could have imagined, especially in a mere two weeks.

"Miss Marchant, if someone else had been watching, someone with a high-powered rifle, that bear would be dead now," he said and felt the weight of his own sadness. "Some of us in this park love those bears. We want them to remain alive. That was one of the mandates set down by President Grant himself, when Yellowstone was made a national park."

He glanced at the young lady, heartened to see she was listening to him.

"Bears are opportunists. The stinkers want the easy way out, because foraging for food in the wilderness can be tough. That bear will be coming back here again and again, because he knows there are cookies somewhere."

She started to cry again. "I didn't know. What will happen?"

"I'm going to post soldiers at this back door all summer if I have to, to make sure the bear gets the message that handouts are over," he told her. "It's a bear's nature to act this way and he won't be shot for it. Not on my watch."

She was silent then, and he waited. "I'm truly sorry," she whispered. "I just wanted Granny to let me have fun."

"I understand, Miss Marchant, but you've got to realize this is an animal preserve, not some wonderland."

"But people feed bears all the time."

"I know. They shouldn't," he said. He thought of serious Alice and her concern for wildlife and contrasted her with this silly girl—silly, but maybe repentant.

"I predict that in a few years there will be so many people and towns, and horses and railroads, that the wildlife will need a safe haven. I know it's hard to imagine, but that time is coming. Think about that for a while and grow up."

He heard voices in the corridor, and opened the door on an elderly woman in a nightgown and robe, looking fearful. Her eyes softened when she saw her granddaughter huddled in the chair, crying again, but maybe not for herself this time. Ramsay could only hope.

"Sergeant Major Stiles, Mrs. Evans," the hotelier said and retreated to the safety of his chair behind the desk.

"Tell your grandmother what you were doing," Ramsay said, offering his chair so Mrs. Evans could sit down.

In fits and starts, the granddaughter admitted a short lifetime of crimes and misdemeanors, going all the way back to ink in her teacher's tea in primary school. *I put the fear in her*, he thought and was not disappointed. The older lady sat with her arms folded and her back rigid. As Ramsay watched, her expression softened.

When Miss Marchant was silent, her grandmother put her hand on her arm. "I'd be remiss if I didn't tell you how much you remind me of your mother," she said finally.

"Mama did things like this?"

"Other things."

The matter could have teetered in any direction, but Ramsay had to give the palm to Mrs. Evans, who was made of sterner stuff than her granddaughter. Fixing her own stare on Miss Marchant she shook her finger at her. "Evie, did you ever wonder why your mother ended up going to school in a convent?"

Evie Marchant gasped. "You wouldn't!"

"Try me," her grandmother said. "You will behave from this moment on or so help me, it's Saint Thomas Aquinas's School for Young Ladies for you! One word to your mother and my son will suffice."

Bravo, Ramsay thought, impressed. "I think my work is done here," he said. "If you have any more trouble in the park, Mrs. Evans, I'll refer you to Judge Meldrum. He runs the district court and is located at Mammoth Hot Springs. He's a personal friend of mind. Mr. Bell? Maybe you and I should have a chat in the lobby and leave these two alone."

They walked into the lobby. "Would you like a room for the night, courtesy of the Fountain Hotel, Sergeant Major?" Mr. Bell asked. "A stiff drink?"

Ramsay said no to both, but he couldn't deny personal pride in getting the tightfisted hotelier to actually offer him a room. "With your permission, I'll return to the back porch. I think I'll stay there with the broom."

"You'll be sending soldiers for a few nights?"

"I will. I'll also tell them to train a few of your men to take over when the season gets busy and the troopers are needed to patrol the geyser basin," Ramsay said. "Good night."

Wrapped in a thick blanket with the Fountain Hotel crest on it, Ramsay dozed and watched until the sun came up, his broom ready. When it was light enough to see, he had the stableboy saddle Xerxes. He arrived at the Fountain Station in time for poached venison, which the corporal insisted came from a deer on his last legs.

"It was a mercy killing," the corporal insisted, and Ramsay gave him no argument. The boys at the Fountain Station knew how to cook venison.

Halfway through as tender a steak as Ramsay had ever eaten, the corporal remembered a telephone message from last night. "I wrote down the message from Major Pitcher," the corporal said and handed it over. "I had to ask him to repeat himself several times. I think he was laughing, but it could have been a bad connection. Lots of crackle."

Heaven spare me, Ramsay thought. *What now?* He read the note and suppressed the most impressive swear word he could think of, only because he was a leader of men.

Sergeant Major Stiles, you are needed here immediately, Ramsay read. *I have a directive from the president of the United States about a visitor, and it is the assignment of a lifetime. Yrs, Major John Pitcher.*

He followed the arrow and turned over the note. *P.S. Everyone on the staff will be watching this one with bated breath. How are you at escorting rich old musical theatre stars? Pretty good? JP.*

Chapter Eighteen

Thank goodness Xerxes had the good training to travel north on the Grand Loop with a sleeping sergeant major on his back for a portion of the journey. Years in the saddle had made Ramsay adept at dozing and riding.

The sergeant at the Fountain Station hadn't helped matters with his cheerful comment, "Better you than me, Sergeant Major." Ramsay had bit back another evil word or two and earned a reproachful look from Xerxes when he applied his spurs more firmly than usual as they left at a fast trot.

Deciding that no one would like him at all pretty soon, he didn't stop at the Willow Park Wylie Camp. He would have whined to Carrie, which he knew wouldn't prosper his cause, whatever that might be.

Still groggy from sitting up all night, alert for a cookie-loving bear, he crested the hill into Mammoth Hot Springs in early afternoon and sat there a moment.

He collected what thoughts he could muster that weren't profane in the extreme and tried to steel himself for what was to come.

All he wanted to do was stomp over to the barracks, toss out the perfectly competent sergeant of B Company and resume his former position there. Someone else could be sergeant major if it meant turning into Major Pitcher's designated idiot for stupid assignments.

Xerxes gave him a most meaningful look and started down the slope on his own volition. Nothing like a horse to keep a trooper humble.

"You win, Xerxes," he said.

He took his time over his horse, grooming his faithful mount. When he couldn't stall any more, Ramsay put his hat back on, cocked it at the proper angle, squared his shoulders, and went in pursuit of Dame Duty, that fickle mistress.

Major Pitcher looked up when Ramsay knocked on the doorframe. "Good to see you, Sergeant Major Stiles," he said most formally, then ruined it with a slow smile. "You're probably loathing the air I breathe, aren't you?"

To be diplomatic or something else? That was the question. "Not quite yet, Major," Ramsay replied, depending on their long acquaintance to smooth over any potential misunderstanding. "Better give it to me straight while I'm on my feet. I was up all night with a bear."

"Mission accomplished?"

Ramsay thought of Miss Marchant's white face, indignant at first, then filled with remorse. Little Alice and her promising future occupied his weary brain next, followed by Carrie pinning his medal of honor ribbon back on his uniform. "All in all, yes, sir. I'll write a report," he said, knowing there wouldn't be a word about Carrie McKay in such a document.

"This business might take precedent." Major Pitcher rummaged through the envelopes on his desk and held one out to Ramsay. "I don't get these very often, for which I am supremely grateful. Read it and tell me what you think."

Even though he already knew it was from the president of the United States, Ramsay still paused to look at the embossed return address. He opened the letter, impressed with the simplicity of "White House, Washington" in the upper left-hand corner, followed by the word "Personal."

The letter was handwritten, but readable. President Roosevelt spent a short paragraph asking after Major Pitcher's health and that of his wife. The next paragraph stopped him cold.

John, I am requesting that all the stops be pulled out for Madame Louise LaMarque, Ramsay read, *a former star of the musical stage.*

"The musical stage? Heaven help me," he said.

"New York is a wicked town," Pitcher said, not even trying to suppress a smile growing wider by the minute.

His cup already running over with dread, Ramsay kept reading. *She was the second wife and now-widow of an advisor to President McKinley's cabinet, who died a year ago. She wants a tour of the park and insists someone of her prestige needs an escort.*

"She surely means an officer, Major Pitcher," he said.

"Nope. She might, but Teddy doesn't. Keep reading."

My choice is Sergeant Major Stiles, Ramsay read and then read it again. *After all, he saved my life from a drunk in Gardiner. He's the one.*

"Sergeant Major Stiles, you're anointed," the major said. "Bet you wish you'd left that drunk alone now, eh?"

Ramsay set the letter down on the major's desk, seeing in his mind's eye anything meaningful he planned to do fly away on little fairy wings. The old trot would probably demand every moment of his time. His project condensing Captain's Chittenden's book would languish on his desk and wither away from neglect. Bears would roam Fountain Hotel's lobby and corridors unchecked, searching for cookies.

Ram, you whiner, he thought. *How bad can this be?* "When is Mrs. LaMarque expected to arrive?"

"According to this letter, tomorrow." The major held up a second letter of several pages. "You'll want to study this tome. It lists all her demands."

"Demands, sir? Is it a ransom note?" Ramsay thought those days when his voice was changing were long past, but apparently not. His voice shot into an upper register he hadn't heard in years. Major Pitcher raised his eyebrows, but wisely said nothing.

"You heard me right, Sergeant Major." He handed over the other letter. "She'll bring her own satin sheets, but there will be Earl Grey tea every afternoon on some hotel terrace or another, no whistling or humming in her presence, and complete silence after ten o'clock at night. She will initiate all conversation. She likes to dance. Uh, can you?"

"The waltz, two-step, polka, and schottische under duress, sir," Ramsay replied, grateful for the first time in his life for his mother's insistence on dancing classes, even though he hated it. "It's been a few years, though." Gadfreys, more like twenty-five.

"Better and better! Keep this instruction manual, or ransom note, or whatever you want to call it handy," the major joked. "Take along your best uniform, because you'll be staying in the hotels and dancing, taking tea on the veranda and doing a lot of listening to an old battle axe, I gather."

"Yes, sir," Ramsay said, because there was no other answer.

"There will be a maid accompanying her. According to that letter, a coach and driver have already been hired from the YP Transportation Company. They will fetch the two of them from Cinnabar. You will be waiting at the Gardiner Hotel by noon, with a smile on your face and a spring in your step."

"Yes, sir." Ramsay saluted and went to the door. "Sir, is Captain Chittenden still around?"

"I believe his wife and children arrived today. I doubt he'll want a visit."

Disappointed in all ways, Ramsay dragged himself to his quarters and flopped down on his bed. He started to read through the letter. In mere minutes, he slept.

He slept through mess call for supper and woke up in time for Extinguish Lights. Sour of face, mind, and body, he cajoled B Company's cook out of leftovers and then walked to the bathhouse by the lower terrace. Usually a good soak in a thermal pool could cure what ailed him, but not this time. He sat in silence, dried off, dressed, and walked across the parade ground toward his quarters.

The lights were on in Captain Chittenden's quarters. He walked up the path to the house but changed his mind. Major Pitcher was probably right; a man with a newly arrived family probably didn't want to hear him whine about Carrie McKay. He stood there a moment, listening to laughter and happy chatter, then turned and quietly retraced his steps.

He sat on his front steps until the chill of evening drove him indoors. He stared at himself in his shaving mirror, saw the sun and wind wrinkles and the hard look in his eyes. Had his face always been this thin? He thought about Carrie McKay and watched his eyes soften.

"My word, Ramsay, you old dog you," he said to his image. "Get through the next five or six days—how bad can it be—then get serious about courting Carrie. Figure out a way."

It was a cheerful thought. He took it to bed, read a few chapters in *The Moonstone* (one of his favorite books), turned out the light, and tried to sleep.

After a night of running away from a bear dressed like a woman in a linen duster wielding a cane, Ramsay took extra care over his grooming, which included patting some bay rum on his face. He wore his best undress blouse and khaki jodhpurs and polished his cavalryman's boots to a mirror shine. He packed what he needed, but left his duffel inside his front door, ready to grab and go, perhaps while milady and her maid were promenading on the Mammoth Terraces.

The five miles to Gardiner were accomplished with time to spare. According to the letter, Mrs. LaMarque and her maid would be waiting at the town's best hotel, which meant to most people the hotel which offended genteel visitors the least. He arrived in the lobby of the Gardiner Hotel and looked around for someone elegant with a maid. No Mrs. LaMarque. He went to the door and looked out, hoping she had changed her mind east of Cincinnati and turned back.

As he waited, indecisive, he saw a rider coming from the north, moving fast, hunched over his saddle. From instinct not called upon since the end of the Indian wars thirteen years ago, Ramsay looked beyond the rider, wondering who was following the man.

The horse and rider practically slid to a stop in front of the hotel. Ramsay couldn't ignore the wild look in the horseman's eyes, as though he had seen too much.

Ramsay came closer, taking hold of the exhausted horse's bridle. "What's wrong?"

The rider thrust a note in his hand at Ramsay. "She's not too happy, Sarge," he said, "and she's all yours, if you're from Fort Yellowstone. I never saw anyone hold the Northern Pacific hostage before!"

Ramsay released his hold on the horse's bridle and the rider headed toward the closest bar, where he threw himself from the saddle, flashed through the swinging doors, and disappeared inside.

He stared at the folded note in his hand and resisted a powerful urge to wash his hands of it like Sergeant Major Pontius Pilate and join the rider in the bar. With serious misgivings, he flicked it open and read, *Things are at their worst. Hurry up. Dave Lassiter.*

Ramsay mounted Xerxes and rode north toward Cinnabar, full of misgivings and cursing the moment he intercepted that harmless drunk at the arch dedication.

Cinnabar came in sight too soon to suit him, and there was the train. He saw a YPTC carriage nearby, with Dave Lassiter sitting there, his booted foot propped against the footboard, a stunned expression on his face. Ramsay knew the man as not someone easily rattled.

He heard a woman screaming inside the train. Alarmed, he dismounted, and wrapped Xerxes's reins around a hitching rail by the carriage.

"Dave, what's going on?" he asked.

"A spectacle of unusual proportions," the driver said. Dave Lassiter was a man well-acquainted with hyperbole, which he called "high purple-ease," because he knew his own foibles better than most.

Perhaps Dave was right this time. When the screaming stopped, Ramsay leaned closer to him. "Is anyone in real trouble?"

"Just you, Sarge, if you've been sent to gather up these women," Dave replied, his long face longer than usual and verging on mournful. "And me. I'm the lucky driver."

The shrieks began again and the conductor, a man Ramsay also knew as calm and unflappable, leaped from the train. He puffed over to Ramsay. "You'd better do something!"

"I'm not so sure the army pays me enough," Ramsay said, attempting to inject a little humor into a situation where no one was laughing.

No one even smiled. Ramsay took a deep breath and stepped onto the back of the train, a private car tacked on in Bozeman for Yellowstone's wealthiest visitors. He knocked on the outside door, listened as it became quiet, and entered the car.

A tall, handsome woman glared at him. She carried a cane and she shook it at him. Startled, Ramsay stepped back.

"I was expecting at least a lieutenant," she snapped.

"All you get is me, ma'am," he said. "What can I do? Is someone in need of a doctor?"

"No," she replied, injecting several syllables of disdain into the word. "My maid refuses to leave the train because she is afraid she will be scalped and dragged into captivity."

"That won't happen," he assured her, looking at a woman in a maid's uniform, her eyes wild in her face, and her hair every which way on her head. "There haven't been any Indians in Yellowstone Park since 1877. Well, not too many. She's perfectly safe."

He might have been a cricket chirping on the hearth for all the impression that he made on either woman. "She is also convinced that if she leaves the train, she will roll off the mountainside."

Ramsay couldn't help himself. He laughed out loud, which made the servant burst into tears again and the well-dressed dragon favor him with an elegant sneer. She was ten times worse than the lady in the lobby of the Fountain Hotel, and she was his, for the duration of a Yellowstone Park visit. No, the army didn't pay him enough.

As the old lady glared at him as though he were dog poop she would scrape off the bottom of her shoe, Ramsay thought about life as a private citizen. He thought of combat and the need for quick decisions.

Suddenly, he had an amazing idea, one that nearly hit him on the head like a sledgehammer wielded by one of the Katzenjammer Kids in the Sunday funnies. He knew better than to discard it out of hand, because it was the perfect solution to everyone's problems in the super-expensive rail car. Mostly it would solve his biggest problem, and for a change, he didn't think of other people first.

Hoping for the same control over two overwrought women that he was accustomed to as a sergeant of no mean ability in the US Army, he raised his arm and pointed at the maid. "Stop it. Just stop it," he commanded, and she obeyed. "Thank you."

He looked the battle-ax right in the eye until she shifted her glance. So far, so good.

"I can solve your problem, Mrs. LaMarque."

"I doubt it," she snapped, on the attack again.

He had to give her points for indomitability, but he wasn't about to surrender the field, not when everything he cared about was at stake. Maybe he could tell Captain Chittenden about this in the near future, or his own children someday.

His heart in his throat, Ramsay turned to the rail car door and opened it. "Then good-bye, Mrs. LaMarque, if you won't even listen to my proposition. Go back to Washington with this nitwit you employ and complain to President Roosevelt." He walked out the door and closed it behind him, then he gave her five seconds before he left the platform and rode Xerxes out of Cinnabar. Maybe.

The door opened when he was two steps down the few stairs that led to the depot platform.

"What do you have in mind, Sergeant?" he heard behind him, the voice frosty enough to freeze his backside.

He turned around but did not take a step up. "That is Sergeant Major to you, Mrs. LaMarque," he said in what he hoped was a quiet voice of command. A man can only feel his way through life as best he knew how.

They glared at each other, but mercifully, the maid had not resumed her caterwauling.

"Sergeant Major." She bit off the words like a grizzly would rip the guts from a trout.

He took a step up. "I can get you a useful maid from the Wylie Camp at Willow Park. It will take a day and some persuasion."

He took another step up until he stood on the platform with her. "She is not a maid, either, but a cook. The first time you raise your voice to her I will personally escort you right back here to Cinnabar. It comes down to this: How badly do you want to visit Yellowstone Park?"

There it was, laid out neatly in front of a woman used to her own way. "Take it or leave it."

"I could have President Roosevelt yank you right out of the army," she said.

He folded his arms and knew he stood on sure ground. "No, you can't. Send this crybaby to Bozeman to wait for you, and I will escort you to the National Hotel at Mammoth Terraces. You'll have to make do on your own for a day while I convince a sensible young lady to work for you temporarily." He pulled out his timepiece. "I need an answer now."

"Yes," she said quickly, somewhat to Ramsay's surprise. "You are unpleasant and already a cross to bear . . ."

"So are you, Mrs. LaMarque," he interrupted.

He thought he saw a tiny twitch of her lips, and maybe even a gleam in her eye, but he had to be mistaken. Then again, maybe the old warthog liked to do battle and no one had challenged her recently.

"I will overlook that," she said. "What will this paragon cost me?"

"A year's tuition at Montana Agricultural College, plus whatever fees and books are required," he said promptly.

"How much?" she demanded.

He had no idea. He also knew he was fighting with a woman well-endowed with a fortune who probably had no idea, either. "One hundred dollars. Fifty paid right now to me to convince her when I argue your case. Fifty when we all survive five or six days together, because survive it we will."

"Done, you irritating man."

He held out his hand and wiggled his fingers. "Let's see that fifty."

Chapter Nineteen

The last dish was washed and put away and Carrie took off her apron, ready to rush back to her tent and change for the evening campfire. She was going to sing, "Why, No One to Love?" again. After several days of including it in her repertory, she discovered it earned her more tips than "Old Dog Tray."

Beyond more dimes than nickels, she knew she sang the song to be reminded of the cavalryman who liked to think of his mother. She wanted to see Ramsay Stiles again. If there was another reason, she was equally certain she was mistaken. A lifetime of expecting nothing wasn't something easily amended, even though this summer of 1903 was full of surprises.

The night after Ramsay left on that horse so improbably named Xerxes, Jake Trost, the campfire magician, had asked her to dance in the first impromptu hop of the season, now that scheduled tours were bringing more visitors to Willow Park. The camp men moved back the tables in the dining hall and Bonnie Boone set up the a punch bowl and cookies on a side table. Mary Ann Wylie herself came down from Gardiner with her handful of sheet music, and the tourists assembled, those who weren't worn out from hiking Mammoth's Terraces.

Mrs. Wylie started with a polka, which segued into a waltz, because some of the visitors and savages used to lower altitudes were starting to gasp from the speed and energy required, Jake Trost among them. He finally cried uncle at even the slower pace, and sat Carrie down on a bench.

Any thoughts that the civil engineering major from the University of Washington was a lightweight were quickly dispelled by the man himself.

"Carrie, I have to be honest." Jake's face was serious, and she steeled herself for the worst. "I'll admit it. We have heard some rumors about you."

"I know," she said and started to rise. "I'll go."

"No," he said and she sat down. "Before he left our tent the other morning, the sergeant major told us not to believe everything we heard."

"Did he? My goodness," Carrie said.

"In no uncertain terms!" Jake said, not so serious now and more like the Jake she knew. "He has a way of looking you in the eye and making a statement that couldn't be anything but the truth, and you had darn well better believe it."

"I think it's called command," Carrie teased. "Thanks, Jake."

She couldn't overlook his wry expression. "Carrie, he said if we have any questions, just to ask you."

That was her cue to tell him that yes, she had lived on the second floor of the Railroad Hotel, but that she had been just a child and she and her mother had cooked and washed dishes in the restaurant below. "I worked there a few more years after my mother died, and then the Wylies took me in hand because I was an orphan," she finished, figuring even Ramsay would agree that was enough of the dirty details.

Jake nodded, and gave her his own look of command, not as forceful as Ramsay's but strong enough to assure Carrie she was still in good hands. "With your permission, I'll drop the word to the other savages."

"I'd appreciate it," she said simply. She stood up. "All right, Jake, you've had long enough to rest, and I like to two-step."

"You're on, Carrie," he told her and whirled her away.

There was more dancing the second night, and not just with Jake. The other camp men of Tent Twenty led her through a waltz, another two-step, and then the hesitation waltz back with Jake again. The dance was new to most of them and required instructions from one of Jake's tentmates and the shy teacher from her own tent who turned out to be not so shy on the dance floor.

"I'm not too good at this," Carrie finally confessed to Jake, who promptly turned it into a standard waltz.

"Neither am I," he whispered. "Carrie, do you dab almond extract behind your ears?"

She giggled. "No! You're smelling faithful application of Jergen's hand cream, a necessity if you wash as many dishes as I do. It goes everywhere." *Now that was too much information*, she thought. *I hope he overlooks it.*

"I like it," he said, and whirled her to a chair, because he was starting to puff again. "How long until I can breathe and not gasp?"

"Another two weeks."

Carrie looked around in surprise to see Sergeant Major Stiles perched on the edge of a pushed-back dining table. As she smiled at him, he straightened up, crossed the space between them, clicked his booted heels together and bowed.

"Since your dancing partner is about seven-eighths dead, will I do?" he asked.

She glanced at Jake, who smiled and waved her off. "Go on, save yourself," he called out, as she found herself in the arms of an unexpectedly good dancer.

Why he should make her shy, she couldn't have told a tentfull of roommates, but shy she was, at least until she found the courage to look up at his face. She had never seen eyes so tired, but there he was, dancing with her anyway.

"Ram, you look worn out with half a foot in the grave," she said, then realized she had given him a nickname. "I mean, Ramsay."

"Ram will do. I like it," he replied as he whirled her away. "Maybe I'll call you Caroline, because I like that. No particular reason. And by golly, I am absolutely knackered."

His obvious exhaustion didn't stop him from finishing the waltz. Their dance ended in a quiet corner of the dining hall. He sat her down and collapsed in genteel fashion beside her.

"Where in the world did you learn to dance?" she asked.

"In Iowa first, then here and there. Some of those isolated garrisons in the Southwest, mainly, because we were bored," he said. "My mother insisted on dancing classes, even though we barely had two pennies to rub together, when I was growing up."

"Why?"

183

"She liked to dance too," he said simply.

He closed his eyes for a moment that stretched into a longer moment. There was no ignoring his exhaustion, and she let him be, watching because there he was, and she liked the way he looked. Those wrinkles she thought at first that might be age lines, were probably wrinkles caused by scouring winds and sand or snow pellets. The West could do that to a person.

He hadn't shaved, either, which surprised her, because her brief acquaintance with Sergeant Major Stiles had shone her a man fastidious about his grooming. Something was up, and she wanted to know. When he woke up, he would probably tell her.

He sat with his eyes closed for the better part of five minutes, or enough time for a polka. She thought the livelier music and stamping feet might rouse him, but he was past that. When his head started to tip forward, she thought she had better wake him before he fell on the floor. She gently touched his arm and gave him a little shake.

"At least I'm not drooling," he said, which made her laugh.

"What in the world is going on?" she asked, with no pointless commentary.

He seemed wide awake now. She wondered what he looked like in the morning when he woke up. She liked to face the day gradually, with a stretch and a sigh, and maybe a snuggle deep in the covers again, if it was cold out. Ramsay Stiles didn't seem like that kind of sleeper. Just thinking about it made her blush, and wonder where her mind was wandering.

"I'll tell you, Caroline. I need to borrow your services for five or six days."

"Whatever for?" she asked, intrigued.

"Take a look at this letter." He pulled out a letter from an inside pocket.

She stared, open-mouthed, at the words "White House," read the letter, and read it again. "You stood in front of President Roosevelt and saved him from a dangerous man?"

"He was just a harmless drunk."

"You didn't know that," she said.

"No, I didn't. It's nothing, Carrie."

"Hardly." She scanned the letter again. "And you're the lucky escort."

He sighed. "She's a dragon in a designer gown. Her maid is too hysterical and fears being scalped if she leaves the train. Don't laugh. Hysterics are ugly customers, Caroline."

He suddenly looked contrite. "I probably should apologize to her someday, but what do I know about soothing rich widows? Mrs. LaMarque is determined to tour the park, and she insists on a maid. Mr. Wylie gave me permission to ask you. Please help me."

He said it so simply. Carrie wanted to say yes immediately—he was that kind of a commander—but she had her doubts. "I'd love to, but I need every single nickel and dime I can scrape together here, if I'm going to get through one semester at college. Even a few days would set me back, and I have two semesters to worry about."

"You don't quite grasp the measure of my desperation, do you?" he asked. His expression held so much humor in it that it cut through every layer of exhaustion on his unshaved face. He reached in his pocket, pulled out a wad of bills, took her hand and slapped it in her palm.

She stared down at the money and felt the blood drain from her face. He must have noticed, because he reached behind her and started to push her head down.

"Breathe," he commanded.

She leaned forward and breathed. He took his hand away, but draped it casually near her shoulder. "Where? How? What?" she asked.

"Cinnabar. A convincing argument. Fifty dollars," he replied, which made her laugh.

"I am serious, Sergeant Major Stiles," she said.

"So am I. I told the dragon I could get her a maid if she would pay your tuition at Montana Agricultural College. She asked me how much. I had no idea. I'm learning not to think small."

Carrie stared at the money in her hand. "This is two semesters' tuition, plus fees and maybe books. I'm not going to Vassar, just an ag school." She couldn't help the smile that threatened to break her whole face. "But she doesn't know that."

"It gets better," he told her. "Are you prepared for this? I told her I wanted another fifty dollars for you when the whole excruciating experience was over. She agreed."

She didn't want to cry, but there wasn't any way she could stop the tears that slid silently down her face. His loose grip tightened until it became a gentle caress. She turned her face into his uniform blouse, which wasn't a good idea. He hadn't shaved and also hadn't been near a bath tub in recent days. To her surprise, she decided she didn't care. For the first time since she was thirteen, she didn't feel completely alone. Such a feeling could easily survive a man's sweat.

"Will you do it? You'll earn every dollar. She's imperious and disagreeable and we've already butted heads."

"Is my job also to sweeten her up?" she asked and blew her nose on the red bandanna he handed her.

"I believe you can," he said. "Yes or no?"

"Yes, absolutely," she told him. "My goodness. I won't have to scrub lavatories and clean halls this year."

That was a bit indelicate, she thought and sneaked a peek at the sergeant major's face, ready to apologize for plain-speaking. His expression surprised her, because a man who had a remarkably soft heart was suddenly looking back at her, not the same man used to command and obedience. She doubted it was a face anyone had seen except her, and she felt the gentle mantel of privilege settle on her shoulders.

It took him a moment, but when he spoke, she heard big scoops and dollops of kindness. "You might even have more time to study, and have fun with friends."

"I might," she said. "Thank you, Ram."

She sat back and looked up, startled to see everyone in the dining hall watching and trying to listen without appearing obvious. True to form, Millie Thorne was already whispering to the girl next to her, one of Carrie's tentmates. Aghast, she looked down at the money in her hands, and knew what Millie was thinking.

Sergeant Major Stiles must have noticed Millie too. When he stood up, that warm-hearted man disappeared. He held up both hands for silence. Mrs. Wylie lifted her hands from the piano keys and put them in her lap, her eyes lively with interest.

"Before anyone looks at the money I just handed Miss McKay and starts gossiping, let me explain what's going on." He looked directly at Millie Thorne and picked up President Roosevelt's letter from the table. "President Roosevelt has requested an escort through the park for a widow whose late husband advised President McKinley's cabinet." He handed the letter to the nearest savage. "Read it and pass it around." He looked around the quiet room, his gaze stopping on Millie again. "The lady's maid is afraid to enter the park because she somehow thinks Indians are going to scalp her."

"We're not called savages for nothing," someone said. The resulting laughter broke the unspoken but plainly felt tension.

"I have to admit I laughed out loud when the maid said she was also afraid she would fall off the mountain if she left the railcar."

More laughter. This time, Jake Trost spoke up as he handed on the letter. "Most of us engineering majors could talk to her about Newton and gravity."

"I daresay you could. The lady insists on seeing the park, but her maid won't budge." He turned to Carrie. "I know Miss McKay, because she made me pie, the first pie since the Philippines. I can't tell you what that meant to me. She's close by here in Willow Park and I haven't time to hunt around. I asked her, after getting Mr. Wylie's permission, if she would fill in for the maid. She agreed. This is money up front from Mrs. Louise LaMarque."

Gasps and exclamations came from more than one of the savages. "Louise LaMarque?" one of the girls asked, breathless.

"You've heard of her?" he asked, surprised.

"My word, yes," someone else called out. "She was the highlight of the Broadway musical theatre for years and years!"

One of the girls started singing, " 'Sweetly, sweetly, my lover's kiss, fills the moonlit air,' " while one of the men answered with, "Which makes no earthly sense, but it rhymes with sunlight fair." Everyone laughed. Mrs. Wylie turned back to the piano and began playing while the girl, after looking daggers at the jokester, sang, " '. . . which makes my happy heart bloom with sunlight fair.' " She shrugged. "You're right, but what a melody. You should hear it on a Victrola."

More laughter. Amazing how everyone grew quiet when the sergeant major held up his hand again. "I'm going to deprive you of your pie maker for probably six days." He smiled when everyone groaned in unison. "I will return her! I just want you know what is going on, so there won't be any inclination to spread rumors about a lady who doesn't deserve it. As you were, savages."

The dancing resumed. Carrie watched as Millie Thorne left the room alone. The relief she felt was so enormous that it threatened to bring on more tears, which would never do, not when the sergeant major was expecting her to be mature about this. She blew her nose on the red bandanna again. If she washed it out tonight, she could return it tomorrow.

"Plain speaking, sir," she said.

"I wanted to make this situation perfectly clear," he said. "Millie's eyes were on you like a hawk when I handed you that money."

"Thank you," Carrie said. She had never meant anything more in her life. "Do we leave for Gardiner in the morning?"

"We do. I was tempted to ask you to ride back tonight, but it's dark and I am about to drop dead at your feet. Caroline, I'm too old for only six hours of sleep in the last three days."

"You'd better sack out in Number Twenty, sir," Jake Trost said.

"My thought precisely." He was the efficient sergeant major again. "Pack whatever clothes you have that are civilian clothes, Caroline."

"I only have two skirts and shirtwaists," she said, hoping Louise LaMarque wasn't looking for style in her impromptu maid. "We usually just wear, well, what you see."

"You'll do, Caroline," he said, noticing Jake. "I mean Carrie. Leave at six o'clock?"

"All right." She gave him a good, long look. She measured his exhaustion, but knew it wasn't her place to comment. "I'll meet you here in the morning. How're we going? I'm no horsewoman."

"Not sure then. I was hoping to borrow a docile nag here," he said.

"There's not much opportunity to learn to ride if you work in the Railroad Hotel kitchen," she reminded him, hoping the whole scheme wouldn't unravel because she couldn't ride and didn't have a riding skirt anyway.

Mrs. Wylie played a major chord, a minor one, and then a major chord again. "Problem solved. I came here in a buckboard to drop off some paperwork, and I'll return in one tomorrow. At six o'clock, you say, sergeant major?"

"You are a lifesaver," Ram said. He nodded to them both and then left the dining hall.

"Go help him," Mrs. Wylie said. "That man is really tired."

Carrie nodded. She saw that Jake had already taken Ramsay in hand, so her help wasn't needed. As she stood there, Ramsay looked back at her and gave a little nod. He must have heard Mrs. Wylie. She hurried to his other side, wanting to scold him for not taking better care of himself. She would have, except she understood the necessity of doing what had to be done. She wanted to tell him all that, but there was Jake, and besides, she didn't have any business scolding anyone.

The three of them walked to the tent. Jake let go of Ramsay's arm. "I think you're good for the rest of the way,

Sergeant Major," he said. "I'm going back for the rest of that popcorn by the campfire. I love stale popcorn."

Carrie let go of Ramsay too. She stepped back, shy, but determined to say what was in her heart. She cleared her throat and he looked at her with that same kind smile. If she had ever thought him intimidating, that silliness had flown away squawking like a magpie.

"Ram, thanks for thinking of me," she said. "You have no idea what this money means."

"You're long overdue for a change of fortune."

She couldn't disagree, but what else he had done made the money seem almost paltry in comparison. She took a deep breath. "Thank you from the bottom of my heart for smoothing my way in there. I don't think I would have been brave enough to speak as plainly as you did."

"You're brave enough," he said. "I'll see you in the morning. Louise LaMarque is a dragon, and I mean it."

Chapter Twenty

Daylight came at four o'clock, and Ramsay lay there wide awake, constitutionally unable to sleep once the first bit of daylight poked over the mountains. He pulled on his trousers and boots, rounded up Xerxes, and lit out casually and bareback for the Norris bathhouse.

He dunked himself first in the frigid Gibbon River, which brought him back to life. Trust those icy streams to either start your heart or stop it. A quick wash in hot water did the job. He hadn't time to scrape away at his whiskers, but Caroline had already seen him scruffy. At least he didn't smell so bad now.

Why on earth Caroline? He thought about that bit of impertinence for a moment, wondering why he needed a private name. He smiled inside. At least it was more discreet than Honey Bunch. *Caroline in private, Carrie in public*, he thought. *Just because.*

He put on the rest of his uniform for the return ride, arriving as Caroline came out of the kitchen, holding a bowl of oatmeal for him. It touched his heart to think for one tiny moment she had been watching for him.

"Jake said you weren't in the tent, and I was afraid you had changed your mind," she said as he dismounted. "It's already sugared and creamed. Here's a spoon."

"Bail out? Not me. I can't face that woman alone," he said. "I rode to Norris where we have a world-renowned bathhouse."

"That good? Do your soldiers ever loan it out?" she asked and then blushed. "Forget I said that."

"Miss McKay, it could be arranged," he said, then he had the good sense to shut up and eat.

By six o'clock they were on the road to Mammoth, the buckboard reins in Mrs. Wylie's capable hands and Caroline sitting beside her. He rode ahead, looking back once or twice to make sure Caroline hadn't turned tail and left him to face the dragon alone. He heard the women laughing and then singing together.

He gave his usual salute and shout, "Thank you, Lieutenant Kingman!" at the gateway to the cantilevered road. Both ladies clapped, so he bowed elaborately from the saddle. He was still smiling when they descended into Mammoth past the terraces.

The smile left his face and his stomach started to hurt as they rode directly through Mammoth and continued down the slippery slope to Gardiner, where he knew Mrs. LaMarque, along with her luggage of spite and umbrage, waited to pounce. He toyed with the idea of insisting that Caroline give him back the cash, which he would lob into the foyer of the Gardiner Hotel and then run. He could easily pay Caroline fifty dollars and call the whole thing a mistake on his part. Even fifty dollars would put her well ahead of her usual summer's scrimping and saving.

Instinct told him the girl—no, woman—riding in the buckboard would never show the white feather, so he couldn't. Five days, six days at most, equaled one hundred forty-four hours. Some of that time would be logically committed to sleeping. After too many long days in the Philippines, he knew he could manage six days in Wonderland. He looked down at his little Medal of Honor ribbon, which seemed to mock him. *I am a coward*, he thought. *An overbearing woman brings out the worst in me.*

The first order of business was to drop off Mrs. Wylie at the modest building the Wylies leased as the summer main office, even though both of them spent more time in the park. He helped Mrs. Wylie from the buckboard, thanked her for her assistance, and stood back while she hugged Carrie and wished her good luck.

Asking Carrie to wait, he tied Xerxes to the hotel hitching post next door and walked behind the building to see if Dave Lassiter was ready with the carriage. He wouldn't have been surprised to see Dave gone, after he had been forced to drive the dragon and her luggage to Gardiner once Ramsay left in a hurry to fetch Caroline. But there he was, brave man, the carriage and team ready.

He made some comment to Dave that he forgot as soon as he uttered it, so unnerved was he to face Mrs. LaMarque again. There was nothing to do but return to the porch of the Gardiner Hotel where Carrie stood beside her carpetbag, a modest bit of luggage looking as though it had been passed down from many a traveler. She wore a simple straw hat with a narrow brim that Western girls favored. She had tucked her pretty hair into a bun in the back, which meant the hat tipped forward at a pleasing angle.

He joined her on the porch, ready to gird his loins and warn Carrie one more time. She stopped him. "Is Mrs. LaMarque by the front desk?" she whispered, as if the old trot could hear through walls.

He nodded. "That's the lady of my nightmares," he whispered back. "You ready?"

"As I'll ever be."

To Ramsay's ears, she sounded remarkably serene, which puzzled him. "I've been warning you, but you don't seem too worried," he said, still unwilling to move toward the front door.

"I've been observing her," Carrie told him, coming closer so she could keep her voice low. "She isn't too much taller than I am, but look how she carries herself."

He looked, reluctant to see anything admirable in a battle-ax, but Carrie was right. He couldn't deny the woman had a certain confidence, and she wore a handsome, wine-colored traveling suit. "Pretty elegant," he had to admit.

"I should learn to do that," Carrie whispered back.

"Do what?"

"Learn to carry myself with more dignity. Watch me. Is this right?"

He looked at Carrie, and saw her straighten her already pleasing posture into something a little grander. Her chin went up, but not out, creating an elegant line, even in a well-worn skirt and shirtwaist that had seen plenty of laundering.

"I would say so," he admitted.

A man walked past them and went into the lobby. Carrie leaned closer. "See what she does when someone moves into her orbit."

He watched and saw Mrs. LaMarque raise her shoulders slightly and seem to will herself taller. "I think it's a learned reflex," Carrie said. "We talked about this in one of my classes. My professor said it's something women of a certain class do. Short ladies somehow know to stand taller when anyone looks their way."

"The upper class?" he asked, interested.

"No. My class," she said simply. "I imagine Mrs. LaMarque has had to learn to be impressive, to survive in her business. Life isn't so kind to ladies who strike out on their own, Ram. I know this for a fact. She might be wealthy and accomplished now, but I doubt she started that way."

Impressed with Carrie's understanding of a woman only observed through the window, he couldn't dispute her. He couldn't help his own skepticism, but he saw no point in stifling someone who might be a superior judge of character.

"I hope she doesn't yell at me," Carrie said, sounding uncertain.

"I already told her not to," he said. "I told her if she did, the deal was off and you wouldn't be returning the money."

Caroline smiled at him. For the smallest moment, he felt a little better, a little nobler, a little kinder. "Are you determined to be the best friend I ever had?" she asked.

That and more, he wanted to tell her, but this was neither the time nor the place. Where or when that would be, he didn't know. "Why not?" he settled for. "You're not that hard to help."

She waved a hand at him, as if to ward off more inconsequential chatter. Good enough. He could live with that. Maybe he needed a friend too, someone who didn't see a uniform and duty. That was probably all either of them had time for this summer anyway.

He took a deep breath, which made Carrie put her hand to her mouth so she wouldn't laugh, and opened the door into the lobby.

Mrs. LaMarque saw them immediately. Ramsay watched her shoulders, and sure enough, she gave them a lift, as though steeling herself. It happened quickly, but Carrie was right. He glanced at the woman beside him and saw the same small gesture.

Mrs. LaMarque stayed where she was, but he expected that. What he didn't expect was Carrie to move from his side and approach the battle-ax first, a smile on her face that looked genuine.

"Carrie McKay, let me introduce you to Mrs. LaMarque," he said, and crossed his fingers behind his back.

He didn't expect Mrs. LaMarque to extend her hand and she didn't. He held his breath, hoping Carrie hadn't put her hand out first, to be rebuffed. It calmed his soul to see Carrie had kept her hands at her side. She knew Mrs. LaMarque had no intention of shaking hands.

He glanced at the ogre and saw disappointment in her admittedly lovely eyes. He wondered if his own rudeness to her two days ago, his roughshod trampling of her dignity, had made her want to hurt Carrie. He knew he would never know the answer to that, but he resolved right then to hold his tongue and trust his friend.

Carrie waited for Mrs. LaMarque to speak, which was proper. Again Ramsay wondered if the socialite wasn't still disappointed, hoping to catch Carrie in a gauche act and confirm her suspicions about Western lack of social graces. Heavens knows he must have confirmed a few. He watched both women, curious to know how this would play out, but not afraid, because Carrie was braver than he would ever be.

"I hope you know a few things about what someone like me expects in a servant," Mrs. LaMarque said at last. "I'll admit I am not hopeful."

"I understand, ma'am," Carrie replied, with nothing in her voice of subservience or irritation. "I've never worked as anyone's maid before." She smiled. "I'm usually in the kitchen. I do know this: I learn quickly, and I'm not afraid to ask questions."

"Do you know anything about arranging hair?"

"Very little. I am not stylish, as you can plainly see," Carrie told her. "We'll have to make a lot of this up as we go."

"What can you do?"

"Whatever you need, with clear instructions," Carrie said. Her chin came up and she looked like the bravest human being on the planet to Ramsay. "I don't like to be yelled at, I'm good at polishing shoes, and I make excellent cherry pie."

"She does," Ramsay said. "Best I ever ate."

"Oh, really?" Mrs. LaMarque could not have sounded less interested. She raised her skirt an inch or two. "Are these shoes proper enough for the park?"

Carrie shook her head. "You need sturdy shoes." She raised her skirt. "Something more like this, but if I were in Bozeman right now, I would probably kill for shoes like yours."

Mrs. LaMarque laughed, a hearty, genuine sound that startled Ramsay. She must have noticed, because she pointed a finger at him.

"Carrie, he doesn't think I know how to laugh."

"He probably has no appreciation for absolutely beautiful shoes, either," Carrie said serenely. "He's a man."

Ramsay stared at them and realized that Carrie McKay was not only the bravest woman he had ever met, but maybe the most clever. In one sentence, she and Mrs. LaMarque had become allies. He didn't mind being the enemy.

"Pardon me, ma'am, but may I ask you something, or should I wait until I am spoken to?"

"Ask away, Carrie. Let's not stand on ceremony," Mrs. LaMarque said. "This rough and tumble area where you live is too rustic for much pomp, I suspect."

"We are completely pompless in Montana, where I live most of the year. You'll have to ask Sergeant Major Stiles about Wyoming," Carrie said promptly. Ramsay turned his head and coughed, so he didn't laugh. "I was wondering: I kept my last pair of shoes, because you never know when you might be desperate. If our feet are the same size, I'll loan this pair to you because they're newer. You'll be more comfortable."

Mrs. LaMarque frowned; maybe Carrie had gone too far. But no, she was raising her own skirt again and angling her foot next to Carrie's. "You might be right," she said. "Let's go upstairs and find out. You can also advise me on what I should take along for the journey."

Ramsay smiled at that. The journey. He had a vision of Lewis and Clark guided west by an Indian woman with a baby on her back, followed by a Washington, D.C., socialite with a walking stick and a fur boa, but in sensible shoes.

"What, pray tell, is so funny?"

Caught. He could lie or tell the truth. He chose the truth, since he wanted to remain Carrie's friend. To his relief, Carrie laughed out loud and even Mrs. LaMarque awarded him a faint smile.

"We'll show him, Mrs. LaMarque," Carrie said. You can be comfortable and stylish."

"Excellent!" Mrs. LaMarque said. She took her room key from her purse and started for the stairs, looking back at Ramsay. "You can summon the carriage. But wait. Will I need an evening dress and that fur boa you think is so amusing?" She narrowed her eyes and glared

199

at him. "I did bring along a fur boa, just in case you're wondering."

Standing behind Mrs. LaMarque on the stairs, Carrie crossed her eyes and sucked in her cheeks. It took every ounce of US Army discipline not to double over with laughter. He couldn't give her The Stare, because Mrs. LaMarque would think it was for her, and not the woman standing behind her.

"One evening dress," he decided. "There are hotel dances. I'm taking the two of you to dinner tonight at Major Pitcher's house at Fort Yellowstone."

"What a relief," Mrs. LaMarque said. "That means you will have to look a little better than a soldier just out of . . . of . . . the jungle."

She could have said anything, but she said that. All he could do was nod and turn away.

"The nerve," she said, but Carrie saved his life again, as she had probably been saving it since he met her peeking out of a privy.

"He's had some recent experience with jungles, Mrs. LaMarque. I'll tell you about it," Carrie said, her voice low, but loud enough for him to hear. "Give us twenty minutes, Sergeant Major Stiles, and we'll be ready for the journey."

Chapter Twenty-One

*H*e has some nerve!" Mrs. LaMarque said as she pounded up the stairs, Carrie right behind.

Between the two of these alley cats, I am going to earn every cent of this fifty dollars, Carrie thought, her mind on the matter ahead, but her heart on the wounded look in Ramsay's eyes.

"Mrs. LaMarque, let me open the door for you," Carrie said, as the woman fumbled with the key in the lock. "Hotel locks can be tricky." The lady's hand shook, and Carrie wondered if it was from anger or something else.

The lady put the key in Carrie's hand and stood back, her eyes militant. "He is going to try me within an inch of my life," she declared. "How do you tolerate him?"

Carrie opened the door. The small room was nearly overwhelmed by a steamer trunk that looked almost as large as the room she and her mam had shared in the

Railroad Hotel. *This is going to take more than twenty minutes*, she thought, dismayed. She had a larger concern, one she knew would be with her long after this imperious woman was on the train back to Bozeman and the ordeal finished. She set the key on the bureau.

"He didn't mean to be rude by turning away," she said, hoping for the right tone, somewhere between placating and informing. "You need to know something about the sergeant major. I also read it in the *Avant Courier* last winter."

"The *Avant Courier*? That poor excuse of a newspaper I read over breakfast in Bozeman? I am impressed," Mrs. LaMarque snapped. "I'll have you know my late husband owned twenty percent of the *Washington Post*!"

"Please, ma'am."

Mrs. LaMarque folded her arms across her chest, her eyes no less militant, but at least her mouth shut.

"Sergeant Major Stiles won a Medal of Honor in the jungle," Carrie said. "After his lieutenant was beheaded with one swoop of a sword, Ramsay took over the patrol and fought his way into a cave full of insurrectionists. Into it! I'd have run so far and fast in the other direction. They routed out hundreds of rebels who were stopping travel on the only road. The jungle still bothers him. I know it does."

Mrs. LaMarque looked down at her hands. She removed her kid gloves, tugging carefully at each finger until the tight gloves were off. "Should I apologize, do you think?" she asked, in a normal tone of voice.

Or it could have been a neutral tone, the kind where the issue could still go either way. Maybe Carrie had read her wrong from the wretched start.

"No. That would make him self-conscious," she said, and plunged ahead, because matters probably couldn't be worse. "Now that you know, be kind, please."

"No one has asked me to be kind in a long time," Mrs. LaMarque said.

She's going to fire me, I know she is, Carrie thought. *She's going to demand her money back.* She waited for that reality to terrify her, but it didn't. Sometimes a girl needs to stick up for a friend. Her head went up. "Maybe we all need reminders, now and then."

Mrs. LaMarque shook her finger at Carrie. "I'm not used to being told what to do, young lady."

"I am," Carrie said. "I get told what to do all the time, and it hasn't ruined my life. You might have to listen to me about your clothing for the park. I know a steamer trunk won't fit in the carriage Sergeant Major Stiles has arranged."

Fire in her eyes, Mrs. LaMarque opened her mouth to reply. To Carrie's mystification, she closed it and just stared at Carrie through narrowed eyes. *I can play this game too*, Carrie thought, and gazed back with all the kindness in her heart, which, she was discovering, seemed to be quite a lot lately. *If she had the nerve, she would give Ram Stiles the credit.*

"What would you recommend?" Mrs. LaMarque finally asked.

Carrie looked around the room. "Those two suitcases will do," she said, pointing to two perfectly lovely matching bags. She looked closer and gasped. "Is this alligator?"

"Yes, of course," Mrs. LaMarque said, trying to sound bored, or maybe she was bored. Carrie didn't care. She wanted to touch the alligator skin.

"Only two suitcases? That is absurd," Mrs. LaMarque said. Even to Carrie's ears, it sounds like a last-ditch protest. "Very well! Open the trunk and let us get this over with." She fished around in her purse and handed Carrie a key. There was no mistaking the tremor in her hand this time.

Carrie opened the trunk and pulled the two sides apart. She stared with real delight at the cloth-covered drawers and the neat row of shoes at the bottom of both sides. Carrie thought of her two pairs of shoes, one old and one newer, and felt almost light-headed at the sight of shoes for each day of the week. The other side of the trunk had a clever rod across the top for hanging dresses, skirts, and evening frocks. Everything was anchored in place with a criss-cross of stiff fabric. None of the dresses looked practical.

"Let's start with one serviceable nightgown. Do you have such a thing?" Carrie asked, after she emptied the alligator bags of mostly miscellany, as far as she could tell. "I hope you have a warm nightgown. Something in flannel?"

"I have a nightgown and robe for each day of the week," Mrs. LaMarque said, sounding like a woman on solid ground again. "My maid uses flannel to wipe my shoes."

"Flannel is nice when the weather's cold," Carrie replied, thinking of the nights when she had hunkered down in a bed with too-few blankets.

"Look in that top drawer."

Carrie opened the drawer and sighed with pleasure. "My goodness."

"Made in France at some convent or other. Nuns are skilled with lace," Mrs. LaMarque said casually. "See if you can find anything suitable."

Hoping her fingers, rough from kitchen work, wouldn't snag on so much perfection, Carrie picked up the first gown, a dream of lace and silk a color *McCall's Magazine* called sea foam. She wondered what variation of The Stare Sergeant Major Stiles would use on such a flimsy bit of bedtime coverage. You're getting wicked thoughts, she told herself, devoting her attention to the gowns until her face didn't feel on fire.

"See anything useful?" Mrs. LaMarque asked. "You said we had twenty minutes before that sergeant major is going to drag us out of here."

I don't want to think about Ram Stiles right now, she told herself. It's not healthy. She rummaged carefully through the drawer and finally found a long-sleeved gown, still silk, that might work. "This one, although I wish you had a flannel gown."

"I don't," the woman said with finality. "We can't take them all?"

"One only, if we're going to fit what you need into those two cases," Carrie said just as firmly.

"I have never slept in the same nightgown two nights in a row," Mrs. LaMarque said, that militant tone returning.

Was she suddenly feeling brave? Did thinking about Ram Stiles in whatever context bring out the bravery in her? "Perhaps you haven't in recent years," Carrie said.

Mrs. LaMarque looked at her for a long moment, eyes narrow again. The look softened, to Carrie's relief.

"No, not in recent years, Miss Smarty Pants," she replied. "I like my comforts now, though. Only one gown?"

"Only one."

"A robe and slippers?"

It was hard to overlook the sarcasm, but Carrie did her best. "Certainly. If you have perhaps three simple skirts and shirtwaists for daytime, that would work."

"Look on the other side."

Carrie unclasped the fabric that held the dresses tight against each other and searched through gorgeous fashions. Her heart in her mouth, she stopped at one evening gown labeled House of Worth. She found sensible-enough skirts and shirtwaists, plus two petticoats, and carried those to the bed.

"I have been informed there will be dances in the hotels," Mrs. LaMarque said, seeking for control again. "There will be room for an evening dress."

She walked to the steamer trunk and flicked through diaphanous bits of lace and silk.

"It's chilly here until August," Carrie ventured, pretty certain her credit, never massive, was about to run out with Lady Imperious.

The socialite stopped at a deep green dress with gold-crusted sequins on an overskirt and bodice. "This one," she said. "Make it fit in that suitcase. Open that center drawer and I'll show you which corset."

She did, and Mrs. LaMarque pulled out a low-cut corset. "These stockings too, plus this petticoat."

Carrie fished out the required items, wondering how it would all fit, and closed the drawer. "Underdrawers, Mrs. LaMarque?"

"Next drawer down."

Carrie attempted some humor. "I suppose you will insist on one for each day."

Mrs. LaMarque gave her a down-at-the-nose glare and ruined the effect by smiling, to Carrie's astonishment. "You are a rascal, Carrie McKay."

Carrie laughed out loud and opened the next drawer. Those same French nuns must have been hard at work. She took out six delicate drawers with lace on the legs. She stroked the fabric. A girl wouldn't even know she had any drawers on.

"Take out another pair for yourself," Mrs. LaMarque said. Her voice sounded gruff, as though she didn't want to be found doing something kind. "We're much the same size, and there is a drawstring."

"I won't argue," Carrie said, and took out a cream-colored pair. She held it up to her waist. "Seems a shame to bury it under all my other clothes."

"Save it for your wedding night then," Mrs. LaMarque said, and there was no denying the humor in her voice. "You'll find some wild-eyed cowboy in this state to marry. He'll probably have a heart attack if you parade around in those."

"Mercy on us, ladies! I'm shielding my eyes and heading back downstairs before I go blind!"

Carrie gasped and stared at the open door, which neither of them had thought to close. "You . . . you . . . you told us twenty minutes," she stammered, and jerked the silk drawers behind her back.

"That was fifteen minutes ago," Sergeant Major Stiles said. He held his lips tight together, and Carrie knew he was desperate to laugh.

"Go ahead and laugh," Mrs. LaMarque said. "If you don't, you'll probably rupture yourself."

That did it. Ramsay Stiles, dignified noncommissioned officer, ducked into the hall and started laughing. Carrie put her hand to her mouth, looked at Mrs. LaMarque, and started to laugh too.

"We should have closed the door," Carrie said, which for some unaccountable reason sent Mrs. LaMarque into another peel of laughter, which meant Carrie had to laugh too.

"I'll close it for you," they heard from the hall. "Ten minutes and then I'm coming in, underdrawers or not."

"Mercy," Mrs. LaMarque said. She looked at the skirts and shirtwaists on the bed. "Bring over that suitcase. Let's get started."

'I don't think I can ever leave this room again," Carrie said, her hands to her face.

"You can and will," Mrs. LaMarque assured her. "Let me try on your shoes."

Relieved to do something, Carrie took off her shoes. Mrs. LaMarque tried to appear more disdainful than ten or twelve queens, but she clapped her hands when the shoes fit. "I can outrun bears now," she declared. "You'll get them back in a week. Where are your other shoes?"

"Downstairs in my carpet bag," Carrie said. "I'll be right back."

She opened the door, ready to go to the lobby in stockinged feet, but there was her carpetbag right outside the door. *Thank you, Ram*, she thought. *I guess I'll have to face you again.*

It took them longer than ten minutes, but even a brave man like Ramsay Stiles probably did not wish to shock himself again. The suitcases bulged dangerously, but maybe that was the nature of alligators, bagged or not.

"There will be a hatbox," Mrs. LaMarque said. She looked around the room, her hands on her hips. "What do you suggest we do with this steamer trunk? It's not going to disappear."

"We can store it here," Carrie said. "My boss, Mr. Wylie, reserves a room downstairs for steamer trunks."

"I am not with the Wylie Company," Mrs. LaMarque assured her. "Camping is vulgar."

"No it's not. It's fun," Carrie said.

"Ask the desk clerk, and then tell Sergeant Major Stiles we are ready."

Suddenly shy to face him again, Carrie went down the stairs and saw Ramsay hiding behind a newspaper in the lobby. She sat down beside him, and stared straight ahead. "We're done upstairs."

He rolled the newspaper into a tidy stick, looked around to make sure the lobby was empty, and tapped her on the head with it. She couldn't help smiling.

"There's a quartermaster wagon headed back to Fort Yellowstone," he said, all business, but with a bit of lurking humor in his voice. "I've arranged for two privates to haul that monstrosity to National Hotel in Mammoth, where she, and I imagine you, will be staying tonight. I'm certain the manager will trip all over himself to store it somewhere until she returns in all her splendor."

"I've cut down on the splendor," she said, still too embarrassed to look him in the eye.

The sergeant major took care of her shyness by turning her cheek toward him with one finger. "I'm glad to know you two are laughing. We might survive this ordeal yet."

She nodded, unsure of herself and wishing she were in Bonnie Boone's kitchen making pies, or singing Stephen Foster songs at the campfire. "I'm wishing I hadn't agreed to this," she admitted.

"I know you are," Ram said. "I also strongly suspect that you have more backbone than you think you do." He couldn't help smiling. "And a smashing pair of silk drawers."

Carrie took the newspaper from his hand and hit him on the head with it. "Go get those privates and wrestle that trunk downstairs," she said, laughing now. "This had better be the fastest six days in the history of the universe."

"Chronology doesn't work like that," he said as he went to the door and motioned to the soldiers outside. "By the way, I meant it about dinner at my commanding officer's house tonight."

"You and Mrs. LaMarque?"

"And you."

"All I have are skirts and shirtwaists. Not me."

"It's an order."

"I don't work for Major Pitcher," she said, feeling her courage dribble away.

"I do, and you're my guest," he said. "Caroline, just be yourself. It's too late to start worrying about what you're wearing."

"Just once I'd like to impress people," she said.

"You already do."

She wanted to brain him with the newspaper this time. "Do you have an answer for everything?" Carrie asked, exasperated.

"Nah, just the important stuff. Didn't your mother ever tell you that your eyes will get stuck if you roll them like that?"

Chapter Twenty-Two

*I*f the dinner at the Pitchers' house was a success, Carrie gave all the credit to the amazing, infuriating, domineering Mrs. Louise LaMarque, formerly of the Broadway musical stage.

If Carrie hadn't known better, she would have thought Mrs. LaMarque went out of her way to be charming and deflect all attention from her temporary maid, who wanted to sink beneath the floorboards because she felt more at home in kitchens. All her recent dancing partners, Jake Trost among them, had commented how light on her feet she was. Now Carrie wondered why she felt like she wore clown shoes, accompanied by hands too large and out of proportion.

One bright moment was her introduction to Mrs. Chittenden, an angular-looking woman with bright eyes. Ram introduced them, and Mrs. Chittenden held out her hand immediately, even though it was obvious to Carrie that the engineer's wife was several rungs up the social ladder from anyone who ever cooked in the Railroad Hotel and scrubbed floors to help pay her tuition.

"Mrs. Pitcher suggested I bring along some of my sheet music," Mrs. Chittenden confided. "Sergeant Major Stiles says you sing at the Wylie Campground fire each evening."

"Mrs. LaMarque is the singer," Carrie reminded her, feeling a wave of dread march up her spine.

"That's true. What was I thinking?" Mrs. Chittenden said, and introduced Carrie to other officers' wives.

Carrie shook hands, wished herself elsewhere, then found herself drawn into conversations about Yellowstone in the summer, rumors of excellent pie at Willow Park, and bears. Always wary of slights because of her social status, she found none. She stopped looking and enjoyed herself.

Dinner was simple fare—government beef, tinned beans, potatoes on the venerable side, and a custard with peaches to sum it up. All the while, she kept up conversation, watching for cues when to turn the discussion to the person on the other side of her. She silently thanked Miss Janeway of Montana Ag's Domestic Science Department, who had insisted her students would need this information someday. "You won't always live on isolated ranches," Miss Janeway had assured her pupils, even though most of them would probably do precisely that.

Thank goodness it was Ramsay on one side and Captain Chittenden on the other. The engineer wasn't above drawing on the linen tablecloth with the blunt edge of his knife to demonstrate the challenge of the corkscrew road at Sylvan Pass to the officer's wife next to him.

Her only mistake was to stand up when Mrs. Pitcher asked if anyone wanted after-dinner coffee, rising out of habit to serve as she would have done in the Wylie dining hall. She started to sit down, red-faced, when Mrs. Pitcher gestured to her.

"My dear, you are kindness itself to help me," the major's wife said. "My cook has a hip complaint, and the maid just married to a teamster in Gardiner. Poof, gone."

The way the other wives laughed told Carrie all she needed to know about the precarious nature of domestic help in Yellowstone Park. She excused herself and hurried into the kitchen. She saw the major's wife talking to the cook, who suddenly sat down and rubbed her hip as though it ached.

Carrie felt tears well in her eyes at Mrs. Pitcher's kindness in creating an instant excuse for her rising inadvertently, as though she had planned the whole thing. She thought of slights and gossip at her lower-than-low status and realized she had an ally. She couldn't fathom why, but it was enough to know.

Under Mrs. Pitcher's directions, Carrie filled the silver coffee pitcher from the enamelware on the range. "I'll be right behind you with the custard," the major's wife said.

Serving coffee put Carrie further at ease, because she was efficient and skilled in something so simple but satisfying to her. She watched Ramsay as he spoke to Captain Chittenden across her empty space, seeing animation she hadn't noticed when he talked to others at the table. Her heart went out to him as she realized he was probably no more comfortable in this setting than she was.

She suspected the sergeant major would rather be sitting at his own table in his kitchen, eating something simple. *I prefer it too*, she thought, as she served coffee. She couldn't deny the wisdom in learning how to better herself, and then have the freedom to choose how her life went. She knew she owed the Wylies an unpayable debt for taking in a terrified girl, weeping at the back of the First Presbyterian Church.

Mrs. Pitcher served custard in cut glass bowls. Before she sat down, she thanked Mrs. Chittenden for the loan of her own dessert bowls. "Mrs. LaMarque, that's how things are in the army," she said, singling out her august guest. "My bowls broke on this most recent return to Fort Yellowstone. Share and share alike, ladies?"

Everyone laughed at this apparently common facet of army life, and the major raised his coffee cup in an impromptu toast: "To the ladies of the army, who make do, from broken dishes to husbands who are never home when they are needed."

Carrie raised her cup too, and caught Mrs. LaMarque's eye. The socialite beamed on the assembly of ladies and gentlemen in rugged circumstances, enjoying the novelty of her rustic surroundings. And may we survive six days together, she added silently.

In a matter of minutes, Carrie wondered if she would even survive the rest of the evening. As the table talk declined, the major ushered all of them into the parlor, nodding to Ramsay to bring in some of the dining room chairs.

"I choose a back seat any day," Ramsay said as he sat beside her on the chairs closest to the dining room they had just vacated. "I am never going to get used to so many officers in one room."

"You'd rather be anywhere but here too?" she whispered.

"Give me a log by a campfire," he replied.

Mrs. Pitcher asked Louise LaMarque if she would favor them with a song. The parlor grew silent in anticipation. With a glance at her husband, she said, "John had the pleasure of hearing you on Broadway once. We don't often have a treat like this. Nettie Chittenden told me earlier she would be happy to accompany you. Would you humor us?"

Mrs. LaMarque looked as though she heard requests like this all the time. Carrie settled back next to Sergeant Major Stiles to enjoy the pleasure of a veteran songstress, not a Montana Ag girl with a tip jar. Mere moments later she was on her feet, terrified, and faced with the dread knowledge that Mrs. LaMarque, all sweetness to this assembly, was determined to make her earn every dollar of her wages.

"I'll be delighted to sing, but only if Carrie McKay sings with me," Mrs. LaMarque said, and gave her a triumphant I-dare-you look.

Carrie sucked in her breath and Ramsay started in surprise. "That old trot," he murmured under his breath. "You can always say no."

"Don't think I can," she whispered back. "Wish me luck."

"You've got it. Tally-ho, Miss McKay."

She touched his shoulder to steady herself, and threaded her way through the chairs to stand next to the piano, and hoping her knees didn't knock together.

"How sweet of you to agree to this, Carrie," Mrs. LaMarque said. She turned to Mrs. Chittenden. "Do you know 'Nellie Gray'?"

"We probably all do," Nettie Chittenden said as she rose gracefully and went to the pianoforte. She seated herself and gave Carrie a "poor you" look so full of sympathy that Carrie felt her heart start beating again. Nettie ruffled through the stack of sheet music she had brought with her. "Here it is."

"Carrie will harmonize on the chorus," Mrs. LaMarque announced. She cleared her throat. "Any time you're ready, Mrs. Chittenden."

Tuition, books, fees, and living expenses, Carrie reminded herself as she looked over Mrs. Chittenden's shoulder at the music of a song she didn't know well.

As terrified as she was, or maybe as irritated—the exact emotion eluded her—Carrie relaxed under the spell of a truly lovely voice, well trained and experienced. Mrs. LaMarque willed herself taller, as Carrie had seen her do earlier, and clasped her hands together in that tender-longing pose found on theatre bills throughout the musical world, up to and including Bozeman. The words poured out of her with impeccable grace and diction. If she was exacting revenge for Ramsay's Turkish treatment, or Carrie insisting on two suitcases only, so be it, Carrie decided, as she listened to vocal yearning and longing for Nellie Gray.

As Carrie joined her in the chorus, her fear left her. She sang for a future she might have, if she could stay in school. Halfway through the song, she realized she was singing for the sole pleasure of it. A glance at Ramsay Stiles, sitting there with his chair tipped back and a smile on his face, told her he understood.

By the time Louise LaMarque hit the home stretch with, "'Oh! I hear the angels calling, and I see my Nellie Gray. Farewell to the old Kentucky shore,'" the former Broadway star of America's fledgling musical stage had her audience where she wanted them, the women sniffling and reaching for handkerchiefs, and their warrior-husbands taking surreptitious dabs at their eyes.

If you can do it, I can do it, Carrie thought grimly. She clasped her hands too, and took that maudlin chorus home: "'I'm a-coming-coming-coming, as the angels clear the way, farewell to the old Kentucky shore!'"

"Charming, my dear Miss McKay," Mrs. LaMarque said to her, as their audience applauded. She bowed gracefully, indicated her accompanist, who inclined her head, and then looked at Carrie with merriment in her eyes.

While admirers circled Mrs. LaMarque, Mrs. Chittenden took Carrie aside under the guise of helping to organize the sheet music.

"Why do I get the feeling you were shanghaied into that little musical tableau?" the engineer's wife asked. "When she summoned you so imperiously from the back row, you had a look on your face like a sailor drugged and shanghaied."

"I was shanghaied," Carrie said. "I think she wants to punish me for forcing her to put her Yellowstone Park touring clothes into two suitcases instead of a steamer trunk."

"You're equal to it," Mrs. Chittenden said. "I'm impressed."

"Ram . . . Sergeant Major Stiles bullied her out of an enormous sum of money for me to be her maid through the park," Carrie whispered back. "It's going to pay half my expenses for the whole year at Montana Ag."

"He's a good man," the engineer's wife said. "When your ordeal ends, stop by to visit. Hiram is going to be mucking about all summer on a bridge across the Yellowstone and a road through Sylvan Pass."

"I wish I could visit, but I'm heading right back to the kitchen at the Willow Park Wylie Camp when this is over," Carrie said, with real regret.

"Then duty calls," Mrs. Chittenden told her as she gathered up the rest of the sheet music. "We army wives understand that better than anyone. And here is the

217

aforementioned Hiram to escort me home. Goodnight, my dear. It's a pleasure to know you."

"I am tired," she heard behind her back, and sighed inwardly.

"Walk me back to the hotel," Mrs. LaMarque demanded. "I'm tired, and I suppose Sergeant Major Stiles will want to leave at some unheard of hour."

"We can change his mind," Carrie said. "You and I should promenade on the Terraces, first thing after breakfast. I've never been there either. Mostly I just work at Yellowstone, and that doesn't leave time to be a tourist."

"Go ask the tyrant," she commanded.

She found the tyrant in the dining room, talking to Major Pitcher, who gave him a thumbs up sign and then went into the kitchen calling his wife's name.

"A thumbs up for tolerating the dragon?" she asked, wondering why Ram's face was so red, that curse of the strawberry blond she was personally well-acquainted with.

"Yes, that's it," he said and turned even more red. "You sounded wonderful. You're a game goer. Pardon the slang, but it's true."

"Thank you." Better to leave it at that.

"Is the dragon talking to you?"

"Yes. She wants to inform you that she will not leave here at the crack of dawn, and you will find us on the Terraces around ten o'clock."

"Fair enough. I have some paperwork in Admin calling my name. This means lunch at Willow Park, if you think Bonnie won't mind interlopers encroaching on the Wylie Way."

"She'll manage."

"If I distract the dragon with a visit to Apollinaris Springs, might there be time for you to make a pie?"

"There is every chance, Sergeant Major Stiles."

Chapter Twenty-Three

Carrie and Mrs. LaMarque took the short walk in silence from Major Pitcher's house down Officer's Row to Mammoth Hot Springs's National Hotel.

Carrie decided to plunge ahead. "A little warning about what you expected would have been kind."

"I know," the woman said, serene in her superiority. "You and that sergeant of yours have been ordering me about and I was tired of it."

"He's not my sergeant," Carrie said.

"I rather think he is, whether you know it or not," Mrs. LaMarque said.

Might as well squash that one right away, or this week would be worse than unbearable. "Unlikely. I am returning to college in September, and I know he is more than a little frustrated learning new responsibilities," Carrie said. "I'm happy to help him out, because you need a maid and I need tuition money."

"This is a business arrangement?" Mrs. LaMarque asked.

Would anyone willingly work for you any other way? Carrie wanted to ask, but knew better. "I believe it is."

"Fair enough," Mrs. LaMarque said, after a lengthy silence that took them up the stairs of the hotel and into the lobby. "In the morning, you will run me a bath in that regrettable tub down the hall, then lay out my clothing on the bed. Now, you will help me get out of this dratted corset and go in search of a cup of Earl Grey tea."

"I will hunt down Earl Grey and make him howl for mercy," she assured the socialite.

Mrs. LaMarque smiled at that, but just barely. Carrie wanted to continue feeling uncharitable, but the lady did look tired.

"Meanwhile, I will get into the one solitary nightgown you have allowed me, and read a chapter in one of the two books you let me cram in my luggage."

Feeling sorry for ourselves are we? Carrie thought. "Will that be *To Have and to Hold*, or *The Battle-Ground?*"

"Not *To Have and to Hold*," Mrs. LaMarque said. "I don't know why I selected that one. Perhaps I did it because you were standing over me with a stopwatch!"

Patience, patience, Carrie told herself. Think of a blissful fall semester with no lavatories to clean. She kept her mouth closed.

"That's how it is, Carrie? You're just going to smile about everything?" Mrs. LaMarque said. "I'll have you know Mary Johnston is a dreadful suffragette. I met her at a garden party once that lasted two years because she never stopped talking."

"She might be a bore, but I cried all over her book," Carrie said, unwilling to remain silent, and truth to tell, impressed at Mrs. LaMarque's circle of acquaintances. "You actually met her?"

"I actually did," Mrs. LaMarque replied.

Carrie laughed, even though she knew the dragon was mocking her. Mrs. LaMarque managed a smile.

"Would you permit me to look in my steamer trunk for a different book? Here is the key," Mrs. LaMarque said, still not over her pique.

Carrie opened the trunk and pulled out the bottom drawer with its books. Mrs. LaMarque unbent enough to rummage through the selection. She pulled out a battered copy of *The Virginian*, and brandished it at Carrie like a trophy.

"President Roosevelt's personal copy," she said in triumph. "What do you think of that?"

"I am impressed," Carrie said, and meant it. "Would you let me borrow *To Have and to Hold* and reread it?"

"Not if you plan to cry all over it."

"Cross my heart I won't."

"Read it, you silly girl," Mrs. LaMarque said, her tone mild now. "About that tea?"

"After I get you out of that corset," Carrie said. "I know I hate to be uncomfortable."

"Do you even own a corset?" Mrs. LaMarque asked as she turned around so Carrie could unbutton her.

"Certainly. I have one on now," she said.

"If you pulled the strings tighter, you would have a tidier figure."

"I'd rather breathe," Carrie said. "There we are. A few more hooks . . ."

She helped the dragon from her corset and petticoats and into her nightgown and robe, then went in search of tea. She had no trouble talking the night cook into hot water and Earl Grey, plus two macaroons on a small tray, to be charged to Room 25.

Mrs. LaMarque was reading *To Have and to Hold* in bed when Carrie returned. She slammed the book shut and tried to push it away before Carrie saw her.

"Aha! I caught you!" Carrie exclaimed and laughed.

Something happened. Mrs. LaMarque's expression settled into a deep, unnerving stare. "I told you I didn't like this book," she snapped and threw it across the room. "How dare you make fun of me."

"But I . . . I thought since you were looking at it, I could tease you a little," Carrie stammered, wondering what had gone so strangely wrong. "It wasn't malicious, I assure you."

"Set down that tray," the woman demanded.

Carrie's mouth went dry. She wanted to do anything but continue under such cold-eyed scrutiny, because she was suddenly back in the kitchen of the Railroad Hotel, and George Thorne was coming toward her. She set down the tray and backed away from Mrs. LaMarque's bed. Maybe the lady would drink her tea and feel better in the morning.

"D . . . do you need anything else?"

"No. Go away."

"Yes, ma'am, but where?"

"Surely there was some sleeping arrangement made for you," Mrs. LaMarque said, her eyes boring into Carrie.

"Not unless you made it."

"I didn't. Go away."

For the first time in the long day, Carrie had to swallow down tears. "Where would your maid have slept?" she asked when she had regained some measure of control.

"Go away," the socialite told her again. She tried to pick up the tea cup, but her hand shook so badly that she dropped it on the bed. "This is all your fault," she said. "Get me a towel!"

Carrie went into the dressing room and picked up a towel. Her fingers seemed to have no nerves and she dropped it, picked it up and dropped it again. She grabbed it with both hands and hurried to Mrs. LaMarque's bed, where she pressed the towel against the damp spot. All she wanted was to leave as fast as she could.

"Now what are you going to do to fix this mess you caused?"

No, you don't, Carrie thought, as her blood started to flow through her body again. All the hard work and the slights and the innuendos boiled in her brain. She forced them down and backed away from the bed.

"I did nothing to cause any of this, Mrs. LaMarque," she said, her voice steel.

The woman gasped. "Don't let me ever see you again!"

"Very well," Carrie said, calm now.

Numb, Carrie found her carpetbag in the combination dressing room and closet, nearly out of sight as though it had crawled away in embarrassment. She picked it up and left the room without a backward glance at the woman in the bed. She wanted to keep walking all the way back to Willow Park but it was dark and no one traveled at night on Yellowstone roads unless it was an emergency.

Now what? she asked herself, unwilling to cry right there in the hall. She started down the stairs, wishing she hadn't left her fifty dollars in Mr. Wylie's safe in Gardiner, confident she would be taken care of on what had changed from a five-day ordeal into a heavier burden than she chose to shoulder. She tried not to remember her horrible night spent between two ash cans in an alley in Bozeman, but suddenly she was there again, in all its terror.

She sank down in the middle of the stairs, unmindful of curious stares from two guests heading upstairs, followed by a bellboy struggling with their luggage. *What did I do to cause this?* she asked herself in amazement.

"You can't sit there."

She opened her eyes and saw the manager staring at her.

Carrie leaped to her feet and clutched her carpetbag. "I am Mrs. LaMarque's maid," she stammered. "She seems to have neglected to make any arrangements for my lodging."

The man threw up his hands. "Oh, for heaven's sake! Just go to the kitchen. What's the matter with people? And so early in the season!" He shook his head and went back into the lobby. She heard a door close.

"This won't do, Caroline," she said out loud, and drew a small measure of comfort using Ramsay's name for her. She would have to tell him some day that her real name was just Carrie, because Mam liked it. She touched the collar of her dress and pretended the Medal of Honor ribbon was still pinned there.

Ramsay Stiles hadn't quit in that awful cave and she couldn't quit now. Dazed, she walked back to the kitchen where the nice chef's helper had found her hot water and tea. She explained that Mrs. LaMarque had made no sleeping arrangements for her, and was there a room off the kitchen?

"I cook in the Willow Park Wylie Camp and I am filling in for Mrs. LaMarque's maid," Carrie explained. "Are you on duty all night in case a guest asks for something?"

"That's my job," the woman said. She sighed and Carrie saw sympathy on her dark face. "People with

224

money can be mean." She pointed to a door next to the kitchen range. "Two cots in there. I try to lie down on one, but you can take the other. Mind you, a bell rings in there if someone wants something, but it's all I have."

Carrie sighed with relief. "I can make this up to you after I get paid," she said.

The woman shrugged. "It's happened to me too, dearie, and in a not-so-nice place as this one. Don't worry."

They looked at each other, blue eyes into brown eyes, and found the sisterhood. Carrie held out her hand and the assistant shook it.

To Carrie's gratification, the woman opened a jar and handed her two macaroons. "They're pretty good. Better still, sit down. Time to take a load off."

The cook brought over two glasses of milk and a plate with more macaroons. She was right; they were more than good. They ate all the macaroons, drank milk, and talked about cooking until Carrie felt her eyes growing heavy, no matter how much she blinked them.

"Go to bed, child," the cook said finally. "You'll figure out what to do."

Chapter Twenty-Four

The bell rang three times in the night. Carrie woke up, thought about what she would do in the morning, and went back to sleep each time. The first bell found her calling down great Scottish maledictions on the head of the spoiled, self-absorbed, complicated woman it was her misfortune to tend. The second bell had her walking away in the morning and thumbing a ride back to Willow Park. Sergeant Major Stiles could find someone else and not bother to stop by the camp for cherry pie again. That scenario brought her close to tears. By the third bell, she reminded herself that Ram had no idea what was going on. By morning, she resolved to earn the rest of that one hundred dollars, if only to spite Louise LaMarque.

Early morning kitchen sounds and fragrances woke her. She dressed quickly, thinking about a pompadour, but decided on one braid down her back. Mrs. LaMarque would probably have something cutting to say about that, but since Carrie knew she might be fired, what did it matter? She liked to wear her hair that way. The sleepy-eyed assistant pointed her toward the employees' lavatory, where she finished her morning preparation.

When Carrie returned to the kitchen, a bowl of oatmeal and toast waited for her. A simple thanks was all she could manage, when she really wanted to put her arms around the cook's kindness. She ate with gratitude in her heart.

"Thank you," she said simply, and left the kitchen.

She would have made it out the side door, but Ramsay stood in the lobby, slapping his cavalry gauntlets from one hand to the other, a frown on his face. When he saw her, she felt his relief as a living, breathing entity. He was so tall and comforting and she wanted to throw herself into his arms and sob.

"Caroline, where have you been?" he said, crossing the lobby in three steps to take her hand. "I've been looking everywhere."

She didn't try to stop her tears, because she knew she couldn't swallow fast enough or press hard enough against the bridge of her nose. She did know how to cry quietly and she did that as he put his arm around her shoulder and led her to a sofa in an empty corner of the lobby.

She told him what had happened last night, squeezing back on his hand as he held hers. "I went to the kitchen because the manager said to." She managed a watery chuckle. "I have a sixth sense about cooks, Ram. I thought she would help me, and she did."

She sat up straighter. "Why were you looking for me? Surely she didn't . . . She told me to go away and I did. I mean, I'd like to try again, but I don't know . . ."

He put his hand gently on her neck and tugged her closer. "Somewhere along about midnight, someone from the hotel banged on my door and said the guest in Room 25 was having a royal fit. It seems her maid was missing."

"Oh, my goodness, Ram. Have you been looking for me all this time?"

"Almost."

"I'm sorry."

"Not your fault."

His hand felt good on her neck, even though she knew her mother never would have approved, not Mary McKay. She knew she could have sat that way with the sergeant major for hours, or maybe the better part of the summer, but she had to know more.

"What did she tell you?" Carrie asked, prepared for the worst and knowing she wouldn't be disappointed.

He let go of her and leaned back. "When she could speak without foaming at the mouth?"

"Don't exaggerate! It's bad enough," she declared, and he just grinned at her.

"There was high drama in Room 25," he assured her. "She said you were impertinent and then snuck up on her and scared her so badly she dropped her cup of tea. Let's see: you were making fun of her dear friends . . ." He grinned at her again. "If memory serves me, there was something about overthrowing a Central American banana republic . . ."

Carrie laughed in spite of herself. "Oh, there was not! Is a serious conversation impossible with you?" she asked.

"Not at all," he said. "Anytime you want. I would like to know what really happened in that room."

She told him, starting with their earlier banter about *To Have and to Hold*, and Mrs. LaMarque's over-reaction when Carrie found her reading it and attempted a good-natured tease. "It went downhill from there," Carrie said. "She ordered me out and tried to pick up the teacup, but her hand was shaking and she spilled it."

"That sounds far more truthful than what I heard. Tell me: Did you strew all those clothes around the room, or was that her added drama?" He held up a placating hand. "My goodness, Caroline, your expression tells me the answer to that one. What do you want to do now?"

"I'm going upstairs to try again," she said.

"You don't have to," he told her. His tone became more businesslike, more like a sergeant major. "I'm perfectly willing to tell her she'll be making this journey on her own."

"What would President Roosevelt think?"

"Not sure I care," he said. "I'm not losing my job, and I won't have you humiliated like that again."

"It's tempting to throw in the towel," she admitted. "I can't, though, because I don't want to give back the fifty dollars."

"That's yours to keep," he reminded her. "That was the deal I made with Madame Battle-ax."

She shook her head. "Ram, I couldn't anymore keep fifty dollars I haven't earned than I could split that tip jar with Jake Trost any way but down the middle."

"I figured you'd say that, Caroline."

"And my name's just Carrie. That's all."

"Humor me, friend. I want to call you Caroline, at least when it's just you and me, because I like it," he said. He stood up and held out his hand, pulling her to her feet. He steered her toward the front door.

"You should know that the dragon managed to get herself dressed," he said, his tone army-brisk now. "With a massively wounded expression, she told me she cleaned up the mess you made. She's out walking the terrace, *Haynes Guidebook* in hand. I'll come with you."

"No," she said quietly. "You probably have work to finish. If I can't face her alone, what good am I? Is the plan still to leave around ten? Provided I'm still employed?"

"Far as I know." He pointed to her carpetbag. "I'll put that in the coach on my way back to my office. See you on the terrace in half an hour."

Brown eyes into blue ones again. This time Carrie touched Ramsay's Medal of Honor ribbon. "For luck."

Without a word, he took it off again and pinned it to her collar.

Carrie thanked him and left the lobby. She had never been to the terraces. As she walked with purpose, she decided to go up the steep wooden stairs past the Liberty Cap, a distinctive, long-dormant hot spring Ram had pointed out yesterday. She stood a moment in admiration of the odd formation, then mounted the steps.

Drat it if she didn't start worrying that Mrs. LaMarque might try this steep route and twist her ankle, or otherwise hurt herself. *Why do I even care?* she thought as she made her way slowly up the steps, across the boardwalk until she stood in front of Palette Spring and Terrace, according to the marker.

"My goodness," she said out loud, which made a dapper old gentleman walking up the path chuckle.

"It's that and more, miss," he said, and tipped his hat to her. "Watch your step."

She smiled at him, thankful for his kindly admonition, feeling charitable again. She breathed the sulfur air and let her eyes trail over lovely terraces of dripping water containing calcium carbonate, according to the sign. White, orange, and brown colors had flowed separately and then mingled together, who knew how many years ago, to create the masterpiece before her. She knew it was only one terrace of many, but there wasn't time for more right now. It didn't matter. With the whole hundred dollars she was determined to earn, she could take a day off now and then, hitch a ride like the other savages, and see something of the park. She didn't have to work every single day.

She felt her whole body relax as she gazed on the glory before her. No matter how badly Mrs. LaMarque continued to behave, she, Carrie McKay, was still in Wonderland and seeing it through a tourist's eyes this time. In the distance she saw more terraces, some of them deep red, or a blue bluer than blue.

She also saw Mrs. LaMarque sitting by herself at the end of the long boardwalk stretching east and then rising to another set of steps. She touched the service ribbon and walked toward her employer, if such she still was.

She knew Mrs. LaMarque saw her because the woman turned away. "So that's how you feel?" Carrie murmured. "You can't dismiss me that easily. I have to hear from your own lips if I am fired."

She would have to tell Ram when she saw him next—whether it was to continue on this already shaky journey or to say good-bye—that the fear left her the moment he pinned on the ribbon. She did not falter as she came closer to Mrs. LaMarque, who still wasn't looking at her.

There was room on the rustic bench so she sat down. Mrs. LaMarque had stated in that lengthy letter that she did not wish her maid to speak first, so Carrie said nothing.

"You could have stayed in the room last night. I was about to tell you what to do," Mrs. LaMarque said finally.

"You told me to go away, and I did," Carrie replied. "I found a place to sleep."

"You didn't think I would worry about you?"

"It never crossed my mind," Carrie answered truthfully. To bluff or not to bluff? she asked herself. "As soon as I can get that fifty dollars from Mr. Wylie's safe in Gardiner, I will return your money. I'll leave it in an envelope at the front desk, and you can get it when you finish your trip. Good day, Mrs. LaMarque."

She stood up and walked away, trying to decide whether to go higher up on the terraces to see more, or to retrieve her carpetbag from the coach and find a way to Gardiner, which she knew would not be difficult. Or maybe just stay. The matter was in Mrs. LaMarque's hands.

She decided to climb higher. Mrs. LaMarque could continue with Sergeant Major Stiles and the money would be waiting for her later. The elderly gentleman who had said hello to her had been carrying a guidebook. If he didn't think her too forward, maybe she could catch up with him and look at his guidebook too.

"Carrie, don't leave."

She turned around. Mrs. LaMarque was walking toward her. Carrie regarded her, feeling no fear, no matter the outcome. She waited, her hands clasped in front of her waist, the way Mam had taught her when she was a little girl. *Nothing you can say will hurt me*, she thought, and meant it. *I have a medal.*

Mrs. LaMarque was wearing her neutral face, the one Carrie trusted no more than her angry face. She hadn't seen any other side to the woman. That wasn't entirely true. Carrie smiled a little to remember their give and take over the steamer trunk. That was a nice moment to recall, if she ever decided to think of this person ever again.

As Carrie watched her calmly, Mrs. LaMarque's expression softened. In any other person, Carrie might have thought she saw contrition, but who could tell with this woman? She remained silent, waiting.

"Don't leave," Mrs. LaMarque repeated.

Carrie's eyes opened wide as Mrs. LaMarque held out her hand. "I will try to do better."

Carrie extended her hand, half expecting the old witch to withdraw hers at the last moment. She felt a pang as she saw Mrs. LaMarque's tremor that ended when they clasped hands.

Carrie tried to release her hand after a moment, but Mrs. LaMarque wasn't ready to let go.

"Shall we try again?" the lady said.

"I believe we should," Carrie answered. "Sergeant Major Stiles probably knows absolutely nothing about laying out clothes or cinching up a corset."

Mrs. LaMarque released Carrie's hand and laughed out loud, not a simper but that full-bodied sound Carrie had heard earlier. She knew the lady would never actually apologize. They could stand here awkwardly or they could move on. She doubted Mrs. LaMarque knew what to do right now, because she had probably never been this close to apology in her life and it wouldn't come.

"Mrs. LaMarque, you said something at the major's house last night about teaching me to get more volume when I sing," Carrie said and changed the subject. She started walking, hoping that the lady would walk with her. "If we have time on this trip, maybe you can help me."

"It's simply a matter of breathing deeper from your diaphragm, and not your chest," Mrs. LaMarque said as she fell in step with Carrie, apparently willing to close that page in her book of umbrage. "We should have a moment for that in the next few days."

Mrs. LaMarque looked up at the terraces above them and shook her head. "It's too much for me," she confessed.

Carrie nodded and gazed at the terraces she wouldn't have time to explore on this trip. They would probably still be here later. What was another week in the scheme of a few thousand years?

They walked slowly down the boardwalk. Carrie touched the service ribbon when she saw Sergeant Major Stiles waiting for them by the Liberty Cap. He sat on Xerxes, and the coach was behind him, with the driver standing ready to help Mrs. LaMarque up the single step he had just pulled down. The luggage was already strapped on behind the second seat.

"I will sit in the second seat, and you will sit next to the driver," Mrs. LaMarque announced. "And look, are there two linen dusters for us?"

"I believe so."

Carrie looked at Ram Stiles, who touched his finger to his campaign hat. *I believe someone is looking out for me*, she thought.

Chapter Twenty-Five

$\mathcal{R}$amsay kneed Xerxes closer to Carrie. "Mrs. LaMarque will want you to sit beside her when we get to the Golden Gate," Ramsay whispered to her, bending down from Xerxes and keeping his voice low. "I'll wager you."

"Betting what?" she whispered back.

He blushed and she wished she hadn't asked. He surprised her then by not looking away. "You dance with me at one of the hotels if I win."

This was no time to hang back; she felt it in her bones. "What if I want to wager the same way?"

"Then we will definitely dance. I don't change wagering rules. You're on, Caroline."

And the doubt. "I don't have an evening dress."

"We'll dance on the ballroom balcony. This sergeant major takes no excuses. Offers none, either."

He leaned over so close to her, and her heart felt less battered, much less. Any closer and he would be out of focus. She decided this was going to be the best five days of her life so far. When she had a leisure moment, she would study the odd fact that the worst day could change on a dime to the best one.

He spoke next to Dave, the driver, then led out. Mrs. LaMarque tapped her shoulder. "What was he saying? I want to know."

Carrie turned around. Mrs. LaMarque had resumed her superior air. Contrition was obviously not a lasting virtue with the Empress of Washington, D.C. "He said nothing about you, Mrs. LaMarque. He spoke only to me." She couldn't help a smile; she knew that road called the Golden Gate. "Better hang on tight. You might even want to close your eyes."

She turned back around and caught the driver's eye. He winked at her. "We could make it a real doozy of a ride," he whispered.

"Only if you don't scare me too," she whispered back.

"Wouldn't dream of it." He gave her a big grin. "Besides, I'm under orders from Sarge to treat you as I would my own mother."

"He never said that!" Carrie exclaimed.

"Wanna bet?"

"I've been betting enough lately," she replied, hopefully with at least the semblance of dignity. All it earned from Dave was a snort he turned into a cough.

Carrie sat back, content because she had made a wager with Ram Stiles she could not lose, and the air was pine scented. She breathed deep, tired down to her stockings, because it had not been a restful night. She looked ahead at Ramsay on Xerxes, amused to see the sergeant major's head bowed forward. He had perfected the art of sleeping in the saddle. The poor man had been up since midnight, soothing an irrational woman and looking for a missing one.

Carrie smiled to herself at the gasps and exclamations from the seat behind her, as they drove through the Hoodoos, where a mountain's burden of dripping water had collapsed, leaving honeycombed caves. Hoodoos on either side of the road looked as though they had been tumbled there by giants, ready to topple.

Carrie watched Ramsay sit up in the saddle, wide awake and alert to what she knew was directly ahead, and vanished behind a great block of limestone. Nearly one hundred feet high, the stone loomed over the narrow road, as though trying to crash into an equally tall stone on the other side. Mrs. LaMarque clutched the front seat. "Where did he go?" she asked with a distinct quaver in her voice that bore no resemblance to the singer's well-honed vibrato.

"Just around the bend, ma'am," Dave said as he gathered the reins tighter. "We're going in now, and up a steep grade. It's called Silver Gate, in case you're interested. Here we go!"

Mrs. LaMarque shrieked and wrenched Carrie back against the seat by both shoulders as Dave took the rise a little faster than he ordinarily would have, if his passenger had been a nice person, and not Louise LaMarque. The coach swayed from side to side, and the singer started to moan.

"Well, imagine that," Dave said when they passed through Silver Gate. "Horses are a bit spry today."

"Stop. This. Coach," Mrs. LaMarque demanded.

"We're heading into a great view, ma'am," Dave said. "Right now?"

"Immediately."

With a sidelong glance at Carrie, the driver pulled back on his hand brake and spoke to his well-mannered horses, who weren't any more spry than usual.

"Ma'am?" Dave asked. "We can't turn around here, if that's what you have in mind."

By now Sergeant Major Stiles had threaded his way back to Silver Gate's opening. "Is there a problem?" he asked, careful not to look at Carrie or the driver, but at the rocks above their heads.

"Mrs. LaMarque wanted me to stop, Sarge." He shrugged.

"He is driving like a maniac," Mrs. LaMarque declared. "Do something."

"Not much I can do," Ramsay said, all business. "He's contracted for your trip and Dave is the best driver with the Yellowstone Park Transportation Company. The road is a bit rough here; that's all. There's a truly splendid view ahead."

"I have no choice?" she asked, the martyr now.

"No, ma'am," Ramsay said cheerfully. "The view is amazing—canyon walls some three hundred feet high, and a drop off to the Gardner River . . ." He reined in closer to the driver. "What do you think, Dave? About five hundred feet straight down?"

"More," Dave said, and spit. "Seven hundred if it's an inch."

"Great view," Ramsay assured everyone's favorite tourist. "We should probably move along."

"Not until Carrie gets in back with me," Mrs. LaMarque insisted.

"Not a problem." Ramsay dismounted and let down the metal step. He helped Carrie down, squeezing her hand. "Mrs. LaMarque, are you sure? I know from your manifesto . . . uh, letter . . . that you don't like to be crowded or spoken to."

"I will make an exception," she said with some dignity. "Sit with me, Carrie."

"Yes, ma'am," Carrie said as Ramsay helped her up, his hand on her waist this time, which meant a little pat when she was almost aboard.

"All right now," Ramsay said, the brisk sergeant again. "Dave, you might want to drive close to the edge so Mrs. LaMarque can see the yellow moss above and below the road. One of the many ways Yellowstone gets its name, I believe."

"No! Not necessary! I can see just fine from the center of the road," Mrs. LaMarque said, in tones not so round and declarative this time. "Seriously."

"It's a great view, ma'am," the sergeant major said.

Carrie couldn't even look at him as the carriage passed ahead and he rode Xerxes closer to the edge. *If I start to laugh I'll never stop*, she thought. *Somebody should smack that man.*

Mrs. LaMarque started to whimper when a freight wagon began its approach to Golden Gate from the other end.

"No fears, Mrs. LaMarque," Ramsay said, cheerful to a fault as he edged Xerxes beside the carriage. "You should have driven this road when it was wooden and butted way out over the river. Come to think of it: Dave, did we ever lose a wagon on this stretch of highway?"

"I'd rather not say," the driver replied, sounding to Carrie like the soul of rectitude.

"True. I don't want to worry anyone. Captain Chittenden and his crew built this beauty a year or two ago. As you were, Dave."

With that, the cavalryman and thorough joker moved Xerxes ahead on the beautiful viaduct that cantilevered over the Gardner River far below.

Carrie felt Mrs. LaMarque's arm twine through hers and clutch her close.

"You really should open your eyes, ma'am," she said, feeling wicked and vindicated at the same time. "There's such a long drop that if you look down, you'll see eagles swooping below us on the air currents. Imagine that."

"I'd rather not," Mrs. LaMarque whimpered, her eyes squinted shut.

Carrie patted her hand and enjoyed the view. Mrs. LaMarque gasped when Carrie leaned forward to take Dave's worn out copy of *Haynes Guidebook* from the front seat. "Oh, now, now," she soothed. "I suppose you don't have to look if you don't want to. Let me read to you from the guidebook, so you won't miss anything."

She took a strangled yelp as agreement, and turned to page twenty-two. "You'll find this interesting," Carrie said as the freight wagon thundered by and Mrs. LaMarque scrunched down in the seat. "We're at Rustic Falls now. Let's see: '. . . adds a charm to this beautiful spot . . .'— You really should open your eyes, ma'am. No?—' . . , and when seen in the early part of the season is especially fine.'"

I should be ashamed of myself, Carrie thought, but the guilt lasted no longer than the sight of swallows swooping and diving in and out of the canyon. She stopped reading and leaned against the seat, pleasantly tired and inexcusably happy. Mam would have scolded her and called her exhibition the revenge of the little people. It was enough, coupled as it was with the equally satisfying sight of a uniformed man on horseback. *Can't stare at him too long,* she thought. Puzzling how the day had grown so warm, even in the shade of the canyon.

She convinced Mrs. LaMarque to open her eyes once the carriage left the Golden Gate viaduct and drove through Swan Lake Basin. "You might see some deer and elk," she coaxed, and the singer opened her eyes, first one then the other. Gradually the woman loosened her grip on Carrie and looked around at elk in the distance, and a moose heading with some purpose toward the Gardner River, her baby gamboling along.

"Goodness, those are ugly creatures," Mrs. LaMarque said, leaning out for the first time to stare at Mama Moose, who stared back.

"One of my professors at Montana Ag says moose look like deer designed by a faculty committee," Carrie said.

Mrs. MaLarque laughed that wonderful laugh of hers, which caused Ramsay to swivel in the saddle and stare. She glared at him. "I do laugh, young man," she said. "Maybe you need to loosen up a bit yourself."

"Yes, ma'am," he said and turned back around.

Mrs. LaMarque focused her attention on the moose. Carrie put her hand over her mouth to keep from laughing out loud when she saw Ramsay's shoulders shaking with silent laughter of his own.

The terror of Golden Gate was followed by the serenity of Swan Lake Basin. One would think the park's civil engineers had planned it that way. Carrie relaxed and leaned back again, enjoying the rare luxury of doing nothing, while her seatmate appropriated the guidebook and stared across the meadow, looking for whatever Mr. Haynes claimed she might see.

Her reverie ended when the sergeant major called a halt at the Willow Park Wylie Camp. He dismounted and came back to the carriage when Dave set the brake.

"Mrs. LaMarque, I propose that we drop off Carrie here and . . ."

"Oh, no," Mrs. LaMarque said in her frostiest tone. "She is mine for another four days at least."

He held up a placating hand. ". . . and see if she will make us a cherry pie and have a meal ready. You and I, Mrs. LaMarque, ably assisted by your estimable driver, will continue to Apollinaris Spring for a look and a drink. We will return to Willow Park, eat, and continue to Fountain Hotel."

"I prefer to remain here for the evening. Will you arrange that, Carrie?" Mrs. LaMarque said. "I suppose you can stay in your own tent here, although I wonder— could we share a tent?"

"Possibly, depending on if there is a spare tent," Carrie said warily. "It will cost you."

Mrs. LaMarque arched her eyebrows and fixed Carrie with her patented stare. She fished in her purse and handed Carrie a ten dollar bill. "I cannot imagine it will cost more than a dollar to stay in . . ." She looked at the row of red and white striped tents as if they were medical school specimens. ". . . these things."

"We can continue on," Ramsay reminded her. "We could be at Fountain Hotel by seven and it will still be light. You do have a reservation there tonight."

"Inconsequential," the lady said. "I am tired now, not in three or four hours." She did something then that Carrie would never have dreamed of, not after the fury of last night. She patted Carrie's hand and touched Ramsay's arm, connecting the three of them. "I think we are all tired, sergeant major."

"I think we are," he agreed. "No one got much sleep last night."

"No, we didn't," Mrs. LaMarque said, her voice soft with no threat in it. Carrie glanced at Ramsay and saw a half smile. She wondered if he was thinking her same thought: *Mrs. LaMarque was on the verge of apologizing.* It didn't happen.

"Carrie? Can you follow through?" Ramsay asked.

"Sir, yes sir," she said, which made him laugh. "I can engineer pie, secure some dinner, and procure suitable lodging."

"Give me a salute and I'll think you're making fun of me," he said in amused protest. "Do I really sound like that?"

Carrie and Mrs. LaMarque looked at each other. "Bravo, Carrie," the lady said. "Yes, you do, Sergeant Major. If I must be forced to do without my steamer trunk, and Carrie must . . . must keep me in line . . ." Again that half-apologetic glance ". . . then you can loosen up too."

"Yes, ma'am," he said promptly.

Carrie opened the carriage door, pleased when Ramsay put his gauntleted hands around her waist and swung her down. "Go work your magic," he told her.

"Which would be . . ." she began, not too tired to tease a little.

"Making my world a better place," he said, without a single blush. She watched his eyes lose their hard squint—he probably didn't even realize he did that—. "I can loosen up too. Madame LaMarque demands it."

Chapter Twenty-Six

*W*hile Carrie admitted to vast relief to see Mrs. LaMarque ride away, she knew better than to pretend it was permanent. "Four days," she murmured, thinking it might cheer her up after last night. All it did was remind her that when the four days were up, Ram Stiles would be back to his business as usual, and so would she.

She watched until the carriage with its US Army escort continued toward Apollinaris Spring, then she went in search of Betty Lackey, camp manager, a well-seasoned Wylie employee who spent her winter months teaching English at Bozeman High School.

"Two dollars for a two-compartment tent, and one dollar for her dinner," Miss Lackey said as she took three of Mrs. LaMarque's ten dollars. "You tell Mrs. LaMarque if I hadn't had a cancellation, there wouldn't be anything for her."

"I'm not brave enough to tell Louise LaMarque any such thing," Carrie said as she pocketed the money.

The militant light in her eyes suggested to Carrie that the teacher was just warming up to a favorite topic. "Some people just expect the rest of us ordinary folk to do what they want, without your leave," Miss Lackey said.

"Some people do," Carrie replied. "Thanks, Miss Lackey. You're a total peach for helping me."

The no-nonsense woman rolled her eyes. "No peaches! Go make us all some cherry pie," she directed. "You realize you've created an unhealthy dependency."

On an average day, Carrie knew she would have blushed and denied. For some reason, the days weren't so average now. "Thank you," she said simply.

"I hope you will sing at the campfire tonight," she said. "Sophie is too shy to sing alone, and you know that Jake Trost's magic tricks are stretched pretty thin." She looked out the open door of the Wylie Store, where she worked and kept the camp books. "There he is. He told me the place is no fun without you."

"Without me?" she asked in amazement. "I've never impressed anyone as the life of the party."

"Maybe you're not paying enough attention to you. Scat now. You have pies to make and I need to get ready for a tour."

You might be right, Carrie thought. She relished again the realization as they rode through Swan Lake Basin that she had nothing to do except ride in a carriage and see Wonderland, just like a tourist. *When did I last take a moment for myself?*

Jake was painting the trim on the dining room windows when she hurried toward the kitchen. He put down his brush and gaped in open-mouthed wonder, as though she had been missing in action for the better part of a year. He gave her an elaborate bow, which made her look around, hoping no one had seen him.

"I am under orders to make cherry pie," she said. "Then I'll be back on the trail with my employer. Jake, she can be a dragon." *Except when she's not*, she thought, surprised at herself, as Jake laughed. Maybe she shouldn't be so petty about the lady who was going to pay her more than anyone in the park probably made in five days. Maybe she could be nicer.

Jake picked up his brush when Miss Lackey looked out the door and cleared her throat louder than she needed to. "You'll have to dish the dirty details later," he said.

"Maybe not," Carrie said. "She's imperious and always expects her own way, but she's been treated like royalty for a lot of years. How would you or I behave in similar circumstances?"

Jake shrugged and returned to his work. Before she hurried away, she heard him say in a low voice, "I missed you, Carrie."

Bonnie Boone listened to Carrie's greatly shortened account of the last two days. She quickly cleared the prep table and set out pie tins. The bin of flour came next, followed by lard.

"The menu is beef burgundy, served on sourdough bread," Bonnie announced. "I hope that is grand enough, even if Her Highness expects to eat dinner before everyone else."

"Bonnie, you're a peach too."

"Silly! It's on the menu. Get busy with those pies!"

By the time the carriage with its one elegant rider came in view two hours later, the pies were done and cooling, and Carrie's arm was stiff from whipping cream. Bonnie had scrounged up a nicer tablecloth than usual, and even found brass candlesticks.

The four o'clock arrivals had just finished staggering through the dining hall for tea and whatever restoratives would keep them going until dinner at six, so the place was blissfully quiet—no banging of cutlery and clicking of thick white coffee cups to disturb the empress.

Carrie hurried forward when they entered the dining hall. With the sergeant major on one side and the carriage driver on the other, Mrs. LaMarque looked suddenly small and supremely exhausted. When she reached them, Dave Lassiter relinquished his hold on the lady and muttered something about horses to grain and groom.

Carrie took her arm, dismayed to feel the tremor. "I have tea ready to pour," she said. "It's your old friend Earl Grey."

"You're always going to be snappy and impertinent, aren't you?" Mrs. LaMarque asked, with just a shadow of her usual tart commentary.

"Probably," Carrie replied, after a worried look at Ram Stiles, who returned the look with a half smile. "I'm not always going to be a kitchen flunkie, but that's what I am right now. Here we go. Have a seat."

She went for the tea and returned with it bearing the weight of a lump of sugar and a small slice of lemon, just as Mrs. LaMarque had demanded in her manifesto.

Mrs. LaMarque sighed and took a sip. Another sigh. She looked around, and her gaze landed on Carrie. "Still that regrettable braid down your back?" she asked, with something resembling her usual asperity.

"Yep. I like it," Carrie replied. "Ramsay, can I get you some tea or maybe coffee?"

"Just water."

"My dear Miss McKay, he is Sergeant Major Stiles," Mrs. LaMarque reminded her.

The tea was working wonders. Carrie didn't falter. "He's Ramsay to me," she said. "I'll bring out some water for the sergeant major, and then the beef burgundy," she said.

To her delight, Ram followed her back to the kitchen. He tugged on her braid. "I like it too," he said.

"Good." She undid the clasp on the service ribbon and pinned it back on his uniform. "I might not even need this anymore," she said.

She poured him a glass of water from an industrial strength metal pitcher. He drank it down and held out the glass for more. "What happened to you in two hours?" he asked. "You were getting pretty tight-lipped in Gardiner."

"I decided to be kind and enjoy the journey," she replied. "How many opportunities do I have to see the park through a tourist's eyes?" She nodded her thanks to Bonnie, who brought out a tureen of beef burgundy. "I love this stuff. You carry the bread."

"Sir, yes sir," he replied.

She served Mrs. LaMarque and Sergeant Major Stiles and returned to the kitchen for stewed tomatoes with chunks of bread soaking up the tomato goodness, and applesauce, reconstituted and boasting cinnamon and raisins.

"I've never eaten this combination before," Mrs. LaMarque commented, but she didn't stop eating. "You would never see this at Delmonico's."

"Nope. This is a national park and we're doing this the Wylie Way," Carrie said. "When you spend the night at the Fountain Hotel, and certainly Lake Hotel, it'll seem just like you're back East."

Mrs. LaMarque smiled at that. "I can tell you're not impressed."

"Not at all. I like it here and I like the way we do things. More tea?"

"You are a scamp."

"Completely. We have cherry pie for dessert, with whipped cream." She beamed at Ramsay Stiles, who looked about ready to laugh. "Bonnie said you can come back to that holy of holies—the kitchen—and slice off as large a hunk as you would like."

"I'll take her up on that," he said as he stood up. "Mrs. LaMarque, a little pie or a lot? Choose wisely here."

"A little," she said. "Oh, go on. Carrie can get it for me."

He saluted and walked to the kitchen. Carrie stayed where she was, concerned with the severity of Mrs. LaMarque's tremor. "If you'd like, I can help you to your tent and you can eat your pie there."

"I would like that," the lady said, and managed a self-conscious laugh, the quiet kind intended to travel no farther than the two of them. "That way I can dribble and spill without a concerned audience."

When she went to the kitchen, Ram looked up happily from the half-pie he was consuming, whipped cream on his cheek. She took the end of her apron and wiped his cheek and cut a slice of pie for Mrs. LaMarque. A lady-like dollop of whipped cream went on top, after Ramsay made a great show of grabbing the bowl so she couldn't have any.

"I'm going to help her to her tent," she said. "She's not very steady."

In an instant he was a sergeant major again. "Need any help?"

"No. She would only be more embarrassed."

He nodded, ready to keep eating, but put down his fork. "I'll tell you what happened at Apollinaris Spring, but it'll keep until I've had a nap."

"Good or bad?" she asked, wishing comments like his wouldn't send her back upstairs to the Railroad Hotel, afraid of everything.

"On the whole, good. Don't worry," he told her, telegraphing to the deepest part of her heart that he knew why she worried. "Stand back now. I'm on a mission." He continued where he left off.

"Don't indulge him too much," she teased Bonnie, as she carried the pie into the dining room. "He won't fit into his uniforms."

"Will too," he said, his voice muffled by whipped cream, but surprisingly commanding anyway.

She returned to the dining hall, deserted except for Mrs. LaMarque, who sat with her head bowed over the table. Too much late-night distress for all of us, Carrie decided, and felt sympathy she hadn't expected.

The dining hall seated one hundred visitors. Carrie felt her heart go out to the solitary figure, and wondered how many meals she had eaten precisely this way. Carrie thought of her own lonely bites of lunch and dinner in the Railroad Hotel Café, when the lunch crowd had dispersed and the evening diners weren't expected for a few hours. Maybe they weren't so different.

She helped the unprotesting lady to her feet. Pie in one hand, Mrs. LaMarque leaning on the other, Carrie led her carefully across the road between the dining hall and the first row of tents. She noticed how the lady hesitated at the flap to the tent, as though it were an actual barrier, and not a piece of canvas to be flung to one side.

The lovely alligator luggage sat in the front room, with its pot-bellied stove and two rocking chairs. Her carpetbag was there too, looking like a red-haired stepchild in such proximity to tanned and subdued reptiles.

It was the work of minutes to get Mrs. LaMarque into that sole nightgown and robe,—thank goodness she didn't complain about it—turn back the coverlet, and help her into the bed in the next curtained-off room.

"Would you like to sit up and eat your pie?" she asked, then took a good look at the lady. "I suppose you wouldn't." She gently tugged the blanket higher, feeling surprisingly concerned, considering her rough treatment of the night before. She stood in the doorway to the partitioned room, then she sat in one of the rocking chairs, worn out, wondering if she should return to the kitchen and help out. While she was trying to decide, she fell asleep.

When she woke up, the sun was much lower. She wanted to go back to sleep, but the sound of Wylie guests talking as they walked into the dining room across the way caught her attention. She heard footsteps on the wooden porch outside the tent and pulled back the flap.

"Nothing to knock on," Ramsay said. "Do I just say 'knock, knock'?"

"Why not?"

"I know I ate only a few hours ago, but by golly, I'm ready to eat again," Ram said.

She looked at his face, happy to see the exhaustion gone now. He was looking back just as intently. He put his hand to her cheek and turned it slightly.

"Caroline, you have little wicker crosshatches on your cheek. Doesn't this tent come with another bed?" he teased.

"Of course it does. Like a ninny, I thought I would just sit in that rocking chair for a minute and then get up and . . . and do something," she said.

"What?" he asked. "Worry some more? Rush across the road and help out, even though you're not assigned here this week? Stew about Mrs. LaMarque? Why do you always have to be doing something?"

She couldn't help the tears that welled in her eyes. How did he know exactly what she was wondering was wrong with her? She rubbed her eyes. "I've never had a time in my life when I can remember having nothing to do. I think it frightens me a little. That's all. I'll be all right."

"When?"

"I don't know," she said, irritated with herself or him; she wasn't sure.

"How about right now? Is that soon enough to be all right?"

Bless his generous heart. He stepped inside the tent, and did the only thing she really needed, without knowing what it was she needed. He took her in his arms. He pulled her close and patted her back in what felt like a big-brother way. She hesitated only a moment then put her arms around him, which meant the big-brother patting went away immediately and he simply held her close.

He didn't try to kiss her, or put his hands anywhere but on her back. She had never felt so safe, an emotion she barely understood. She wondered for a moment just what she did feel, but the only thought that came to mind was safe.

"I don't want to ever move again," she whispered into his chest. "You're going to laugh, but I feel safe."

"Never move again? You'll change your mind when a few weeks pass and I start to reek," he whispered back. "And no, I'm not laughing. I feel safe too."

She let him go, but not too far, just far enough to stop the edgy feeling and the distinct knowledge that Mam would be clearing her throat, if Mam had lived long enough to see her now. *Mam, I wish you could know this kind man*, she thought.

"Ram, do we just sort of pick our way through life and hope for the best?" she asked, when he just stood there looking at her face as if she either had a leaf plastered to it, or he wanted to memorize what she could have told him wasn't anything remarkable.

"That's been my understanding, Caroline. Are you hungry?"

For you, I think, she told herself, and knew that wasn't going to come out of her mouth. She took a good look at his face. She already knew he was a soldier without an ounce of fat on him, but did he have to look halfstarved? She thought of her own dodgy life and knew why she always had a handful of bread or crackers to look at before she went to bed at night. What was his life like? Was it her business to ever ask?

"Yes. Let's go eat," she said. "I'll peek in on Mrs. LaMarque first."

She wasn't aware she had been holding his hand until she had to let it go to cross the partitioned room. She pulled back the curtain, relieved to see the lady asleep, the lines on her face smooth. Her hands were tucked under her cheek like a child would sleep.

"She's out," she whispered.

"What are we waiting for?"

"You'll be getting beef burgundy again, and probably those regrettable canned tomatoes with bread chunks that Mrs. LaMarque sniffed at," she said.

"Which I recall she ate," Ram said. "I'm nuts about breaded tomatoes. It's even better with Worcestershire sauce."

She looked down at the Wylie girl dress and apron she still wore, and sent him across the street to save her a space. "I'm changing first. If I show up like this, Bonnie Boone will think I want to work." She hesitated.

"But you don't, remember?" he reminded her. "I think the expression is 'off the clock.' In the army, we have a bugle call, 'Recall from fatigue.' That, Miss McKay, is your status right now. Hurry up and change. I told you I was hungry."

Chapter Twenty-Seven

*R*amsay had saved her a place in the dining hall, where she sat and enjoyed the novelty of being served by others. Carrie focused her attention on the plate of beef burgundy in front of her and the humble breaded tomatoes. She realized she had been so busy making pies and helping Bonnie before her complicated employer returned from Apollinaris Springs that she hadn't eaten since breakfast, that lowly bowl of oatmeal.

"I paid for your dinner and mine," he said as he reached for the rolls and butter. "Ever-scrupulous and a leader of his troops, that's me."

Carrie looked around the hall half-filled with diners, because the season was still early. "I like this."

"You're supposed to," Ramsay said. "Think of the satisfied sigh that will rise from diners' throats when they eat your cherry pie."

"Ramsay Stiles, I didn't know you were such a smooth-tongued operator," she said. "All indications didn't point that way, the first time I met you."

"Just you and me and a privy," he said, then he ate the roll he had over-buttered. He discreetly brushed the crumbs off the table when he finished. "Tidy too."

His self-assurance deserted him then, because Carrie noticed that tell-tale blush, the curse of all blondes, inching its way north of his collar. She decided not to focus on him, to give him some room. He would speak when he felt like it; she already knew that much about him from their brief acquaintance, privy or not.

"When we're done here, and you don't allow yourself to be dragged away by Bonnie to wash dishes, let's sit by the campfire. I learned a few things at Apollinaris Spring."

"About Mrs. LaMarque?"

"Partly. Maybe about me too."

She nodded and looked up when Jake Trost tapped her on the shoulder.

"Could you sing some Stephen Foster for us tonight?" he asked, holding his hands together as if in prayer. "You already know how pathetic my magic tricks are." He leaned closer and lowered his voice. "Sophie is good and she's game, but she's a little shy in front of an audience."

"I can do that," Carrie said. "Even better, maybe I can prevail upon Louise LaMarque to sing. She's sleeping right now in Tent One."

"Louise LaMarque? Here right now? That would be swell," he said. "Is she as wonderful as I imagine?"

"She exceeds all my wildest imaginings," Carrie said, figuring that was as close to the truth as she could manage. It seemed to be enough for Jake, who clapped her on the back and returned to his seat across the dining hall.

"Well done, Caroline," Ramsay said, reaching for the last roll. "That was a masterpiece of diplomacy."

"It was, wasn't it?" she replied. She stood up and worked her way out of the bench. "I'll take some dinner to Mrs. LaMarque and see what she says."

The tourist in question sat in the parlor portion of the tent, finishing her piece of cherry pie. Carrie held out the beef burgundy and stewed tomatoes, plus rolls and applesauce. "Can I interest you in dinner?"

Louse LaMarque eyed it with some disfavor. "Set it on this wobbly table," she told Carrie. "The sergeant major has encouraged me to be more flexible."

Carrie smiled inside at that and did as she was asked. She sat in the other rocking chair. Might as well get right to the point. Her employer didn't seem to relish small talk any more than Carrie did. "I mentioned to the savage who does magic tricks that you might be prevailed upon to sing for us tonight at the campfire."

"He said more flexible, not stupid," Mrs. LaMarque said. She picked up a fork and stabbed the breaded tomatoes as if they were guilty of a felony.

"I told him I would ask," Carrie replied, unruffled. Maybe she was finally beginning to understand Mrs. LaMarque. "If you don't need anything else right now, I'll go to the campfire."

That wasn't so hard, she thought, as she smiled and left the tent. She stood a moment in the street, wondering about something else, then she went into the kitchen, where Bonnie was organizing her kitchen crew.

"You don't belong in here right now," was Bonnie's greeting.

"I love you too," Carrie teased. "Tell me, Bonnie: where is Millie Thorne?"

"That Thorne in everyone's side? She was here one day and gone the next. Mr. Wylie's been too busy to bother, but the gossip mill says she asked for a transfer to . . . where was it?"

"Greenland?" Carrie asked. "That might be far enough."

"No, silly! Somewhere closer. Whichever it was, she didn't go smiling." Bonnie scraped a few more plates into the garbage can with such fervor that Carrie wondered what else she was scraping away. "No one seems to be missing her."

"That should simplify my life when I'm back here sometime late next week," Carrie said. "I may never be out of Sergeant Major Stiles's debt."

"Good," Bonnie said complacently. "Scram now."

She hurried to the campfire circle, which had been swept and tided, but the logs left still unlit. Ram sat there, his back to her. She stood a moment in silent appreciation, wondering how he bore all his responsibilities so efficiently, wanting to know more about him, but shy to ask.

Perhaps for the rest of this little odyssey, she could pay more attention to the guidebook in her lap, and not entertain herself watching him on horseback. That would be a better use of her time, she decided, even as the other side of her brain laughed and hooted at her.

He turned around before she got any closer. This wasn't a man to sneak up on. She sat beside him, leaving what she considered a proper six inches of space between them.

"I was afraid I'd have to storm the kitchen, weapon in hand, and demand that Bonnie let you go," he said.

"No. I left Mrs. LaMarque not precisely rejoicing in a tray of dinner. She did inform me that you advised her to be more flexible on this trip."

"I did, but I don't hold out any high hopes."

"Wise of you. She pretty much vetoed my suggestion that she sing tonight, which didn't cast me down too far. I didn't think she'd agree."

"We're learning, Caroline, we're learning."

She waited a moment, then moved an inch closer, which she knew was still proper. "What did you learn at Apollinaris Spring?"

"That it didn't kill me to apologize to her," he said.

Startled, she looked him full in the face. "What on earth did you apologize for?"

It was his turn to inch closer, as if unconsciously seeking comfort. She had no objection. "You didn't hear me at Cinnabar, when I rode over her like a troop charging the enemy. I'm not proud of that. I apologized," he concluded simply. "We sat there a long time in silence, just watching how the water spouts from that little spigot—it looks so out of place."

"No apology from her?"

"I didn't expect one. I decided to tell her what had happened to me a week or so before in Fountain Hotel, when an overbearing lady—I didn't mention she reminded me of anyone we know—called me a bellhop and demanded that I help her with her bags."

The little gap narrowed even more. "So unkind," Carrie murmured.

"When I told her I was a sergeant major in the army, she told me to leave the park alone and go chase troublemakers."

Carrie moved closer and ended the little space between them. They sat together almost hip to hip, nearly touching, but not quite. "Any comment from Mrs. LaMarque?" she asked, even though she knew the answer.

"Certainly not. I had long ago arrived at the conclusion that people in the higher social orders aren't much interested in folks like us, Caroline."

"They're missing out," she said, and bridged that last tiny space by resting her head against his shoulder, which gave him permission to put his arm around her waist.

"I hope you don't mind, but I told her about you, and tough times at the Railroad Hotel," he said, half-apologetic, maybe uncertain of her reaction.

"I don't mind," she said, and she meant it. Leaning there with a good man's arm around her and her head on his shoulder felt almost as safe as his arms around her in the tent.

"I also reminded her not to ever shout at you." He gave a self-conscious laugh. "And that's what I did today, Colonel McKay, to further the aims of the US Army in peacetime and wartime."

His arm came up higher when she turned her face into his chest. "I'm too proud, Caroline, and she reminded me. That's not a bad thing. I wish she had some idea, her and that lady at the Fountain Hotel, how hard I work and how doubtful I feel, at times."

"No one talks about that much, do we?"

"We should."

They sat there in the peace and quiet of the empty campfire circle as the sun continued its descent behind the Gallatin Mountains to the west. He told her about taking the cave in Luzon Peninsula, about the noise and the shouting and the darkness, and how they crawled on their hands and knees. "We were demons, Caroline," he said. "The Moros whip themselves into frenzies before they attack, but we were even worse. The sight of Lieutenant Bonham losing his head was plenty of incentive."

Her arm went around his waist at that. He breathed deep until she felt his shaking stop. "The night before, Lieutenant Bonham read us a part of a letter from home. His wife had just delivered their first child. Said she was going to wait until he returned to name the boy. We gave him all kinds of great suggestions and we laughed a lot. Lieutenant Bonham truly was a great leader of his troops. Caroline, it broke my heart."

He cried as quietly as she cried. He stopped first and blew his nose on his red bandanna that seemed so out of place with his usual spit and polish. "Here's a good corner," he said and handed it to her. "I can't even imagine what the etiquette book would say about this," he told her, with a hint of his usual humor.

"I've never seen it in any book on manners," she assured him and blew her nose. "I'll wash it. No argument."

"None given."

He took his arm away from her waist and she straightened up. "I'd better make sure the Wylie savages know how to take care of Xerxes," he told her. "I'll be back. Wouldn't want to miss the magic tricks. Oh, and your singing."

"Ram, you're nutty, even if no one knows it but me," she said.

"You're enough," he replied but then stopped before he had gone more than a few steps. He came back and squatted on his haunches to be close to her. "I nearly forgot. I told—no, no, I'm learning—I suggested to Mrs. LaMarque that we start early enough tomorrow to take in the Norris geysers, plus the lower geysers, before we get to Fountain Hotel for the night."

"A sergeant major suggesting?" she joked. "I'll never tell."

"You're a bigger nut." He turned serious. "The odd thing is, she doesn't seem to be interested in geysers or hot springs. Not even Old Faithful."

"I'm looking forward to seeing it," she said.

"There's this: She said quite emphatically, 'After your unfortunate incident at the Fountain Hotel, we will skip that one entirely. Shake the dust off our feet.'"

"That might be her way of apologizing," Carrie said.

He stood up. "I think you're right. I'm starting to wonder why she is really here at all." He touched the brim of his hat to her. "See you in a few minutes."

"I'm starting to wonder about a lot of things," Carrie whispered to his retreating figure, "Like if maybe I'm in love with you."

Chapter Twenty-Eight

*X*erxes was in excellent hands, but Ramsay brushed him again, enjoying the effort because every trooper knows the value of a good remount. As he brushed, he thought about the mechanized vehicles he was seeing more often now, especially in the larger garrisons.

Even when he was a little boy, he had thought ahead, imagining a farm where a man like his father didn't have to go to an early grave from overwork. He remembered entertaining his parents with stories of hot and cold running water in every house, and threshing machines that ran on steam power. They laughed, but even at age ten, he knew a wistful laugh when he heard one.

Just as he knew what would happen if all the wolves, coyotes, and mountains lions were eradicated from the park, he knew that eventually motorized vehicles would turn cavalry horses out to pasture.

"It won't be anytime soon, Xerxes," he promised, as he groomed his remount. "I know it's coming. You ought to give the matter some consideration."

"Do you always talk to your horse?"

He turned around to see Jake Trost with a shovel in hand, mucking out a loose box.

"I always talk to Xerxes," he said, not in the least embarrassed, because he knew most troopers did what he did. "How else is a man to get a good conversation going? I didn't know you worked in here."

"We savages take our turn at nearly everything," Jakes told him. "My dad agrees with that philosophy."

"Smart man."

"There's this: Mucking out stables makes me happy to be a civil engineer major. You know I can't count on magic tricks to see me through."

They laughed together over that little stretcher. Jake leaned on the shovel. "I wanted you to know the rumors have stopped dead in their tracks."

"I'm glad. High time."

"You like her, don't you?"

It was a simple question. Why did he blush? "I do, plus Carrie's certainly helping me out right now."

"I like Carrie too," Jake said. He leaned the shovel against the stall. "See you at the campfire."

When Jake was out of earshot, Ramsay returned to the business at hand, conversation with Xerxes. "I guess he spelled that out, didn't he? Any suggestions? Nothing?"

Ramsay lingered outside the stable until the sky darkened and he smelled a campfire. He glanced toward Tent One, where Mrs. LaMarque sat on the wooden porch. Her head leaned a little to one side, and he thought she slept. He felt a momentary pang that maybe this trip, as simple as it seemed, was proving too much.

He decided not to worry about her, not with Carrie already at the campfire. He walked to the fire and sat beside her.

"What are you going to sing?" he asked, when he really wanted to ask Carrie what she thought of Jake Trost, and how her life was going, and if he was wasting his time. *Ram, you're an idiot*, he thought, mildly disgusted with himself.

"I'll sing your song, and then probably 'Old Folks at Home,' because I like it."

"Have you planned an encore with Mrs. LaMonster?" he teased.

"No, indeed," Carrie said with a shake of her head. "She made it clear to me that she had no intention of singing tonight."

"Give me a winter patrol any day, with a blizzard thrown in," he said.

He meant it as a joke, but Ramsay saw worry in her eyes. "Don't even tease about that," she said and touched his sleeve for a far-too-brief moment. "I'll worry about you this winter."

"No need. I know what I'm doing," he said, which was, at that moment seated beside a lovely woman, about as far from the truth as he had ever wandered in his life. He nudged her shoulder. "Here comes our magician."

She nudged back and whispered, "Bonnie Boone says he's calling himself The Great Trostini now. I haven't seen his show in several days so who knows?"

Trust Jake to be more clever than Ramsay would have supposed. He did his same talent-thin tricks, except that he made a great show of flubbing even those until his audience was laughing and demanding more nonsense. *Be advised that this man is no fool*, he thought.

"Smart fellow," he whispered in Carrie's ear. My goodness, but she smelled so sweetly of almonds. "He's turned his deficits into assets."

For his finale, Jake called a little girl from the audience and performed one last trick. Without a single flub, he tugged a nosegay of paper roses from what looked like a hollow log and presented it to her with a deep bow. The laughter turned into *oohs* and *ahhs*, followed by applause.

"My turn," Carrie said when the clapping died down. "Wish me luck."

He wished her all kinds of things, up to and including a lingering kiss. "Good luck," was the cleverest thing that came out of his mouth.

There she stood in front of the campfire, hands clasped in front of her, her lovely hair in its single braid. Always the observer, Ramsay noticed something different about her before she said a word. As she beamed on her audience, she seemed more confident. Something about her was different.

"I'd like to sing two songs for you," she began. "We may be called Yellowstone Park savages, but we love being here, and we want you to enjoy Wonderland as much as we do."

Her comments drew a round of applause she obviously hadn't expected, because he saw her surprise and then the pleasure on her lovely face. *She has no idea how charming she is*, he thought. A glance at Jake Trost told him the University of Washington student was thinking the same thing.

She put up her hands. "I'd like to sing a favorite song for Sergeant Major Stiles, sitting here on the front row. I could tell you more about him that would impress you, but he'd be embarrassed if I did. Let me just say he's one of the many troopers in our park who keep order and look out for bears."

Audience members chuckled. Ramsay had to smile. The woman did love her bears, even if they queued up at a privy. He privately applauded her wisdom in not sharing medals and Moro insurrectionists with campers out to have fun in Wonderland.

After a pitch pipe note from Jake, she sang "Why No One to Love?" and she sang it to Ramsay this time, not the couple to his right who were holding hands and mooning over each other, and not even to the older lady and gentleman he had noticed as he came to the campfire. Just to him.

She curtsied gracefully when she finished and didn't seem embarrassed by the enthusiastic reception her song received. Who was this Carrie? Ramsay had to admit he liked her even more.

"And now, a song for me. You all know it, and you're welcome to sing along on the chorus." She hesitated and he tensed, simply because he was so tuned to help anyone in trouble, especially Carrie. "Here it is," she said. "I'm an orphan. I earn money here in the summer so I can attend Montana Agricultural College in Bozeman." She flashed a smile in Jake Trost's direction. "We're not as well-known as the universities of Oregon or Washington, which some of my fellow savages attend, but we'll grow."

She stepped toward her audience, not away, as a less confident Carrie from only a few days ago might have done. "I don't have a home, really, unless it's right here in Yellowstone Park. Join me on the chorus, if you'd like."

She looked to Jake, who gave her another note. " 'Mid pleasures and palaces, though we may roam, be it ever so humble, there's no place like home.' "

She sang the verse so pure and lovely and gestured for her audience to join her on the chorus. Ramsay joined in too, thinking of Iowa farms and hard times, and parents who loved him. "'Home! Home! Sweet, sweet home! There's no place like home, There's no place like home!'"

Carrie sang the next verse, then gestured again. As her rapt audience joined in, Ramsay noticed a figure leave the back row and join Carrie on her impromptu stage.

Well, Hades froze, Ramsay thought, amazed, as Louise LaMarque put her arm around Carrie's waist and harmonized. To his further amazement, Carrie kissed her quickly on the cheek, which made Mrs. LaMarque stop and visibly gather herself together before she could finish the chorus.

Thunderous applause followed. Ramsay suspected that many of the campers knew exactly who this dignified lady was, even though she had not graced a Broadway stage in years. Carrie turned and applauded her fellow singer, who bowed gracefully to her and then to the little audience, likely a far cry from legions of devoted fans she had once commanded.

When the applause faded, Carrie held up her hand. "You obviously know who this charming lady is," she said and waited a moment for more applause to end. "Louise LaMarque is touring Yellowstone, the same as you. Can we prevail upon her to sing another song?"

More applause. As he watched the grand old dame, Ramsay knew she was being nourished by her little audience's acclaim. The fact was written all over her face. His heart did a little dive when he saw how tightly she had clasped her hands together, to stop any tremors. *You're a tough old warhorse*, he thought with admiration. *Gallant to the last.*

Everyone looked at Louise LaMarque with evident anticipation. She did not disappoint. "While it is true I have not graced the stage in recent years, I have a favorite too. It's also a song you have heard of, although some of you might not admit it if Grandma were here."

What is this rascal up to? Ramsay asked himself, concerned. She had better not be bamboozling Carrie. I'll stop her before she does that.

She made an elaborate show of putting her hand above her eyebrows and looking through the group of campers. "Let's see: No one younger than fifteen in this unruly mob? Perfect. I'll sing Lottie Collins's version. If you want the laundered version, go somewhere else!"

Some of the older men in the audience applauded. Ramsay laughed inside to see one wife shake her finger in her husband's face in a silent scold that did nothing but amuse the others. To everyone's continuing delight, she tugged at his arm. The old boy wouldn't budge.

Mrs. LaMarque turned to Carrie. "You, my dear, will join me on the chorus, and I expect to see some ankle. At the very least."

The savages and younger men in the campfire circle whooped and applauded and Carrie blushed. She whispered in Mrs. LaMarque's ear, and the old songstress-turned-socialite just laughed. With all the aplomb of a duchess, she looked around, gave herself a note, and Ramsay knew why Carrie's cheeks had rosied up.

Mrs. LaMarque raised her skirt just far enough to show off a well-turned ankle. She swished her skirt and sang, "'A sweet Tuxedo girl you see, A queen of swell society, fond of fun as fun can be, When it's on the strict QT.'"

She paused and gave a most knowing leer in Ramsay's direction. "Right, Sarge?" she asked, and her audience whistled and hooted.

The skirt went higher. "'I'm not too young, I'm not too old, Not too timid, not too bold, just the kind you'd like to hold, Just the kind for sport I'm told.'"

Predictably, the more straitlaced among the women gasped at that line. Carrie's eyes were huge in her face, but he knew she was also a tough little fighter. He couldn't help smiling as she lifted her own skirt up to her ankle, and a very fine ankle it was.

"Ready everyone?" Mrs. LaMarque asked. "Ready, Carrie?"

"As I'll ever be," Carrie said. She gulped visibly, which made Jake Trost laugh out loud, and raised her skirt to her knee. Ramsay smiled to see that the very fine ankle was connected to an equally excellent knee. His agile brain reminded him to store this bit of information for future reference.

"Everyone? We'll start slow. 'Ta-ra-ra-boom-de-ay, ta-ra-ra-boom-de-ay.'"

If a can-can performed in a Wylie Camp by a woman on the shady side of sixty could be called sedate, Mrs. LaMarque swished her skirt and waggled one leg and then the other. Her eyes full of fun, Carrie joined in, singing and dancing as Ramsay sang along. Watching Carrie and clapping along to the rhythm with the others, Stiles realized those Moro insurrectionists in the cave had finally given up. He sang, clapped, and couldn't remember his last nightmare.

Each verse was a little more naughty, but even that irritated wife whooped on the line, "'Though not too bad I'm not too good.'"

He knew precisely how good Carrie was, how kind, how hard-working, and how determined. Watching her sing and dance with a twinkle in her eye, Ramsay realized that after two years, some of it spent in a bad place, he didn't feel old and ready to gum his bread and warm milk at night. He wanted to sit with Carrie McKay in a quiet parlor and see where things went, not that he could find such a venue in a place dedicated to geysers and bears.

He looked at Mrs. LaMarque, who happened to be watching him, and gave her a thumbs up. She threw back her head in silent laughter, and he knew he had an ally instead of an enemy.

The applause went on forever, which meant one more chorus, this one involving a kick or two, instead of just a waggle. Ramsay watched gleefully as the little tip jar filled to overflowing. Some of the campers walked away singing "Ta-ra-ra-boom-de-ay," while those younger among them capered about, practicing their own high kicks.

"Well, Sergeant Major Stiles, did we set back respectability in Wonderland a few years?" Mrs. LaMarque asked him. She tucked escaping pins into her pompadour and fanned herself with her hand.

"A generation at least. What would President Roosevelt say?" Ramsay teased in turn.

"He would be applauding, I am certain," she told him. "Carrie, come East with me. I can see a life on the wicked stage for you."

"No thanks," Carrie said. As he watched in simple appreciation, she undid her tangled braid, shook out her hair, then started braiding it again. Impulsively, he put up his hand and stopped her.

271

"Leave it this way," he said. "That's not an order, but pretty near to one."

Too shy to look at him, she did as he said. She ran her fingers though her hair to attempt some order, then pulled it over her shoulders.

She patted the log beside her and Mrs. LaMarque sat down. "Come now, I don't think that song has been around more than ten years," she said. "You never sang it on the stage."

Mrs. LaMarque gave one of her full-bodied laughs. "No, my dear, but I wanted to!" She patted Carrie's knee. "Ten years ago when everyone from Lottie Collins to organ grinders were singing it, I was holding sedate social evenings in my husband's house on Fifth Avenue. What a bore!"

Ramsay smiled as the two entertainers leaned toward each other and giggled. He heard Mrs. LaMarque sigh and saw her place her hands on her skirt, one hand trembling, the other at rest. She looked down at her hands. "But time moves on, my dears." She leaned out and looked around Carrie, Ramsay her target now. She spoke quietly to him as if no one else were present. "Don't waste it," she said and then sat back, her attention on Carrie again. She held out her hand. "Help me up, my dear. Time for these old bones to find a mattress!"

Carrie helped her to her feet. Mrs. LaMarque gestured toward the first row of tents. "I can point myself in the right direction. Don't you loiter out here too long, Carrie. A girl can get a bad reputation doing that."

With a laugh and a wave of her hand over her shoulder, she walked to Tent One, humming "Ta-ra-ra-boom-de-ay."

Jake Trost must have wandered off too. Ramsay stood up, wired but pleasantly tired at the same time. "I will walk you home, milady, then head to Number Twenty," he told her. "Miss McKay, you are a wonder."

"I decided today that since I am a lady of comparative leisure for a few days, I might as well have fun," she said, as he escorted her toward Tent One. She turned back and picked up the tip jar. "I'll divvy this up right now. Sit down. You can take Jake his share."

Delighted with her scrupulous, no-nonsense attitude, he helped the lady of comparative leisure divide the coins and even dollar bills, to Carrie's wide-eyed amazement.

She caught him in silent laughter. "See here, Ram, you don't appreciate the finer points of show business," she teased in turn. "My goodness, five dollars each!"

She stuck her share in her pocket, put the rest back in the tip jar, and handed it to Ramsay. He took it in one hand, considered Mrs. LaMarque's admonition not to waste time, and put his other hand around Carrie's waist. She touched his heart by blending into his side.

"Feeling safe?" he asked.

She nodded. They walked in silence to Tent One, up the single step and onto the porch. "What a day this has been," she said. "I almost don't know what to say."

"Don't say anything," he told her and kissed her.

He could have done the endeavor more justice, but he had a tip jar in one hand. He found it simple enough to haul her close with one hand and then kiss her. It might have been the easiest thing he ever did.

She kissed him back, which he found entirely gratifying. Too soon to suit him, she let go and opened the door. "You're just the best man, Ramsay," she said.

He knew he wasn't, but suddenly he wanted to be.

Chapter Twenty-Nine

$\mathscr{M}$rs. LaMarque had managed to get into her night-gown and robe, but she held out her brush to Carrie. "It's a bit tangled from that dancing. Would you?"

They both sat on the edge of the bed as Carrie brushed Mrs. LaMarque's white hair until it snapped and popped. Sitting so close to her employer, Carrie couldn't overlook the grayish tinge to her face and her heavy eyelids, as though it took supreme effort to keep them open. She put down the brush.

"Mrs. LaMarque, this trip is too much for you, isn't it?"

The lady sat up straighter and opened her mouth, probably to object. Carrie put her arm around her and Mrs. LaMarque leaned into her. She nodded.

"And there you were, kicking up your heels for us!" Carrie joked. She wanted to take a light tone, because she could tell something far heavier was weighing on this complex woman.

"I'm an old warhorse," Mrs. LaMarque said finally, even though it seemed to take more energy out of her with every syllable. "Give me something that approximates footlights and even a tiny audience, and I am ready to go." She squeezed Carrie's hand. "If I must be honest, my life has been rather dull lately."

"We don't have to continue this journey," Carrie said, even though her heart told her otherwise. When would she have another chance to spend time with such a splendid man as Ramsay Stiles, but for this trip?

Mrs. LaMarque said nothing. She closed her eyes. *What else?* Carrie thought. There was something at stake; she could almost reach out and touch it.

"Why are you here, Mrs. LaMarque? I could tell you weren't impressed with today's walk to Mammoth Terraces. Some visitors tell me that's their favorite view in the park. You didn't seem interested."

"I wasn't," she replied. "Hot springs, geysers, even bears—oh, I don't know."

"Yes, you do," Carrie said firmly. "Why are you here?"

Mrs. LaMarque sighed. She put the hairbrush on the end table and gestured for Carrie to help her to her feet. "Pull back the coverlets. I need to lie down."

I want you to tell me, Carrie thought, but she did as Mrs. LaMarque ordered. Carrie helped her from her robe and took her hand to assist her into bed. She propped both pillows behind the lady's head and then pulled up the chair close to the bed.

"I need to hear what you should be telling me," she said. "We can stop this trip right now. I'll return that fifty dollars and—"

"No, you will not!" Mrs. LaMarque declared in a voice surprisingly strong, even though Carrie could see it cost her. "No," she repeated. "You have college plans and you need every cent."

"I can't argue that," Carrie said with a shake of her head. "Still . . ."

Mrs. LaMarque reached for Carrie's hand. "I suppose you won't leave until I tell you what you want . . . need . . . to hear."

"Pretty much."

To Carrie's dismay, Mrs. La Marque closed her eyes. "I'm just regrouping," the lady declared. "I swear you sigh loud enough for two people and a hamster."

Carrie laughed. "Especially that hamster! Why are you here?" she repeated, in what she hoped was her kindest voice.

"I want to see the Grand Canyon of the Yellowstone," Mrs. LaMarque said suddenly, almost as though she was blurting out the words against her will. But now that they were said, she seemed to relax.

"I hear it's amazing," Carrie said, at a loss. "We can be there tomorrow."

It was Mrs. LaMarque's turn to sigh. "Just one hamster sigh. I'm tired." She tried another tack. "You'll think I'm silly."

"I doubt you've done a silly thing in your life."

"Yes, I have. I fell in love with Thomas Moran." She opened her eyes and sat up, full of determination again. "Fluff up these pillows, Carrie! I have a story for you, since you won't go to bed until I tell it. Such determination! Yes, Thomas Moran, the artist who painted the Grand Canyon of the Yellowstone."

"There are lithographs of that painting all around," Carrie said. "Mrs. LaMarque, I have to hear this."

"Then hush and let me tell you. First of all, let me state that he had absolutely no idea I fell in love with him," Mrs. LaMarque said. "He was newly married." She sighed again. "That's a two-hamster sigh, my dear."

"It will get you every time. One minute." Carrie went into her own partitioned-off room and found her brush and comb. She came back and sat cross-legged in the chair, which made Mrs. LaMarque roll her eyes.

"You truly are a savage," the woman scolded. "For heaven's sake, sit on the end of my bed, if you have to sit like that."

Carrie obliged, and started brushing her hair. "The artist Thomas Moran. Keep going."

Mrs. LaMarque made herself comfortable. "When your sergeant . . ."

"He's not my sergeant," Carrie said softly.

"He is too! Don't be a goose." Mrs. LaMarque cleared her throat. "When your sergeant took me to that smelly spring . . ."

"Apollinaris Spring . . ."

"Be quiet. How can I concentrate? He told me about the Railroad Hotel and your hard times. He insisted that I never raise my voice to you." Mrs. LaMarque reached to the end of the bed and touched Carrie's knee. "Talk about determination! He was absolutely adamant that I never raise my voice to you."

What a kind man, Carrie thought. She attacked her hair and brushed it vigorously. "He looks out for me, doesn't he?"

"It's obvious to everyone on the planet, I think," Mrs. LaMarque said.

"He told me that every trooper in Yellowstone Park is responsible for every animal, geyser, hot spring, and every person, except maybe poachers." She touched her warm face. "It's his duty."

Mrs. LaMarque rolled her eyes. "Carrie, did he or did he not kiss you on the porch before you came in here? That is not part of his duty."

"How did you know?"

The lady laughed. "What a pair of sillies! I heard you two talking, then it got quiet for a few moments, and then you came inside. I wasn't born yesterday. Whether you're aware of it or not, he stood on that porch a while before I heard him leave it."

"My goodness." At a total loss, Carrie cast wide for the thread of conversation and to her relief, reeled it in again. "We were talking about you, missy," she said, which brought a smile to Mrs. LaMarque.

"All right then! Can't a lady have some fun? Here's my story: After that unfortunate war started with those ridiculous Southerners, I was living rather hand to mouth in Philadelphia."

"I thought maybe you had some hard times," Carrie said. "There is something about the way you straighten up and try to look taller that reminds me a bit of me. We do that to protect ourselves, I think."

"I suppose we do," Mrs. LaMarque said, and her voice was kind. "You're an observant girl, Carrie."

"Mostly just trying to get through life like you," she said. "I'm sorry. I keep interrupting. Hard times in Philadelphia."

"I was singing in a saloon." Her eyes grew bright. "Come to think of it, do I get a share of those tips tonight?"

Carrie laughed, happy to tug the conversation farther away from Sergeant Major Stiles. "I already gave the Great Trostini half the jar, so you and I can split the five dollars remaining."

"Silly goose." That sigh again. "There was a time when half of five dollars would have looked really good."

"I know," Carrie said softly. "It still looks good."

"There I was, hungry and it was January." Her face hardened. "The saloon owner had suggestions about how I could earn more money upstairs."

"I know about second floors," Carrie said. "I couldn't do that, and you couldn't either?"

Mrs. LaMarque shook her head. "I came so close. I had already agreed to . . . to go upstairs. That morning, I spent my last nickel on a buttered roll and coffee. Someone at the lunch counter had left behind an *Inquirer* and it was opened to the classified ads."

She looked at Carrie, her expression gentle. "Child, you want this to end well don't you?"

"I hope it does," Carrie replied. "Too many things don't."

"I won't argue that. The Philadelphia Academy for the Arts was hiring live models. I answered the ad and that afternoon, I found myself wearing nothing more than a wrap you could see through and a smile. I did this three times a week for art students. Every few mornings they hired me to clean paint brushes. In the evenings I kept singing in that saloon."

"I don't think I could be that brave," Carrie said, feeling her face flame. "I mean . . . I don't mean that to sound, well, the way it sounds."

"I don't think you could, either," Mrs. LaMarque said. "The only man who ever sees you in the altogether is going to be a husband. You already suspect who I think that should be."

"Yes, but . . . "

"Yes but, yes but! You're trying my patience! Where was I? Ah, yes. Thomas Moran was one of the students, even though he was already painting with his older brother, Edward, who had a small gallery. Edward told Tom he needed to improve his human figures, so there he was."

"Did he talk to you?"

"None of them did, not at first, but it was always Tom who made sure there was coal in the stove and the window was closed. He didn't want me to be cold."

She looked into the distance, and Carrie knew Mrs. LaMarque was back in a drafty classroom, wearing next to nothing, while students sketched her. *Life is hard*, she thought. *When someone does something nice . . .* She couldn't finish the thought, because it was going to make her eyes fill with tears, and that wouldn't do.

"You are such a softy," Mrs. LaMarque said, also the observer, but with no unkindness in her voice. "One day class dismissed early, and both brothers invited me to eat lunch at the restaurant next door." She laughed at the memory. "I dressed, and waited out front. They both walked right past me, then Thomas stopped, turned back, raised his hat, and said, 'I almost didn't recognize you with your clothes on.' "

Carrie laughed and Mrs. LaMarque joined in. "I still remember we ate beef sandwiches and soup with pearl barley in it. The menu proclaimed it was lamb stew, but Tom said the lamb must have run through on stilts. He had a lovely English accent."

"You said he was married?" Carrie asked.

"Both brothers were. Imagine this, Carrie: neither of them wanted anything from me except friendship. Don't look so skeptical, you prude!" she declared.

"Can't help myself," Carrie admitted, thinking of the Railroad Hotel. "Are artists different from other men?"

"I rather think they are, Carrie," Mrs. LaMarque said. "They see a different world. Where was I? Ah, yes. Friendship like that had never happened to me before." She raised her knees under the covers and hugged them. "Come to think of it, maybe I was more in love with that idea than I was with Thomas Moran. He was kind and he was a friend."

"What happened when the class ended?"

"It was spring, and my life improved," Mrs. LaMarque said. Carrie sensed the woman felt she was on more sure ground. "I answered an ad for a singer in an upper drawer supper club. An impresario from the New York City musical stage heard me and put me in the chorus of his latest Broadway revue. Such a tiny role! When that ended, he put me in another show, with two songs to sing this time. Another year and my name was on the marquee."

"How glamorous," Carrie said.

"I suppose. I was making two hundred dollars a week." She sat back, her eyes in the distance again, seeing something Carrie couldn't see. "All that meant to me was that I wasn't going hungry ever again and I didn't have to work on anyone's second floor."

Carrie nodded. She looked down at the hairbrush in her hand. "I . . . I . . . always take some crackers to bed, or a handful of dried apples. It used to be I would wake up in the middle of the night, panic, and gobble them down."

Mrs. LaMarque made a sound deep in her throat, and reached for Carrie's hand this time. She squeezed it, then she let it go.

"Now I think it's a luxury to wake up and see those crackers still on the nightstand. It means I made it through the night," Carrie told her.

They both sat in silence. Carrie knew she should let Mrs. LaMarque go to sleep. She had an overpowering urge to snuggle next to her as she used to sleep with her mother, just the two of them against Bozeman, Montana, and every injustice practiced on a deaf woman and her child.

"Did you ever see Mr. Moran again?" Carrie asked, not ready to go to her solitary room, even if it was only on the other side of the canvas partition.

"I did." Mrs. LaMarque laughed, a wistful sound. "I married that impresario. He died in '73, and I was a rich widow—not too respectable because I was a theatre person, but fine looking and well off. I sang and danced and even financed a show or two myself. I caught the eye of a Wall Street financier with some Washington ties. He married me and I became even more respectable."

"Your own carriage and a Park Avenue mansion?" Carrie asked. "I read the rotogravure section of the eastern newspapers when I clean the library at Montana Ag."

"You may have even seen me promenading with my distinguished husband," Mrs. LaMarque said. "We were quite the couple. It wasn't all stocks and bonds with Harry Lyndon; he had another side. He was interested in art. He heard about a government-sponsored expedition to this area."

"Yellowstone?"

"Among other places. We went to an exhibit of some of the paintings, and there were Thomas Moran's watercolors, sketches, and that one magnificent painting. The photographs of another expedition member by the name of William Henry Jackson formed part of the exhibit too."

"Was Mr. Moran there? Did you see him?"

Mrs. LaMarque's eyes filled with tears. "He was and I did." She dabbed at her eyes. "He didn't recognize me."

"Surely he had heard of Louise LaMarque," Carrie said, feeling irritated at a man she had never met. "That should have rung a bell somewhere."

"Perhaps. Mind you, I was Elsie Krank in Philadelphia, Louise LaMarque on Broadway, and now Mrs. Harold Lyndon." She chuckled, and leaned forward to tug Carrie's hair. "Silly! My hair was a different color too."

"Didn't you . . . didn't you say something?" Carrie demanded. She felt tears welling in her eyes. To her horror, they spilled onto her cheeks and she cried, "I want you to tell me you said something!"

She put her hand over her eyes, embarrassed, ashamed. She may have been tired, but Mrs. LaMarque threw back her covers and sat closer to Carrie, taking her in her arms, as no woman had done in years, not since her mother had comforted her when she was little. "You were supposed to say something," Carrie cried.

"Oh, my dear, plans change, people change," Mrs. LaMarque crooned, her voice soft and gentle, a far cry from the woman who had frightened her in the National Hotel.

"I want to know that things got better. I have to know."

Mrs. LaMarque held her off and then pulled her closer. "Go ahead and cry. It's hard being alone, and hungry, and afraid, but still determined, isn't it?"

Carrie nodded, unable to speak. The humiliation and embarrassment left her as she clung to a woman who knew precisely how hard life could be, how unforgiving to women.

Finally, she relaxed in Mrs. LaMarque's kind embrace. "Goodness. You thought you were going to get a tour of Wonderland, and you end up with at least one silly."

"Two," Mrs. Lamarque said. "Your sergeant major is going to give me a case of the fantods! Well, maybe three sillies. I should have told him right up front that all I wanted to see was the Lower Falls of the Yellowstone."

They laughed together. Carrie blew her nose and straightened her dress. "I still have to know more."

"And you'll hear it," Mrs. LaMarque said. "I'm a proud woman, and I only want to say it once. Go get your sergeant major, and that's an order."

"He'll be asleep. It's too late."

"I doubt it. That quiet time on the porch went on long enough to tell me that he's probably wide awake and wondering what to do now."

Chapter Thirty

$\mathcal{T}$he dispatch from Major Pitcher was waiting when he walked back to Tent Twenty after kissing Carrie McKay. It was a short walk from one end of the Wylie camp to the other, but the revelation that he had been in love with Carrie probably since his first visit to Willow Park and her rescue took no time at all. It was simply a matter of admitting it to himself. After that heartfelt kiss, who was he kidding?

There it was, the dispatch he had half been waiting for since his return to Fort Yellowstone last winter. There was a note from the Norris soldier station scribbled on it from the corporal in charge, reading, *Hope this finds you. Major P's adjutant brought it here, and he didn't look happy.*

Feeling numb and nerveless, he took the dispatch out of the envelope. Never one to put off bad news, he opened it and had his fears confirmed. Major Pitcher had written his own note to the official dispatch ordering Sergeant Major Ramsay Stiles to report with all deliberate haste to Fort Clark, Texas, to explain himself. He read the major's note and took heart, but not much: *Just as we feared. Sergeant Lafferty tattled on you, as was his perfect right. As soon as you can finish your current assignment and leave for Fort Clark, the better. I'll be sending a letter ahead that might help, but it's a serious accusation, Ramsay. Yrs sincerely, John Pitcher.*

"Goodbye, army," Ramsay said out loud. "Hello stockade."

Ramsay heard the light tap on the door to Tent Twenty. He had been lying there, wide awake, wondering what to do next. From the sounds of snoring, no one else was awake. He buttoned his pants, scuffed his bare feet into his moccasins and pulled back the flap, knowing who was standing there before he even touched the canvas.

"I'm making a muddle of things, but Mrs. LaMarque has ordered me to fetch you to her tent," Carrie said, with no preamble.

He tucked in his undershirt and ran his fingers though his hair. "This will have to do."

"You look fine. Better'n me."

He came closer and saw the tears on her face. He touched her shoulder. "What did she do to you?"

"Nothing like that. She's been telling me . . . oh, sit down a minute."

They sat on the edge of Tent Twenty's porch. Carrie didn't bother with a discreet six inches from him, but sat close. He listened in sympathy, eager for something to take his mind off his larger trouble, and then in astonishment as she told an amazing tale.

"My word, she knows Thomas Moran and just wanted to see the Lower Falls? Why didn't she tell us right away?"

"I think that's why she wants to see you now. She's a proud woman."

He finished her thought. "Who never should have come here, because her health is precarious."

"I think so. That tremor . . ."

To Ramsay's gratification, Carrie leaned against his arm, which gave him complete permission to put his arm around her shoulder. Maybe he didn't even need her permission any more. That was a matter he could stew over later, and probably stew over until dawn. Mercy, but he was a fool for this woman. Why on earth had Major Pitcher told him to look for a wife? This was more trouble and heartache than he needed right now since his affairs had suddenly turned south.

And yet there she was, depending on him. In his positions, others depended on him. In battle it was a life or death dependency. Carrie's dependency was different. If he were to play her false, she wouldn't die, as one of his privates or corporals might die in battle. Uneasy at the thought, he knew it would be a different kind of death, and he did not relish even the thought of so much anguish for her, or if he was honest, for him. And so he stewed.

"That's what she told me," Carrie concluded. "She has more to say, but she wants to say it only once. Do you mind?"

"Not at all. I wasn't asleep. Let's go."

They were inside Tent One in no time. Carrie dragged in the chair from her room, because Louise LaMarque was back in bed, her eyes so tired now. He almost hated to admit it, but he felt a twinge of pity. He saw what Carrie saw, a lady worn down and tired who probably had no business touring Yellowstone Park, which, while not a hard slog, could be a challenge.

"It's this," she began, also with no preamble. She held out her right hand.

He watched the tremor, and his sympathy grew. He saw the irony—a woman with wealth and connections (she knew Theodore Roosevelt, after all), looking forward to a decline in health she could not control.

"What I have is named after James Parkinson, a physician in the eighteenth century, who first described the symptoms," she said, putting her hand into her lap and covering it with her other hand. "My handwriting has gotten smaller and smaller, and I know you have both seen me hesitate to enter a room."

"I wondered if you see a barrier than no one else sees," Carrie said.

"Hard to describe, but that is close," the lady replied. "I don't know what to do when I see a doorway. You've seen how I can hold a spoon and it shakes, but the tremors stop once I get the spoon close to my mouth. This is a most vexing disease, and truly, these dratted tremors exhaust me."

"You want to see the Lower Falls of the Yellowstone before such a trip would be impossible," Ramsay said. "Thomas Moran's painting needs to come to life for you."

"Precisely, Sergeant Major." She seemed to straighten up then, and the pride returned. "My husband was instrumental in arranging for the government to purchase the painting. I heard President Grant say that painting, plus Mr. Jackson's photographs, convinced him to set aside this wonderful place as a national park."

"We can go there tomorrow," Ramsay said. He glanced at Carrie and saw the frown line deepen between her eyes. He said what he thought she was thinking. "This will shorten our trip by two days. We can have you on the train to Bozeman by the end of the week. You'll be in the comforts of your own home soon."

He heard Carrie draw a deep breath and knew he didn't want to look at her, because he knew he would see someone already resigning herself to working hard at the Wylie Camp, while he went to Texas under a dark cloud. Their time together was going to be over too soon to suit either of them.

"It will be a relief to be home," the lady said. She looked down at her hands. "Maybe I thought I could grasp a little glimpse of an earlier time in my life. I've seen Versailles. I've even been presented to Queen Victoria. I don't know . . ."

"Maybe Elsie Krank wanted another glimpse of Tom Moran," Carrie said. "I'm eager to see the falls and the canyon too."

Only not quite so quickly, Ramsay thought. He saw how Carrie's shoulders drooped, and how she couldn't hide the disappointment in her eyes. He hoped he wasn't so transparent, but she seemed to know him well enough to know something bothered him. Heaven help him if she thought it was something she had done.

Some hero he was. She's too young. She has her own plans for her future. They probably don't involve following a sergeant major into a suddenly insecure future. All the reasons ran through his mind, and he writhed inside under his own cowardice.

What else could he do? Mrs. LaMarque had made up her mind, and he had orders to see that she visited the park. Carrie had never figured in those orders and she knew it. This was a business arrangement between them. He knew he had to tell her what had happened, but he didn't know how or when.

"We'll start out early," he said, getting to his feet. "It's been gnawing at me that we wore you out today. We'll get to Canyon Hotel in good time and you can rest tomorrow night. We'll see the canyon the day after, then start for Gardiner."

Mrs. LaMarque held out her left hand to him, the one that didn't shake. "Thank you, Sergeant Major, for indulging this old lady. Maybe later you can see that Carrie gets to visit Old Faithful and those hot springs here and there."

"I'm sure it will happen," he said vaguely, and hated himself. "On the road by eight, Carrie? Could you cajole Bonnie into packing box lunches for us? That's a fairly empty stretch between here and Canyon."

"Yes, certainly," she replied and didn't look at him. "We'll be ready in the morning. Good night, Ramsay."

She said it kindly, but she dismissed him. He walked back slowly to his tent, trying to tell himself he should be grateful he hadn't committed himself to anything, even though a kiss was a powerful indication that a man, an honorable man, was serious enough to think of a future involving a wife and children.

Just how honorable do you think you are? ran through his brain as Ramsay tossed and turned and finally slept.

Heavy-eyed, he met Mrs. LaMarque and Carrie in the dining room, just finishing breakfast. Mrs. LaMarque looked rested; Carrie did not. *She sees right through me*, Ramsay thought in misery. *She knows me.*

Other tourists were already seated and deep into flapjacks and sausage. He paid for the same and sat with his ladies, focusing his attention on the food, then drinking two cups of coffee, in the hopes it would keep him awake until they reached Canyon Hotel.

He worked up his nerve to glance at Carrie. He had never seen her drink coffee, but here she was, holding out her mug for another cup as the server came around. Carrie looked at him and raised her cup to him in a salute remarkable for the wooden look on her face.

"Looks like neither of us slept too well last night," she said.

He heard the sorrow in her voice, which pained him more than a slap across his face. She knew something was wrong and he wasn't talking to her.

"Do you think we can find a moment to talk about . . . about whatever it is that's eating you?" she whispered to him when Mrs. LaMarque's attention was taken by the Great Trostini himself, who sat on the lady's other side to chat.

"I don't know when," he managed to say.

"That's a poor answer," she said, and got to her feet. She touched Mrs. LaMarque's shoulder. "I have to gather my things together. You're already packed. Jake, could you help me get Mrs. LaMarque's luggage to the stable?"

Jake stood up and gave Mrs. LaMarque an elaborate salaam that made the lady laugh. "Your wish is my command, Scheherazade," he said. "Lead on."

They left together. Ramsay's misery deepened when he heard Carrie laughing at something Wonder Boy was saying. Great gobs of monkey meat, but were all University of Washington engineer majors so insufferable?

"You look like the very last rose of summer," Mrs. LaMarque said.

Somehow, it was easier to talk to this woman he knew would be out of his sight and mind in a few days. "I received a dispatch last night from Major Pitcher. It's bad news for me."

"Is it something Carrie might want to know about?" she asked, and he heard all the sarcasm in her voice.

"I can't tell her," he said. He stood up and helped her to her feet.

"Will it make her unhappy?"

"Probably."

She waited for him to speak, but he knew he could out wait her. Finally, she narrowed her eyes and glared at him. "You are a coward," she snapped and flounced ahead.

"I am, indeed," he said, loud enough for her to hear. From the startled looks he saw, they had both spoken loud enough for others to hear too.

Furious with himself, he saddled Xerxes. He was rougher than he should have been, cinching up the old gentleman, who gave him a wounded look. "Sorry, sir," he muttered. "If you only knew my troubles."

They started out from Willow Park camp, Ramsay leading, and Dave Lassiter following with the carriage. Mrs. LaMarque and Carrie sat together in the second seat, which at least cheered his heart.

He rode steadily without looking back, his stomach already beginning to hurt as he contemplated what lay ahead at Fort Clark. When he looked back after several miles, he realized he was alone on the road. Cursing himself, he turned Xerxes around and cantered back the way he had come, wondering if Mrs. LaMarque had suffered a relapse of some sort, and worried because he knew nothing about Parkinson's palsy.

But there they were in the little turn off at Roaring Mountain, guidebook in Mrs. LaMarque's hand while Carrie took her picture with the grand dame's Kodak. They were tourists, and not just part of army duty. He couldn't help smiling at them.

"That's better, young man," Mrs. LaMarque said as Carrie helped her into the carriage. "Carrie wanted to see this . . . this whistling mountain."

"Roaring Mountain," he said automatically, and quoted from Captain Chittenden's book, the one he was probably never going to modify for the use of the troopers who patrolled this Wonderland that had turned on him.

"'. . . a high hill on the left of the road, with a powerful steam vent near the summit.'"

"Bravo," Mrs. LaMarque said. "We're ready to drive on now."

Dave tipped his battered hat to Ramsay and returned to the Grand Loop. Ramsay took his place at the head of this puzzling caravan. The turn off at Norris Junction to the cutoff for Canyon couldn't have come soon enough to suit him, except Dave was calling to him to stop. He dismounted and walked back to the carriage, happy enough to be off his horse. For the last mile or so, he had been wondering why he had thought drinking so much coffee was a good idea. He could send them on their way and catch up, after he found a convenient clump of trees, an easy task in Yellowstone.

"Yes?" he asked.

To his surprise, Carrie leaned out of the carriage. "I absolutely refuse to pass up Emerald Spring at the geyser basin here," she said, sounding uncannily like Mrs. LaMarque. She held out the *Haynes Guidebook* and pointed to the page. "'The sulphur-lined basin with coral walls, most beautifully shaped, can be seen to an appalling depth.'"

"Twenty-seven feet down," he said, and felt the beginning of a relief so overpowering that he wanted to sink to his knees in gratitude. What a woman! She wasn't going to let him get away with melancholy pouting.

"Mrs. LaMarque is going to sit here and you are going to take me to Emerald Pool," Carrie said, her voice serene now because she sensed she had won.

He knew she wouldn't care for what he had to tell her. "You're not going to like it," he said, in his last feeble attempt to spare her. "I suppose you're not going to take no for an answer."

"I am not," she replied. "Help me down. We have an Emerald Pool to visit."

Chapter Thirty-One

*H*e helped her from the carriage. "That's Porcelain Geyser Basin to the north. We're going to the Back Basin. It's not far."

Silent, he led her to Emerald Pool. He watched her face as she stared in delight at the astonishing color created when the deep blue met the yellow and created a green seldom seen in nature.

He was already going to make a fool of himself in the next few minutes, but staring at all that water was only exacerbating his other problem, the temporary one.

"Just watch the water, if you please," he told her. "I drank way much coffee for breakfast. I'll be back."

She chuckled, but didn't turn around. He found an obliging clump of trees and took care of business. He stood there a long moment after he buttoned up, wondering how to tell her.

She had walked a little way on the boardwalk, the better to admire the pool so serene, colorful, and deadly hot. When he joined her again, he took a deep breath, and pulled the dispatch from an inside pocket on his uniform. He handed it to her.

She hesitated before opening it and then took her own deep breath. She read Major Pitcher's note first, as he had done, then the dispatch. He watched her face and saw the confusion. She closed her eyes for a moment, then she faced him and touched his chest.

"I knew I had done something wrong and couldn't figure out what it was," she said and leaned her forehead against his chest.

If she had punched the air out of him with a battering ram he could not have felt more startled. He stared at the top of her head against his chest, then put his arms around her. He closed his eyes in pleasure as she encircled him with her arms.

"Promise me that whatever happens in the rest of your life, you won't ever automatically think you did something wrong," he ordered. "Don't let any man anywhere ever make you feel that way."

"I believe it's how women think," she said.

"I wish they wouldn't, Caroline," he said into her hair. "I took a wrong turn this winter. I am going to be court-martialed and thrown in the stockade for it."

She gasped and pulled away as he knew she would, but only to give him that clear-eyed look he was already familiar with. She took his hand and tugged him to a wooden bench just off the trail. "Tell me what happened," she said. "Tell it all. Don't leave out one single thing."

He still tried to weasel out of an explanation, but Carrie stopped him with a fierce look. "Mrs. LaMarque told me not to move until you tell me everything."

"Mrs. LaMarque?" he asked, dismayed.

"Yes! Do you think we didn't notice how glum you were last night, and how pathetic you looked in the dining room?"

He winced at "pathetic," but she was right. After years of keeping his own counsel through every wave that washed over him, he decided to obey another set of orders: Carrie McKay's.

"Remember my little red book, and how you turned by chance to that page about wolves?"

"Yes."

She was quick, but he already knew that. She tightened her grip on his hand that she hadn't let go of when they sat down. She scowled at some tourists who stopped to gape at something. Maybe they had never seen a sergeant major holding hands with a pretty girl. How did he know? They hurried on.

"You're fierce," he said.

"You're stalling. Did you tell your men not to poison or otherwise kill wolves?"

"And coyotes and mountain lions," he said. "It had been a long winter. When I returned from Washington, D.C., with that . . . that blamed medal, I was tasked with taking an additional pound of strychnine to each soldier station because everyone was running low. I delivered it, but I told them it was folly to be killing predators, because in a few years, the park will be overrun with elk and deer the wolves should have eaten."

"We talked about survival of the fittest in one of my classes," Carrie said.

"There's more to it than that. I strongly suspect that when the ungulates—elk and deer for you less informed—"

She chuckled at that, as he hoped she would.

"The ungulates will start stripping the bark from the trees. I've seen it happen in bad winters. Trouble is, too much of that and the trees die. Maybe I'm out in left field here, but it's only logical that killing the predators is going to change things." He couldn't help a self-conscious chuckle of his own. "I've been studying the wolves and making field notes."

"That hardly surprises me," Carrie said. "What happened with the—oh, I can't even say the word."

"Strychnine. Since the winter was nearly gone, I, uh, shall we say, encouraged them to put away the strychnine until next year and not make a conscious effort to kill any more predators that season."

"They didn't argue?"

"Most didn't. By March, the wolves had retreated to safer spots in the park, probably in Lamar Valley. It's hard to say about mountain lions; they come, they go. No one argued until I came to the Lake soldier station," he said, remembering the incident so well. "Sergeant Lafferty, F Company, took me aside and said he wasn't going to disobey an order. He said he was going to continue putting strychnine in winterkill deer and elk carcasses. I told him to suit himself."

"He reported you," Carrie said.

"He certainly did." Ramsay gave a dry half-chuckle. "He's an ambitious man, Sergeant Lafferty, and I was in the wrong."

Carrie tightened her grip on his hand. "Do you spend a lot of time just watching animals?"

"More than I probably should," he admitted. "They fascinate me, especially the wolves, with their packs. Did you know they seem to have a pecking order? My observations indicate they typically kill the weak and the old who would probably die anyway, and the very young, but that's nature. They are magnificent animals and they don't deserve to die because someone in the Department of the Interior dictates otherwise."

Carrie let go of his hand and walked back to Emerald Spring. She stared into the water. He watched her with deep appreciation, admiring her small waist and general air of compact vitality. He knew she had plans of her own and another year of school to complete her degree. He also wanted her to be the mother of his children, because they would be the luckiest kids in Wyoming. Ramsay, you think too much, he told himself.

He thought she might return to the carriage, but she turned around and looked at him, as though measuring him. She walked back to him and sat down. "What do you think will happen in . . . where is it?"

"Fort Clark. It's not too far from the Big Bend area of Texas. For starters, I'll probably receive a blistering, profane scold from the regiment's lieutenant colonel. I already got a good one from Major Pitcher, but the colonel's will be even worse, I have no doubt."

"You stand there and take it?"

"I do, Caroline," he said. "I was wrong and I committed the worst sin a non-commissioned officer can commit, except that of striking an officer—I disobeyed an order."

"What happens after the scold?" she asked in that clear-voiced, realistic way of hers. Praise the Almighty that a man would never have to question where he stood with this woman. She could probably manage four or five sons with the efficiency of a drill sergeant, and the added dollop of motherly fondness. He would never know.

"I've seen what happens to soldiers who disobey orders. I can probably expect a court martial with perhaps two or three years in the stockade at hard labor, and the loss of all rank," he said, flinching when she flinched. "And I will be commanded to relinquish my enlistment, once I serve that sentence."

"And then?"

He shrugged. "I'll be thirty-nine or so years old by then probably, unemployed and stuck in Texas. Or I'll be thirty-nine years old, a private again if the army is lenient and I am broken by them, and earning thirteen dollars a month."

"Can privates marry?" she asked and blushed, because she was Carrie McKay.

"No."

Better drop the hundred pound sand bag on her now. He grasped her hands. "Caroline, I want you to know there is no other way this ugly scenario I caused can end." The thought of never seeing her again sent a wave of pain over him equal to the knife wounds he suffered in that cave. "I wish you well, and I will never forget you, but this is the end of whatever it was that we began a month ago."

She gave him a sharp look. "What we began a month ago was love, and you know it."

"We haven't talked about it." Sweet suffering saints, what a whiner he was.

"We didn't need to," she said, and he heard all the sorrow in the world. He also heard her peculiar strength, she who should have none, not after her hard times. "I understand that you have to leave as soon as possible. Mrs. LaMarque will be too tired to see the falls today. We'll see them tomorrow morning, and then if you feel you must ride ahead, I can get Mrs. LaMarque onto the train for Bozeman."

He nodded. What could he say? His intransigence and stupidity had come full circle. In any other year he wouldn't have cared as much, but this summer he had fallen in love. He could almost see the great cosmic housekeeper sweeping up their lovely little moment into a dustpan and dumping it outside the universe.

Carrie took his hand and tugged him upright. "We have to get to Canyon now. One thing more, Sergeant Major Stiles: you and I made a foolish wager that we both won. If there is a dance tonight at the hotel, we're going to be there and we're going to dance."

He turned the hand holding into a hand shake. "You're on, Caroline."

They started back to the carriage where he saw Mrs. LaMarque watching for them. He could hardly bear to glance at Carrie, but he saw serenity on her face, her chin up, her shoulders proud. He knew he was watching a woman forged in a fiery furnace equal to any of Yellowstone's hot springs or geysers. He knew she deserved someone far better than him. Before he left for Texas he would leave a note for Jake Trost. He smiled inside. Not that Jake Trost needed a note.

Halfway to Canyon on the cutoff from Norris, he stopped the carriage and dismounted. He ignored Mrs. LaMarque's sharp look and his heart broke to see tears on Carrie's face.

"Give me a minute here, ladies, and let me hand you down," he said. He pointed north, across the road. "Off that trail is my favorite place to look for wolves. I want to see it again."

Praise heaven, Mrs. LaMarque gave him no argument. He took the binoculars from his saddlebag and led the way, with Dave Lassiter curious and bringing up the rear. Moving slowly for Mrs. LaMarque's benefit, he led them to a clearing. He heard Carrie's satisfied exclamation, which made the whole trek worthwhile.

"We're on the Solfatara Plateau," he said and pointed north. "This was one of my favorite places to watch wolves last winter. I'd ski here and sit until my bum froze. It was worth it. Want to sit a while?"

No one objected. Mrs. LaMarque's only comment was that she would need help getting up. He sat next to Carrie, rested his forearms on his upraised knees and glassed the landscape. Nothing yet, but he was a patient man.

No one said anything. He felt his heart leap and then settle comfortably in his chest again when Carrie ran her hand down his arm.

"Will you forgive me for being stupid?" he whispered, even though he knew Mrs. LaMarque could hear him.

"Forgiven," she said promptly, with some of her usual spark. "We're dancing tonight, remember? Louise said she could take a few tucks here and there in her evening dress."

"Louise?" he asked, somehow not surprised.

She nodded, her eyes on the nearer distance. She clutched his arm. "Look. Over there by that single tree."

Eyes to his binocs, he followed where she pointed and let out a sigh he had been holding since last March, when he came this way through the snow and cold, determined not to encourage the use of strychnine. He nodded in satisfaction and handed her the binoculars. "Count them for me, will you? Something's in my eyes."

She looked. "Two large ones, and other wolves about as big. My goodness they have long legs. And one, two, three little ones."

"There were five pups last March. Ah, well. Hand the binocs to Mrs. LaMarque."

"Louise," he heard from the lady he thought he would dislike forever, until he didn't.

"Louise. Hand off to Dave when you've had a look."

"I never imagined a sight like this," the grand dame of Broadway and secret admirer of Thomas Moran said.

"Enjoy it now." He couldn't help the quaver in his voice and didn't try. "In ten or fifteen years there won't be a single wolf in this park. The coyotes might last longer, and who knows about mountain lions? They march to a different drum."

When the glasses came back to him, he watched a few more minutes. The pups fake-charged each other and tumbled in the tall grass, almost out of sight. Mama Wolf sunned herself on a warm rock and watched her brood, while Papa began to edge out and around, looking toward the plateau where they sat.

"He's onto us," Ramsay said. "Watch what he does now." He handed the binoculars to Carrie.

"He's nosing Mama Wolf," she reported, "and look, they're retreating into the trees. They sort of fade away, don't they?"

"Ghosts on the wind," Ramsay said. "That's what Jack Strong calls them. I wish you could have met him, Carrie."

"Maybe I will yet, Ram," she said. "Don't be such a nut."

He smiled at that, aware how lucky Jake Trost was going to be if he was as smart as Ramsay thought he was.

She handed the glasses to Louise, who watched a long while, then handed them to the carriage driver. Dave shook his head. "I don't need them. Take another look, Sarge. I don't think Dad's so concerned about us."

Ramsay didn't need glasses to see a lone male bison making his stately way from Grebe Lake toward the trees. He wondered if this was one of the bison of the paltry twenty-nine remaining that Captain Chittenden had counted one fall.

"I was going to help Jack Strong's cousin round up a few more bison this fall and try to coax them north, closer to Fort Yellowstone," he said and put the caps on the lenses.

"Maybe you'll be back from Fort Clark in time to do just that," Carrie said.

"I doubt it. I really do."

"Maybe you need to have more faith, Sergeant Major Stiles," she replied. "Am I the only one who wants to fight a little harder?"

Chapter Thirty-Two

*U*nless you want me to pin your ribs to this dress, stop wiggling."

"I am not wiggling," Carrie insisted. She held still for a second but then craned her neck to see the clock on the mantelpiece in their suite of rooms in Canyon Hotel.

Louise LaMarque thumped Carrie with the thimble on her finger. "Do you want to fall off this footstool, break your ankle, and be forced to stay in bed tonight? Hold still!"

"Is it really five o'clock?" Carrie asked, certain she was going to have a forest of bumps on her head from that thimble. "Is he going to be back in time for the dance?"

"I doubt it. He probably took a fast, er, moose or elk to Gardiner and is waiting for a train to whisk him far from young women who fidget. Don't cry, Carrie!" The thump was more of a tender pat on her head this time.

"I doubt there are enough cucumbers in the hotel to help you if your eyes start to swell. That's better."

Carrie stood still, her head down, feeling every single day of her twenty-three years. Here she was, standing in an evening gown with the discreet label, Worth, sewn in the lining, and all she could do was sniff back tears.

"He said he wasn't going far," she said, trying to convince herself. "Only to that bridge construction site by the upper falls. Captain Chittenden is working there."

"That nice bearded man from the party at Major Pitcher's?" Louise mumbled, pins in her mouth. "Raise your arm. Higher."

"Yes, ma'am," Carrie said as she raised her arm. "Ram said he likes to spend time with the Chittendens. What kind of advice can the captain possibly offer? Ram knows what's going to happen."

"Don't you have anyone to confide in when things are at their worst?" Louise asked. The pins were in place, and she began to sew.

Carrie thought of Bonnie Boone, the Willow Park cook, and wished herself back there making pies. It seemed a pity that a person couldn't reset a summer and begin it again, without a sergeant major this time. No, that would be worse.

She wanted to mope and feel sorry for herself as Mrs. LaMarque sewed and hummed, but that would never do. It was also nearly impossible to mope, standing in front of a mirror and admiring what an understated but obviously expensive evening dress could do for an ordinary mortal.

"Mrs. LaMarque, I've never worn anything like this," she said. "No matter what happens tomorrow, I intend to enjoy this evening."

"That is more like it," the lady said. "Make a quarter turn. Other arm up. You have a fine bosom. I've noticed

Sergeant Major Spit and Polish taking little peeks at you. I don't think he's mooning over your non-existent cheekbones."

Carrie knew Louise LaMarque well enough that there was no point in denying such a statement. Better to forge ahead. "I admit to too much enjoyment in watching him sit a horse."

"You are not alone there, missy," Mrs. LaMarque teased.

"Mrs. LaMarque!" Carrie declared but then giggled. "I needed that," she said, serious again, but not quite so melancholy. She looked down at the dress and Mrs. LaMarque's sure eye for alteration. "You're good at last-minute stitching."

"Just a little something I learned from that first Broadway revue: If a dress tears, you'd better be able to fix it fast. Turn around slowly. Now back the other way. I think we've done it."

"I am perfection in a gown worth more than half of Bozeman." Carrie joked.

"Silly! Every lady in that ballroom will know you are wearing a Worth dress," she said. "The trick is to act like you don't care at all."

"I don't really," Carrie said. "I just want to see Ramsay right now. Louise, he's leaving us after we see the falls!"

She tried not to cry, she really tried, but there was no way to convince her tears. Mrs. LaMarque held her close. "Somehow this is going to be all right."

"You don't know that!" Carrie cried.

"No, I don't," Louise said quietly. She held off Carrie and gave her a measuring look, the kind Carrie knew her own mother would have given her just then, if she could have. "He's heading into the unknown, and you had better buck up and not make it worse, Miss McKay."

Carrie nodded. She held the handkerchief to her eyes and kept it there until her eyes were dry.

"That's better," Louise said. "Let me help you out of this little piece of heaven. Lie down and I'll bring a washcloth for your eyes."

Carrie held still as Mrs. LaMarque unhooked the dress. "You need a better corset, missy," she scolded.

"I really want one of those gorgeous lace brassieres I see advertised in *McCall's*," she said.

"Don't we all! You have the figure for one. I used to." Mrs. LaMarque kissed her cheek. "Earn that degree next spring and you'll get a good job so you can buy a black lace brassiere that will take Sergeant Major Stiles's breath away! Lie down now."

Carrie went into the smaller bedroom in the suite. She looked around at the comfort, even in this rustic place, and still wished herself back at the Willow Park Wylie Camp, among people more like herself. This hotel was pleasant, to be sure, but it wasn't home, wherever home was. Her determination to enjoy herself seemed to float away like steam from a hot spring.

The window was open and she went closer, careful to not show herself in her camisole and petticoat. Ramsay said she could hear the falls from the hotel, and he was right. Tomorrow he was leaving, riding ahead to catch the train out of Gardiner. Tomorrow was also Mrs. LaMarque's day to see what had inspired Thomas Moran, an artist she met at a low ebb in her life, and who put the heart back in her body when she needed it.

She lay down and closed her eyes, wanting a home of her own, one with Ramsay Stiles in it. How could she possibly sleep with Ramsay on her mind, in her heart, crowding aside every careful plan she had made in the last few years, when she had dared to start making plans?

Exhausted with worry, she thought about the stories she read in women's magazines, with their happy endings for ordinary people, or even ladies who wore Worth gowns—all those happy endings. Why did writers even dare write drivel like that? Didn't they know how hard life really was? Maybe she would write a letter to the editor about the matter. Right now, she was tired right down to her soul.

When she woke, the sun was still barely above the mountains. Her stomach signaled that she was hungry, so she knew it was late. She raised up on one elbow and stared at the bedside clock, which registered small hand on the eight. She listened, nerves alert, to hear Ramsay Stiles talking with Mrs. LaMarque in the sitting room. She got out of bed and opened the door a crack.

My goodness, there he sat in what had to be his best uniform, holding a gold medal on a red, white, and blue ribbon.

"I'll hurry and get my dress on," she said, the door open a crack.

"You'd better, Caroline. I'm depending on you to fix this ribbon just so for me."

Mrs. LaMarque stood up and walked to the door. "Shoo! I'm coming inside to help you into that gown."

She blinked back tears. Mrs. LaMarque took her by the chin and gave her a little shake. "That's enough now. I could help him with that medal—heaven knows it would be an honor—but he insists you must."

Carrie dressed in record time, then fixed her hair in a simple bun at the back of her neck. It was old-fashioned and probably out of place, but she knew no one would look at her, not with a sergeant major in blue and gold standing beside her.

She borrowed the one pair of useless shoes Mrs. LaMarque had insisted upon, back at the National Hotel in Mammoth, which seemed like months ago, and not just days. *I must remember this entire evening*, she thought. *This will probably never happen again.*

"Ready?"

She nodded, and Mrs. LaMarque opened the door with a flourish. Ramsay stood up. She was suddenly too shy to look at his face, and stared down at his shoes. She had never seen him in ordinary shoes before; it was either boots or moccasins. They were shined to a blinding polish.

"They're wonderful shoes, Caroline, but I'm up here," he said.

Full dress uniform was precisely that. From his shoes to his tight collar with the crossed swords insignia, he left her nearly unable to breathe. Medals, gilt buttons, and those intimidating chevrons and rockers on his sleeves and hash marks galore, to the yellow stripe on his trousers—she gazed and admired, then walked into his arms because it was all too much.

He held her close. "You look splendid," he said. "I never saw a prettier Carrie McKay, but I miss the single braid."

"You're a fine specimen yourself, Sergeant Major Stiles," she said.

He held her off for a better look. "I've been telling Mrs. LaMa . . . Louise . . . about our bet at the Golden Gate."

"It seems so long ago," she said to Louise. "We were both pretty sure you'd want me to sit beside you, once Dave Lassiter took you through Kingman Canyon. The wager was a dance."

"You are both rascals and should be chained up in a side show," Louise declared. "Stick that bauble on his chest, Carrie! There's a dance going on and you're both standing here with a shaky old dame."

In deadly earnest, Ramsay handed Carrie the Medal of Honor. "For a little thing, some days it weighs too much."

She looked at the medal for a long moment, thinking about a brave man in a frightening place. "Where did you find the courage, Ram?" she asked softly.

"I dug deep, same as I am doing right now. You'd better dig deep too, Carrie."

She put her hand on his shoulder to steady herself. "I promise I will. Hold still now."

She centered the medal where he pointed, then fiddled with it until the medal looked perfectly squared away.

"Every single man in my patrol earned this," he said. "I wear it for them and for my lieutenant. It should be his."

He stood up and crooked out his arm. She put her arm through his, then she took it out when Louise LaMarque handed her a pair of long evening gloves. They wrestled them on while Ramsay watched, amused.

Finished with the glove struggle, Mrs. LaMarque stepped back and eyed them both. "You'll do," she said, sounding haughty as ever, but betraying the condescension with her eyes bright with unshed tears. "Go on and have a good time. Don't stay out too late or I will worry." She clasped her hands to her heart. "I must be a doddering idiot, but I feel as though I am sending my children to a cotillion."

"Do you like the feeling?" Ramsay asked.

"I believe I do," she said. "Go on now."

"Yes, ma'am," Ramsay said, and clicked his heels together. "We're headed for the Grand Canyon of the Yellowstone tomorrow at eight in the morning sharp."

"I've been looking forward to this all my life," she said. The starch returned. "Scram now! I have some letters to write tonight. I am shockingly overdue on some correspondence. Take his arm, Carrie, hold him close."

"Yes, Mam," Carrie said. She thought to tease her, but it didn't feel like a joke in her heart and it didn't come out of her mouth in a flippant way. She meant it with all her heart.

Mrs. LaMarque blew her a kiss and held open the door. "Scram, I say," she said softly.

Chapter Thirty-Three

$\mathcal{D}$on't look now, Caroline, but everyone is staring at me and wondering how on earth a guy with a wind-scoured face ever managed to find such a peach of a lady."

His dear Caroline looked up at him and frowned, which meant she pursed her lips. *My word, what an invitation*, he thought.

"You're a nitwit," she replied. "Everyone is staring at me and wondering how some little snip with dishpan hands managed to snare such a prize. Just so you know."

"You have on gloves. They can't see your hands," he whispered in her ear. "You smell like almonds."

"Jergen's lotion, ten cents a bottle," she replied and laughed. "Just something to go along with this evening gown worth more than Captain Chittenden's new bridge he's building. Ramsay, I'm scared to death."

"No need. You know I'm a good dancer, and by all that's holy, we look pretty impressive. A waltz, ma'am?"

"I thought you would never ask," Carrie replied. "We earned this in our devious little way."

His hand firmly on her waist, he pushed off. "By deliberately frightening the dragon? The one we've grown surprisingly fond of?"

"My goodness yes," she said. She gripped his hand tighter and looked into his eyes, unable to speak. He hauled her in closer so he didn't have to stare into her beautiful, sorrowing eyes. They danced in silence.

A polka and another waltz and then Ramsay escorted her off the dance floor. He took her hand and walked her to the veranda. The air was cool, after the ballroom. Arms around each other's waists, they stood in more silence. He knew she was close to tears, by the way she drew in one shuddering breath after another. He had never been more grateful for darkness.

He looked around and led her toward one of the rustic benches lining the front of the hotel. "I rode over to the bridge Captain Chittenden is building," he said, not relinquishing her hand. "It's a marvel, Caroline. It's poured concrete, which means his crew is building a wooden framework to hold the concrete in place when it's poured sometime in August. I don't know how he's going to do it, except that I know he will."

Silence. He pulled a handkerchief from his pocket and she took it without a word. "I told him what had happened. He's writing a letter tonight too, but I did a bad thing and it's come back to bite me."

She leaned against his shoulder, silent, the handkerchief tight in her fist.

"Nothing to say?"

She shook her head and they sat quietly together.

"One thing," she said, her voice so shaky. "Just tell me you care about me."

How kind is this woman, he thought in anguish. *She could rail at me for being stupid and ruining everything, but she isn't doing that.*

"I love you more than I can say," he told her. "I never thought something like love would happen to me, but it did."

"Fight a little harder then," Carrie told him, and he heard the fierce core to her soft-spoken words.

"It doesn't work like that in the army," he told her. "There is no gray, only black or white. I disobeyed an order. If I were a pea-green private, things might be different. I'm almost as high-ranking as a man can get and still remain a noncommissioned officer. I have absolutely no excuse and I cannot pretend one."

"You have nothing to offer me?" she asked, her voice rising.

"Nothing. By the end of this month I will either be in the stockade, eventually busted to private, or out of the army, disgraced, and unemployed. Who would hire me?" He closed his eyes as she shuddered and burrowed closer. He wished he could blend into the trees and fade away like the lone wolf he was destined always to be.

"You want me to consider this whole crazy month as an experience and nothing more?" she asked, her voice soft again. "I'm to forget you, even though I wouldn't mind if you were unemployed? All I know are hard times. You know you can find a job. I'm sure you have savings . . ."

"Forget me, Caroline." He hated to say it, but he had to. The last thing he wanted was for the shame of what he had done to taint her in any way.

"I'll start right now. Stop calling me that, Ramsay," she whispered into his sleeve, the one with all those hashmarks that were probably going to be ripped off one at a time by an officer.

He had watched men drummed out of the army and it was not a pretty sight. At least no one would lash his back, something he had seen too, in the old army. She didn't need to know that.

"You'll be in school in September," he reminded her. "Your path is smoother now."

"I thank you for that," she said formally. She stood up. "When bad things happen to me, I get quiet. I usually throw myself into hard work so I can sleep from exhaustion at night. I'll study hard this year and mind my own business. It's going to take me awhile to forget you."

She turned away and he watched her shoulders shake. If the earth could have swallowed him right there, on the porch of Canyon Hotel, he would have counted it a tender mercy he did not deserve.

"Hopefully not too long to forget me," he said, and felt like an idiot saying something so vapid. He made it worse, of course. "I'm probably somewhere high on your list of cads right now, and more easily forgettable."

"Maybe by the time I draw my last breath, I'll think of you only every other minute. Good night, my dear. We'll be ready at eight tomorrow morning. Let's give Louise LaMarque an excellent day."

She walked away, her beautiful gown making a swishing sound that he knew he would hear until he drew *his* last breath.

Sleep was out of the question. Ramsay lay in bed and stared at the ceiling, then he remembered something he could do, which gave him some relief. When he took the train to Bozeman before transferring to a southbound line, he would stop at his bank and move his funds into an account for Carrie McKay, care of Montana Agricultural

College. He had always been frugal, not a hard thing, considering the isolated garrisons he lived in, far from ways to spend money. In more recent years, he had dallied in stocks and bonds thanks to Captain Bouvier, who knew how to invest. Granted, Ramsay had lost a fair amount during the Panic of '93, but he had recouped modestly. However things came out at Fort Clark, he didn't want the army to garnish any of his money in further retaliation. Better it went to gallant Carrie McKay.

He knew such a gift was the only concrete thing he could do. On a whim, he got up and looked through his saddlebags, which he had brought to his room, much to the eye-rolling amazement of the room clerk. He pulled out the confounded etiquette book Mrs. Pitcher had given to him. He knew there was a chapter on letter-writing.

His first instinct was to chuck the blamed thing out of the window. Knowing his luck, some well-meaning soul would find it and return it promptly to him. He thumbed through the book, a wry smile on his face, wondering how an initiation prank had turned so serious, then gone so wrong. He had found a woman; he had found *the* woman, and here he was, mooning like an idiot over something that wasn't going to happen.

He turned to Courtship and Marriage, laughed out loud at the heading, "Proper Manner of Courtship," and shook his head as he read silently, *It is impracticable to lay down rules as to the proper mode of courtship and proposals. The customs of different countries differ greatly in this respect.*

Obviously the experts had no idea of the rules of courtship. And if Yellowstone Park could be viewed as a "different country," he had always been on shaky ground. Visitors came and went; Wylie girls cooked, cleaned, sang, and then departed for their real lives. He stayed here, off and on for several seasons, studying wolves until he knew their habits were of no serious danger to animals in the park. No one cared to listen to what he had observed.

On the other hand, no one knew how watching the wolves at play through the snow had calmed his heart, still racing wildly after a bad time in a faraway country and suffering through a serious injury. The wolves, bears, elk, and even noisy magpies and uppity chipmunks had soothed his mind. Carrie McKay had put the heart back into his body.

"'There may be such a thing as love at first sight, and if there is, it is not a very risky thing upon which to base a marriage,'" he read out loud, then read again, surprised at the absence of vague superiority, which filled the other 417 pages. He turned to the title page and wondered which of the four professors and three additional experts who had come together to write this ridiculous book had fallen in love at first sight.

"Good for you, whoever you are," he said. "I did the same thing. I hope your results were better. Now where is your equally useless chapter on letters?"

Knowing sleep resided on some distant asteroid in another galaxy, he dressed, pulled up a chair to the desk and rummaged in the drawer. He stared at the Canyon Hotel stationery and tried to compose a letter to Carrie, just a factual one stating he was creating an account for her and transferring his savings into it. At a loss, he turned to the book once more, and came to, "The Love Letter."

Ramsay swore under his breath and frowned at the silly statement: *A love letter should be dignified in tone and expressive of esteem and affection. It should be free from silly and extravagant expression.* Mercy, it was a wonder anyone ever wrote a letter or courted a lady or married the same.

How in the world did anyone ever get around to having babies? Hogwash.

Holding the book between thumb and forefinger, he lifted it high over the wastebasket by the desk and dropped it, well past needing to read one more word. He had already agonized over the section on gift-giving which suggested nothing fancier than flowers or a book. He was giving Carrie McKay his life savings, along with his whole heart.

He crumpled the letter that so far said no more than "My dearest Caroline," and tossed it into the wastebasket too. In the Bozeman bank, he could write a businesslike note, stick it in his savings book, and add her account number, once he secured one. If he sent the packet to Gardiner, care of the Wylie summer office, Carrie would get it.

Saddlebags repacked, his dress uniform in its own satchel, he made his way downstairs and out to the stable, where Dave Lassiter harnessed the horses and Xerxes looked on with some interest. He strapped the satchel behind his saddle and spent a moment with Dave, thanking him for his help.

"I have to ride ahead on fort business after we get to Lower Falls," he told the driver. "Just get'um to the National Hotel and Mrs. LaMarque on the train."

"Happy to, Sarge," Dave said. "I expect I'll see you out and about the fort in the next day or so."

Don't count on it, Ramsay thought. "I expect you will," he lied. "I'll move the ladies along now."

He stood in the entrance to the dining room, only because Carrie hadn't spotted him yet, and he wanted to watch her, maybe memorize her. He smiled at the way she cocked her head a little to one side when she listened to Mrs. LaMarque, and how she leaned forward with conversation. Her little straw hat was perched a bit forward, which meant the mass of hair in the back glowed with its blond and red highlights as the morning sun moved into the room.

His fingers almost itched to tug out the hairpins he knew were poised here and there, and watch the beauty of unconfined hair cover her shoulders. He sighed, knowing that would be another man's happy task in the future, when Carrie found someone of like mind far more suitable than he was. He thought of Jake Trost, hating the engineering major for a brief moment, and then reminded himself that Carrie already liked the amiable fellow. Something could happen there.

Was this harder than taking a cave full of angry insurrectionists? Quite possibly. He pushed away from the doorframe where he leaned and crossed the dining room. Carrie pulled out a chair for him and he sat next to her.

"Some coffee?" she asked, still not a girl for preliminaries. "Here's an egg, bacon, and toast."

He nodded and let Carrie capably organize him. "Do you know what's really good?" she asked, looking at him, but not letting her eyes linger.

Bravo, Carrie, he thought. *You'll forget me soon enough.*

Deftly she sliced the toast and the egg, and laid the halves on the toast. The bacon went down on top, and she sprinkled some grains of salt from the salt cellar. The other half of toast went down. "An egg sandwich," she announced.

He smiled at her. For a small moment, all the uncertainty and pain he had seen last night crossed her face. She returned her attention to Mrs. LaMarque while he ate his sandwich.

When he finished breakfast, he looked closer at Carrie. He knew he was never going to enjoy the fragrance of Jergen's lotion again, because it would only mean Carrie.

She gave him a businesslike glance. "Shall we go? Mrs. LaMarque isn't getting one second younger . . ."

". . . Carrie . . ."

She grinned at the lady in question. For the smallest second he saw the hurt in Carrie's eyes that even a joke couldn't hide. He wanted her to start forgetting him, because he hadn't given her any other choice.

"And you have business elsewhere, Sergeant Major Stiles."

Chapter Thirty-Four

After Carrie took off the beautiful dress last night, picked out the alterations, and returned it to the suitcase, she and the woman who had begun a journey in animosity had talked and cried until the early hours, arriving at no conclusions.

In the early hours, she began to feel the deepest gratitude for the woman whom she thought would plague her very existence, and all for the promise of one hundred dollars by the time the ordeal was over. Where she had sobbed over Ramsay's intractable situation, Mrs. LaMarque had comforted with serenity, and even an element of good cheer that, while startling Carrie at first, ended up soothing her to sleep, her head resting in the socialite's lap.

Carrie knew she had turned some cosmic corner when she woke in the morning to see Mrs. LaMarque watching her with the deepest concern. For a moment, she forgot her own sorrow when the lady gently rested her steady hand against her cheek.

"You know, my dear, I never wanted children," Mrs. LaMarque said.

Carrie managed a weak laugh. "After my ridiculous lamentation, you must be supremely grateful you never had a daughter. I should apolo—"

"No, no. Don't misunderstand me," Mrs. LaMarque said. "I realize I might have been good at this." She showed a spark of her former starch. "I know I could have managed a daughter, you silly child."

Carrie sat up, her heart filled with affection. Maybe Ramsay was right. Maybe she would eventually forget all about him. She could allow him a corner somewhere in her heart, but there was room for others too, even difficult people who might become excellent friends, if given a chance to blossom.

"There is no doubt you have managed me nicely through a trying time," she said. "I will be all right now."

"Not until your . . . that . . . sergeant major is a little farther away," Mrs. LaMarque said firmly. Barely suppressing a smile, she raised her hand that shook and waved it at Carrie. "See here, I'm shaking my finger at you."

Carrie stared at her and then joined in Mrs. LaMarque's laughter. They both laughed until they had to wipe their eyes.

"If a body can't laugh at a little tremor, then what's the point in having Parkinson's palsy?" Mrs. LaMarque said. "Maybe I should look at things in a different light too."

Carrie put out her hand and they shook together, then they laughed some more. Her resolve to put her feelings for Ramsay Stiles into some dark corner of her mind had lasted no longer than the moment after breakfast when he helped her into the carriage.

She looked into his tired, serious eyes and knew she was seeing a reflection of her own eyes. She met his gaze as long as she could bear and then turned her attention to Mrs. LaMarque, who was already seated and needed no assistance. "Are you comfortable, ma'am?" she asked, not willing to say anything more to the sergeant major because she knew her tears would fall again. Better he should think she was going to do exactly what he told her to do and forget him.

She looked down at her hands until he spoke to Dave and mounted his horse.

"Louise, may I hold your hand? I'm having a hard time," Carrie said, her eyes now on the horse and rider in front of the carriage. Without a word, the tourist from Hades who had become so dear twined her fingers through Carrie's.

"Brave talk is easy in the middle of the night, isn't it?" she whispered to Mrs. LaMarque.

"There is hardly anything simpler," the lady replied. "You should have heard my late-night conversations with Tom Moran through the years. It's like writing a heart-felt letter and then not mailing it."

Carrie nodded, aware that in her own misery, she had forgotten the sole purpose of Mrs. LaMarque's trip was this visit to the Lower Falls of the Yellowstone. She glanced at her companion's self-possessed, calm face, knowing she should model herself after such courage and serenity. Sometimes all a woman could do was forge ahead, never forgetting, but at least not remembering relentlessly, when there was no other alternative.

The enormity of the task ahead of her made Carrie quail inside. Love could be a dreadful burden. Maybe that was the summer lesson. As they came closer and closer to the Grand Canyon of the Yellowstone, her heart ached for the man on horseback, heading toward court martial, the stockade, and humiliation he did not deserve, simply because he had disobeyed an order that made no sense. Unlike everyone in the Department of the Interior, he had made a personal study of wolves, perhaps even a scientific study, and arrived at different conclusions.

She knew she couldn't think of the years ahead because that was too hard. Better to take the rest of the summer day by day, minute by minute if she had to. After a while, the false front of serenity might become easier to wear. She glanced at Mrs. LaMarque, who had covered up her love for Thomas Moran until it turned her hard. *I don't want that*, Carrie thought suddenly. Although I greatly admire her now, I dare not become hard and brittle.

Carrie looked up, startled to see they had stopped. She was alone in the carriage and Ramsay Stiles was holding out his hand for her to step down from the carriage.

"We're here?" she asked, feeling like an idiot.

"We have been for several minutes," he said, so serious. "Mrs. LaMarque told me to leave you alone until you . . . you felt like getting out. Do you?"

"Oh, yes," she said. "Goodness, this was the whole purpose of this trip, wasn't it?"

"I'm not sure anymore," he said, and helped her down.

What could she say to that? Standing next to the one man in the world who could make her completely happy, she knew she could hide behind that façade she needed to build, similar to Mrs. LaMarque's façade, or be honest. She chose honesty.

"I'm not sure either, Ram," she said, raising her voice to be heard above the sound of millions of gallons of water pouring over a ledge. "I wish I could carry some of your burden. Since I can't, or you won't let me, just know I'll be writing you in Texas."

Not for me the midnight letters I never send, she thought. *I can't do that.*

"Not the wisest use of your time, Caroline," he said as they walked toward Mrs. LaMarque, who waited with less than stellar patience at the top of the gently sloping trail.

"It's my choice," she said simply. "Whether you read them or not is your business. She doesn't look very patient. Let's move it."

He smiled at that, as she hoped he would. She told him to hurry ahead and take Mrs. LaMarque's arm to steady her on the path, and Carrie took her time. Above and beyond her own misery, she knew this was a moment to relish and remember from the summer when she fell in love and learned that life, while not fair or easy, was worth the trouble of living right.

Another turn in the path and she gazed with open-mouthed amazement at the fairest sight in Wonderland. Other visitors stood by the low wooden barrier, their Kodaks trained on the gorgeous, sumptuous feast of color and light, depth and sparkle.

Why do you bother to look down into a camera? she thought, entranced. *What is the use of a black and white image? Trust your minds, silly people.*

Mrs. LaMarque stood at the barrier with the others, staring in silence. "What are you thinking?" Carrie whispered, knowing her voice would never be heard over the rumble of the waterfall.

She smiled inside as another tourist raised his voice and held up the *Haynes Guidebook*, shouting to read to his companion.

Be quiet, Carrie thought. *Enjoy this sight like no other.*

With all the other savages who worked in the park, she had seen countless postcards of the Grand Canyon of the Yellowstone, as sketched first by Thomas Moran, then painted at leisure in his studio. Like all savages, she knew the basic facts to tell visitors at Willow Park, who already anticipated the sight reserved for the last day of their five-day tour. She knew the Lower Falls was some one hundred feet from side to side, making it far less in width than Niagara Falls. Even knowing the water funneled through the narrow space with boisterous abandon had not prepared her for the drop of three hundred feet. The thunder and roar stunned her.

She stepped back, wanting a bit of puny distance, and felt her hand suddenly clasped in Ram's hand. He had removed his gauntlets and she sighed with the pleasure of his skin against hers.

"I've seen this for years, but I never get over it. And look at the color of the canyon walls. No wonder it's called Yellowstone."

He whispered directly into her ear in order to be heard. She closed her eyes when his lips touched her ear, knowing deep inside that even if she visited this spot over and over in the coming years, this moment would be forever burned on her heart.

So much for her plans to be serene and calm and completely artificial in the face of his departure, which she knew was only minutes from now. Carrie circled his waist with her free arm and leaned her head against his chest. She thought of a sermon heard years ago in the First Presbyterian Church, that sanctuary to her in Bozeman, when Reverend Gillespie spoke of needing eyes that see and ears that hear. Those eyes that saw took in the yellow, gold, pink, and faint green of steep canyon walls and lodged them firmly in her heart, admittedly an odd anatomical juxtaposition. Through the noise of falling water, her ears that heard caught the faint, steady beat of Ramsay Stiles's kind heart as she leaned against his chest. And wouldn't you know, that sound found its way into her heart too.

She stood close to the man she adored who was soon to walk out of her life, hopefully without a backward glance, because that would undo her. After minutes of silence, he tugged her hand and started her toward the path up to the waiting carriage and Xerxes.

They walked together in silence. She should never have looked at his face as they came to stand beside his horse. Such a thin face, such a worn expression, as silent tears trickled down his cheeks.

Then it was good-bye, his hands firm on her shoulders, looking her right in her brimming eyes. He pulled her close. "I wasn't going to do this," he whispered.

"Shut up and kiss me," she whispered back.

He kissed her and she clung to him, as she tried to press her hands through his back and into his heart. If he never kissed her again, she knew she would never forget this kiss. Her ears roared, but not from the sound of falling water. She felt his gilt buttons against her breast and she tried to memorize every second that sped past.

He released her first, his hands on her shoulders again and not around her back. "Write me. I thought I didn't want that, but I do."

She nodded, and took several deep breaths until she grew light-headed. "Where will you be sent?"

"Probably to Fort Leavenworth," he told her. "It'll be hard labor for a few years and constant humiliation. Everyone will want to pick on the sergeant major who disobeyed orders because he had mush for brains and cared about wolves."

"Do you think you will be allowed visitors?" she asked.

"I imagine. The army isn't entirely heartless," he replied, and she heard all the bitterness.

"I'll graduate next spring. I'll move to Fort Leavenworth. I will find employment and I will visit you," she told him.

"I know there is a good man majoring in civil engineering at U-Dub who is interested in you. I'd rather you got on with your life," he said.

She couldn't help a watery smile. "That's what I will be doing, Ram. And I will see you again."

She kissed his wet cheek quickly and then turned and ran back down the path toward Yellowstone's second greatest miracle. The first was the man she left behind.

Chapter Thirty-Five

Carrie spent the day at the Lower Falls, sitting with Mrs. LaMarque in the picnic area, then walking with her to the wooden barrier to gaze in silent wonder. They watched the light change as the earth moved through its orbit. Carrie remembered a class in art appreciation during her prep school days at Montana Ag, when the instructor showed them chromolithographs of Rouen Cathedral, as painted various times during the day by Claude Monet. *You should come here and paint, Monsieur Monet,* she thought.

The give of light and shadow in the canyon reminded her of the timelessness of the hand of God. It in no way diminished her own trials, but she saw them in a different light, the light of the canyon. No matter what happened, she knew she could be strong too. She knew she could endure.

She cried when she couldn't help herself, walking alone down a quiet path away from the waterfall. By the end of the day, she did not feel at peace, but she felt calm. Because her only remedy for anything in her life was hard work, she longed to get back to the Wylie Camp at Willow Park.

Both of the ladies slept from exhaustion that night at Canyon Hotel. They left after an early breakfast, fortified with box lunches, and under the careful and sympathetic eye of their driver.

Carrie wanted to fulfill one of Ramsay's wishes and insisted upon a detour to the nearby construction site of the bridge over the upper falls of the Yellowstone River, where Captain Chittenden worked. She did not know him beyond that one evening spent in Major Pitcher's parlor, but she knew in her heart she needed to make a good report to Ramsay Stiles, when she wrote him that first letter in distant Fort Clark, Texas.

Captain Chittenden met them at the stone abutment of the bridge that would soon arch over the Yellowstone River. He wore muddy corduroy trousers, knee high boots, and a sweater with the elbows worn out. Despite his dishevelment, the dignity of the man came through. Carrie held out her hand. He looked at his hands.

"D'you mind a little grit?" he asked.

"Not if dishpan hands don't bother you," she said as they shook hands. She looked beyond him where the workers were building a wooden frame around the steel girders that formed the core of the bridge with its graceful arch. "I don't know how you do what you do, sir."

"I could say the same to you," he told her, his expression changing from welcoming to serious. "Be of good courage, Miss McKay."

He still held her hand. He squeezed it and then released it to renew his acquaintance with Mrs. LaMarque as though he greeted visitors in his own parlor back at Fort Yellowstone.

She made herself smile, forcing back any emotion to hamper the incredible awe she felt at the work of this genius engineer. No wonder Ram spoke so highly of the man.

When she felt in control, she turned back and joined his orbit as he held the sketch of what was to come, once the cement was poured into the framework and allowed to set.

He gestured her closer. "I have to tell you: Ramsay twitted me about insisting on bells, whistles, and a marching band, when an ordinary bridge would do," he said in great good humor. "I told him the Yellowstone River deserved my best. He agreed with no more argument."

She listened as he described the cement pour to come. "It'll be in August at the full moon," he explained, this engineer by training with a poet's heart. "Canyon Hotel is loaning us a bank of electric lights. We'll work in continuous shifts until the job is done."

"How long will that take?" Carrie asked.

"Probably four days and nights. I worked the numbers. I'll pull in other workers from the corkscrew road toward Cody." He chuckled. "We'll have a grand old time."

"It fairly takes my breath away," she told him.

He touched her sleeve. "Come back and see it before you leave for school, Carrie. I'll give you a photograph to send to Ramsay."

Why did her eyes fill with tears at the mere mention of his name? She took the handkerchief Mrs. LaMarque gave her and dabbed her eyes. "I will, Captain," she told him. "Thank you for what I suspect you are trying to do for him."

"Many of us are trying," he said. He studied her a moment, as an engineer would. "Ramsay has already lost heart. Don't you lose heart, and that's an order."

～❧

Twelve long hours later as dusk poured its shadows onto Mammoth's magnificent terraces, Dave Lassiter pulled his tired team to a stop in front of the National Hotel. He and Carrie helped their exhausted passenger from the carriage, and a team of bellhops sprang into action, the desk clerk running along beside him, assuring the socialite of every comfort.

While the others waited in their hotel room's parlor, Carrie helped her friend into bed and promised her tea and biscuits. Mrs. LaMarque nodded. When Carrie turned to go, she took Carrie's hand.

"In my purse I have an envelope for Mr. Lassiter," she said and closed her eyes, as though a mere sentence overpowered the drive that Carrie knew was weakening and would continue to weaken as Parkinson's palsy took its toll.

After tipping the bellhops, reassuring the night clerk that all was well, and asking for refreshments from room service, she did as Mrs. LaMarque said and handed Dave an envelope with his name on it in tiny, spiderlike handwriting.

"I've been paid by the transportation company for my service," he protested.

"Apparently Mrs. LaMarque didn't think it was enough," Carrie said. "Between you and me, I wouldn't argue the matter."

"Yup, we know the lady, don't we?" Dave grinned at her and accepted the envelope. "I'll be by at nine in the morning. The tracks are through to Gardiner, so we'll try out the new depot. You coming too, Carrie?"

"Most certainly," she said. "I'll have her ready to go. On behalf of Sergeant Major Stiles and me, thank you, Dave."

A shadow crossed his normally cheerful face. "Sarge finally told me what was going on. I can write a letter on his behalf too," he promised. "I'm no great shakes at putting pencil to paper, but it can't hurt." He scratched his head. "Trouble is, I don't think anyone pays much attention to us little people."

"I know, but we try. Thanks, Dave."

Once she downed her tea and nibbled at a macaroon, Mrs. LaMarque made Carrie sing, glaring at her when she said she couldn't. "You told me you wanted some help with projection," she said.

Carrie nodded and sang "Ta-ra-ra-boom-de-ay" with the speed of a funeral dirge.

Mrs. LaMarque flicked thumb and forefinger against Carrie's head. "Like. You. Mean. It," she ordered.

Carrie sang again as her employer, friend, and now-mentor pressed against her diaphragm and gave her basic instruction. She sang it over and over until Mrs. LaMarque was either satisfied or tired.

"Just remember—deep breaths from down below," Mrs. LaMarque. "My word, you have worn me out."

Carrie sat beside the sleeping woman all night, dozing and then watching her charge, wondering where Ramsay was right now, wishing he weren't alone to face what had to be a dreadful, humiliating experience, all because he loved wolves and had a soft heart.

As morning came, she washed her face and brushed her hair, arranging it into another tidy bun. By tomorrow she would be wearing her one braid down her back again, dressed in her shapeless cotton work dress with the big apron. Too bad she could not move backward in time to early summer and do things differently.

But would you, Carrie? she asked herself. She doubted it.

Before they left the suite in the National Hotel, Mrs. LaMarque insisted that she hurry down to the laundry and borrow a tape measure. By the time she came upstairs, tape in hand, Mrs. LaMarque had collared one of the maids to write down Carrie's measurements as the former toast of Broadway and widow of a Wall Street tycoon measured her.

"Shush now, Carrie," Mrs. LaMarque said as the tape went around Carrie's chest. "Thirty-six bosom," she commanded. "Write that down, miss. Every woman needs a good traveling dress. You're going to graduate next year and make a name for yourself. Potential employers expect their staff to look elegant. And no braid down your back!"

Carrie laughed and raised her arms again for the waist measurement.

Neither of them said much as the faithful team, guided by Dave Lassiter, made its way down from Mammoth's heights to scruffy little Gardiner. The arch wasn't complete, but a crew was setting the stones in place. Ramsay had told her about President Roosevelt's visit, with all of the troops on parade with shiny boots and well-buffed brass buttons. Others had told her how he stood in front of the president when a rowdy drunk waving a pistol approached the speaker's stand.

You can't help but be a hero, Ram, she thought, then turned her attention to Mrs. LaMarque, because she was a safer subject. Mrs. LaMarque was looking at the bleak landscape, windblown and full of sagebrush.

"It doesn't look like much here," she commented and then took Carrie's hand. "Wonderland begins at the Terraces, doesn't it?"

"When the arch is done, it will begin right here," Carrie contradicted. "Captain Chittenden said the words 'For the benefit and enjoyment of the people,' will be set in stone. I like that."

"I do too," Mrs. LaMarque said. "The big people and the little people like us, eh, my dear?"

Carrie nodded, too full to speak. She wanted to beg Mrs. LaMarque not to leave, which would have been childish. When her dear friend departed and Dave Lassiter returned to his usual duties, there would be no one besides her who would remember the trip that began in discord and ended in an aching kind of sweetness. She, Carrie McKay, would be the only one left in Wonderland who knew how people could change, given the right setting and the inclination.

The depot was built solidly of logs that improbably still smelled freshly cut and sawed. Mrs. LaMarque stood on the platform and watched Dave carry her alligator bags into the sleeper car and then help two porters in impeccable uniforms trundle her steamer trunk into the baggage car. Mrs. LaMarque tipped them, Dave blew her an impudent kiss good-bye, and then she and Carrie stood alone.

"I don't know what to say, except thank you from the bottom of my heart for giving me a day at Tom Moran's masterpiece," she said finally. "I also enjoyed Ta-ra-ra-boom-de-ay!"

They laughed together. "Tell the Great Trostini to work on his magic tricks," Mrs. LaMarque said. Her eyes filled with tears and she gathered Carrie close. "Don't worry too much about your sergeant major," she said. "There are probably more people than you know who are concerned about his welfare."

"I will do my best to keep breathing and hoping," Carrie said. "May I write you?"

"You had better!" Mrs. LaMarque reached into her purse. "I wrote my address on this envelope. You'll find what I owe you inside."

"Thank you, Mrs. LaMarque," Carrie said and kissed her cheek. "It's a big help."

"A kiss is not sufficient," the lady said as she embraced Carrie, holding her close.

The conductor walked by, cleared his throat and hollered, "Board! Board!"

"You don't need to shout in my ear, young man," Mrs. LaMarque said in her best stage voice, the one that in earlier days had smacked the back wall of Broadway's finest music halls and theatres. "Give me a hand up and don't be so noisy!"

Carrie stood on the platform, watching as the thoroughly cowed conductor helped Mrs. LaMarque to her seat. "Don't change a single thing, Louise," she whispered and waved as the train left the depot, bound for Livingston, then Bozeman, and then east to New York City and Washington. Carrie hoped to remember every detail of her time with that remarkable, brittle, witty, exasperating woman.

She looked down at the envelope in her hand, happy to see the Washington, D.C., address, where the woman who had modeled for art students and sung in saloons now held teas and dinners as a respected widow with money to burn, and unspoken love for an artist of some renown. What a life.

The envelope felt too heavy for a mere fifty dollars. Her heart in her mouth, Carrie opened the sealed envelope. "What have you done, Louise LaMarque?" she murmured as she counted two hundred and fifty dollars.

Head up, she marched to a quiet corner of the depot and cried, thinking how smooth her path would be this year at school with such generosity, plus the fifty dollars Ramsay had extracted from Mrs. LaMarque, plus whatever she earned this summer. She wouldn't have to work at all. Since she was going to be a woman of leisure at Montana Ag, she could talk her department head into letting her take another typewriting class from the secretarial arts department. She would graduate and find a good job near Fort Leavenworth. She could work and wait as well as any woman.

If Mrs. LaMarque did as she promised, Carrie could look forward to a tailored traveling suit, something all successful women needed.

Carrie dried her eyes and raised her chin. "I am a successful woman."

Chapter Thirty-Six

After she splurged on a glass of lemonade from the lunch counter, Carrie tucked Mrs. LaMarque's envelope down her shirtwaist front and walked the two blocks to the Wylie Camping Company office, hoping Mrs. Wylie would be there to help her find a ride to Willow Park.

"There you are!" the lady in question said when she opened the door. "How did you fare? I hear she was a terror."

"Only until we got to know her," Carrie said. "Mrs. Wylie, for my services, she gave me enough money to pay all my expenses this coming year."

"That is good news, indeed, Carrie," Mrs. Wylie said, beaming at her. "Have a seat. I have something here for you that I suspect a certain man mailed from Bozeman."

"Oh, dear," Carrie said as she sank into the chair.

Mrs. Wylie regarded her with sympathy. "We heard what happened. Say the word and William will write a letter on his behalf. So will I."

"Yes, thank you." *Please don't make me say anymore*, she thought. She held out her hand for the package and rested it in her lap.

"I doubt it will bite," Mrs. Wylie said as Carrie sat there staring down.

Carrie opened the package and took out a bank book from the Bank of the Rockies. She opened the letter stuck inside the little blue book and spread it on her lap.

My Dearest Caroline, I closed my savings account here, opened one in your name, and deposited my life's savings in it, she read. "Mrs. Wylie. Please help me," she said.

Mrs. Wylie quickly came around the desk and sat beside her.

"I've been crying so long that my eyes hurt," Carrie said, embarrassed to admit such weakness. "Please, could you read it out loud."

"I will after you take a deep breath and then a sip of water. Carrie, you're as white as milk."

Mrs. Wylie handed her a paper cup of water. "That's better. All right, here I go. " She began the letter again. " 'My Dearest Caroline . . .' He calls you Caroline?"

"He likes it," Carrie said simply.

" 'I closed my account here, opened one in your name, and deposited my life's savings in it.' My word, Carrie, how much is that?"

With shaking fingers, Carrie opened the bank book and stared at the last entry. "Mrs. Wylie, two thousand dollars!"

Mrs. Wylie got herself a drink of water from the cooler. She sat down again with a plop. "I need a deep breath too. Here we go. 'I have no idea what the army is going to do to me, but I don't want them to come after my savings. If you're going to continue to be stubborn and visit me after you graduate next year, it would give me some peace to know you have funds for whatever you might need.' Going to be stubborn?" Mrs. Wylie asked. "Good for you, Carrie. He's a fine man. Where was I?"

"I'm stubborn," Carrie said, wondering when that happened.

"'It isn't a huge amount,'" Mrs. Wylie read. "'Like others, I lost money in the Panic of '93. It's recouped a bit since then, and I want you to have it.'"

"I can't possibly accept this," Carrie said.

"Yes, you can, missy!" Mrs. Wylie insisted. "He's protecting his interests by giving them to you. Pretty smart, if you ask me."

And kind, Carrie thought. So kind. Carrie thought of Mrs. LaMarque's money stuffed down her shirtwaist, and all her years of scrounging about to get enough money for the necessities, let alone college. Now this. It was Ramsay's money, hers to protect, because she was stubborn.

Mrs. Wylie cleared her throat and turned over the note. "Just a little more to read, Carrie. 'The army might try to take this away too, but they can't have it. I earned it. It's yours. You're as brave as any trooper I ever led, and a darned sight better-looking. All my love, Ram.' What is he talking about?"

Carrie took a rectangular red box from the package and pressed the button to open it. She gasped to see Ramsay's Medal of Honor, with its tricolor ribbon and the spread eagle perched on a cannon. She gently touched the five-pointed gilt star.

"This is what he is talking about, Mrs. Wylie. This is his Medal of Honor."

"That's what they look like? Oh, Carrie."

They stared at the medal together. Stunned, Carrie closed the box and set the bank book back on top of it. "I don't have a good place to keep this. May I leave it here in your safe?"

"You can, but I think you should store it in the Willow Park safe."

"Why?"

"Something tells me you might like to take that medal out and look at it now and then," Mrs. Wylie. "You know, just to remind you how brave you truly are, and stubborn. He's right, Carrie."

They sat close together in silence. "I can do that," Carrie said finally. She took the contents of the box and put them in her purse. "You're right. I wouldn't want these so far away from me." She closed her eyes against the pain that rolled over her. "He is far enough away."

She gathered herself together. "Mrs. Wylie, I stopped here to see if you could recommend a way for me to get back to Willow Park. I have work to do."

Her heart sank when Mrs. Wylie hesitated. "Is something else wrong?" Carrie asked.

"I honestly don't know," Mrs. Wylie said. "Major Pitcher from Fort Yellowstone sent a note to me by courier ordering you to report to him at the administration building as soon as Mrs. LaMarque is on the train."

"I will not," Carrie said, getting to her feet as if pulled by strings. "I won't. It's still a free country and I owe nothing to the US Army. I'll walk to Willow Park before I will have anything to do with Major Pitcher. Good day, Mrs. Wylie, and thank you for your help."

"Carrie . . ." Mrs. Wylie began. She smiled then. "I'll claim I never saw you. Someone will let you hitch a ride."

"I wasn't worried," Carrie said, serenely in charge of herself again. "See you around the campfire soon?"

"Of course!" Mrs. Wylie blew her a kiss.

She picked up her carpetbag, opened the door, and started walking, confident someone would give her a ride before she walked too far. People heading to the park were kind that way.

Am I stubborn, Ramsay Stiles? she thought as she strode along, breathing in great lungfuls of Montana air and feeling surprisingly liberated. She thought of the Medal of Honor safely stowed in her purse and knew its home from now on would be under her pillow.

For the fun of it, she walked through the construction site that was going to become what people had already dubbed the Roosevelt Arch. She smiled at the masons who tipped their hats to her and went back to work, mortaring the stones in place.

She didn't have to walk far. She couldn't recall his name, but he was one of the older drivers for the Yellowstone Park Transportation Company. He pulled his team to a halt beside her.

"Fred Lonnigan, at your service," he said with a tip of his hat.

"Are you going to Willow Park?" she asked.

"Eventually. One quick stop first at Mammoth. I'll give you a hand up."

He helped her into the seat beside him. Carrie turned around. "No tourists?"

"Not right now," he said. "This won't take long."

Carrie settled back, thinking about the four weeks to come before she took the train back to Bozeman and her senior year. By the time she left Wonderland, fall would be making its presence known, with the elk bugling their challenges to other bulls and keeping a sharper eye on their harems. She thought of Ramsay's wolves in the Lamar Valley and wondered how they would fare this winter, with no advocate.

She hoped it might snow before her last day at Willow Park, because she enjoyed the fumaroles of steam that seemed to pop up, unannounced, through Yellowstone's white blanket. In early June, a solitary buffalo had strolled into Willow Park during a spring squall and hunkered down by the creek until he was covered with snow. She remembered that Jake Trost had watched the solitary bull with her and wondered out loud if they ever got lonely.

She hoped with all her heart that Ramsay Stiles wasn't sitting in the stockade, staring up at a postage stamp of sky through iron bars. He was a man used to the out of doors, a patient observer of wolves, an admirer of cherry pie, the man she wanted to marry and have her children by.

She closed her eyes, tired of everything, wondering if she would ever have a good night's sleep again. She couldn't help but lean against Fred Lonnigan, who put his arm around her in an avuncular way and said, "You've had a trying time, missy." It was the last thing she remembered as Fred spoke to his team and they took the steep grade to Mammoth Hot Springs.

"Miss McKay? Carrie? I need to speak to you."

Carrie opened her eyes and sat up, alarmed to realize that the traitor driver had taken her directly to the administration building at Fort Yellowstone. She blinked her eyes to get the sleep out of them and found herself staring down at Major John Pitcher.

"Oh, no," she said and tried to scramble over Fred to escape out the other side. The driver grabbed the waistband of her skirt and she realized she wasn't going anywhere.

"I don't know anything and I have nothing to say to you," she told the major when Fred Lonnigan, grinning, deposited her on the boardwalk next to Yellowstone Park's acting superintendent.

"Thanks, Fred," the major said. "Hang around and you can drive her to Willow Park when I'm done."

"I'd rather walk than ride with someone as sneaky as Fred Lonnigan," she declared, which made Fred laugh and the officer turn away and cough.

"Carrie, Major Pitcher put out a memo telling all of us drivers to look for you. I got lucky. Will you still make pie for me?"

"I might," she said, unwilling to cooperate. "Maybe in a year or two."

Carrie folded her arms and glared at the major, too tired to care what impression she made and thoroughly disgusted. "As for you, Major, I currently have no use for the US Army," she said.

"Carrie, all I want is to let you know what we're trying to do for Sergeant Major Stiles," Major Pitcher said. "Come into my office. Please?"

"Since you said please, I suppose I must," she told him, searching for dignity when all she wanted to do was find a dark corner to lick her wounds.

He showed her to a seat in his office and closed the door. Rather than sit behind the desk, he took the other chair. He gave her a look so full of sympathy that Carrie felt wretched tears gathering again.

What could she say? "Major, I'm so tired." *Well, that's a bit of brilliant repartee*, she thought, almost past caring what the major thought of her, but not quite.

"I imagine you are," he said. "I didn't mean to send out scouting parties for you, but everyone here at the fort wants you to know we will do our best to see that Sergeant Major Stiles is not incarcerated for what, to the US Army, is a most serious offense—disobeying an order."

"He told me he was looking at a court martial and years of hard labor at Fort Leavenworth," she said, wondering where she found the courage to even say the words, let alone think them. "Major Pitcher, it's wrong."

"No, it isn't, Carrie," he said, and took her by both hands. "Disobeying orders is a terrible offense. He knew that when he told his troopers not to use the strychnine at the soldier stations."

She looked away and withdrew her hands. "I know you're right, but I hate that you're right."

"Is it any consolation that I agree with you?" the major asked.

She felt her shoulders droop and exhaustion claim her. She nodded, unable to speak.

The major seemed to have trouble with his throat. He cleared it several times. "Carrie, nearly every trooper at this fort has sent a letter, plus all the Yellowstone Transportation drivers—yes, even Fred Lonnigan." He reached behind him to a packet of papers on his desk and took out a thick document. "I also sent a typewritten copy of this, plus a lengthy letter, to Colonel Ward who commands our regiment. I sent another to the Department of the Interior. This is your carbon copy, plus Ramsay's handwritten copy."

Her curiosity outweighed her sorrow. She accepted the handkerchief Major Pitcher gave her, blew her nose, and looked at the document. She scanned the pages, her heart opening wider, as she thumbed through what seemed to be field notes dating back three years.

"My goodness, he kept a record of his wolf observations in Lamar Valley," she said. "Summer and winter. Everything."

"It's amazing. He brought it to me the morning of his departure for Fort Clark. Told me—ordered me, actually—to read it and make sure it was given to you. I read it and took the liberty of having my clerk type it and provide carbon copies."

"He's been watching the wolves for years," she said, alert and interested.

"The notes date from Ramsay's arrival here three years ago as First Sergeant of B Troop. There's a year's gap during his time in the Philippines and then in Letterman Hospital in San Francisco. Carrie, he was badly wounded in that assault on the cave," Major Pitcher said. "I'm certain you haven't seen his injury." He chuckled. ". . . At least not yet."

"Major Pitcher," she said and blushed.

"One of the insurrectionists took a real slice at his ribcage. He said fifty stitches closed the wound. I know he nearly died of the infection."

"I didn't know."

Major Pitcher tapped the documents in her lap. "One of the entries states how the wolves helped him heal. He watched them and wrote that something happened to his heart."

He leaned back in his chair, staring out the imaginary window that only men who have seen combat seemed to look through. Ramsay did it too. "He was so weak and thin when he came back here in November. I didn't think he'd survive the winter. Gradually, he began to perk up and did mention to me that he was watching the wolves. When he and I went East for that medal ceremony, he seemed almost himself again. Yellowstone healed him."

"The wolves did," Carrie said.

Through a blurry film, Carrie pressed the handwritten set of notes to her breast, holding them close as she yearned to hold their author close. She thought about the past month. To her infinite relief, serenity began to replace anxiety. Maybe the wolves would be kind enough to heal her too.

She smiled at the major, unable to speak.

"Are we friends again?" he asked.

"We are. I do have a favor to ask."

"Ask away."

"I want one more copy to send to Mrs. Louise LaMarque. She's knows what is going on, and this will soothe her too. And may I have another copy of your letter, as well?"

"Done and done, Miss McKay." Major Pitcher turned around and picked up what she requested from his desk. "We're doing what we can. I'm perfectly willing to go to Fort Clark and see if my presence will help."

"Thank you," Carrie said. "In fact, if I scribble a note on this copy for Mrs. LaMarque, could you mail it as soon as possible? If I have to do that at Willow Park, that adds another day or two until it gets going."

"Done again. I'll get an envelope from my clerk's desk."

She wrote a note to Louise LaMarque. In Major Pitcher's absence, she took the envelope from her shirtwaist and copied the Washington, DC, address on the note. When he returned, she handed him the note and documents.

"Very well, Carrie," he said as he put everything into the large envelope. "It'll be on tonight's train."

He escorted her to the boarded sidewalk, where Fred Lonnigan waited.

"Will we succeed, sir?" she asked after Fred handed her up to the driver's seat.

"I wish I knew," the major said. "Write him every week, and stay busy yourself."

"I can do that. Thanks, Major Pitcher," she said as Fred gathered the reins. "I'm sorry I was difficult."

"No need to apologize," the major said. "Ramsay is far too valuable to languish in prison. Now, we wait."

Chapter Thirty-Seven

$\mathcal{B}$onnie Boone was the first person Carrie saw at Willow Park Camp. With tears on her face, the cook opened her arms and grabbed Carrie into an embrace that went on and on.

After a loud session with handkerchiefs, Bonnie sat Carrie down in the empty dining hall and made her recount the whole wonderful, miserable trip. By the time she was finished, the cook told her to report for work when she felt like it. "Just this once," she teased and then hugged Carrie again.

Carrie let herself be escorted to Tent Twenty-Six by her roommates and the Great Trostini, who insisted on knowing who he could write to at Fort Clark.

"I've spared you this bit of snobbery, but my father is president of Seattle Electric Light Company. He knows General Nelson Miles quite well from Civil War days," Jake Trost told her.

"General Miles?" Carrie asked. She thought Ramsay had mentioned him once, but she was stupefied with exhaustion and misery.

"My dear, he is General of the Army," Jake said with a smile. "Touché! Never hurts to throw around a title."

"Whatever you can, Jake," she said, then put up her hand to stifle a yawn. "My word, but I am tired."

He gave her a Great Trostini salaam at the door to her tent, so she was smiling as she went inside. In a matter of minutes, she had shucked off her clothes and succumbed to sleep.

Carrie slept around the clock, waking at four the next afternoon. Eyes still half-closed, she lay in bed listening to the rain as a late-afternoon storm bullied its way over the Gallatin Mountains and through Willow Park, heading east. Hands behind her head, she lay there wondering what was happening to Ramsay. Knowing her leisure would end the moment she poked her head outside the tent, Carrie read the army clerk's transcription of Ram's years-long observation of the wolves. She started reading the neatly typed pages and then changed to the dear man's original account, desperate to be as close to him as she could by reading his own handwriting.

His meticulous attention to detail touched her heart as he described watching pups play under the watchful eye of their parents and other pack members. He wrote of eagles swooping low on the air currents in Lamar Valley, curious and wondering in that way of birds of prey out for possible misadventure, as Ram wrote, . . . *if there might be a meal somewhere in it for them.*

He described the wolf pack, noting subservience among younger males, and then the rejection of a *low-on-the-totem-pole* male. *The top wolf and his mate drove him out with nips and bites,* she read. *Tail down, dejected, he slunk away to try his luck with another pack, if he can find one. He is a lone wolf, and I understand him.*

Her heart increasingly tender, Carrie read of Ramsay's own struggles through the past winter, when he lamented the eradication of wolves by troopers stationed at isolated cabins. *No one seems to understand the role of the wolf here,* she read. *When the packs are gone—I give them twenty years—the elk and deer will overpopulate Wonderland. I have to wonder what else will change. The water? The land-scape? The trout in the streams and lakes? I wish I knew more.*

She read one section over and over, the page in early spring of this year where Ramsay Stiles seemed more at peace with himself. *I woke up one morning thinking of wolves, as I often do,* he had written. *I laid in bed and realized I haven't been in that awful cave in a long time. I rejoice. I thank the wolves.*

His final entry called out those silent tears again. He must have written it just before he turned his field notes over to Major Pitcher and left for Fort Clark and likely punishment. The entry told of his last sight of the wolves, seen with Carrie McKay and Louise LaMarque. *We watched in silence as the meadow below us turned into a wolf playground, with the pack at ease and enjoying the fellowship of wolf companions. I have watched this pack for three years. I suspect that wolves mate for life. I was in the same mood, as I sat by Miss Carrie McKay. I can write no more.*

It seemed so unromantic, callous even, but as she sat up in her cot, Carrie felt her stomach growl. She was hungry, she was wide awake, and she wanted to work. She neatly shuffled and tapped the papers until they were orderly, because she needed order. She put them in her cubbyhole to be close at hand. Even a touch in the middle of the night might be soothing.

She washed her face and dressed, content to be in her shapeless work dress with the big apron. She subdued her tangled hair with a stiff brush and then braided it into one braid. She couldn't help laughing when she realized that Mrs. LaMarque still had her better pair of sturdy shoes, the no-nonsense brogans that had taken her through the park. *Mail them back, Mrs. LaMarque*, she thought and then realized when she returned to Bozeman, she could splurge for a new pair.

The Medal of Honor went under her pillow. She put Ramsay's note and bankbook in a spare envelope and took them to the Wylie office where Miss Lackey put them into the safe.

Without saying a word, Carrie took her place in the kitchen, helping with the last-minute preparation of tonight's Idaho baked potatoes and homely meatloaf and gravy that always seemed to vanish because everyone liked it, especially the wealthier visitors who came to the Wylie Camps because they wanted to rough it. The crusts on someone else's apple and peach pies didn't survive Carrie's critical scrutiny, which meant her job as pie maker was secure for the remainder of the season, starting tomorrow morning at four o'clock.

She worked silently and efficiently, grateful for the peace that cooking never failed to give her. By the end of the dinner shift, Carrie found herself laughing at the latest foible of one of the tourists, reluctant to leave her three cats in cages in Bozeman while she toured the park.

"She brought them along, and one of them escaped. It was an awful sight," Bonnie told her as they scraped leftovers into a bucket for the bears. "He climbed out on a tree limb. One of the Norris soldiers fetched him back, but not without scratches. I think all of us learned new words."

Dressed in black trousers, white frilly shirt, and sporting a red sash, the Great Trostini made a special kitchen visit, asking if she felt up to singing tonight after his performance.

"Only if you feel like it, Carrie," he told her. He glanced at Bonnie and moved closer. "Sergeant Major Stiles stopped here and told me to keep an eye on you the rest of the summer. Said he didn't want to hear of any more tall tales. I told him we'd be vigilant. It did put a smile on his face."

"He's been kind to me. I'll sing, but I won't sing 'Why, No One to Love' anymore," she said, too shy to say more.

Singing was harder than she thought it would be. She faltered on the chorus, 'Home, home, sweet, sweet home,' thinking of Ramsay in shackles staring up at a postage stamp sky through iron bars.

To her relief, Sophie sitting on the front row leaped to her feet and joined Carrie. Soon everyone was singing, and Carrie knew two things: she had friends, and she could manage.

Day by day, Carrie settled into camp routine again. She cooked, she smiled, she was polite about tourists' sometimes-odd questions, and she even sang a much tamer version of "Ta-ra-ra-boom-de-ay" with Sophie. She did her best and fooled even herself, until she could retire to her tent, prepare for bed, and take the Medal of Honor out from under her pillow for a long look.

If sleep wouldn't come, she had permission from Bonnie Boone to go into the dining hall, light a lamp, and write a letter to Fort Clark. She poured out her heart to Ramsay Stiles, writing how she missed him and loved him. She didn't mention his bank account and medal, because she feared someone in a position to do him further harm might open his letters first. She told him the

stories of odd questions and strange doings that constituted a season with tourists.

She wrote every other day, because during one long
night she woke up, tears on her face, convinced that only
her letters were keeping army justice at bay. It was irrational, but she couldn't help herself.

As August edged toward the downward slide to
September, she received her first mail from Fort Clark,
three letters that arrived on the same day.

"It's not your imagination that everyone in the Wylie
Company wants to know when you hear from your sergeant," Mr. Wylie said when he dropped off the mail for
Willow Park. "Humor your boss. Open it and at least
reassure Old Man Wylie that he's not behind bars yet."

Carrie did as he asked, breathing her own sigh of
gratitude that after the words " 'My Dearest Caroline,' "
fast becoming her favorite salutation in the history of
writing, Ramsay wrote, " 'I'm still twiddling my thumbs
in my room and not the guardhouse.' "

Mr. Wylie waved her to a stop. "That's all I need to
know," he said. "Every stop I make, the savages want to
know how he's doing." He thought a moment. "Come to
think of it, the soldiers at the various stations have been
flagging me down for news from Texas."

He took her letters to mail to Fort Clark and went on
his way. Since it was early afternoon and all the evening's
prep work could wait a half hour, Carrie took her letters
to her tent, kicked off her shoes, and lay down to read in
comfort.

My Dearest Caroline. There were only three thin
letters, so she rationed them to last her the entire half
hour before she had to report to Bonnie Boone for
dinner. She read those three words over and over
until they blended into one word: Mydearestcaroline.

Mydearestcaroline. She said them softly until the little trio began to hypnotize her in much the same way Coleridge's perhaps better-known poem did: "InXanadudidkublaikhanastatelypleasuredomedecree," which made her laugh.

As much as you worry, I am not shackled and in chains, although I am confined to barracks, he wrote in the first letter. *At least I am until one of the officers gets permission to take me to one of Fort Clark's classrooms, where I instruct brand new lieutenants in the art of war in the Philippines.*

"My goodness," she said out loud, and read the words again slowly, thinking of her darling man, there for punishment, teaching others because he had experience they needed. "I can't imagine that pleased the colonel too much."

She read more. *Colonel Ward was upset in the extreme when he found out what his captains were doing, but then he stayed and listened. That can't hurt my cause.*

She finished the letter, reading over and over the last two paragraphs where he asked her to go to Solfatara Plateau if possible, and check on his wolves. *Dave Lassiter shouldn't be too hard to convince. Take along Jake Trost too.*

"You keep pushing Jake on me, Ram," she told the letter.

In the second letter, he grew more serious, telling her of the humiliation of a monumental dressing down from Colonel Ward in front of the entire garrison. *I was the prize pig, the bad example,* he wrote. *It was a blistering scold, administered with me standing at attention on the parade ground in the Texas heat and everyone listening from the shade of the porches.*

She read through a film of tears, wondering if the army was the cruelest organization in the world since the Inquisition. She did hear the triumph in his final words, at least before he started those last few paragraphs telling her how much he loved her. *I took his abuse for an hour and was marched back to my room in the barracks. I closed the door, then threw up all over the place. What a mess, but at least I didn't embarrass myself in front of the entire garrison.*

His third letter was a restless one, full of doubts as the time dragged on and still the colonel didn't assemble the officers for a court martial. The only bright spot was her letters, and the whispered word from a fellow sergeant who brought Ramsay an evening meal and told him, "You should see the letters coming in from everywhere in your favor."

So that's where it stands, dear heart, he concluded. *I walk back and forth in my room, and up and down on the veranda when I can wangle permission. I clean out latrines and scrub floors, and police the parade ground with my burlap sack and sharp-pointed stick. I'm becoming immune to humiliation, especially when some of the lieutenants and their sergeants walk along with me and ask me about the Philippines, and jungle warfare. They know they must understand what to expect before they ship out, and I oblige them. I think of my lieutenant and want these men to come home in one piece. I am doing my duty. It could be worse, dearest Caroline.*

Campfire singing was purgatory that night, fearing every moment that her cheerful façade would rub off and expose her pain, sorrow, and longing to people who were here for an adventure in Wonderland. She forced herself to warble Stephen Foster's sentimental tunes, flirt a little and belt out "Ta-ra-ra-boom-de-ay" with Sophie, determined to please. All the while, her mind and heart remained centered on a brave man in Texas, suffering daily shame all because he could not kill wolves.

That was the last of the letters. Nothing followed nothing, until the August afternoon when one of the drivers tipped his hat to her and dropped off a box with a Washington, D.C., address. All the housemaids, kitchen staff, and laundresses hanging around the Wylie store for mail call gasped in unison as Carrie pulled out a dark blue traveling suit wrapped in tissue paper. It was simple, elegant, and understated. So was the light blue silk blouse that practically slithered from a smaller box.

Everyone chuckled over Carrie's work shoes, which the grand dame returned. The darling dark blue hat with its small feathers and curled brim was greeted with open-mouthed wonder. More sighs—Carrie's the loudest—greeted the froth of silk drawers and two silk nightgowns.

"It'll take more than silk to keep you warm in Montana," one of the savages teased.

"That's what Carrie is hoping," another maid said. Everyone laughed and Carrie blushed.

Silent astonishment accompanied the last item, a black lace brassiere that sent Bonnie Boone into an excellent imitation of a swoon.

The attached note read, *I think you'll have your sergeant major's full attention with this little number. Love, Louise.*

There was a post script in the lady's increasingly small handwriting that Carrie saved until her friends trooped away to read their own mail.

She held it up to the light, her heart full with gifts that had come exactly when she needed them.

Don't lose hope, she read. *This isn't over.*

Chapter Thirty-Eight

*H*opeful, Carrie waited for more letters. None came. Tired of tears, she started walking Willow Park meadow alone, humoring Jake and Bonnie by taking along a pot to bang on and a wooden spoon. "Sing too," Jake said. "Bang that pot and scare those bears."

No idiot, she did as they said and was rewarded with bears seen at a distance and no closer, even though she knew she had a good voice—Jake laughed over that when she told him. She sat on a small boulder and watched distant mama bears and cubs grown fat on cutthroat trout and berries, as she imagined Ramsay used to watch the wolves.

She knew it was the time of late summer when bears started eating everything in sight, bulking up for a long winter's hibernation. She contemplated hibernation, wondering if she could eat a lot, sleep all winter, and wake up to find Ramsay Stiles back in Yellowstone.

No letters. Then came the day when two of her letters were returned, stamped "Not At This Address." Wordless, she showed those to Bonnie as they were prepping dinner and then threw herself into Bonnie's kind embrace. Sophie sang in her place that night as Carrie lay in bed, the Medal of Honor in her hand and Ram's wolf observation field notes on her stomach. Her eyes were dry; she was finally beyond tears.

Before dinner on the following day, Captain Chittenden surprised her in the kitchen as she banged out yeast rolls, kneading with ferocity aimed at the evil US Army that didn't know how to treat a good man with sense. She jumped when he tapped her on the shoulder, then she forgot herself and grabbed him by the arms.

"Where is he?" she demanded but let go and stepped back, appalled at herself.

Apparently not an easy man to ruffle, the engineer took her hand and led her into the empty dining room.

"I don't know where he is," he said after she apologized profusely and sat down. He had an envelope tucked under his arm, labeled like her most recent letters, with that pernicious, we-know-but-you-don't stamp. He opened the envelope and took out a photograph of a major portion of his summer work. "I had Jack Haynes develop this right away and I mailed it to Ramsay. Look at it."

Her own social error forgotten, she gazed in open-mouthed delight at the graceful bridge that was labeled "Melan Arch of the Yellowstone."

"Melan?" she asked.

"An Austrian engineer. I admire his work and I wanted that shallow arch," he said.

"This is beautiful, Captain Chittenden," she said, thinking of the bridge work she had observed with Louise LaMarque. She mentally moved on because it was either that or dissolve into a puddle. So much for her resolution on no tears. "You know what Ramsay would say."

"I think I do."

"'Captain, you can call it what you want, but people here will name it the Chittenden Bridge, whether you like it or not,'" she said, imitating her dear man's clipped speech. "You know that's what he would say." She took a deep breath. "Where is he?"

"I wish I knew. I'll be honest, Carrie, because you deserve that—he's probably en route to Fort Leavenworth."

She nodded, unable to speak but unwilling to cry. "Will he be allowed letters eventually?" she asked when she could talk without choking up.

"Eventually."

She tried to hand back the photograph, but he shook his head. "Keep it. Send it to him when you get his address. I'm on my way to see Nettie and our children. I'll be another four days on the corkscrew road toward Cody and then back to Mammoth to accompany them to Sioux City."

"If you hear anything, let me know," she said. "I don't care how bad the news. I have to know."

"Absolutely. When I get to Fort Yellowstone, I'll ask Major Pitcher what he knows."

She walked with him to his horse, waved good-bye, and stood there until he was out of sight, going home to his family. For a moment she imagined herself standing on a porch at Fort Yellowstone, watching for Ramsay coming home from hearing tourists' complaints, advising the troopers under him, observing wolves—whatever Yellowstone threw at him. She would sit him down in the kitchen, give him hot buttered bread or maybe pie, and listen, chin in hand, while he described so meticulously what he had done that day or week in Wonderland.

" 'Why, No One to Love'?" she said softly and returned to her kitchen duties.

In a hurry, Mr. Wylie stopped by on his weekly circuit of his tourist camps, telling his assistant manager to begin dismantling one row of red-and-white-striped tents. "It's been a good summer with satisfactory numbers for us," he told all his Willow Park savages assembled in the dining hall. "You've done your best. I'd like to hear from you this winter, if you wish to return."

He promised them a little bonus in their last paycheck next week, which brought cheers, and he ate cherry pie with the housemaids, kitchen flunkies, and camp men who were headed back to the college grind, or classrooms of their own.

"No word, Carrie?" he asked when he held out his plate for another slice.

"Not even a paragraph, Mr. Wylie," she said. "If I've learned nothing else this summer, I've learned patience."

"You've learned more than that," he said, gesturing her to sit down. "Mary Ann told me about Mrs. LaMarque's generous tip. You're going to have a good final year. I hope you'll still find time for Sunday dinner at the Wylie house."

Her smile was genuine. "I wouldn't miss it. Thanks for everything, sir."

"Any time." He started to rise but then sat down again and leaned closer. "Here's some news that might interest you—Millie Thorne resigned from the Lake Camp a month ago and headed back East to stay with her cousin."

"I honestly hope she'll be careful," Carrie said, unwilling to imagine any sort of proximity to the terrifying man who tried to ruin Carrie in the Railroad Hotel kitchen. "She won't be at Montana Ag?"

"No. You sound surprisingly charitable to Millie Thorne, who did her best to make your life miserable," Mr. Wylie said.

"Life is full of lessons," she replied, and held out her hand. "I'll stop by your Gardiner office before I leave."

For once, she didn't mind the tedium of the kitchen inventory. Bonnie Boone packed what supplies she could, even though a few days remained with a dwindling number of tourists arriving and departing. As Carrie was checking off foodstuffs that could be safely stored, she realized it had been more than a month since she had taken extra bits of food to her tent each night.

"Bonnie, I haven't needed any crackers or peanuts lately," she said.

"You did at first. What changed?"

"I did," Carrie said softly. "I met Ramsay Stiles and didn't feel so frightened. Why is that? Maybe I should be afraid again, but I'm not."

Bonnie seemed to consider her question. She flicked idly at spice jars and wiped the lids. "Did he give you confidence?"

"I think so," Carrie said. "So did Mrs. LaMarque. So did you. I can always have a career in Yellowstone making pies!" They laughed together. "I feel like a grown woman now," Carrie said after more reflection. "After all, I have a traveling suit, a black brassiere, and a plan when I graduate." She smiled at Bonnie. "And friends."

"Give yourself more credit," Bonnie said. "You're saying all of us made you brave. My dear, it started with you."

What was easy to say in the quiet of the afternoon was more difficult to remember as that final campfire

363

approached. Sophie had packed her valise because she was leaving in the morning to return to Ashton, Idaho, and classroom duties. The other two maids had already left for Eugene, Oregon, and school, so Tent Twenty-Six was almost empty. Two more days of cleanup would end Carrie's stay in Wonderland. Jake Trost was catching the same train as Sophie, but heading west to Seattle and his final semester.

He had taken her aside that afternoon before the tourists arrived for dinner, inviting her to Seattle in October for homecoming. "U-Dub has a pretty good football team, plus I'd like you to see my city and meet my parents," he told her. "What do you say, Carrie McKay?"

What could she say? With the exception of a sergeant major in prison in Fort Leavenworth, no other man had cared for her that summer as well as Jake. She shook her head, even though Ram had told her civil engineers had good careers ahead of them in this new century, and a comfortable life.

"I'm sorry, Jake, but no," she said, dismayed to see the chagrin in his eyes, but firm in her resolve. "My heart wouldn't be in it."

She already knew Jake was a solid fellow, confident even with a turndown. "I didn't think you'd accept," he said, serious enough this time to touch her heart. "I wish you would, but there's a sergeant major on your mind."

"He'd probably tell me that wasn't the wisest choice I'd ever made," she said.

"He probably would, and you'd ignore him in that polite way of yours," he told her. "You know who you want." He kissed her cheek. "If you ever change your mind, just write me care of Seattle Electric Light Company."

She began the final campfire more lighthearted than she would have thought possible. Two more mornings of pie making and bread baking lay ahead, then it was time to pack, think about the fall semester, and head for Bozeman. She had finalized plans to stay in one of the new co-ops closer to campus where everyone pitched in and saved money by doing all the cleaning and cooking. She knew she could afford a regular boardinghouse, but she was still Carrie and mindful of her funds.

The tourists who assembled on the logs in the campfire circle were bundled up more heavily, as they had been at the beginning of summer. The Great Trostini began his by-now expertly inept magic tricks, but stopped as a V of geese flew overhead. Carrie watched them too, with that mixture of anticipation of a new season and realization that winter was coming fast. The summer had turned into autumn, which in Yellowstone meant a brief respite before cruel winter. She had given her heart to a sergeant major, met a perfectly delightful old Broadway star turned socialite, and begun what she knew would be her own annual pilgrimage to the majesty of the Grand Canyon of the Yellowstone. All in all, not a bad summer.

She sang "My Old Kentucky Home," first, which always brought applause and some sniffs in handkerchiefs from the more sentimental visitors. "Nellie Was a Lady," kept the tears flowing, which she dried out with her solitary rendition of "Ta-ra-ra-boom-de-ay," and a little ankle and knee.

Then it was over. She stepped forward as she always did and asked if anyone had a favorite. Silence and then from the back row came a familiar voice.

" 'Why, No One to Love?' Sing that for me, Caroline."

Chapter Thirty-Nine

*C*arrie shook her head to clear it, then put her hands to her mouth as Ramsay Stiles walked toward the dying campfire.

If anything, he looked even thinner in the face. Her eyes went to his uniform sleeves, which still bore the usual chevrons, rockers, and hash marks.

"If you can't sing it, will you at least give this sergeant major a hug?" he asked as the tourists looked around, wondering what to expect.

The time to be shy was long past between her and Ramsay. Her face still but her heart racing, Carrie kept walking toward him until she was wrapped in his arms. He put his hand on her head and tucked her close to his chest in a gesture of protection that took away in amazing short order the awful pain of separation and fear of the unknown.

"I've been so worried," she whispered, for his ears only.

"You're not alone in that," he replied. "I have quite a story for you."

She looked around, startled, at the sound of applause. The little group of late-season tourists cheered and applauded.

"And that, ladies and gentlemen, is our season finale," the Great Trostini said. "It looks like a happy ending to me."

The tourists dispersed to their tents, passing Carrie and Ramsay so close together, his hand still protective on her head. Jake stopped to shake Ramsay's free hand.

"I tried to convince her that engineering was a lot more secure than whatever you're up to, sir, but she wasn't buying it," he said.

"Maybe she's not as bright as we thought," Ramsay teased and kissed the top of her head.

"She is," Jake said. "The campfire, such as it is, is all yours. See you later in Tent Twenty, sergeant major?"

"More than likely."

Everyone was gone. Carrie looked up and he took his hand away. "I don't care how bad or good things are," she said, "but you'd better kiss me right now."

He did, starting with a gentle kiss, then proceeding to a more inspired one, a kiss long and deep and full of the promise of more to come. He took her breath away. Everlastingly practical, she had read that phrase in many a short story in *McCall's* or the brand-new *Redbook* and deemed it impossible. Standing there and enjoying a thorough kiss, she wasn't so certain.

"Gotta breathe, Caroline," he said, sounding breathless.

He stopped her when she moved toward the campfire. "Nope. Bonnie Boone just told me we could use the dining hall and she promised not to peek. I need to see your face while I convince you to marry me, and it's too dark here."

"I won't require much convincing," she said.

"There's more to it than that."

Hand in hand, they walked to the dining hall, where some of the tables and chairs were already stacked on top of each other, ready to be moved to winter storage in Gardiner.

"Looks like the end of summer in here, as sure as geese overhead and elk bugling and fighting," Ramsay said as he surveyed the evidence. He pointed toward a table closer to the kitchen, the one with a kerosene lamp lit and glowing.

"You sit down," Carrie said. "I have something for you."

She walked to the empty kitchen and took a plate and fork from the cupboard. The slice of cherry pie she had saved from each day's baking went onto the plate. There wasn't any whipped cream, but Ramsay Stiles wasn't a man requiring frills.

She put the cherry pie in front of him and sat beside him. "I've been saving a piece back every day. I didn't know I would see you again, but I hoped."

He gave her a look that said more than words, and ate the serving. She watched him eat, enjoying the sight of a pleased man, her man no matter what. After he finished and wiped his lips, he turned around on the bench. "Come on. I have a good lap."

She sat on his lap. "This is nice," Ramsay said when his arms went around her. He held her off a little, the better to see her face. "I love you, Caroline," he said. "There's no fancy way to say it."

"You just covered the subject," she replied. "I love you too. Heavens, when those last letters of mine were returned, I was certain you were on your way to Fort Leavenworth."

"Actually, no, but I was told not to contact anyone," he said. "I fear Lieutenant Colonel Ward has a mean streak. There was nothing he wanted better than to court martial me and send me to Fort Leavenworth to break up rocks for paving stones." He sighed. "He would have been within his rights, I have no doubt."

"Then why in the world are you here?" she asked simply.

His hand went to her head again and he pulled her close. "I owe a debt to everyone at Fort Yellowstone. You should have seen the stack of letters on his desk when he hauled me into his office for that final time before kicking me loose. Letters from officers, men, drivers, the Wylies, Captain Chittenden in particular, and most important, Major Pitcher's letter with my wolf field notes."

"I read them," she said. "Well, I read them every night. I have a carbon copy, plus your original notes. Major Pitcher thought I should have them."

"Nice to know where they are," he told her. "There were an equal number of letters from officers and sergeants garrisoned right there at Fort Clark, getting ready to ship overseas to the Philippines. Those guerillas refuse to show the white flag."

He held her off again. "Caroline, I spent so much time talking to officers and noncoms about jungle warfare. We've never fought like this before and there are huge gaps in everyone's education."

"Knowing you, you probably wrote a little manual," she said, only half in jest.

"I did. The wolves were more fun," he said.

He looked at her for a long moment. Carrie realized, perhaps for the first time, what a patient observer

Ramsay Stiles was. She knew he was watching her expression, much as a wolf studied his landscape, unblinking, cautious, but confident, because wolves were made that way. She had learned a lot reading and rereading his wolf study.

"Is this where I nudge you and lean in like the top lady wolf?" she asked, and he laughed out loud, a sound that filled her with joy. He was free; he was happy.

"Yeah, this would be a good time for that. I need to figure out a better term than 'top lady wolf'."

Laughing, Carrie nudged his chest and leaned in. His arms tightened around her and she felt rather than heard his laugh.

"One of the captains garrisoned at Fort Clark told me later of the rousing arguments between Colonel Ward and his officers, but I have to tell you what tipped the scales for me. It came from an unexpected source, but if you think about it, maybe neither of us should be surprised—Louise LaMarque."

Carrie gasped. "I . . . I wrote her and sent her a copy of your wolf study," she said when she could speak.

"Thank goodness you did that. President Roosevelt is quite the conservationist," Ramsay said. "The president himself told me Mrs. LaMarque stormed into his office, slapped down that report, and demanded he read it."

"I can see her doing precisely that," Carrie said. "She's impossible to ignore."

"Indeed! President Roosevelt then telegrammed Colonel Ward and asked what in the Sam Hill was going on at Fort Clark. A few lengthy telegrams went back and forth, which led eventually to my freedom. For the record, let me state that Colonel Ward is not a happy man right now." Ramsay shook his head. "What a dilemma!

The colonel would love to hand me my head on a platter, but he knows I have the president's ear. "

Carrie pulled away for a comprehensive look of her own. "Wait a minute. 'The president himself,' you said? You talked to President Roosevelt?" She gave him a less-genteel nudge then poked her finger in his chest. "Where have you really been, Sergeant Major Stiles? It had better be a good story."

"Wow, Carrie McKay, if I were a wolf, I'd be on the floor right now on my back and groveling! That's a hard tone to take with the man of your dreams."

"You are a goof," she said. "Don't stop now, mister."

"That's why I couldn't tell you where I was headed. National security and all that," he said. "I spent three delightful days at Sagamore Hill with the president of the United States," Ramsay said, and Carrie heard the awe in his voice. "He generally spends a portion of the summer at his estate there. We talked about Yellowstone and wolves, and protection for animals, and the army and war. He wore me out."

"My goodness," was all Carrie could say.

"He made me an offer, and so did Colonel Ward," Ramsay said, serious now. "Hold off a bit and look me right in the eye. This is going to be your decision."

She put both hands on his chest. "No, Ram. You're the man doing the work. I'll be home making cherry pie and probably growing babies." She blushed. "Well, it's true."

"Most likely. But if you're not happy with my choice, ten to one, you won't be happy with me," he told her. "You have the worst poker face in the history of the game. You'd never earn a dime."

She laughed and kissed him.

"Wow, Caroline," he said finally. "Pay attention now. Against his will I am positive, Colonel Ward offered me the position of Command Sergeant Major of the regiment. CSM Fuller recently retired and the spot is open. What else could the colonel do, with Roosevelt breathing down his neck?"

"From miscreant to command sergeant major," Carrie said. "You amaze me, Ram."

"In this position, I will be immediately posted back to the Philippines, where we are still fighting," he said. His shoulders relaxed. "I see a big 'no' your eyes, Caroline."

"What a great honor for you, but no," she said firmly. "No more Philippines."

"Good choice, dear heart! Fort Clark is hot and dry and doesn't look anything like Yellowstone," he said. "You'd be living there while I was overseas, and you'd hate it as much as I do."

"Are you somehow going to stay in the army?" she asked.

"Patience, patience, Miss McKay. Here's the next offer. You ready for this? President Roosevelt offered me a position in the Secret Service."

Carrie gasped and grabbed him around the neck. "What an honor!"

"My word, yes. I spent another week in Washington, learning about the operation of the Secret Service."

"Ramsay, do you always land on your feet?" Carrie said.

"Only since I met you," he assured her. He touched his forehead to hers.

"President Roosevelt told me he'd been thinking about it since that little kerfluffle at Gardiner during the dedication of the arch. Apparently Mrs. LaMarque assured him

I was a steady fellow who didn't mind apologizing when in the wrong, and was ever-watchful otherwise."

He turned deadly serious then and took her face in his hands. "Carrie, we'll be living in Washington, D.C. I have to tell you—Colonel Ward informed me that whatever I decide, I won't be allowed to return to Yellowstone Park in any official capacity. I'm here to clean out my quarters." He kissed her. "And propose. The president found that amusing, but Colonel Ward did not. Will it be Washington? Think about it."

Carrie thought about it. "I won't be able to see the mountains, or Bozeman, or anyplace that matters to me." She stopped speaking, angry with herself. An offer like that from the president of the United States wasn't something to carelessly turn down.

Ramsay rubbed his cheek gently against hers. "I see another 'no' in your eyes."

Agitated, Carrie stood up and walked to the door of the dining room and then back again, rubbing her arms, ready to cry. She stopped in front of the man she adored, knowing he was watching her traitor face. "It's an honor and a privilege to serve this president, and the ones to follow. You should take this offer."

"I still see a 'no,'" he told her. "Carrie, you're also a dreadful liar."

She sat down with a plop, closer to him, but only if he reached out, which he did. She edged toward him. "I think I would be . . . I know I would be sad to leave this area, but you're not allowed here anymore. I have to have you. What are we going to do?"

It was his turn to stand up and walk. "Don't leave," she said, suddenly alarmed. "I'll learn to like wherever you are. Please don't leave me."

"I'm not leaving, not ever again, Caroline," he told her and sat next to her, their hips touching. "When I left here under as black a cloud as a person can think of, I rode Xerxes to Jack Strong's place before I got on the train."

"I still need to meet that man, don't I?" she asked, trying to lighten the mood.

"You might, depending," he replied. "I knew Xerxes would be okay if I left him there. Earlier today, I had the train drop me off at Jack's. Xerxes was happy to see me. I sat at Jack's kitchen table and told him what I told you, and whined about my choices." He nudged her. "I whine sometimes."

"Ramsay Stiles, everyone does," she said patiently.

"He wrote a little note for you. Told me not to look at it." He reached into his pocket. "Here it is."

"Confess. You peeked."

"I did," he said, which surprised her, but there was nothing in his bland expression that suggested a hint of his own feelings. Ramsay could probably have made a fortune at a poker table. "Command sergeant major, the Secret Service, or what's in that note, Caroline. I mean when I say it has to be your decision. I value you far too much to not consider *our* future, not just mine."

She took the note with her name printed on it in almost childlike block letters. She opened it, read it, and couldn't help her tears. Wordless, she handed it to the man she was going to marry, and watched his expression change. He let out a deep sigh and leaned back against the table. Then he looked at her.

"I see yes in those pretty eyes."

She nodded, too overcome to speak. She watched his eyes this time, and knew she was looking at "yes."

He read the note silently, then out loud, as though he still didn't think it would be real to either of them until he spoke the words on the page. "'Miss McKay, I'm deeding this ranch to you and your whiner of a husband. I have no children. I know he likes it here. We'll see how Ramsay likes it at three on a February morning when he's pulling calves. He says you're a Montana girl through and through, no matter how you got here. You decide and tell me soon. Jack.'"

"It's a deal, Ramsay Stiles," she said. "You'd better propose to me."

"I know you have another year of college to finish," he said, watching her eyes so closely.

"Plans change," she said firmly. "I'm not waiting a year to marry you."

"I need you too much to wait," he said frankly. "Maybe you can finish college later."

"Our children will finish in my place," she told him. "We need to get started on those children, Ram. You're not precisely a young man."

"And she makes cherry pie, President Roosevelt," he said to an imaginary audience. "I believe she had a pair of silk drawers too. Don't tell anyone except your friend, Louise LaMarque, sir."

"Several pairs now, and a silk nightgown! Mrs. LaMarque has been taking care of me too," Carrie said. "Well?"

"Miss McKay, it has come to my attention that a man of property needs to marry to ease his lot in life. Would you, could you, consent to matrimony?"

She kissed him. "Yes." He was going to be a fun husband. She could tell already.

"That blamed etiquette book that I studied at length earlier this summer says that you can refuse me once. Apparently young ladies are sometimes overcome with the idea of matrimony."

"I'm not overcome," Carrie said, because she was practical and in love. She kissed him again. "I hope you threw away that stupid book."

"Threw it away at Canyon Hotel. Our children will have to wade through their own matrimonial waters without the advice of nincompoops."

She sat on his lap again, and ventured to slide a few fingers inside his uniform blouse. "What's going to happen when wolves start to eye your newborn calves?"

"I'll figure it out." His hand went to her head again in that protective gesture. "You're buying into a hard life, my dearest Caroline."

She closed her eyes and thought of hard times in the Railroad Hotel, hard work earning nickels and dimes to scratch her way to a college education, hard labor from before dawn to after dusk at Willow Park. She balanced it on the scale of her love for Ramsay Stiles and smiled to herself as it tipped in his favor.

"It would be infinitely harder without you," she said. "Just take me to the Lower Falls now and then, and drive me across Captain Chittenden's Melan Arch Bridge when I get grumpy or you start to whine."

"Done, my love."

They sat close together. The wind picked up and she heard the pines start to whisper. Winter was here. Her mind was at rest. Her heart was full. Whether Ramsay was aware of it or not, Carrie knew she had been courted by a master.

Epilogue

After a night of no sleep in Tent Twenty, wishing he were in Tent Twenty-Six cuddling Carrie, Ramsay returned to his office at Fort Yellowstone. He wrote a letter to President Roosevelt declining his generous offer and told him about the ranch in Paradise Valley near Yankee Jim Canyon where he would always be welcome. The next letter went to Colonel Frederick Ward, declining his unwillingly given promotion as command sergeant major. The third letter went down the hall to Major Pitcher, stating his intention of not reenlisting for another five years, and severing his ties with the US Army, effective in one week on the annual date of his original enlistment.

The fourth letter took more time and thought. He wrote to Louise LaMarque, describing what had happened, thanking her for her role in all of it, and inviting her to visit them on the JBar81. He didn't have to ponder long before he signed it, "With love, Ramsay."

Ramsay's mother generally had a saying for most occasions. He recalled "Marry in haste, repent at leisure," but he didn't think his wedding to Carrie McKay in Major John Pitcher's parlor four days later would fit that description. Time, tide, and the army wait for no man. They had to move fast because Captain Chittenden was escorting his family home to Sioux City in six days, and the best man really needed to be in that parlor.

The Wylies brought their Presbyterian minister from Bozeman for the event, which Ramsay knew pleased Carrie to no end. Mrs. Pitcher scrounged silk flowers from somewhere to decorate an improvised altar, and her cook put together an impressive wedding cake on short notice.

They were married in Major Pitcher's parlor just as the first snow shower of the season pattered against the windows. Ramsay wore his dress uniform for the final time before it went into mothballs. His sweet Carrie had pinned the Medal of Honor in its accustomed place and kindly dabbed at the tears in his eyes.

She came into the parlor on Mr. Wylie's arm, looking charming in a blue traveling suit with a hat that tipped toward her forehead. Her hair was a mass of red and gold, carefully pinned. He thought about removing those pins one by one and brushing her hair, probably mere minutes after the ceremony, a little reception, and then a short walk to his house. He reconsidered; he could brush her hair later.

He may have started to twitch and fidget at the thought (he knew his face was red), because his best man suggested in a whisper that a deep breath now and then was a good idea. Captain Chittenden was wise enough to say no more, but his lips kept twitching during the mercifully brief ceremony.

To Ramsay's satisfaction, Jack Strong arrived for the wedding. When they were man and wife, the old Mountain Crow rancher put his arms around Ramsay and Carrie and assured her they would begin building a new house in the spring. Ramsay had to laugh when his brand new bride kissed Jack Strong's cheek and promised him that her brand new husband wouldn't be whining so much now.

Two days and two nights in noncommissioned officer's quarters were not the stuff of romance that a newly minted wife probably dreamed of, though he heard no complaints from Mrs. Stiles. On Day Two, she insisted on singing "Ta-ra-ra-boom-de-ay" barely dressed in an amazing black lace brassiere and silk drawers that made him feel considerably younger than his thirty-four years.

More snow held off long enough for a quick trip to the Upper Geyser Basin and Old Faithful, which Ramsay knew his wife wanted to see. He liked the way she leaned back against him as they watched the eruption. He had already learned how pleasant it was to rest his chin on her head, his arms around her.

Work had begun on a new hotel near Old Faithful. When it was done next summer, he and Carrie might be able to abandon ranch life for a few days and pay a visit.

On their return trip, he had no trouble convincing the Norris soldiers to let the Stiles commandeer the bathhouse. This led to the inexpressibly wonderful discovery that someone with gentle hands was willing to scrub his back.

He wanted one thing more, and it happened on the last night before he put away his ordinary uniform, dressed in civilian clothes, and shut the door on his quarters, a rancher now.

He lay awake, Carrie safely tucked close to him, asleep. At first he thought he imagined it, because he wanted so badly to hear from his wolves before his exile from permanent duty in Yellowstone began. No, there they were, howling their drawn-out lament to winter coming, and maybe their own demise. Hide, my friends, he silently ordered them. I can't help you now.

He only thought Carrie slept. There she was, wiping his eyes with a corner of the sheet and kissing his chest.

"You hear them, my love?" he asked, his heart breaking.

"I do." She rested her head on his chest, her arm tight across him. "They'll be back some day."

"You're certain?" He had to know.

"Plans change. Give it time. Rules change. Can you live with that, Ram?"

He could. He would.

Afterword

In his prediction to Carrie McKay, Sergeant Major Ramsay Stiles was not far off the mark on the extirpation of wolves in Yellowstone Park. By 1926, the last wolves were killed in the park.

In a 1986 article, "The Wolf Mystery," from *Playing God in Yellowstone Park*, the author states that the army didn't begin a systematic destruction of wolves in Yellowstone until 1914. My research in the summer of 2016 found something different. A 1907 edition of *The Red Book*, given to all soldiers in the park and first issued a few years earlier, plainly states, "Scouts and non-commissioned officers in charge of stations throughout the park are authorized and directed to kill mountain lions, coyotes and timber wolves. They will do this themselves and will not delegate the authority to anyone else."

Ramsay Stiles was also right about what would happen when the park's predators were gone. The elk population in particular proliferated to a degree that soon caused alarm among naturalists. The overgrazing of the range in the summer and the wintertime stripping of bark from trees and shrubs changed the entire landscape of Yellowstone National Park, and not for the better.

For years, attempts were made to regulate the elk population, leaving no one happy. From the 1940s on, there was a steady, persistent drumbeat by conservationists, biologists, and environmentalists to reintroduce wolves to Yellowstone Park. In 1995, it finally happened. By March, fourteen gray wolves imported from Canada were turned loose in the park's remote Lamar Valley. A similar number from the same source came in the following year.

Since then, the wolves have aligned themselves into some ten packs, numbering roughly ninety-five animals. These packs have distributed themselves over a wide area, with concentration still mainly in that north/northeast portion of the park. Wolves are protected in the park, but are subject to regulated hunting in nearby states, as their numbers have steadily grown. There are conflicts with ranchers, to be sure, but the wolves are back and destined to stay.

The return of the wolf has considerably altered the number of coyotes, who had returned to the park of their own volition years earlier. They tend to cluster more cautiously now in steeper elevations. The elk population has declined as predicted, which has meant improved grassland and trees in Yellowstone. The beaver have gone from one colony to many, since the elk population which used to eat the willows that beaver require has diminished. This fact has improved the park's streams and rivers.

And so Nature goes. My comments here barely touch the surface of what has changed so dynamically since the wolves returned, but then, you didn't read *Courting*

Carrie in Wonderland for an environmentalist's treatise, did you? And I didn't write it for that either.

Just as the wolves soothed Ramsay Stiles during a difficult time in his life, they have done the same for me. I suppose I should have known I would be writing a book that included wolves as characters since my own experience with one in October of 2010.

In April of that year, my dear father died. Dad was from Cody, Wyoming, Yellowstone's east entrance. As a family, we enjoyed Yellowstone vacations whenever Dad, a Navy man, had leave and we were not on the other side of the world or somewhere in between.

I happened to be in Yellowstone that October, right before major portions of the park closed for winter. I had been visiting Bob Kisthart, a back country ranger in the Old Faithful District, and I was on my way east to Cody early that morning.

I stopped at Fishing Bridge, one of Dad's favorite places. I stood there and watched the Yellowstone River flowing north out of the lake. My heart was heavy when I got back in my car and continued east on an empty road.

I can only credit kind Providence for what happened next. I was driving, thinking of Dad, when what should I see striding along in the westbound lane but a wolf. Let me tell you, that wolf owned the road. Once I realized I was staring at a wolf and not a coyote—wolves are a lot bigger, have different-shaped snouts, and really long legs—I smiled so big I thought my face would break.

The sight of that wolf, no longer being hunted out of existence or driven away because of misguided ideas, put the heart back in my body. I have largely told this story from Ramsay Stiles's viewpoint, because I know how he felt.

The more I researched Yellowstone Park—tough work, but I did it so you don't have to—the greater my appreciation grew for Lieutenant Dan Kingman and Captain Hiram Chittenden, US Army Corps of Engineers. In 1883, Kingman was first assigned to the park to survey for roads. He graduated second in his West Point class in 1874, which meant he was encouraged to go into the Corps of Engineers. Throughout the nineteenth century, West Point was the best engineering school in the United States.

It was Kingman who envisioned what became the Grand Loop, the road still followed today by all visitors. He created it to move tourists in logical fashion past all of the park's wonders, not necessitating any repetition. He also built the trestle viaduct in what became known as Kingman Canyon, on the road north from Norris to Mammoth and Fort Yellowstone, the park's headquarters then and now.

After Kingman moved on to other assignments, he was eventually followed by Captain Hiram M. Chittenden, US Army Corps of Engineers. Graduating third in his West Point class in 1884, Chittenden is arguably the most brilliant man to wear those distinctive Corps of Engineers turreted castles on his collar. In addition to stellar engineering in Yellowstone Park, he wrote the first major opus on the United States fur trade. An excellent scholarly work, *The Yellowstone National Park*, followed, as well as other books. Where he found the time, I have no idea.

A persuasive man with some pull in Congress, Chittenden achieved what no other engineer in the park managed—a huge appropriation to get the park's engineering on sound footing, instead of piecemeal dabs of funding.

In remarkably few years, Captain Chittenden made the existing roads better. He replaced Kingman's scary wooden trestle viaduct through the canyon that bears his name and turned it into a concrete wonder. His corkscrew road in the park's steep east side was a marvel of nineteenth century engineering, as well.

Nothing has ever surpassed the captain's splendid Melan Arch Bridge, which spanned the Yellowstone River just above the Upper Falls of the Grand Canyon of the Yellowstone. It was a masterpiece of engineering, constructed faultlessly in the wilderness under difficult conditions.

In 1961, the lovely arched bridge was torn down, despite protests, and replaced with another bridge more suited in width and structure for the park's modern traffic. I doubt the National Park Service wanted to demolish Chittenden's bit of poetry in concrete, but safety constraints necessitated it. The replacement bridge was fittingly named Chittenden Memorial Bridge. Other places in the park bear his name too.

There is more to say about Captain Chittenden, who went on to built the famous Ballard Chittenden Locks in Seattle. His health was never good, and he drove himself hard, which possibly led to his early death in 1917 at age 58. Yellowstone National Park and all of its millions of visitors, whether they know it or not, owe him a huge debt.

What about Thomas Moran, whom Louise LaMarque admired in devoted silence? He was an excellent landscape artist mostly known for his several views of the Lower Falls of the Grand Canyon of the

Yellowstone. The best tribute to Moran would be to go there and see what he saw. It is an amazing sight.

As I read many nineteenth-century tourist accounts of Yellowstone Park, I was struck by the fact that nearly all of them mention the Grand Canyon of the Yellowstone as their favorite place in Wonderland. Not the geysers. Not the hot springs.

I can't argue with them. In October of 2016, I paid a visit to the canyon as I was writing this book. To my rec-ollection, I hadn't been there in sixty years. I remember being highly impressed with the view when I was a kid. I was equally impressed during my more recent visit.

What a sight. What a place. What a park. In 2016, the National Park Service celebrated its centennial. August 25, 1916, was the official date, but rangering got off to a rocky start, plagued by a stingy Congress unwilling to adequately fund this new unit of the federal government. Some of the early rangers came from an existing group of Yellowstone civilian scouts, as well as troopers of the US Army who were allowed to transfer into the new Park Service.

Hired, then disbanded, then hired again, the rang-ers eventually began to make their mark in the national parks. However, not until 1918 did the last cavalry troop ride out of Yellowstone Park, leaving behind a legacy of good management and careful stewardship, in accor-dance with ideas of the time. The Park Service continues to honor the US Army by wearing the distinctive flat hat typical of army campaign hats of that earlier era. (Let me add here that the informal ball caps rangers wear are a lot easier to keep in place in a high wind.)

I was privileged to work in Yellowstone National Park in the summer of 1965 as an employee of the Yellowstone Park Company, making beds in tourist cabins at Mammoth Hot Springs. I learned the fine art of tucking hospital corners, hot potting in the Gardner River, and tolerating the pungent odor of sulfur. I recall making $1.47 an hour, minimum wage plus seven cents.

I might mention here that you've probably noticed the spellings of Gardner River and Gardiner, Montana. Both are correct. Blame some nineteenth century politician or mapmaker, if you wish.

If you are interested in learning more about Yellowstone Park, or the National Park Service itself, there are many good books on the subject. For research purposes, my personal favorite is Chittenden's impeccable work, *The Yellowstone National Park*. I also really enjoyed *Haynes Official Guide: Yellowstone National Park*.

The truly magisterial work on Yellowstone is *The Yellowstone Story*, volumes one and two, by Aubrey L. Haines, former park historian. Both are scholarly but highly readable. I recommend them.

For any of my readers who have persisted this far, let me offer my thanks to Kim Allen Scott, archivist of special collections at Montana State University in Bozeman for his assistance. Carrie McKay would be pleased to know how far her humble Montana Agricultural College has come. It's a fine campus in a lovely town.

I'm equally grateful to Park Service archivists at Yellowstone Heritage and Research Center, Gardiner, Montana, not far from the Roosevelt Arch. I found Wylie Camping Company brochures proclaiming the promise of Wonderland. I looked through many of the Red Books too, which have found their way into the archives. It's touching somehow to see that the little volumes are still shaped as if only recently removed from a soldier's hip pocket.

And thank you, Bob Kisthart, ranger/colleague and friend, for giving me a reason every summer—as if I need one—to visit the park, have lunch at Old Faithful Inn, and argue about which of us should be picking up the tab for that summer's meal. Through the years, you've answered many of my questions.

Carla Kelly
2016

About the Author

Photo by Marie Bryner-Bowles, Bryner Photography

$\mathcal{T}$here are many things that Carla Kelly enjoys, but few of them are as rewarding as writing. From her short stories about the frontier army in 1977, she's been on a path that has turned her into a novelist, a ranger in the National Park Service, a newspaper writer, a contract historical researcher, a hospital/hospice PR writer, and an adjunct university professor.

Things might be simpler if she only liked to write one thing, but Carla, trained as a historian, has found historical fiction her way to explain many lives of the past.

An early interest in the Napoleonic Wars sparked the writing of Regency romances, the genre that she is perhaps best known for. "It was always the war, and not the romance, that interested me," she admits. Her agent suggested she put the two together, and she's been in demand, writing stories of people during that generation of war ending with the Battle of Waterloo in 1815.

Within the narrow confines of George IV's Regency, she's focused on the Royal Navy and the British Army, which fought Napoleon on land and sea. While most Regency romance writers emphasize lords and ladies, Carla prefers ordinary people. In fact, this has become her niche in the Regency world.

In 1983, Carla began her "novel" adventures with a story in the royal colony of New Mexico in 1680. She has recently returned to New Mexico with a series set in the eighteenth century. "I moved ahead a hundred years," she says. "That's progress, for a historian."

She has also found satisfaction in exploring another personal interest: LDS-themed novels, set in diverse times and places, from turn-of-the-century cattle ranching in Wyoming, to Mexico at war in 1912, to a coal camp in Carbon County.

Along the way, Carla has received two RITA Awards from Romance Writers of America for Best Regency of the Year; two Spurs from Western Writers of America for short stories; and three Whitney Awards from LDStorymakers, plus a Lifetime Achievement Award from Romantic Times. She is read in at least fourteen languages and writes for several publishers.

Carla and her husband, Martin, a retired professor of academic theater, live in Idaho Falls and are the parents of five children, plus grandchildren. You may